Mortal Danger

Ann Aguirre

Feiwel and Friends
New York

A Feiwel and Friends Book
An Imprint of Macmillan

Feiwel and Friends books may be purchased for business or
promotional use. For information on bulk purchases, please contact
the Macmillan Corporate and Premium Sales Department at (800)
221-7945 x5442 or by e-mail at specialmarkets@macmillan.com.

Library of Congress Cataloging-in-Publication Data Available

ISBN: 978-1-250-02464-0 (hardcover) / 978-1-250-06426-4 (ebook)

Book design by Ashley Halsey

Feiwel and Friends logo designed by Filomena Tuosto

First Edition: 2014

10 9 8 7 6 5 4 3 2 1

macteenbooks.com

For the survivors:
That which did not kill us made us stronger.

DEATH
WATCH

I was supposed to die at 5:57 a.m.

At least, I had been planning it for months. First I read up on the best ways to do it, then I learned the warning signs and made sure not to reveal any of them. People who wanted to be saved gave away their possessions and said their good-byes. I'd passed so far beyond that point; I just wanted it all to stop.

There was no light at the end of this tunnel.

So two days after the school year ended, I left my house for what I intended to be the last time. I wrote no note of explanation. In my opinion, it never offered closure and it only made the survivors feel guilty. Better to let my parents think I suffered from some undiagnosed mental illness than to have them carry the knowledge that maybe they could've saved me; that burden could drive my parents to the ledge behind me, and I didn't want that. I only wanted an ending.

Earlier I had walked toward the BU T station I used for other errands, like shopping and school. There was plenty of time for me to change my mind, but I'd done all the research, and it was meticulous. I'd considered all sorts of methods, but in the end, I preferred water because it would be tidy and quick. I hated the idea of leaving a mess at home for my parents to clean up. This early—or late, depending on your perspective—the city was relatively quiet. *Just as well.* I'd gotten off at North Station and trudged the last mile or so.

Jumpers loved this place, but if you picked the wrong time, somebody would notice, call the authorities, and then you'd have cars honking, lanes shutting down, police cars . . . pretty much the whole media circus. I was smart enough to choose my opportunity carefully; in fact, I'd studied the success stories and compared the times when the most deaths occurred. Constrained by public transport hours, I arrived a bit later than the majority of those who died here, but my leap would still be feasible.

At this hour, there wasn't as much traffic. The bridge was a monster, but I didn't have to go all the way to the other side. Predawn murk threw shadows over the metal pylons as I faced my fate. I felt nothing in particular. No joy, but no sadness either.

The last three years had been the worst. I'd seen the well-meant *It Gets Better* videos, but I wasn't tough enough to make it through another year, when there was no assurance college would be better. The constant jokes, endless harrassment—if this was all I could look forward to, then I was ready to check out. I didn't know why people at school hated me so much. To my knowledge, I'd never done anything except exist, but that was enough. At Blackbriar Academy— an expensive, private school that my parents thought guaranteed a bright future—it wasn't okay to be ugly, weird, or different. I was all of the above. And not in the movie way, either, where the geek girl

2

took down her hair and swapped her horn rims for contacts, then suddenly, she was a hottie.

When I was little, it didn't bother me. But the older I got, the meaner the kids became, particularly the beautiful ones. To get in with their crowd, you needed a certain look, and money didn't hurt. Teachers fell in with whatever the Teflon crew told them, and most adults had enough secret cruelty to believe somebody like me had it coming—that if I tried harder, I could stop stuttering, get a nose job, dye my hair, and join a gym. So clearly it was my fault that I'd rather read than try to bring myself up to the standards of people I hated.

Over the years, the pranks got worse and worse. They stole my clothes from my gym locker, so I had to go to class all stinky in my PE uniform. Not a day went by that they didn't do something, even as simple as a kick or a shove or a word that dug deep as a knife. I used to tell myself I could survive it—I quoted Nietzsche in my head and I pretended I was a fearless heroine. But I was as strong as my tormentors could make me, and it wasn't enough. Four months ago, the last day before winter break, they broke me.

I pushed the memory down like the bile I swallowed on a daily basis. The shame was the worst, as if I'd done something to deserve this. Being smart and ugly wasn't reason enough for what they did to me. Nothing was. At that point, I implemented plan B. I had no friends. Nobody would miss me. At best, my parents—oblivious academic types—would see me as ruined potential. Sometimes I thought they had me as a sociology experiment. Afterward, they'd retrieve my body and mark my file with a big red FAIL stamp.

The sky was gray and pearly, mist hanging over the river. Drawing in a deep breath, I gathered my courage. To my amusement, I'd passed a sign that read, DEPRESSED? CALL US. Then it listed a number. I'd ignored that, along with a massive heap of pigeon shit, and continued across until I was far enough out that the water would drown me fast, provided the fall didn't kill me on impact. Now I only had to climb over quietly and let go.

The end.

A jagged shard tore loose in my chest; tears burned in my eyes. *Why didn't anyone notice? Why didn't anyone do anything?* So, maybe I was like the other lost souls, after all. I wanted a hand on my shoulder, somebody to stop me. Shaking, I put my foot on the guardrail and swung my leg over. On the other side, metal at my back, the dark river spread before me as if it led to the underworld. For me, it did. My muscles coiled, but I didn't need to jump. All I had to do was lean into space. There would be a few seconds of freefall, and then I'd hit the water. If the impact didn't kill me, the stones in my pockets would.

I'd planned for all contingencies.

I stepped forward.

A hand on my shoulder stopped me. The touch radiated heat, shocking me nearly to death. I couldn't remember the last time anyone had touched me, except to hurt. My parents weren't huggers. So long as I got straight As, they had little to do with me. They said they were rearing me to be self-sufficient. It felt more like they were raising me to self-destruct.

Mission accomplished.

I turned, expecting a corporate drone jonesing to start his cubicle time early, and on target to screw up my careful plans. In that case, I'd have to talk fast to avoid police involvement and incarceration in a mental facility. They'd put me on death watch and stare at me for three days in case I relapsed with the urge to kill myself. The lie hovered on the tip of my tongue—how I was researching suicide to make a sociology essay more compelling—but the guy who'd interrupted my exit also stole my ability to form a coherent thought. His hand remained on my shoulder, steadying me, but he didn't speak.

I didn't either.

I couldn't.

He had the kind of face you saw in magazines, sculpted and airbrushed to perfection. Sharp cheekbones eased into a strong jaw and a kissable mouth. His chin was just firm enough. He had a long, aquiline nose and jade eyes with a feline slant. His face was . . . haunting, unsettling, even. His layered mop of dark hair gained coppery streaks in the halo of passing headlights that limned us both. In a minute or two, somebody would see us. Though traffic was light, it wasn't nonexistent, and eventually some concerned motorist would pull over or make a call. I saw my window of opportunity narrowing.

"What?" I managed to get the word out without stammering.

"You don't have to do this. There are other options."

I didn't try to bullshit. His direct, gold-sparked gaze made me feel that would be a waste of time. Part of me thought I might have already jumped, and he was my afterlife. Or maybe I was on a ventilator after they fished me out of the river, which made this a coma dream. I'd read studies where doctors posited that people experienced incredibly vivid dreamscapes during catatonia.

"Yeah? Like what?"

I figured he'd mention therapy. Group sessions. Medication. Anything to get my butt off this bridge. Right then, only the strength of his biceps kept me from flinging myself backward. Well, that . . . and curiosity.

"You can let me help you."

"I don't see how that's possible." My tone sounded bleak, and it gave away more than I wanted.

I didn't mean to tell a random stranger my problems, no matter how pretty he was. In fact, that appeal made me trust him less. Beautiful people treated me well only when they were setting me up for something worse. In hindsight, I should've been wary that day, but I was just so tired, and I wanted so bad to believe they intended to stop tormenting me. I was ready to accept the apology and move on. *Everybody grows up, right?*

"Here's the deal. We'll get something to drink, and I'll make my proposal. If you don't like what you hear, I'll escort you back here and this time, I won't stop you. I'll even stand guard so nobody else does."

"Why should I? You could be a murdering weirdo."

"You intended to kill yourself anyway."

"I was going to be quick. You might not be. Being suicidal doesn't mean I'm stupid."

He laughed. "See, this is why I didn't bring my car. I *knew* you wouldn't get in."

Weird. That sounded like we were old friends, but I'd remember someone like him. "You got that right."

"You can walk five feet behind me if it makes you feel better."

I wasn't sure it did, but with his help, I climbed back over the guardrail. His argument made sense, and I was curious. What did I have to lose? He might try to recruit me into a cult. Nervous and wary, I trudged behind him, my eyes on his back at all times. I was ready to end things on my terms, not wind up living in a hole in somebody's basement. That would definitely be worse. I shivered, wondering if this was the best idea. Yet curiosity refused to let me back out.

He led the way off the bridge, quite a long walk the second time around; the rocks in my pockets gained weight with each step. Eventually, we reached the street, passing a number of closed restaurants, Italian places mostly. He stopped at a twenty-four-hour diner called Cuppa Joe. The place had a giant mug out front, outlined in red neon. Inside, the vinyl booths were cracked and sealed over with silver duct tape. On the wall, a neon blue-and-pink clock buzzed, a low drone just inside my range of hearing. According to the position of the hands, it was 6:05 a.m., and I'd missed my deadline.

A couple of waitresses wore the ultimate in polyester chic, while old women sat nursing coffee with lipstick imprints on chipped cups, makeup caked into their wrinkles. There were elderly couples as well; men in plaid trousers and white belts, ladies in shirtwaists. Everyone in the diner had an odd look, like they were players on a set, and some otherworldly director was saying, *Now* this *is what a diner looked like in 1955.* I also counted too many customers for this hour. Finally, there was an expectant air, as if they had all been awaiting our arrival. I dismissed the thought as symptomatic of how surreal the day had become.

The hot samaritan sat down next to the window, so that the red light from the giant coffee cup on the roof fell across the table in waves. I took a seat opposite him and folded my hands like I was at a college admissions interview. He smiled at me. Under fluorescent lights, he was even better looking than he'd appeared on the bridge.

It didn't make me happy.

"So is this where you call the cops? You lured me in quietly. Good job." To my astonishment, I got the words out without a hitch. In his company, I wasn't nervous at all, mostly because I half suspected he was a figment of my imagination.

"No, this is where I introduce myself. I'm Kian."

Okay, not what I expected. "Edie."

Short for Edith, who had been my maternal great-aunt. No one used my nickname, except me—in my head. At school, they called me Eat-it.

"I know who you are."

My breath caught. "What?"

"I didn't find you by accident." Before I could answer, Kian signaled the waitress and ordered coffee.

She glanced at me with an inquiring expression. *What the hell.* If I was dying after this conversation anyway—

"I'll have a strawberry milk shake."

"Hey, Hal," the waitress called. "Shake one in the hay."

An assenting noise came from the back and then the woman went behind the counter to pour Kian's coffee. She served it with a flourish, along with a sugar bowl and a pitcher of cream. "That's how you take it, right?"

He smiled up at her. "Good memory, Shirl."

"That's why I get the big bucks." She winked and sauntered to her next table.

I picked up the thread as he stirred cream and sugar into his drink. "Explain how you know who I am and where to find me. It sounds stalker-y, and I'm inclined to bail as soon as I finish my shake."

"Then I have time to make my case," he said softly. "Misery leaves a mark on the world, Edie. All strong emotions do. Rage, terror, love, longing . . . they're powerful forces."

"Right. What does that have to do with me?"

"Your pain came to my attention months ago. I'm sorry it took me so long to act, but I'm constrained by certain rules. I had to wait until you reached the breaking point before I could offer you a deal."

"If this is where you offer a fiddle of gold against my soul, I'm out."

His smile flashed. A little shiver of warmth went through me because he seemed to appreciate my wit. "Nothing so permanent."

"I'm all ears," I said as the waitress delivered my shake, hand-dipped with whorls of fresh whipped cream and a bright red cherry on top—almost too pretty to drink. Deliberately, I stirred it with my straw, ruining the beauty, and sucked up a huge mouthful.

Delicious.

"When humans of exceptional potential reach the breaking point—what we call extremis—we can step in."

I choked on my drink. "Humans. Which makes you *what*, exactly?"

Now I felt sure this was the lead-in to the most spectacular punk ever. I craned my neck, looking for Cameron, Brittany, Jen, Allison, or the cheer mascot, Davina. She had too much melanin for Blackbriar squad standards, so they kept her in a lion costume half the school year, and when she got out of it, she ran errands for the Teflon crew, who treated her more like a minion than a friend. I didn't see anyone from school, but that didn't mean they weren't in somebody's bedroom, laughing their asses off through this guy's button cam. This would probably end up on YouTube.

Like the first video.

Kian shook his head. "I can't answer that unless we come to an agreement."

"Let's cut to the chase," I said tiredly. "I don't know what they're paying you, if you're a struggling actor, or what, but I'm not interested. This isn't even the meanest prank they've pulled. Are they watching right now?"

"Edie—"

"Wait," I cut in. "I bet you don't get paid unless I play along. Fine. Tell me more about this awesome deal. Can I get it for four low payments of nine ninety-five?"

He didn't answer. Instead, he leaned across the table and took my hand. *Now that's commitment to the bit,* I thought.

Then the world vanished, a static skip in an old VCR tape. I remembered those from elementary school, the low-rent one I attended before my parents published, filed their first patent, and could afford a pricey prep school. That fast, the diner was just *gone.*

Brutal wind whipped my hair against my face. My glasses frosted over and my skin tightened with goose bumps in the icy air. A mountain stared back at me, rocky and wild. If I took four steps forward, I'd pitch off the edge. Vertigo spun my head, and I clung to Kian's hand, unable to say a word. This looked like Tibet—or the pictures I'd seen anyway. Deep down, I'd always wanted to go . . . to kneel in a holy place with the silent monks. Could he *know* this about me? I glimpsed no civilization, just trees, rocks, and stars. The cold gnawed through me; I was dressed for late spring in Boston, not in Sherpa gear. Shock paralyzed me for a few seconds.

God, I had to be out of my damn mind. *Hey, coma dream, how you doing? Let's see where this takes you.* But on the off chance it was real, I whispered, "Stop. Make it stop."

Another shift, and we were back at Cuppa Joe. My hands felt like chips of ice. His, still wrapped around mine, radiated the same heat I'd noticed when he touched my shoulder. I glanced around wildly, wondering if anyone reacted to our disappearance. The other patrons showed no signs that anything was wrong, but people didn't *do* that. Vanish and materialize, like somebody was beaming us in a transporter.

But maybe that was key. *People* didn't. Kian had called me an exceptional human, implying he wasn't. I'd been full of breezy skepticism before; it died on that mountaintop. I drew my hand away, took a couple of deep breaths, trying to calm my pounding heart.

"How come nobody even blinked? That was some straight-up *Star Trek* stuff."

"This is our place," he said. "Company owned. I can't tell you more right now."

"Well, that jaunt registers pretty high on the she'll-take-me-seriously meter."

"I don't usually have to resort to it this early in the conversation," he admitted.

My milk shake was still sitting on the table, melting into baby-pink goop. "Sorry I cut you off. You said something about extremis?"

He nodded. "That's when a human is about to die."

Oddly, that cheered me. "So I was going to succeed."

Kian didn't seem so pleased. "Yes. In a sense, you're already gone, Edie. If your fate wasn't currently in limbo, I wouldn't be permitted to talk to you. There's a pivotal moment just before death, when bargains can be made. I'm authorized to offer you three favors now in return for three favors later."

"I don't understand. What kind of . . . favors?"

"Anything you want," he said.

"*Anything?*" By my tone, it had to be obvious I meant things bigger and more impossible than tickets to Tahiti.

"My ability to change your life is limited only by your imagination."

"But then you can ask me for anything," I pointed out. "Three times. What if it's not something I can deliver?"

"The favors requested in return will always be within your power to grant. That's the way it works."

"But there are no parameters of what you might ask . . . or when. It might be terrible. Or illegal." Too well, I remembered "The Monkey's Paw," the burden of being a reader. Somebody who spent less time lost in books might've already signed on the dotted line.

"You were ready to throw your life away," Kian said. "But are you brave enough to change it?"

"You never answered me. What *are* you?"

"How would that help you decide? If I'm a demon, I'm unlikely to admit it, so I could say anything. How would you know if I'm telling the truth?"

He had me there. I scowled and sipped my shake, the possible dangers and consequences banging around my head. Since I'd accepted I didn't have a future, it seemed less scary to consider everything that could go wrong down the line. If my life imploded twenty years later when the bill came due, wouldn't it be worth it to be happy first? It had been so long since I laughed that I couldn't remember what it felt like to walk around without this awful weight in my chest.

"In a theoretical sense, say I agree to your deal. Is there a time limit on when I have to use my favors?"

Appreciation sparked in his gaze. Kian inclined his head. "The first must be used within a year. The rest within five."

"To prevent people from getting what they want with the first, then sitting on the others until they die, thus blocking you from asking anything in return."

"Exactly. The return favors may be collected anytime after completion of our side of the bargain."

"So repayment could be due anytime. Talk about living under the hammer."

"Some people feel that way. Others live in the moment and don't worry about what might come."

I jammed the straw deep into my glass, chewing my bottom lip. "This sounds pretty diabolical. I hope you know that."

"I'm aware." Sorrow threaded his tone, making me wonder what could make someone like *him* sad.

"Can you tell me anything about the people you work for?"

"At the moment, no."

I'd like to glean some more information before making a decision, but his response implied he could only answer questions after I agreed to the terms. That seemed shady; it couldn't be good if my benefactors preferred to hide in the shadows. One thing could be said of this situation; curiosity had supplanted despair as my dominant emotion.

"You said you come to exceptional humans. Why me?" I was brainy, but not the kind of smart that cured cancer.

"If I told you *why* we want to save you, it could screw up your timeline."

"You mean if I learn that I solve cold fusion, then I might not. I might decide to breed rabbits instead."

"You hate rabbits," Kian said gently.

"Yeah." I did—since one bit me in the fourth grade—but how weird that he knew.

"The deal is on the table. Choose, Edie."

From here, I sensed it was up to me. "Can I have some time to think about it?"

"No. I'm sorry."

"It comes down to a leap then, either way. You can put me back on the bridge . . . only this time you don't stop me. Will it be like we never came here or went to the mountain?"

"Yes."

I smiled. For someone like me, there could be only one reply.

THE HOUSE
ALWAYS WINS

"I'm in. Obviously my life sucks. If it didn't, we wouldn't be here."

Kian smiled, a soft breath of relief escaping him, like he truly cared, and he was glad he didn't have to dump me back on the bridge. More likely, he worked on commission. Life had made me cynical, always waiting for the other shoe to drop.

He reached into his pocket and drew out a shining silver coin. At first glance, it could've been a quarter; it was around the same size. But there was a symbol I couldn't identify engraved on one side; more similar to a kanji than any Western language I'd seen, yet I didn't think it was Japanese. Kian flipped it over, revealing an infinity sign on the back.

"Let me have your wrist."

"Why?"

"Accepting the mark formalizes the agreement."

"Will it hurt?"

"Yes. But it's quick."

I appreciated his honesty. A deep breath escaped me as I pushed my right hand toward him. His fingers were warm and sure, exposing my palm, then he slid back my sleeve. As promised, it burned like fire when the metal touched my flesh. A glimmer of light shimmered—almost like a photocopier—and an intense prickle-pain worked beneath my skin. He pressed the coin even tighter to my flesh, until I almost couldn't bear it. I bit my lower lip, blinking hard against rising tears. Just when I thought I'd scream, the sensation eased off.

"Done?" he asked, watching my face.

"You're asking me?"

"When it stops hurting, I can pull the token away."

"It just feels like metal now."

With a relieved look, he removed it and I studied the mark on my arm. My parents would freak if they saw it, since it resembled a tattoo. Oddly, there was no residual pain, and the skin didn't look red or irritated, as I'd seen on people who came to school with new ink.

"There's no special care required," Kian told me. "But I'm afraid we're not finished. I need your other arm."

"The other symbol?" I guessed.

He nodded. "The infinity sign signifies your agreement to the deal. You need the other mark to identify your affiliation."

"I have no idea what that means."

"It tells certain parties that you're an asset, or part of the opposition."

"So showing it could help or hurt me, depending on who sees it?" This crap was getting more complicated by the second.

"Yes."

"Am I allowed to cover these up with armbands or bracelets?"

"Sure. You just can't change them with normal ink or remove them via laser."

"Can't or aren't allowed to?" There was a fairly substantial difference.

"It's not physically possible with existing technology."

"That's the least of my worries anyway." Sighing faintly, I braced and gave him my left arm, wishing I knew what that kanji meant.

This time, I was better prepared for the searing pain. The tears spilled and overflowed despite my best efforts, but I didn't utter a sound while he marked me. At last the coin reverted to cool metal instead of molten lava and I nodded at Kian. He pulled the token away and dropped it into his pocket.

"We're almost done. Can I see your cell phone?"

"Yeah."

It was jammed in my right front pocket. My parents insisted I keep it with me, because we communicated mainly via text. I suspected they'd use my cell like a LoJack to track me if I went missing. *You almost did.* I imagined myself floating in the dark water like Ophelia, only I wouldn't leave a pale and lovely corpse with flowers tangled in my hair.

I dug it out and passed it across the table. Upside down, I watched him enter his name and program his number.

"When you're ready to request your first favor, call me."

"Really?" My brows went up.

"You expected more flash?"

"Well, after the mountain trick . . ."

"I could pop in at random to ask, *Are you ready yet?* but I thought you'd find that startling. And creepy."

Caught off guard, I laughed quietly. "You have a point."

17

"And *you* have a nice smile."

I winced. "Don't. You already got me to agree to the deal."

"I won't apologize," Kian said, "but I'll stop if it makes you uncomfortable."

"It just makes me think you're full of shit."

Taking my words as a sign to wrap things up, he waved at the waitress to get the check, and once he had it, dropped a few bills to cover it. "Let's go then. I'll see you home."

I hurried toward the doors, hating that moment of vulnerability when the rest of the world could stare at me. By force of habit, my shoulders came forward and my head went down. Hair the color of field mice tumbled forward to hide my face. I felt better once I pushed out into the early morning light. Kian caught the door as it swung back, and then he was beside me, another flash of heat and color in a morning warming up in shades of salmon and vermillion, colors I never wore, but whose drama suited him.

"Are you gonna . . .?" I trailed off and waggled my fingers.

He arched an amused brow. "I'm sorry, what?"

I tried snapping my fingers. "You know. Presto! We're at my place."

"Is that your first favor?" Kian tilted his head, and I noticed how tall he was—six feet plus, with a lean build. His muscles were clean and compact, something I rarely noticed about boys before. Admiring guys I'd never date felt too much like a beggar pressing his face against a bakery window in hopeless longing for the delicious things he'd never have. Kian was that kind of forbidden beauty, not for me. *Never* for me.

I covered that feeling as best I could. "No way. Are people seriously that dumb?"

"Not the ones *I* save," he said softly.

18

It was stupid how good that made me feel. Warm. Being smart had never mattered like it should; it never made me happy. It only let me notice how I didn't fit in. I could spend hours on equations, but I didn't know what to say to people my own age. Not that the snobs at school had ever given me a chance. I shouldn't care what any of them thought, but a dark, seething part of me craved payback. I imagined myself, cool and beautiful, sweeping through the halls while the guys who had called me names stared, knowing they'd never get me. Kian could make this happen.

I was startled to notice we'd reached North Station. "What if I'm ready now?"

"You know what you want?" Surprised tone. Kian led the way to the T. Evidently he planned to escort me to my door.

This has been an incredibly weird morning.

Some people might think this was a superficial request, but they wouldn't understand *why* I wanted it. Not just so I'd know—for once—what it was like to be one of the beautiful people. No, once I got inside the Teflon circle, I'd dismantle it brick by brick. A sharp, angry smile cut free, and I didn't care what Kian thought. From this point forward, I had a goal—and *planning* was my forte.

I nodded. "By the time we get to my place, I'll have the verbiage ironed out."

"Let me guess, you're worried about the favor twisting back on you." A faint sigh escaped him, rich with weary impatience.

"You get this a lot, I guess?"

"Often enough."

It was a little odd to be *ordinary*. Predictable. At school, I was the weirdo. Nobody talked to me for fear of coming down with a case of social leprosy. For the last two years, I had been eating in the bathroom, which was disgusting and unsanitary, but it beat the cafeteria, surrounded by empty seats, while the buttholes from the lacrosse team threw pickles at the back of my head.

"I don't need to worry about that?"

He shrugged. "You can. But I'll point out that if I don't make you happy, if I make your life worse, than you'll end up on the bridge again, and we won't get our favors repaid."

That sounded logical, but nothing could've prepared me for how *strange* this day had been. "Isn't there a codicil preventing a human from killing himself when he owes favors?"

"You still have free will," Kian said. "Even under the company's aegis."

Which meant, presumably, it happened. My shoulders tightened with confusion and uncertainty. *Too late for buyer's remorse.* While I wanted to believe that Kian knew what he was doing and he was being straight with me, I didn't have a trusting nature, especially with the beautiful people. Still, I was alive so far, which was more than I'd expected from the day.

We boarded the train in silence and for several stops, I constructed my request. Eventually as we approached Saint Mary's Street, I decided simplicity would serve best. I took a deep breath and followed him off the train. The neighborhood wasn't quiet, even at this hour. A few undergrads laughed as they stumbled home from a night of partying. I lived in the no-man's-land just beyond the bounds of Fenway. If I squinted, I could glimpse how the other half lived, a block away in Brookline proper. This area was a weird mix of broke college students and rich medical professionals, but you could usually tell who lived in which buildings by how well they had been renovated.

The brownstone where I lived wasn't pristine, though residents tried to brighten things up by decorating their window boxes.

Belatedly I realized that Kian was waiting to hear my first request. "I want to be beautiful without losing any aptitude I have. No time limits, no melting face, *no* surprises."

His teeth flashed white as he grinned. "That's easy enough."

"For you, maybe." A thought struck me, and I stared up at him, wide-eyed. "Or did you wish for the same thing, however long ago?"

"Do *you* think I did?"

His features were strong but too symmetrical to come from natural design. Everything aligned just so, lending an exotic cast to his perfection. I hadn't been able to put my finger on what bothered me about him until just now.

"Totally. I'd bet my life on it."

"You'll throw that away at the least provocation, won't you?"

"That's not an answer. Admit it, you weren't born looking like that."

No wonder he had been so nice to me. Beneath the swan feathers, he hid an ugly duckling skin. It made me like him a little more. If he'd been in my shoes, maybe he lacked the natural meanness that I'd experienced at school.

"You're right," he said softly.

"Which means you were in my position once. Doesn't it?"

He sucked in a surprised breath. "People don't usually deduce that so fast."

I imagined him poised on the verge of ending his life, and a chill swept over me. I wanted to touch him—and that wasn't like me at all. Still, my fingers flexed with the urge. Questions boiled in my brain, but we didn't know each other well enough for me to ask what had been so bad about his life that he'd wanted out. Seeing him now gave me hope. One day I could put this misery behind me, right? Eventually I'd look back on this moment and be grateful Kian stopped me from making my final mistake.

It also answered the question about his origins. He might not be human anymore, but he had been, once. It hinted of scary things lurking in my future, yet if I scheduled my favors right, I could enjoy life before I started serving Mephistopheles—or whoever Kian worked for. If I wasn't numb with shock, I'd be more worried.

"In turn, that means you survived your three favors and the repayment."

"There's a limit to what I'm allowed to tell you, Edie."

"It's like a secret society," I guessed. "And I'm only permitted what's available to initiates of my level."

"You're too damn clever for your own good. Are you sure this is what you want?"

"Positive." The moment I said it, my wrist burned like fire, and I whipped it up, narrowly restraining a cry. A dark line appeared across the top of the infinity sign, creepy as hell, like ink working its way out of my skin from the inside. I gasped as the burn subsided, touching my wrist as if I might smear the mark, but it was cool and dry.

"Sorry, I should've warned you. That's a tally. When you have three lines—"

"It means you've used all your favors. Got it. Can I see your wrists?"

He offered them without complaint, and I saw now that he had a kanji similar to mine on his left arm, and an infinity sign struck through with three lines on his right. I frowned.

"Why is one of yours a little different from mine?"

"Spoilers, sweetie."

I was delighted to catch him quoting *Doctor Who*. Smiling, I went into the brownstone and traipsed up the stairs to our apartment. "You can't be serious," I said over one shoulder.

"About what?"

"Not being able to answer. You said you couldn't until I signed on the dotted line. Well, I have. So start talking."

"I was kidding, actually. Ownership symbols are tweaked according to a variety of factors, including the faction represented. This line here," he pointed, "represents Raoul."

"Who's that?"

"The guy who offered me a deal."

For a few seconds, I studied my own wrist, then his. "What part of the mark are you?"

"I'm the curved line crossing these two others." He traced the arc on his left wrist with one fingertip.

"Ah." As that was the only difference, the rest of the character had to relate to the faction Kian represented. *I'm totally getting a handle on this.* Fighting a blush, I asked, "Do you want to come in?"

It was safe to invite him. The day before, my parents had gone to a symposium, something to do with string theory. That was another reason I'd chosen this as the day. My parents wouldn't be home until later, no chance they would've missed me before it was too late.

He nodded. "We have some planning to do."

Music to my ears. Inside, the apartment was small, cluttered with books. There was no television; I had been lucky to persuade my parents I needed a laptop for homework and research. I also watched shows on the Internet—not that they knew. I suspected my parents believed I was too serious and focused to pursue mindless entertainment, but sometimes I really needed to hide out in somebody else's world when mine became unbearable.

The old brown tweed sofa sagged in the middle. Kian didn't seem to notice when he sank down on one end. I sat on the other, hoping I didn't look as nervous as I felt.

"You'll have to go away for the summer," he said.

Talk about lobbing a brick. *"What?"*

"Think about it. Your parents will question the changes if they happen overnight. We need to build a credible framework."

"So I'm going to makeover camp? Or a Swiss finishing school? Somehow I don't think my parents will go for it."

Kian shook his head. "That's why we craft the story to fit the audience. I bet they'd love it if you were accepted to the Summer Science Program, where you sharpen your academics and get college credit at the same time."

"Yeah," I said in surprise. "They would."

"The actual changes? I can knock them out in a couple of hours. But you have to be gone or your parents will question how it's possible."

"And on campus, I'll have a chance to practice being . . . the new me."

"Exactly. It's a no-risk setting for a test run. By the time you go back to Blackbriar, you'll be self-assured, ready to teach them a lesson."

I'd read all the psychology books. In theory, I knew that confidence worked wonders when it came to dealing with other people. That didn't mean I could achieve it on my own; I had spent years doubting my worth on every level except my brain.

But Kian could give me a boost . . .

I put that aside, troubled over his insights. "You knew about the rabbits . . . you know I go to Blackbriar. How much do you know about me, exactly?"

He didn't answer, only offered a level look, which was the only reply I needed. I told myself it was part of his job, and I shouldn't freak out. There were probably a hundred other ugly girls in his phone, assigned by some creepy bureau of supernatural resources.

So I asked something else. "You really think I can pull this off?"

"The assholes at Blackbriar won't know what hit them." For a moment, a cruel light burned in his jade eyes, more catlike in the morning light.

"That sounds almost . . . personal. Do you have a score to settle there too?"

"No," he said quickly. "Of course not. I just want to see them get what's coming, after what they did to you."

Naturally, he'd sympathize with me. If he had been a freak, geek, or misfit before his favors kicked in, he had scars where it didn't show. The bullies *did* deserve this. No question. I hadn't done any-thing to them.

Yet.

I never told him what I planned to do, though. "How do you know I don't just want to be beautiful?"

His chin dropped, eyes sliding away from mine. "I saw the expres-sion in your eyes when you asked. I've seen it before. And there's nothing simple about it."

He was right about that. The Teflon crew had created in me a powerful cocktail of hate, anger, shame, and a burning desire for jus-tice. Maybe somebody like me couldn't get it at Blackbriar, but the new Edie could.

I tapped the arm of the couch, frowning. "Back to the SSP. They require applications for a program like that, usually with references. I don't see how I can get in. It's already—"

"You saw what I could do earlier." Kian chuckled. "You've accepted that I can change how you look. Now you're questioning if I can get your name on a list?"

Heat pinked my cheeks, and I ducked my head. My glasses slipped down my nose. "When you put it that way . . . wait, this doesn't count as my second favor, does it?"

"No. You're not asking to get into the SSP, so it's an adjunct service as the most expeditious way to grant your request with minimal disruption to your life."

"And that's important to your bosses, I guess?"

He nodded. "If parents become suspicious, it complicates the situation. They prefer not to make deals with minors, but extremis happens when it happens."

My head spun with the wild revelations that just kept piling up. By this point, numbness took over. I'd process this stuff later.

Kian went on, "I'll take care of the registration and travel arrangements. It's up to you to convince your parents." He had his cell phone in his hand and tapped away, checking something. "The session I have in mind starts in three days."

So soon. I didn't know if I was ready, but excitement thrummed through me, supplanting the shock. It was three parts terror and one part anticipation, all better than the dread and dejection that had dogged my steps since winter break.

"I'll handle them," I promised. "Text me the flight time?"

Gold flecks sparked in his green eyes when he smiled at me.

Reluctantly I shared his amusement because it was infectious. A laughing Kian was . . . beyond lovely. But he didn't explain what was so funny.

I sighed. "What'd I say now?"

"It's cute that you think I'm booking you on a plane."

Belatedly I remembered the insta-trip to the mountaintop. "Because this is favor-related, you can port me?"

"You're *such* a smart girl," he mocked gently.

"Whatever."

"I'll be back for you in two days, Edie. Pack light. You'll need a new wardrobe before we're done anyway."

"And that's part of the deal?" I asked, fascinated.

"Sure. Clothes impact the perception of beauty."

"Sweet." I'd always hated shopping, but it might be different if I liked looking in the mirror. "You're like a regular fairy godfather."

Pure, ferocious rage flared to life before Kian shut it down. *"Don't call me a fairy. It's risky. Dangerous, even."*

Whoa. What the hell.

"I didn't—"

"Wings, sparkle-dust, mischief. Puck, Oberon, Titania, Tir na Nog, land beneath the hill. That about cover it?"

"Uh, yeah."

"If you call some things, they will come. And then they don't leave."

That sounded scary as hell, *and* like a certain noseless supervillain. A shiver went through me. "Noted."

"Sorry, I didn't mean to snap."

"No prob. I got it. Don't call the you-know-whats." I wondered about the rage-flare, whether he'd had a bad experience with things that didn't go away, but like his almost suicide, I didn't know him well enough to ask.

Maybe someday.

"I should get going." Kian seemed subdued, troubled by his outburst.

I studied him. "Do you . . . live somewhere?"

He looked around my age—eighteen or so—but he must be older. How much depended on what his second and third favors had been. What if he'd asked for eternal youth? He could be, like, a hundred. *Gross.* He didn't talk like a geriatric, but if he hung around kids a lot, that would keep him current. No matter how hot he was, I couldn't get past that age gap. Not that he wanted me to.

"Yes. I live . . . somewhere." Faint sarcasm flavored his tone. Regardless of how exotic it was to me, this must seem like a dead-end customer service job to him, explaining the rules to new clients and feeling annoyed when they didn't catch on right away.

That didn't mean I was putting up with attitude, even from the guy who pulled me off the bridge. "Later, Kian. See you in two days."

After he left, I went to my room and removed my jacket. Years ago, I'd papered my walls with posters of famous scientists like Madame Curie and Albert Einstein. I had the one with Einstein sticking his tongue out, a reminder that genius should always maintain a sense of humor. I was aware this didn't look like a teenager's room. My desk was too clean, organized by type of supplies, and dominated by the high-end printer/scanner plugged into my laptop.

If I had any friends to invite over, they'd make fun of everything, including the books on the floor beside my bed. I was always reading four different volumes, and only one of them was a novel. At the moment, I had a biography of Lise Meitner, a copy of *A Brief History of Time,* half burying a collection of plays by Samuel Beckett. At the bottom of the pile lay a science fiction novel, too dry to hold my interest.

On my desk, I still had the DNA model I'd built for biology. A+ work. Other signs of my nerdery dotted the room: a laptop, a bag of dice, a replica of the Starship *Enterprise*, a Tardis that lit up when you put coins in the slot on top, and some half-painted miniatures. There might be tons of people like me all over the world, but from what I could tell, they didn't go to Blackbriar. If they did, they hid the signs better than I ever had.

I took the rocks out of my pockets and put them in a crate in my closet. On autopilot, I put on pajamas and brushed my teeth. Though I didn't expect to sleep, the nap claimed me quickly and I didn't dream. Well, nothing I remembered anyway, but when I woke, I was oddly stiff and sore, as if the experience had changed me from the inside out. I raised my arms over my head and the marks were still on my wrists. Yet I felt oddly superstitious, like I might be hallucinating.

Coma dream? Dead girl walking? If so, this was the freakiest afterlife ever.

Coming up on my knees, I fought a burst of hysteria and peered at the marks in the mirror on the back of my door: Left wrist, ownership character that looked like a kanji; right wrist, infinity sign with a hash mark across the top. The reflection showed them backward, like they should be. Apart from these symbols and a number in my contacts, I had no proof Kian existed. I rolled out of bed and ran to where my phone was plugged into my laptop, charging. My hands shook as I scrolled through my contacts to the Ks.

You have to be there. I'm not crazy. I'm not.

Then I found it, pushing out a relieved sigh. *Kian. And his number.* Closing my eyes, I pushed out an unsteady breath. Though I had no idea how it was possible, he'd transported me to a mountaintop in Tibet, then brought me back like it was nothing. I might not understand his mojo, but . . .

It's real. It happened. He's coming back.

Or maybe you're dreaming, doped up in a psych ward, while doctors write stuff in your chart like, "Unresponsive to reality," "Becomes agitated when the sedatives wear off." Oddly, that possibility made it easier to move forward, like doing a high-wire act without a net, certain only that you wouldn't get hurt if you fell.

Reassured, I showered and dressed, then put together an impressive package of false documentation using my laptop, the Internet, Photoshop, and my excellent printer. I felt slightly guilty because my parents wouldn't look too hard at these documents. Why? They trusted me. But this part of the plan hinged on a strong sales pitch, and I had to prove I'd earned a scholarship to the university summer science program.

Just before I left my room, I shrugged into a hoodie to hide my wrists, though the day was warm enough for air-conditioning, if we'd had it. Since it was past noon, my parents were home. Soon, the conference circuit would begin, where they presented research to their colleagues. Once I turned twelve, I'd traveled with them because they didn't mind leaving me in a hotel room while they did their thing, but when I was younger, I stayed with Great-Aunt Edith, who called me her namesake and made me walk her Pomeranian.

"Hello, Edith." Dad looked up from his paper with an absent smile, peering at me down the rims of his spectacles. He'd missed part of his jaw in shaving, so it prickled with graying whiskers. That sort of thing was common.

My mother made a noise to acknowledge my existence, but she

didn't look up from scratching on a yellow legal pad. Bowls of half-eaten gruel congealed in the middle of the table, even though they'd presumably gotten home late enough to eat lunch instead, one of my mom's quirks. She worshiped at the altar of steel-cut oats.

Showtime. I set my papers on the table and pulled out a chair. By joining them, I did something odd and worthy of a pause.

My mother looked up. "Yes?"

You've got one shot. Make it good.

"I wasn't sure if it would come through, so I didn't want to get your hopes up . . . but I've been accepted to the Summer Science Program. Full scholarship."

Quickly I summarized the benefits of academic focus, college credits, and keeping my brain occupied during the summer. My parents seemed to think if I didn't use it for those two months, the thing would liquefy and run out my ears. Doubtless they had assumed I'd trail them around all summer, as had become the custom. But since they never paid for another room, maybe they would be glad to have some privacy.

Ew.

My father gave me a questioning look. "You didn't tell us you applied."

"It's pretty competitive. I was afraid you'd be disappointed if I didn't get in."

"But you did . . . and with a full scholarship. Congratulations, darling." Mom leaned toward me and almost hugged me. But she drew up short and offered an awkward pat on the shoulder instead.

"When does it start?" Dad asked.

"In a few days. I know it's short notice, but—"

"Actually, we had been concerned about how much you'd be

alone this summer, even traveling with us. You can only sit through so many symposiums," Dad said.

Mom added, "We'd toyed with the idea of letting you stay home and apply for a job somewhere, but we won't be in Boston much for the next couple of months."

"I wasn't keen on it," Dad admitted.

"You don't trust me?" I pretended to be hurt.

"It's other people I don't trust." His tone was pure cranky.

"So I can go?"

They exchanged a look, beaming information brain to brain and coming to consensus like the Borg.

"Of course," he said. "It's a tremendous opportunity, and we're proud of your initiative."

"Thanks." His praise made me twitch because, of course, I hadn't aimed for better, brighter things. I'd given up. Let the assholes win. The idea lodged in my head; that was so *not okay*. No matter what, I should've kept fighting. I should never have gone to an emotional place where I felt like the bridge offered my best hope.

Never again, I promised myself.

Already, I was better. Stronger. With a goal in sight, I could stand anything.

"Given our conference schedule, this is the best possible outcome for *all* of us. I'm excited for you. Do we need to book your tickets?" Mom asked.

"No, it's all set. Part of the full ride."

She beamed. "You must have really impressed them."

Well, I impressed somebody. Too bad I knew next to nothing about the people Kian worked for, but he seemed to have come out unscathed. I'd take that as my silver lining.

Dad reached over to pat my hand. "It's no secret you've been unhappy at school, and I'm relieved to see you planning for the future. You won't always be surrounded by cretins and knuckle-draggers."

Wow. A small spark of shame went through me. I hadn't realized they noticed my misery. But then, I stayed in my room, mostly. My parents were as weird as I was, and I couldn't take comfort in their company.

Mom nodded. "For people like us, college is the next frontier. This is great, not only for the academics, but this summer, you'll get a glimpse of what the future holds. It's *so* much better than high school."

More guilt, because I intended to abandon their nerd phylum as soon as possible. *For the best reasons,* I told myself. *To give the beautiful people a taste of their own medicine.* I'd get inside enemy lines, then break them down one by one.

"Great job winning over the selection committee," Dad said. "This will look great on college applications in the fall."

He has no idea how apt that is.

I smiled at my parents. "I know. I'm excited they chose me."

SO SVENGALI

The morning I left, my parents tried to see me off. Dad smiled at me, obviously pleased with what he was about to suggest. "We'll go together on the train, have breakfast at the airport, and then we'll say good-bye at security."

Damn. This was a problem I hadn't predicted. "That'll take an hour each way. Don't you guys have to prepare your papers for presentation, pack, and whatever else?"

My mom frowned. "It seems wrong to pat your head and say 'good luck.' What if you run into trouble on the way?"

Seriously?

"I'll be fine, two trains and a shuttle bus." Fortunately, I looked up the route as part of my cover story. "And I don't have much to carry."

They both frowned at me, the long pause making me fear that the situation might become untenable. Kian would likely *not* be amused if I lost half the morning going to the airport and eating breakfast. Once they left, I could probably call him and ask him to meet me there, but what if they wanted to watch me walk through security? I started to sweat.

"Seriously, it's fine," I murmured. "I need to be independent, right?"

Eventually Dad sighed. "If you're sure. This feels like it's happening too soon."

"Be careful." That came from Mom, along with a recitation of things to look out for. "And text us when you get there safely. Remember, we'll be traveling this summer, but we'll have our cell phones if you need anything."

"Will do . . . and I won't forget. Have a productive summer."

They both gave me stiff, awkward hugs that were more like thumps on the back, then Dad pressed some cash into my hands and they let me go. As I stepped onto the street, my phone buzzed. After skimming the text message, I walked two blocks as requested, and Kian met me on the corner.

"You didn't have any trouble?" he asked.

"Not much. I know how to manage my parents."

Barely.

"Good. This way." He stepped off the main walk into an alley, just a narrow gap between two brick buildings. At the end, there was a green Dumpster and some cardboard boxes. If it wasn't a bright, sunny morning, I'd be seriously freaked out and reconsidering my decision. A little voice whispered that none of this was real anyway, so I might as well enjoy the adventure, one of those super vivid dreams that amazed you when you finally awakened.

"Let's get out of sight." The heat of his fingers tangling with mine stole my voice.

I clung, hoping Kian took it for fear or anticipation. I'd die if he knew I just liked holding his hand.

He didn't speak, but once we rounded the Dumpster, he ported us. I expected to land on the campus, but the world came back into focus inside a small, stylish cabin. If *Architectural Digest* ever sponsored a wilderness retreat, I suspect it would look like this. From the view out of the window, it was built on top of a mountain with a river rushing nearby, different from the precipice he'd taken me to first.

"Where are we?" I yanked my hand free and stumbled back a step.

"Relax. I need a quiet place to work on you. As soon as you're satisfied, we'll continue to the university."

"Right." He couldn't change my face in a diner, even if it was company-owned. Whatever that meant. "But seriously, where are we?"

He lifted his shoulders in a shrug, sheepish. "My place in Colorado. Perk of the job. I can live wherever I want, even if I'm working in Boston."

"Don't you have an office?" I joked.

"I do, but . . ." He trailed off, regarding me intently.

Secretly I was glad he'd brought me home with him. A cubicle with fluorescent lights would quell my delusions that this could be more than business for him. So this must be standard procedure, and I shouldn't get my hopes up. I would have loved to poke into the nooks and crannies of the immaculate rooms in hope of uncovering his secrets, but that would be rude, and he had a job to do.

He canted his head toward the couch, pulling on a pair of odd, sleek gloves with textured pads on each fingertip. "Make yourself comfortable. This might take a while."

Yeah, he had a lot to fix. I hunched my shoulders in misery as I trudged over to the sofa. He sat down right next to me, his expression softening. God, yuck, I didn't want him feeling sorry for me, even if he did know how I felt.

"Hey, it's not your fault. And I meant it when I said you have a nice smile. More important, you're a good person. I'm just going to make the outside line up with what you have going on up here." He touched my neck, and soothing heat flooded through me.

Immediately, I felt calmer—and suspicious of that shift. "What did you do?"

"I used an electrical impulse to stimulate your hypothalamus, but I can't make the kind of changes you're asking for without a little pain. It'll go smoother if you're not already vibrating with tension."

"How much pain are we talking about?" I pushed out a slow breath, bracing. "And why can't you make it painless? Or knock me out?"

"Normally, a sedative would be administered, but I'm not an anesthesiologist. This procedure is low risk, but administering medication—well, I'm not doing that. You could be allergic, or it might not work on you the way it's supposed to."

When he put it that way, I saw his point. This was close enough to plastic surgery without a license for me to get scared. I breathed deep, wondering if I should back up. But it was too late; the hash mark had already formed atop my infinity symbol. In this deal, there were no do-overs or takebacks.

"I can handle it."

"Let's focus on what you want. How would you like to look?"

"You can make me resemble someone else?"

"Sure. But it's best if I optimize you. People tend to assume minor cosmetic procedures over the summer, weight loss, gym membership. They'll fill in the blanks as long as you don't have a whole new face."

"Then I'd love to be the best possible version of me."

"Okay, let's start with your eyes. I can change the color or brighten them, as well as correct your vision."

"And people will think I got contacts or Lasik surgery."

"Pretty much."

"There's nothing wrong with the color, is there?" It wasn't like I spent any time staring at my own irises.

"No, they're pretty, like the sun through topaz. You just can't see them too well with your glasses on."

Heat washed my cheeks. "You don't have to say stuff like that."

"You think you're a troll, because the people at school made you feel that way, but you have good raw material. You'll be a knockout when we're finished—and without as much structural redesign as you think."

"Then just do it."

He arched a brow. "You don't want to direct me?"

My shoulders squared, and I sucked in a sharp breath, trying to steady my nerves. Though I half suspected I was dreaming, it was terrifying to consider how much power I was giving him. "You're the expert. Just go for the best version of me. I trust you."

Sweetness and surprise flashed in his face. "People don't, usually. I'm just a means to an end."

"The genie in the bottle?"

He touched my cheek so lightly, as if it were eggshell porcelain. "Something like that."

"Let's get going," I said, dropping my eyes.

"One final question . . . What's your ideal body type?"

I'd never thought about it, mostly because I preferred to believe it didn't matter what I looked like, at least it wouldn't with people who cared about me. Beauty was in the eye of the beholder, right? So all my life, I had been holding out for the day somebody thought I was fine the way I was, but now I was sacrificing that potential for the sake of my plan. My stomach twisted with nerves.

"Slim hourglass, I guess. I always envied girls who look gorgeous in anything."

With great tenderness, he set gloved hands on my face. The heat quickly built to unbearable levels, and soon I was choking back my screams. As he'd hinted, it was like surgery without anesthetic. Tears streamed from my eyes as he stroked shaping fingers down my cheekbones, along my jaws, over my lips and brow. When his thumbs smoothed across my lids, my vision winked out and I followed.

Much later, I awoke . . . and my clothes didn't fit. My muscles burned with a low-grade heat, as if I had been training for a marathon. I lifted a slender, toned arm and marveled at it. Which was when I noticed I didn't have on my glasses. And the world was crystal clear.

"Kian?"

I heard his footsteps on the stairs before I saw him. "How're you feeling?"

"Not bad, considering. Is there a bathroom where I can—"

"Over here." He bounded with an odd, nervous energy that I couldn't interpret, until I realized he was *nervous*. He wanted me to approve of his work. "I left some things for you on the top of the hamper."

Keeping my pants up required one hand pinching the waist. I minced toward the bathroom and shut the door with a quiet terror that I was crazy. Or dreaming. *You're not. You were chosen.* With glowing exultation, I turned to the mirror to meet the new me.

My mouth dropped open.

I *did not* know the girl in the mirror. I mean, she had a few things in common with the person I had been, but it was like someone had removed most of my imperfections in Photoshop. With shaking fingers, I touched my cheekbones. So many minute changes and refinements. The best plastic surgeons couldn't have done what Kian had with his fingertips. From my small, straight nose to my slightly fuller mouth to the piquant point of my chin, I was the best possible version of myself.

He hadn't stopped at my face. Delicate color flared as I stared, imagining him shaping my body like modeling clay. He'd had no choice but to go all the way to third base to do the job right, and it figured I hadn't been awake. *It's just work for him,* I told myself. *Get over it.* My hair was still long, but the mousy brown had gone. Instead, it held a coppery tinge with streaks of gold and red, giving it a gorgeous luster. I shook my head experimentally and it bounced away from my throat in what seemed like a flirty move. Not that I *had* any moves.

I needed some.

Kian knocked on the bathroom door, sounding anxious. "You okay? If you don't like how you look, I can tweak. It'll hurt, of course, but—"

"Relax," I said. "You give good makeover."

"Thanks."

"Let me get dressed, okay?"

"Sure." His steps moved away.

I went to the neat pile of clothes on top of the tan wicker hamper. When I found underwear and bras at the bottom, I almost died of embarrassment. They were the cute kind I'd never worn. I chose a pair of white, pink, and black—striped boyshorts along with the matching bra, then shimmied into my new undies. I had no idea how I would face Kian, knowing he'd bought me underwear, but what the hell, he was so totally my Svengali, that maybe it didn't matter. We were beyond all that. I heard him moving around, pacing it sounded like.

Wow, he's really tense.

I faced my reflection. From the graceful curve of my shoulders to the flat, toned stomach, the mirror showed me a body I didn't recognize and the change was startling, frightening even. Normal weight loss would've given me a chance to get used to being lighter by increments, but I had to get accustomed to this all at once. It would take me a while to assimilate my new shape. By societal standards, I definitely qualified as pretty, but it felt like I was looking at a stranger, one whose body I had snatched. Deliberately I turned away. There were a couple of pairs of jeans, one plain, the other spangled with rips and faded spots. Though I'd never worn anything so stylish, I pulled them out of the pile and checked the size.

"Right." I huffed out a skeptical sigh.

Still, my old pants didn't fit, so why not try? I eased them up over my hips, thighs, and then buttoned them. They fit skinny, but they fit. *No way.* Euphoria sparkled through me, a low-grade fizz in my veins as I rummaged through the tops. I chose a black baby-doll T-shirt with white Japanese characters and a pink dot in the middle of the design. This time I didn't check the size before I pulled it on. Shifting, I assessed myself in the full-length mirror on the back of the bathroom door.

Incredible.

Taking a deep breath, I popped the door open before I could lose my nerve. Kian stopped, arrested in his progress across the front room. His gaze swept me from head to toe, and then he offered an approving nod.

"Obviously I think you look amazing or I would've kept working. But it's more important what *you* think."

"Perfect. I wouldn't have been able to say, *This is what I want,* but you knew."

"I'm good at seeing the potential," he said quietly. "You have any pain?"

"A little. Nothing dramatic."

"There may be a little blood, nothing to worry about. It's a result of the internal shifting I had to do."

I froze. *"Blood?* Like . . . where?"

"I had some when I brushed my teeth afterward, sometimes. And . . . in the bathroom. You know."

The toilet? Oh my God. My parents would rush me to the hospital. "You swear it's not indicative of hemorrhaging or something?"

"No, it's definitely not. It's just a reaction to the procedure. It'll ease back as your body adapts to the transformation."

"Okay. You haven't lied to me so far, though 'some pain' was a massive understatement. It felt like my whole face was on fire."

"Worth it, though, right?"

I smoothed my hands down my sides and thrilled at the way his green gaze followed the movement. "Definitely."

"I'm glad you passed out. It's pretty awful for people with a higher pain tolerance. They scream the whole time."

"Which is why you bring them out here to the middle of nowhere."

To my surprise, Kian shook his head. "I never bring clients here,

Edie. There's a soundproof room at headquarters set aside for this kind of thing."

"But . . . *I'm* here."

He ducked his head. The copper strands in his hair shone against the black, giving him a burnished look in the morning light. His thick tangle of lashes hid his devastating green eyes, but it was easier for me to ignore his beauty, knowing he'd broken the rules for me. I could look at him and see him. From certain angles, I could almost imagine what he'd looked like before someone set burning fingertips to his face and cut away the flaws. That mental image made him seem much more human, less the divine being who'd plucked me off the bridge. I preferred seeing him as a person, not a god.

His silence wasn't an answer. "Kian. If this isn't protocol, *why* am I here?"

"I was afraid the people at headquarters would freak you out." By the way his eyes shifted away from mine, that wasn't the whole truth.

"Bullshit."

This time, he met my stare head-on. "I wanted more time with you."

"Is that allowed?"

"Not really." He ran an agitated hand through his hair. "Just forget it, okay? And before you ask, no, I didn't do anything weird to your unconscious body."

"I wasn't going to ask that." I'd be sore in different places if he had, and while my muscles burned, there was no pain down below.

"So let's get going."

"Wait." I moved toward him and put a hand on his arm. "Do you mean you *like* me? In a normal way. Nothing to do with deals or bargains or favors?"

He shrugged. "It doesn't matter. There are rules."

"The answer matters to *me*."

"For all the good it does either of us, yes, I do. I did before." Bitterness colored his voice, his expression, and I didn't understand why. He'd wished for the *same thing*. Why did he seem to mind changing me for the better?

"Nobody liked me before," I said. "So thank you."

He ignored my gratitude. Maybe I wouldn't want it, either. I tried to put myself in his shoes. How would I feel about the people I met, who were so broken they had been ready to die when I stepped in? It wouldn't be wise to get attached to somebody like that, I thought. Even worse, when you *were* that somebody. *No wonder he's pulling back, minimizing the mistake of showing this much favoritism.* Whatever his motive, I appreciated that he hadn't brought me to headquarters. Intuition told me I wasn't ready to be thrown into the deep end, especially since I wasn't a very good swimmer.

I got out my cell phone, checked the time, compared it with the East Coast, and decided it had been long enough to seem credible that my plane had landed. I texted, Safe and sound on the ground. Thanks for letting me do this.

My mom replied, We're proud of you. Have fun, Edith.

In silence, Kian emptied my backpack and filled it with the things he'd gotten. "There's a gift card in the front zip compartment. You'll have time to buy more clothes before classes start in the morning."

"Oh." I tried not to sound disappointed. "You said *we'd* go, before."

"Yeah, about that. It's not a good idea. You don't need me with you."

But I want you there. I didn't say it aloud. Every fiber of me knew it was a bad idea to get attached to him. He was like a caseworker, almost.

44

"All right, thanks. I'll register, drop my bag off at the dorm, and go shopping, I guess." I couldn't believe I'd just spoken those words voluntarily.

"You ready?" A figurative shutter came down in his expression; he was ready to get on with his work.

"Yep."

There was nothing personal about his hand on mine, just a link required to port me on to the last leg in our journey. We emerged in a quiet corner of what must be the quad. A tangle of branches veiled the grass in filtered green light. Kian let go of me and pushed clear from the foliage.

He pointed, his tone all efficiency. "Registration is in that building. Head over and they can take it from here."

"Can I call if I need you?"

"Of course," he said gently. "But you won't. You need to get used to your new look and develop the confidence to demolish the assholes at Blackbriar, come fall."

I took his point. If I called him constantly, that wasn't self-assurance; psychology books would call it codependence. To hide my nervousness, I joked, "It's also to keep my parents from having a heart attack. I hope the summer's long enough for them to believe—"

"Don't worry." He softened a little. "Parents always want to believe their kids are beautiful. It won't seem like a stretch when the time comes, I promise."

"Then I guess that's it."

"Yeah. I won't contact you until the summer program ends."

"You better come then." I tried for a playful tone. "You're my ride home."

"I'll never let you down when you need me, Edie." His tone seemed so somber for a sunny summer day, as if he saw dark things in the distance and me in the center of them.

"Then there's one more thing before you go." I couldn't believe I was doing this, but the words wouldn't stop. They came from a place of complete certainty.

"What?"

"Kiss me."

I didn't give a shit about rules. A girl only got one first, and I suspected it wouldn't take me long to find somebody who wanted to be the one. But I deserved *more* than that for my first kiss. It had to be Kian—who said he liked me before—even though he wasn't allowed to. I was willing to accept that it couldn't go past this point.

"That's a really bad idea," he whispered.

"If you don't want to . . ."

In answer, he stepped closer so I could smell his soap, just a touch of citrus, and the warm, sunshiny scent of his skin. He dizzied me. Kian tangled his fingers in my hair and drew me to him with just enough hesitation to make me think he was nervous. That helped on my end, though I still couldn't breathe right. His other hand rested on my hip. I didn't know where to put my arms, if I should press close, stand super still, or— *Oh God. It's a good thing I asked him to do this.*

I'd make a fool of myself with anyone else.

"Eyes shut," he breathed in my ear.

I closed them and turned my face up. A trill of pleasure radiated wherever he touched me. Then Kian brushed his lips against mine, and the world stopped.

For this moment, I only knew his heat, his heartbeat. His mouth tasted sweet and lush, like chai tea and cinnamon, and I rose up against him on my tiptoes to sink my hands into his layered hair. This wasn't a perfunctory kiss—no, it was so much more. He caught me against him, and I lost track of everything but Kian. His hands burned through the thin cotton of my tee, roaming my back. For someone who had never been kissed, this was like learning to swim by being thrown off a boat into the ocean.

I couldn't think. Couldn't breathe. His nearness acted on me like a drug, and I clung, wanting only more. Forever, more. Eventually, I registered the hooting behind us in the quad. Fierce heat flashed into my cheeks as I pulled back.

"Something to remember me by." His tone carried a low and lovely ache, as if those moments meant something to him, as if he worried about me forgetting him.

Like that could ever happen.

"I'll see you in six weeks."

"Okay. What time?"

"Let's say eight, West Coast time."

I nodded. "Thanks for everything."

His jade gaze swept me from head to toe, as if committing me to memory. Then he stepped back. The leafy foliage hid his vanishing act, but the air crackled after he went, like charged wind after a storm.

I ached for him already.

A STITCH IN TIME

Going forward, I'd control everything this summer, taking charge of my life just like I had by asking Kian for my first kiss. That resolve made me feel better about being thrown into a college credit program with minimal preparation.

You can do this.

As I strolled toward the red-and-white registration banner, a girl fell into step beside me. She seemed . . . nervous, gnawing at her lip with oversize front teeth. Her mouth was chapped; her hair was dull and needed trimming. And before this morning, she would've considered herself too cool to be seen with me. At least that was my experience; even loners and outcasts preferred not to risk my social contagion because hanging out with me wasn't worth the potential grief from the Teflon crew. But maybe my Blackbriar experience wouldn't repeat here; there was no way this girl could know I had been a pariah.

"Was that your boyfriend?" she ventured, as if I might slap her for speaking to me.

At Blackbriar, this would be a nonstarter, a definite faux pas. People who looked like me did *not* hang out with those who looked like her. But here at the science program, that didn't matter—and I would never crush someone like they had me.

"Nah. Just a guy." That seemed like the kind of thing the new Edie would say.

One who saved my life.

Who liked me before.

"Really?"

"We haven't known each other that long." Surprising and true.

The other girl's eyes widened at that revelation. "But you were kissing."

Somehow I managed a shrug. "I was curious."

My companion didn't know what to say to that, clearly. "Wow."

"Are you part of the science program?" I figured it was better to change the subject because there were so few things I could reasonably say about Kian. Hell, I didn't even know his last name.

"Yeah. I guess you go to school here?"

I shook my head. "I'm heading over to registration myself."

"I never would've guessed." She wore a near-comical expression of disbelief, and if I'd been born with *this* version of my face, along with my brain, I'd find her incredulity offensive. It must suck for smart, pretty girls not to be taken seriously.

"Why?" I dared her to say it out loud.

"Y-you just don't look like the type," she stammered.

Sympathy washed over me. Hours before, I'd been living this girl's life. *Worse*, most likely. "Yeah, well. Looks can be deceiving. I'm Edie."

Belatedly, I realized I hadn't stuttered once. Apparently the behavioral psychologist had been right; I had a psychogenic stutter, exacerbated by stress, mental anguish, and anxiety. Right then, I felt no fear of ridicule, and it was easy to talk.

"Viola. Vi," she amended quickly.

I guessed she didn't want to be known here as the girl whose parents named her after the cross-dresser in *Twelfth Night*. She'd probably be surprised I knew that. I'd seen every film version ever produced, though, including the one with Amanda Bynes and Channing Tatum. That was the last movie of hers I loved.

"Did you come a long way?" I asked.

"I'm from Ohio, so yeah." She went on, "It's cool that I met someone nice my first day. I was a little worried about coming by myself. None of my friends got in."

At least you have some, I thought.

I got in line behind a guy who couldn't stop playing with his smartphone. Everyone at Blackbriar had them, but my cell was cheap and primitive, just so I could text my parents. Though they never said so, they couldn't see the point of buying me an expensive phone when I had nobody else to call.

Vi stood behind me, fidgeting until I turned around, aiming a look at her. She flushed. "Sorry. I'm just nervous about meeting so many new people."

"Me too." I just wasn't showing it at the moment.

"Really? You seem so confident."

Because I'd never see her after this summer, I could be honest. "It's a front."

The line moved pretty fast. There were five people helping out, and they'd divided up the alphabet. I went over to the guy in charge of the *K*s, beckoning Viola to follow me. He was probably a volunteer from the university. His brown hair held a red tinge, and he had a million freckles.

"Name?" he asked.

"Edie Kramer." There was no way Kian would've registered me under a name I hated.

He drew his finger down the list. "Ah, here you are. Wow, you're lucky."

"I am?"

"Yep, you slid right in under the wire. We had a last-minute cancellation."

"What happened to free me up a slot?" An icy chill suffused my skin.

I wondered if Kian had done something to the person whose place I'd taken. Though he'd promised he wouldn't make *my* life worse, he'd said nothing about anyone else. "The Monkey's Paw" flickered in my mind, troubling me. Every too-good-to-be-true situation had a dark side, so I needed to figure out what the catch was—and fast.

"Dunno."

"Really? There's no note in my file?" I tried a smile, feeling like a dipshit. My stomach twisted into a knot. In the past, I'd never have tried to charm my way into anything; my personal charisma wouldn't have filled a thimble.

He hesitated, then flipped a few pages. "Looks like he was in an accident, broke his leg or something. When he cancelled, they pulled you off the waiting list."

"Some people have all the luck," Vi said.

I didn't before. "Thanks for telling me."

"No problem. So here's your registration packet and your dorm keys. You'll need the first for the front door of your residence hall and the other for the room. Room assignment is in the small white envelope. You also need to check in with your RA before the end of the day. She'll go over rules and curfew."

"I was wondering if I could room with my friend, Vi," I said, trying the persuasive smile for a second time.

Life can't be this easy for the beautiful people.

"The rooms are already assigned," he said.

A rule that I can't get around? The old me would've accepted his reply, but if I wanted to be accepted by the Teflon crew, I had to assimilate. So I imagined what Brittany or Allison would do. To have any hope of beating them, first I had to master their weapons of mass destruction.

So I made eye contact, opened mine a little wider, and leaned forward. "But I didn't know Vi was going to be here until just now." Totally true, as we'd just met. "Please, can't you make an exception?"

He weakened visibly. "Let me check the master lists. If your roommates haven't arrived yet, I can swap the names. No harm done."

"Fingers crossed," I whispered to Vi, who seemed astonished and pleased.

A few minutes later, he came back with Vi's packet as well. "They aren't here yet, so they can room together when they arrive."

"Too cool," I said. "Thanks."

As triumph washed over me, I also felt like I needed a shower. *Do those girls have no souls?* I didn't know if I could do this for long, but it seemed to be second nature for them. They considered their ability to control other people an accessory, like a great purse or a cute pair of shoes.

Vi took her envelope as I headed across the quad. "I can't believe that worked!"

"I wasn't sure it would." Especially since I had no experience with manipulation. But I'd watched it happen often enough. Mimicry wasn't tough, apparently.

"This rocks. We're on the fourth floor, it looks like."

"Let's go meet the RA and get that over with."

"Sounds good."

I crossed the quad, which was all green grass and stately trees, to a tall brick building. Two sets of double doors led into what reminded me of a hostel lobby with a rudimentary front desk and a few grubby chairs. A college girl worked behind the counter, answering questions and explaining how the mail situation worked. From there, I ran up four flights, curious how my new body would respond. It didn't leave me short of breath at all, which meant I'd have to work out to keep fit, and I was curious if I'd enjoy doing so, starting from *this* baseline instead of where I was before.

Our RA was all of twenty-one, curly blond hair, good teeth. She looked like a surfer girl, and she seemed laid-back, which boded well. Her idea of going over the rules involved handing us a printout. She ended her short spiel with a grin. "If you *do* decide to break the rules, be smart. Don't let me catch you." At Vi's expression, her smile widened. "Hey, I was sixteen not long ago. I'm not going to pretend I don't remember what it was like."

On the way to the room, Vi bounced with excitement. "This is the most unleashed I've ever been. My parents . . ." She shook her head, words failing her in relation to their strictness. "This will be the best summer ever."

"I hope so."

I unlocked our door and found a simple, Z-shaped space, which gave privacy to each bed. In the middle, there was a double desk, and opposite, we had a dual dresser with drawers on each side. Across from my bunk, I had a closet, and behind the door, we had a sink for washing up. Otherwise, that was it. The walls were cement block and had been painted light blue; the floor was industrial tile, white-speckled with a few interesting stains. I dropped my backpack on the single bed, drawing Vi's attention.

"Is that *all* you brought?" she asked.

Nodding, I dug out the Visa gift card from the front compartment. "My parents thought it'd be fun for me to get stuff here, kind of a belated birthday present."

"Oh my God, that's the coolest thing ever. Your parents are nothing like mine."

I bet they're just *like yours.* But it was such a white lie; what could it hurt? Easier than explaining a hot guy who saved my life had given me $500 to spend on whatever I wanted. I pulled out my laptop and plugged it into the university Internet. A few minutes later, I had directions to the nearest mall.

"You wanna come?"

"Shopping?" She glanced at her baggy jeans and wrinkled her nose. "That's not really my thing."

"We can find a bookstore and a Best Buy too."

I *knew* this girl. I'd been her this morning. The old Edie never went clothes shopping voluntarily. She let her mother buy things and stick them in her room. She wore whatever she found and tried not to think about how she looked. She avoided mirrors and kept her hair so long, it fell into her face. When she walked down the street, she watched her feet, so she didn't see scorn flicker in other people's faces as their eyes slid away. That Edie died on the bridge. I had the freedom to be someone else now, anyone I wanted. The sensation was brilliant but terrifying. If I got it wrong, I had nobody to blame but myself.

"When you put it *that* way," Vi said, grinning.

"Cool. There's a mixer tonight at eight. We'll be back before then."

Her smile faded. "I don't know if I'm gonna go. I'm not here to socialize."

"That's your parents talking. We're here to learn, but we can have fun too. That's why I came." That played better than the real explanation, which no sane person would believe.

Vi shot me a knowing look. "But not the reason you gave at home, I bet."

"Hell, no. You have to know how to manage the parental units. As long as you can work up a rationale consistent with their internal motivations, you're good to go."

"I'm gonna learn *so much* from you."

"Maybe." With a half shrug, I headed for the door.

The mall I'd found was located downtown, kind of a revitalized ultra-chic place with small boutiques, lots of flowers, and Spanish-style courtyards. There were staple department stores, of course, like Macy's and Nordstrom, but I wouldn't be shopping there. Instead I'd hit smaller, lower-priced places. It shouldn't cost too much for jeans and T-shirts. At this point, I wasn't sure enough of my fashion sense to go much beyond those parameters. Deep down, I wished Kian hadn't refused to come with me. He had great taste, cool and elegant, and I'd bet he could dress me perfectly. Maybe that was why he didn't want to do it, though. He'd already made me beautiful.

Anything more might make him feel proprietary, give him a disquieting sense of ownership. I probably shouldn't have asked him to kiss me.

I wasn't sorry I had.

Vi made a noncommittal shopping buddy. She had no opinions on anything I tried on, but I caught a wistful light in her eyes, once or twice. I wanted to tell her how well I understood, but nobody wanted a new acquaintance prying into their personal business. I wouldn't make it better by saying I'd been a "before" picture, too. So I kept a light commentary running on what I intended to buy.

By the end of the spree, I spent four hundred bucks on clothes and cosmetics, forty on a small suitcase to hold it all. I also had the cash my dad had given me, which left me just under a hundred for the rest of the summer. That should be good for random entertainments. From the curriculum, I saw we'd be busy doing telescopic observation of various constellations anyway, so it wasn't like I'd be out on the town every night.

Vi and I ate a quick meal at the food court, and then I kept my promise to locate the nearest bookstore. In the stacks, I browsed for an hour, but I only bought one book: *The Intelligent Negotiator: What to Say, What to Do, How to Get What You Want—Every Time*. The purchase set the seal on my intentions. This summer would be my proving ground.

My new roommate bought a handful of science fiction and fantasy titles. I'd read all of them but one. I touched the second book in her stack. "That one's the best."

"I'll read it first."

Since it was after seven by then, we headed back to campus. Vi fell quiet as we approached the dorm; I could tell she'd rather avoid the mixer altogether. It was a wonder she'd gotten up the nerve to speak to me earlier. But then, I totally understood how one new person felt less intimidating than a roomful of strangers. My stomach churned over the prospect too, but I'd master my fear like a differential equation.

In our room, I didn't change clothes. I brushed my hair and teeth, put on some makeup like the girl in the store had explained. Not a lot. I wasn't confident enough to try advanced tricks, and fortunately, the face Kian had given me didn't require it. *Your face,* a small voice reminded me.

"Ready?" I asked.

She put down her book with a soft sigh. "Not really. But I guess I should go for a while. If it's awful, I can come back up and read."

"Come on, it'll be fun."

On the third floor, the gathering was already in full swing. Some kids looked geeky; others seemed normal. A few were hot. I skimmed the crowd and saw how it had broken down. Techies were comparing toys. Stargazers stood by the windows. A few math types scribbled on napkins. Music played in the background, soft and inoffensive, and the organizers had laid out various canned drinks and cookies. Not much of a spread, but the point was for enrollees to make first contact.

Before I could make up my mind where to enter the mix, a Japanese boy with a shock of black, blond-tipped spiky hair came up to me. He pointed at my shirt. "Are you really?"

I cocked a brow, waiting, trying to look mysterious, because I had no idea what my tee said. I'd just liked the look of it. And how it fit me.

He asked outright, "'Looking for a Japanese boyfriend'?"

Crap. Is that what it says?

I gave him a half smile, praying I didn't blush, because I felt like such a dumbass. *Did Kian get this as a practical joke?*

"Why, are you applying?"

"Maybe." He flashed a smile that said he was a little more self-assured than most of the guys here. "I'm Ryuuto. But Ryu is fine."

"I'm Edie. This is Vi." I stepped sideways so he could see her since she was hiding behind me. She elbowed me to show she didn't appreciate the attention.

She squeaked out, "Nice to meet you."

Come on, Vi. You can do better than that.

But Ryu wasn't paying attention to either of us. He curled his fingers, calling someone else over, a boy with dark blond hair. With his gold, wire-framed glasses, he looked smart . . . and cute. "This is my roommate, Seth. Seth, Edie and Vi."

"Trust Ryu to find the girls right off." Seth had an easy manner, belied by the flicker of his eyes. That was the only cue he gave that he wasn't totally calm.

"We're not the only girls here," I pointed out.

The blond kid grinned. "The ones who'll talk to us?"

"Point," Ryu admitted. "But I figured the shirt was a sign."

I studied Seth. "Programming?"

He nodded. "What gave me away? I'm interested in pretty much all the hard sciences, though. I haven't made up my mind on a major yet."

"Why rush?"

Ryu nudged his roomie. "Let's get them some drinks?"

As they moved off, Vi drew in a deep breath, covered by the music. "I can't believe this is happening. Boys just wander over to you?"

They never did before.

"It's the shirt. Great icebreaker."

And maybe that's why Kian bought it.

She shook her head. "It's because you're gorgeous. I can't do this!"

"Relax," I whispered. "Here they come."

This was all new to me too, but I could learn. I had to. Ryu returned with the drinks and Seth brought cookies. The four of us found some chairs in the corner where we could chill. Vi hadn't spoken a word to the boys, and I could tell by her face that she dug Seth. Maybe we could make that happen by the end of the session.

Ryu was saying, "You ordered your shirt from ThinkGeek, right?"

I nodded, mostly because I had no idea where Kian had gotten it. Fortunately, I was familiar with the store. I'd bought things there before.

"I love ThinkGeek," Seth put in. "I want some of their spy stuff."

"To make stalking easier?" Ryu grinned.

"Shut up!"

Man, I had to get Vi into this conversation. I leaned toward her. "What about you? Ever ordered from TG?"

She shot me a look, but answered, "Yeah, a portable solar charger."

Immediately, both guys turned to her with interest in the specs, whether it was strong enough for a laptop or just an iPod. She fielded their questions with obvious relief; this was something she could discuss. Oddly, her nerves made mine go away because I could see I had nothing to fear.

Vi was right; this was going to be the best summer ever.

INVINCIBLE SUMMER

As it turned out, those were prophetic words. The weeks went quickly, combining work and fun in the best possible ways. The four of us became an inseparable unit, and Ryu did, in fact, become my Japanese boyfriend. My first, though I doubted he'd believe it. Since he was going back to Tokyo at the end of the session, we both understood it was a temporary summer thing.

During the day, we took astronomy, physics, calculus, and programming courses. At night, we teamed up and took telescopic images of a nearby asteroid, then Seth wrote software to determine its orbit around the sun. Twice a week, we had guest lecturers; my favorite was a physics professor with a great sense of humor, and I really enjoyed the Q&A afterward. The instructors worked us hard, but there was time to socialize as well. At first Vi wasn't on board, but I kept dragging her along, and eventually, she relaxed enough to joke around with the guys.

Day by day, it got easier to recognize the face in the mirror as my own, though I still wasn't used to my new body, even the second week in. I kept expecting my legs to be bigger or my pants not to fit when I slid into them. But I paid attention to what I ate, and I got in the habit of running in the morning with Seth. He didn't look like an athlete, another sign that I shouldn't judge by appearances. Maybe if my parents had been sportier, less academic, I would've valued physical activities as much as intellectual ones.

"Good run," Seth said, working slowly through his cooldown. He was teaching me about fitness without realizing it.

"Longest I've ever gone."

"Yeah? We should get cleaned up. They're taking us to NASA's Jet Propulsion Lab today."

I didn't need a second invitation to jog up to my room, where Vi was reading. "Tell me Seth looked super hot."

"I'll do better than tell you." Grinning, I showed her the sneaky photo I'd taken with my crappy phone camera.

"God, I love it here. The weather's gorgeous all the time, it's so pretty, and—"

"Seth," I finished, grabbing my basket of toiletries.

Vi threw a pillow at me, which hit the door as I darted out. My shower was quick, and I still needed to grab some lunch before the field trip. A glance at my phone told me I had thirty minutes to get ready and find food. Fortunately Vi had a sandwich waiting on the desk when I got back to the room.

"You have no idea how much I appreciate this," I said.

"It's just the opposite. You had no reason to be so nice at registration. I'm trying to repay you and prove I know how to be a good friend."

"You're the best." I hugged her with one arm as I ate.

"Hey, you'll get crumbs in my hair!"

"Whatev, Seth will groom you like a bonobo monkey," I teased.

Vi pretended to pout, but she couldn't hide her smile. I'd noticed the way his eyes followed her and the way he brightened when she entered the room. The boy straight up loved how she could hold her own when the tech talk commenced, getting down and dirty with all of the latest robotic trends. Some things were sexier than great hair and skinny jeans.

My old life, along with my problems at Blackbriar, seemed like a dream, a nightmare, really. Though I remembered the misery and desperation, I was happy. Maybe it was too soon to recover and I'd feel crappy as soon as I saw the Teflon crew's faces, but for now, the change of scenery and my first real friends were doing the trick. Even if life was imperfect, it was worth living, every minute, every second, and I'd fight to keep this new tenacity, once I went home. I learned that I had a weird sense of humor, but people liked me any-way—or maybe because of it. I'd spent my life cracking jokes in my head, wondering if anyone but me would laugh.

They did.

As for Ryu, I liked being part of something. I didn't fall wildly in love with him, but he was a great guy: kind, smart, funny, and hand-some. It was cool to sit next to him, looking up at the stars, while Vi and Seth whispered beside us. The first time he worked up the nerve to put his arm around her, I smothered a grin and turned to see Ryu watching me with a goofy smile on his face.

"You act like you've never seen people fall for each other before."

"Not from so close up," I said.

No. I doubted he'd believe me if I said I was operating from what I'd read in books as opposed to personal experience. That truth didn't fit my new look, even if I was more used to it. So Ryu would never truly know me, and that made me a little sad.

"They're pretty cute," he admitted.

"Did you know Seth before the SSP?"

"Only online. We've talked in various forums." From his tone, he'd rather not tell me which ones.

I could guess. "That's cool."

"Hey, do you mind if I take a picture of us, show you off to the guys back home?" His question gave me a weird twinge.

Before, he never would've wanted to do that, even if he liked me. How did I feel about being eye candy? It was bizarre and slightly unwelcome, not because I didn't think I was pretty now, but I wasn't before, and I was still the same person inside.

"No problem."

It wasn't fair to dump my ambivalence on him without context. This was probably a normal request and something he meant as a compliment. Obligingly I leaned in, tilted my head against his, and smiled. The flash blinded me for a few seconds, and when I focused on the girl in the photo with Ryu, it didn't feel like me, more as if somebody had transferred my consciousness into her body.

"We look great. Do you mind if I post this as a status update?"

"Go for it."

He got busy tapping on his phone, so he missed the moment when Seth leaned in and kissed Vi for the first time. They bumped noses, sweet and awkward, and I turned my face away, cheeks hot. Probably they thought I was too wrapped up in Ryu to notice. I liked him, but . . . he was safe. There was no chance of losing myself in him.

"And done." Before he could do more than hug me and kiss my cheek, the instructor called us to attention and directed us to our next lesson.

Possibly because there were only thirty-six of us, no cliques developed, and nobody was left out. And that was just on the social front. School-wise, I learned a ton. By the time the program wrapped up, we had gone to the Jet Propulsion Lab, the Caltech campus, and Griffith Observatory. Of the trips, I liked the last one most. There was something freeing about being surrounded by people who shared my interests. Nobody thought I was weird for being interested in the stars, not that I wanted to study them professionally. I just found them fascinating, so I enjoyed my time in the dome, working on the orbit determination project.

The weeks melted away, and I came out of the program stronger and more confident. *Kian will be proud*, I thought, as I put the last load of clothes I'd ever wash on this campus into the dryer. While I might not be completely used to my new self, I'd gotten good at pretending. *That'll have to be enough.*

The final night in our dorm room, Vi lay on her bed, dreamy-eyed. "Seth and I are going to keep in touch. I have his IM, Snapchat, WhatsApp, and stuff. He lives in Illinois, so he's only three hours away."

I paused the packing long enough to suggest, "You could meet halfway for dates."

She sat up in excitement, got online and found the town that was exactly an hour and a half between them. "Oh my God, I can't believe I never thought of this. It could totally work. I mean, we'd only see each other once a week, but it would be so worth it."

"He really likes you."

And it was so awesome to see that not all guys were assholes. Both Seth and Ryu were decent people, who cared more about what a girl was like than how she looked. But I couldn't help a kernel of doubt regarding Ryu when I considered that Seth had gone for Vi without her getting a complete makeover.

She wore a stubborn look. "Ryu's into you too. Sucks that he lives so far away."

"Yeah, I won't be doing the long-distance thing to Tokyo."

Vi relented with a laugh. "I guess not. I don't even know what the time difference is."

I'd been dorky enough to look it up, but both Ryu and I agreed while we could e-mail, it wouldn't be like we were in a relationship. We'd both be free to date, which was crucial for the next phase in my plan. I couldn't wait to see Cameron Dean—and not because I secretly adored the guy who had been so cruel to me. I had no soft feelings for him. This fall at Blackbriar I'd be a one-girl wrecking crew. And I knew who I'd hit the hardest.

Cameron had been the meanest of the guys, focused on me with an uncanny laser beam of douchebaggery. He was the one who got them to steal my gym clothes. He'd also squirted ketchup on my pants, which led to an endless parade of on-the-rag jokes. Then, of course, there was the worst prank—the one that broke me—but I wouldn't think about that right now. Slowly I shoved down the wave of endless shame.

Vi's here, and she likes me, here and now. She doesn't know any of that, thank God. Not that it would change things, but I needed a clean slate, free of mockery and humiliation. While I strangled memory demons, Vi called to tell Seth the good news and they talked for an hour, making plans. I laughed when I heard her arguing with him about where they should meet, because that would be their place from that point on, and didn't it deserve a little thought, and certainly shouldn't be a random Burger King? This was the girl who couldn't talk to a guy earlier in the summer, and gladness surged through me that I'd played a part in leaving her life a bit better than I'd found it. Otherwise, she hadn't changed. She wasn't prettier. But she had more confidence, which resulted in a boyfriend. The people who wrote articles about self-assurance being a great attractor obviously knew what was up.

"What's so funny?" she demanded, after she hung up.

"You are." Still laughing, I explained why.

She hurled a pillow at me, a habit I'd miss. "You're not wrong, though. It's pretty cool that I'm not freaked anymore. Guys are just people, you know? Some will like me, some won't. That's life."

"You're wise beyond your years, young Padawan."

"Whatever. I'm going to brush my teeth. And you should call Ryu."

Once Vi gathered her basket of bath supplies, I headed for the phone, which rang as I reached for it. Apparently, Seth had been telling Ryu the exact same thing.

"Hey, you," he said.

"Hey, yourself."

A knot formed in my throat. I liked talking with Ryu, laughing with him, his arm around my shoulders on a summer night, while we made notes on astrological phenomena.

"Did Vi lecture you?"

I laughed softly. "Yeah. They don't get that our circumstances are different. Long distance will be hard, but doable, for them."

"But it doesn't make sense for us," he replied.

"I knew that shirt was a good move." Idly I wondered why Kian had bought the thing.

"Are you going to wear it again?" Though he tried to hide it, I could tell he didn't want me to.

If I put the shirt on again, it would become a fetish-thing, like I was obsessed with Japanese guys, and I didn't plan to cheapen what we'd had.

"Nah," I said. "It did the trick. But I've gotta be honest. That shirt was a gift. I had no idea what it said. I just didn't want you to think I was an idiot."

He laughed. "I know. You covered, but I could tell. For the first thirty seconds, you were very *W-T-F?*" Ryu went on, "And of course you're not an idiot. You blew us all out of the water in physics. You're the total package."

I hadn't been, until Kian got his hands on me. My pulse fluttered, thinking about seeing him again. *Bad hormones. Cut that out.* Likely it was just a combination of factors that made me feel this way. He'd saved me, changed my life. How could I *not* feel something toward him? I'd get over it.

"I'll e-mail," I said softly. "With the time difference, it'll be tough to Skype."

"Cool. And who knows where we'll go to college."

"Are you considering the US?"

"Yep. My mom's family lives in Sacramento."

I'd known his dad was Japanese, his mother American, transferred overseas by her company; she met his dad, loved it there, and stayed. Since I hadn't expected to be alive, I'd made no college plans. A spark of remorse popped like a live wire; I had lied through my teeth when my parents checked with me, and because they *trusted* me, they didn't demand to see my scores. Why would they? I didn't deceive them, so far as they knew, and I never got in trouble. I was smart; I had their genes, and I always brought home straight As. So when I made up some results and accepted the accolades, they ordered pizza.

Fortunately, there was still time to salvage the wreck of the SS *University*. "I need to take the SATs again," I murmured.

Lie. I'd never taken them. I told my parents I'd signed up, but instead I went to the movies and ate popcorn all day. Busy with research, grad students, and grant proposals, they let me manage academic milestones because it taught self-reliance. This way, I wouldn't go off to college and end up dying in a pile of my own vomit because I'd never been in charge of my own life. From listening to Vi talk about her parents, I'd come to understand my folks weren't uncaring; they just didn't realize how their hands-off approach felt to me. What they meant as a show of faith registered as indifference, though teenagers with helicopter parents would prize the freedom I'd taken for granted. It was amazing how much I'd learned—and changed—in five short weeks.

He glanced at me, brows raised. "That surprises me."

"It was a bad day."

"I'm sure you'll rock them next time," Ryu said.

"Anyway, yeah, I'll let you know what schools I'm considering."

He sounded more cheerful already. "And vice versa. Even if we never date again, it would be fun to hang out."

I smiled. "You too. Have a safe flight home, Ryu."

"Bye, Edie."

Before he could say anything else, if he would, I put down the phone, and it didn't ring again. I was glad he knew when to let go. A few minutes later, Vi came in, cheeks pink.

I raised a brow at how obviously kissed she looked. "Did you sneak up to see Seth? I hope Barbie RA didn't catch you."

"Nope. I'm a ninja." She couldn't say this with a straight face, or maybe making out with Seth had left her with that can't-stop-smiling expression.

"Don't leave your throwing stars where I can step on them in the morning."

"You're leaving early too? I got my parents to change my flight. I'm going to Chicago with Seth, then I'll catch a connection, and he'll take the bus."

"Sweet. I'll try not to wake you when I head out."

"Then I'd better do this while I can." Vi ran over and hugged me. "I told all my friends about you, by the way. They hope you'll come visit so they can meet you."

"I'll try." I had no doubt Vi's friends were cool and nice.

I could use more of that in my life.

Before bed, I packed and got everything ready to go. I fell asleep thinking about Kian, wondering if he'd look the same, if it would be weird after the kiss. The alarm on my phone went off at seven, and Vi didn't stir. Taking my clothes, I snuck out with my bath supplies. After I showered, I dried off and dressed in the dorm bathroom, and then went back to the room to grab my bags. A quick check verified that I'd left nothing behind, so I slipped out for the last time.

My cell said it was 7:46, early, but no time for breakfast; that didn't matter since I'd be home in ten seconds. I found the spot where he'd dropped me off and pushed into the quiet, leafy cathedral. At least that was how it felt to me with the sun shining through the leaves, all green-cast. It was silent and sacred, divorced from the other side of the hedge.

At precisely 8:00 a.m., Kian appeared. I'd convinced myself he couldn't be everything I'd remembered.

He was.

HOME IS WHERE
THE HEARTACHE IS

His dark hair fell over one eye. In the half-lighted forest, the copper streaks were muted. But his face retained the haunting beauty that made my chest hurt, like it was too much to look directly at him. I wondered if he ever tired of that; if he'd made the wish young and now he wished to be a little more ordinary. Otherwise, how could he be sure it wasn't always his face people wanted and not who he was inside? Or maybe he didn't care. What did I know about him, after all?

Kian made no allusion to the kiss, the smoking-hot, life-changing, why-doesn't-he-do-it-again-right-now kiss. "Did you enjoy the SSP?"

"It rocked. I learned a lot. Made some new friends."

"And got used to the new you?" That had been the point.

"I think so. It feels a bit more natural now." I still wasn't used to the way guys watched me, or how they tried to help me with things I was capable of doing myself.

"Then let's get you home."

My heart dropped a little in disappointment. "I have a couple of questions."

You do? Really? My brain was surprised to hear that. But I couldn't just let him dump me off. I hadn't seen him in weeks; I wouldn't see him until I was ready to ask for my next favor, and I had no idea when that would be.

"About the deal?" he asked in neutral tones.

"Of course."

"Have you had breakfast?"

I shook my head.

"Let's go, then." To my surprise, he pushed out of the leaves.

I followed. "But this is business-related, can't you hitch us somewhere?"

"I could, but every expenditure is tracked. I'd rather not risk running over my monthly power allotment when there are decent places to eat nearby."

"You're not the one hauling luggage," I muttered.

"I am now." He took my wheeled suitcase and backpack before I could protest. "Is this all you bought?"

"Yep. I'm a simple girl."

"No, you're not."

I eyed him. "Like you know me."

"Don't you think we study a person before they reach extremis, Edie? I know exactly who you are . . . and what you've been through."

A shiver went through me. I wasn't sure how I felt about that. Exposed, certainly, but there was warmth too. With Kian, I didn't have to pretend I wasn't a screwed-up mess with a head full of payback plans. He understood. And I'd never face a moment like the one with Ryu, where I realized I was keeping the ugly bits hidden away.

"Okay, I take it back. Thanks for carrying my stuff."

"Edie?"

Before turning, I recognized the voice. Ryu stood forty feet away, looking shocked. Kian and I weren't touching, but he was carrying my luggage in a fairly purposeful way.

"Just a sec," I said.

Jogging, I closed the distance between us. "What's up?"

"Who's that?"

Awkwardness jittered over me, making me shuffle my feet. Kian's gaze bore into my back, but it was impossible to explain him in a way Ryu would understand. Our summer thing might've ended last night when we said good-bye, but I got how he felt. Sort of *damn, it's the next day . . . she didn't like me at all.* I didn't want to leave him with that impression.

A few deep breaths allowed me to be cool, outwardly at least. Inner-Edie was banging her head on a wall. "Kian, my ride. You want to meet him?"

Ryu registered that and relaxed. "I'm on my way to the airport, but I have a minute."

"Did you want to get breakfast with us?"

"I don't have time for that . . . but thanks." He was smiling now. Relieved, even though he didn't want me to know it.

But factoring in this summer, I'd still spent more time watching people than talking to them. My school survival had depended on reading situations correctly and knowing when to get the hell out. I led him over to where Kian stood, waiting with one hand on the handle of my suitcase. His face gave more neutrality; his bearing radiated snow and Switzerland. Still, he waved, as if anything about this was normal.

"Ryu, Kian."

They exchanged some kind of palm-slap, fist-bump thing. We made small talk for a few moments; Kian wasn't rude, just . . . reserved. I couldn't read him, and Ryu didn't seem to notice anything off. Soon, Ryu's cab pulled up to the curb. He leaned down to kiss me good-bye—and I didn't have to ask. I gave my response just enough warmth to send him off happy and he got in with a promise to e-mail me.

"Summer boyfriend?" Kian guessed, as the taxi pulled away.

"Yeah. I needed to date a nice guy before taking on the alpha ass-clown at Blackbriar."

"Good call."

"Why did you give me that T-shirt anyway?" I didn't think he'd pretend not to know what I meant.

He tipped his head back, gazing up at the tangle of green leaves overhead. "My boss told me to."

"Did he tell you why?"

"He said it would put you on the right path."

"That's cryptic. I was supposed to meet Ryu?" If I believed half of this bullshit, it could drive me crazy in short order. "Why does your boss care who I date?"

His eyes went flat. "There's a café down the road, is that okay?"

He totally just changed the subject. He doesn't want to talk about it. It was stupid, but a spark kindled inside me, racing through my veins with irresistible warmth. Though I knew perfectly well Kian meant to keep his mind on business, maybe I didn't. Maybe I wouldn't.

"Yeah, fine."

Jeannine's was nicer than an IHOP, but still reasonably priced, which made sense since they served the kind of food drunk students loved to eat and could afford. The sun was bright, the sky pure azure. I enjoyed the walk, though it passed in silence. I liked physical activity more now. The runs with Seth three times a week had given me a taste for it, and I'd keep it up after I got home. Along the way, I pondered why Kian's employer cared about my social life.

Kian didn't speak again until we settled into a booth. "You said you had questions?"

"Sure. Are *you* on the list of people your boss wants me to date?" *Straight up, put yourself out there.* But it wasn't like I was totally exposed. As far as he knew, I might be asking out of intellectual curiosity.

I wasn't.

"As of now? No. What else?"

I thought fast. "You said I have to use the last two favors within five years. Is that the only caveat? Does there need to be a time lapse between them or can I ask for both together?"

"Within five years. That's all." His jade-and-amber gaze sharpened. "You expect me to believe *this* is why you wanted to delay the trip home? You could've asked that on your doorstep. You said questions. Plural."

Do you ever think about kissing me? Did you miss me? But those weren't business-related, as I'd claimed this was, and I wasn't nearly brave enough. It would take more than the SSP to give me that kind of confidence.

Luckily I had another concern. "The guy who had my slot broke his leg. Did you have anything to do with that?"

Kian didn't deny it. "I told Wedderburn I needed you enrolled as part of your favor. He handled things from there."

Damn. So his boss made it happen. Somehow. That's . . . alarming.

"He doesn't care who gets hurt?"

"Wedderburn's definition of harm is different from ours. 'The leg will heal in six weeks and to him, that's no time at all." I could tell Kian was quoting his employer. "If you're asking if I knew, I didn't. He never shares his plans with me until it's too late for me to do anything about it."

He seems so sad. I wonder how many of us he juggles. Unease trickled down my spine, shadowing a bright and sunny morning. So I changed the subject.

"One last thing, I'm worried about the repayment plan . . . it's just vague enough to make me nervous. Can you tell me how it went for you?"

He thought about it, as if going through a mental rulebook in his head. "Actually, I can, as long as I don't give you specifics about anything else."

"Then tell me, please?"

Before he could, the waitress came back. I ordered a high-protein scramble while Kian chose blueberry pancakes with extra whipped cream. Made me wonder if he'd wished for the ability to eat everything and not gain weight. *Is that even possible?*

Once the server left, he murmured, "Okay. Well, I was fifteen when I hit extremis. And I used all my favors within a year." Faint regret threaded his words.

"Why so fast?"

His silence said he had no intention of telling me that. *Fair enough.* God, I wished I knew why he'd been so unhappy. This wasn't fair; he knew everything about me. But then, we weren't friends. Had no relationship apart from the deal.

I delved elsewhere. "You look so young, it can't have been long before they called for repayment."

"Are you asking how old I am?" He sounded amused.

"It doesn't matter." Except to satisfy my curiosity—and he obviously wouldn't.

"I'm not supposed to share personal information."

"I bet you weren't supposed to kiss me, either." My gaze flew up, unable to believe I'd said it out loud.

"If anyone had been monitoring us then, I'd have been removed from your contract," he said quietly. "And . . . penalized for misconduct."

I didn't want that. "I'm sorry. Why did you do it, then?"

"You know why."

I wasn't sure enough to go there, no matter what I hoped. "Can you tell me about your . . . what? Recruiter? Handler?"

"We're called liaisons. And that depends on what you want to know."

"Name, how you met. That kind of stuff."

"His name was Raoul, and we met at my uncle's fishing cabin." By his expression, that reply skirted the edge of what he was permitted to tell me. It didn't encourage more questions about what happened that day.

"Did you like him?"

Half smile. "I didn't ask him to kiss me, if that's what you're getting at."

"Are you still in contact with him?"

His smile faded. "No."

"What was he like?"

"You've seen *Highlander*, right?"

That was a rhetorical question; I could see that he knew I'd watched it a hundred times and owned the director's cut DVD. But I nodded anyway.

"Ramirez. He was like Ramirez."

I pictured a rugged guy with silver hair and a salt-and-pepper beard, clapping Kian on the shoulder and telling him to stop whining. "It must've been . . . epic."

"It kinda was."

"No wonder you took the deal."

Our food arrived then. We ate in silence while I mulled a loophole that would let him spend the day with me—without burning another favor. I wasn't that dumb.

"Most people do," he said eventually.

"What's the most common favor requested?"

"Money."

"I should've guessed. What if I need your help to research a potential request in ways unavailable to me? Is that allowed?"

He leveled a long look on me. "Edie . . . don't rush the other two favors. Seriously."

What are you trying to tell me with those eyes? I held his gaze, unable to access higher logical functions. When he went back to eating, I felt like I'd been freed from a spell. *Kian casts level 50 hotness. Failed my saving throw.*

"I won't," I said, low.

"But . . ." He hesitated, as if weighing what he was about to say. "If you need help with something contract-related, I'll provide it. Part of the job."

"It could take all day," I said.

This is a bad idea trembled on the tip of his tongue; I saw it hovering and then he said, "My schedule's clear."

"You have other clients?"

"Never more than five at a time."

I squirreled that away with the small store of information I'd gleaned. So he had four people, like me, who had been saved in extremis. I wondered how many favors they'd requested, how old they were, how often he saw them, and if he'd *kissed* any of them. Likely, there was a confidentiality clause; he seemed constrained by all kinds of rules.

"Before, you mentioned monitoring? How often—"

"I don't know," he cut in. "And that's sort of the point. It's meant to keep me honest and on task."

"Is it like when you call the phone company and they tell you your call may be recorded for your protection and in order to provide better service?"

"More or less."

This was frustrating. I wanted to get to know him, but he'd already said he wasn't permitted to share personal information. I didn't want to get him in trouble, or worse, removed from my contract. That meant I'd never see him again. And he must feel the same or he wouldn't be cooperating, especially against his better judgment.

"If I'm pushing, just tell me. I won't break."

I did once. It won't happen again.

"It's not that," he said quietly.

His gaze slipped to his watch, which was unlike any I'd ever seen before. The face sparkled with an unusual crystal, and there were multiple buttons along the side. I could tell I was meant to take a cue from the significant look, so I studied it, but no immediate answers came to me. Then I dug into my backpack for pen and paper. I didn't know what form the monitoring might take; there was a guy on my block who was convinced the government could eavesdrop from space via satellite.

I wrote, *What does the watch have to do with how they track you?*

Kian leaned over, read, and then replied, *It logs everything. They can use it to listen in, anytime they want. It also records my power usage, and there are accountants who resolve my output against the favors I've granted.*

That sounded horrible. *Can you take it off?*

Face grim, he shook his head, and then told me with a tilt of his head to put the paper away before someone got curious. We had been quiet too long. Before, he'd mentioned his headquarters, but claimed he didn't want to take me there because it might freak me out. I was starting to understand why. The shadowy people Kian worked for—with their incredible power and oppressive control—didn't sound like they offered severance packages, unless you meant head from neck.

I realized I might be endangering him with my pursuit, and that shook me. So I finished my food while asking harmless questions about the deal. Relief warred with regret in his expression. Futile wishes rode high in his eyes as he paid the check. With an inner twist, I slid out of the booth.

"You can take me home. My questions didn't take as long as I thought. And I need to think before requesting my next favor."

"Are you sure?" he asked.

While he might be willing to gamble that he wouldn't get caught bending the rules, I wasn't. I nodded. "Thanks for breakfast."

Kian led the way from the restaurant, and like before, he found a quiet alcove, where he took my hand. The world skipped, like we were moving too fast for me to see, and I had that same sense of velocity in my stomach, when I stuttered back into existence in the alley a few blocks from my apartment. He still had my things, so I reached for them. I didn't want to let go of his hand because I didn't know when I'd see him again, but I made myself uncurl my fingers.

He pressed a square of paper into my palm, but he didn't acknowledge the move verbally. "Can you manage your stuff from here?" Polite tone, professional.

"Yeah."

"Then I'll see you." As farewells went, it was anemic and lackluster, but his eyes said other things.

Or maybe I just wanted them to.

Stop it, I told myself. *You had that one kiss, and that's the end of it. You're lucky he didn't get caught.*

I took two steps out of the alley, and when I glanced over my shoulder, he was already gone. It was just as well; I had a lot on my plate. School would be starting in ten days. I had new uniforms to buy, supplies to acquire—then I stopped because I couldn't bullshit myself for another second. I had to read the note he'd written.

Don't trust anyone but me. I'll contact you soon.

Maybe he was trying to spook me into asking for another favor? Protection against his psychotic bosses, perhaps. I wasn't entirely sure I should trust Kian either, regardless of how beautiful or tortured he might be. It didn't hurt to be wary.

And I had to plan, now, for the life I hadn't expected to possess, come fall. Not every kid would receive a magical lifeline, though. As I walked toward the brownstone, I wondered whether I could volunteer at a hotline or something, share my experiences with people who weren't as lucky. Probably I had to be at least eighteen or receive some special training, so I deferred the idea. I could make time during my freshman year of college to pay it forward.

Nerves crept up from my stomach as I got closer to home. I'd only talked to my parents twice this summer, plus a flurry of e-mails and text messages. To preserve my independence, they'd set up an it's-really-you code word that I used to close all my texts. That way, they didn't have to worry that I'd been kidnapped and my captor was using my phone. My parents watched too much *Criminal Minds*, maybe, but the system worked without a lot of phone chatter, and it was easier for them to respond on the road. Last time I heard from them, they said they'd be back a couple of days before me.

Wonder how they'll react to the new me.

They'd be surprised . . . for so many reasons. I told myself it wouldn't help to put it off, so I climbed the stairs to the apartment. After taking a deep breath, I got out my keys and unlocked the door. They weren't in the front room, so they must've slept in . . . and were lingering over their oatmeal in the kitchen.

"I'm home!" I called.

Both my parents came to the kitchen doorway, then drew up short. Their faces reflected pure shock—and in my dad's case, it rapidly faded to horror. "Edith . . . ?"

"How was your summer?" I asked, playing it like I didn't notice their reactions.

"Busy." My dad listed all of the conferences, and it was mind-boggling. It sounded like they'd put a lot of miles behind them. If I had been in the city, I would've been lucky to see them once in two months.

My parents did their brain-sharing thing, trading a look laden with information, and then my mom said, "You look good, honey."

"Thanks. My roomie was kind of a fitness buff, and she got me to work out with her." I spoke the lie with a mental apology to Vi. "We fit in a trip to the salon too."

Results like this couldn't come from a simple summer regimen alone or a cut and color, but my parents, being utterly unconcerned with personal appearance, didn't know that. They fumbled for a few seconds, murmuring incoherent words of support and approval. It was kind of cute how much they didn't know how to react; clearly, they'd never discussed this, as they'd raised me to be a brainy overachiever.

"Well, as long as you're happy," my dad finally said, as if I'd gotten a tattoo or dyed my hair fuchsia. "How was the SSP?"

I could tell they were both eager to get back on familiar footing, so I took them through the syllabus and what I'd learned, which put them at ease. Having good hair hadn't rotted my brain, at least. After I finished my summary, I said, "I've gotta unpack, if that's okay. Then I need to do some shopping before school." At their mutually alarmed look, I added, "Just uniforms. And normal supplies."

I still had to wear the green-and-navy plaid skirt, white blouse, and blue blazer that made up the Blackbriar dress code. There were ways to make the getup seem stylish, though, and if you were one of the beautiful people, the teachers let you get away with infractions, like too much jewelry or makeup, skirt hiked up, platform Mary Janes, that sort of thing. Most of the popular chicks looked like they belonged in a schoolgirls-gone-wild video. I had just over a week to put together my own look without copying them.

"Of course," my mom said. "I'll give you the Visa."

I nodded. "After I put my stuff away, okay?"

"You look perky after being at the airport," my dad said.

They were smart people. If I slipped up, they'd start wondering, and I couldn't afford questions. "Yeah, I took the red-eye, slept all night."

"The only way to travel."

Before they could ask anything else, I grabbed my bags and ran to my room. Once I closed the door, I felt a little safer. Thankfully, we didn't have a close relationship or they'd wonder at how eager I was to get away. But I'd always spent my time alone in my room, so this didn't change anything at all.

First thing, I did as I'd claimed, then I sent quick e-mails to Vi and Ryu. I didn't expect an answer anytime soon as they had lives to get back to, but I considered them my only real friends, which was kind of sad. But at least I *had* some, now. Just knowing they existed—and that they liked me—helped me gear up for the showdown to come. Which totally made me sound like I was strapping on six-shooters and challenging Cameron Dean to a shoot-out at high noon. The truth was way more devious.

For the remainder of the day, I spent time online, learning different ways to style my hair, methods of using shadow, eyeliner, bronzer, and other products I'd only heard of vaguely before this summer. This was stuff my mother never taught me; I didn't think *she* knew. If I'd asked, I was positive I'd receive a lecture on the dangers of vanity versus the value of feminism, but this wasn't strictly for the sake of appearances. No, this was a disguise for my undercover work at Blackbriar. To infiltrate the inner circle, the beautiful people needed to think I'd changed enough to become one of them. Hence, the camouflage. I'd always been an overachiever in the academic world, now it was time to apply that trait to my social life.

My mom knocked on the door around nine. She waited for me to open it before she spoke. "You said you needed some things before school starts?"

"I thought I'd go shopping tomorrow."

"Do you want me to go with you?" Her tone said she'd rather be summoned to jury duty, but that she felt like she needed to make the offer.

"No, it's fine."

"Then here's the card. Save your receipts, please." That was Mom, always concerned about making the numbers in all columns tally up; she must drive her grad students crazy.

God knew what she'd say if I confessed the true explanation for my transformation. Best guess? She'd decide I had taken some dangerous, highly illegal weight-loss drug and ship me off to rehab. And from there, I couldn't accomplish the one goal I'd set myself this summer—to make Cameron Dean pay, along with the rest of the assholes in his group.

So I smiled at her, and it must've made her suspicious. She hesitated in my doorway. "Do you want to talk about . . . anything?"

I pretended to misunderstand the question. "No, my schedule is already programmed. I'm taking Advanced Calculus, physics, AP Literature, World History, Introduction to Japanese, photography, and computer science."

"Sounds like a balanced curriculum. Good night, then."

She let herself out, doubtless praising herself for raising such an organized, rational child. The truth would devastate her, both of them, actually. My computer beeped, telling me I had an e-mail. It could only be Ryu or Vi since there was nobody else.

Are you home yet? I forget how long the flight is to Boston. Anyway, I'm back. My mom threw me the lamest WELCOME HOME party. There was Jell-O. You said you go to Blackbriar, right? I bet you missed your real friends, but I'm glad I met you. Talk soon! Vi.

"Real friends?" I said aloud.

Right. In a month or so, I might have people who *pretended* to like me, who want to know me, but they would be a means to an end. The Teflon crew had *no* idea of the Armageddon bearing down on them.

BLOOD IN THE
WATER

I n the morning, I completed the getting-ready process and went out
to face the world. Deep down I was a little uncomfortable with my
new clothes, even if I'd been wearing them all summer. Part of me still
wanted to pull my hair into my face and hunch my shoulders and walk
too fast, as if that could keep people from looking at me, judging me.
It took all of the confidence I'd built up at SSP to step out of the brownstone. Our downstairs neighbor smiled at me as he came up the four
steps that led into the building; Mr. Lewis was a notorious crank, but
I thought he might actually doff his cap. I braced and headed for the
T station.

My first stop had to be Blackbriar; the school uniform store was
open as of today, and none of the clothes I had from last year fit me.
My stomach churned as I went underground, used my Charlie Card,
and got on a car that wasn't as packed as it would've been earlier in
the day. Plus, I was heading away from the city center.

Blackbriar had an Auburndale address. The school was the size of
a small private college, "lush, pastoral grounds where the curriculum

is . . ." and some shit in the mission statement about respect and diversity, but there sure were a lot of white faces at Blackbriar. It went along with the country club nearby, and the price tag on my annual tuition.

My parents lived relatively close to the university without paying the prices of Beacon Hill or Back Bay. Which left me twenty minutes from school on the T, and the walk from the station wasn't so bad, unless it was raining or snowing. On those days, I could count on some asshole to splash me when he went past in his expensive sports car, paid for with Daddy's money. Since my parents were college professors, I had good health coverage and excellent academic resources but no car. Their patent paid enough to keep me at Blackbriar, but my folks weren't swimming in cash, unlike the majority of the school. People at school had summer homes in Martha's Vineyard and jetted to Europe on winter break.

And I live in a walkup and ride the T.

For the first time in my life, I had trouble on the subway. Homeliness was like a cloak of invisibility. People often pretended they didn't see me or if they got caught looking, their gazes slid away. Sometimes I used to overhear whispered jokes or throwaway insults, and I was pretty inured to it. But today, two frat guys jostled over the seat next to me, and the victorious one immediately sprawled into my space, so I had to touch my bare knee to his or pull my legs closer together. *Good old lavaballing.*

I was supposed to look at him, I think, or acknowledge him in some way, but instead I sat silent through the ride despite a couple of attempts to catch my attention. Apparently, that merited a mutter of "Stuck-up bitch," as I got off the train.

Pass, jackass. Not interested.

I considered the purchase of uniforms a dry run, so to speak. Most of the students around today would be underclassmen or those who gained weight or lost it over the summer, but this should help me gauge people's reactions. I was betting most wouldn't recognize me. Since I was dressed in Converse, shorts, and a tank top, I ran from the station to the front gate, mostly to see how long it took.

Six minutes.

The black wrought-iron gate was open, inviting alumni and current students to enter the magical land of learning. During the school year, there would be guards here because the children of politicians, dignitaries, and executives attended Blackbriar. At pickup, the cul-de-sac would be full of black SUVs and bodyguards collecting the under-sixteen offspring of important people. I followed the paved drive toward the brick building with white trim and matching colonial columns.

Funny that my personal hell could look so charming.

The main building housed the administrative offices, the library, auditorium, and a few freshman classrooms. Green manicured lawns crossed with stone paths led between the various departments, each built in a unique architectural fashion. The athletic complex, also known as the Stinkatorium, was built in what I'd call Greek Revival style, with white stone facing, pillars, and a dome over the swimming pool.

The sheer scale of the campus sometimes made it hard to get to class on time, and it was worse when some jackass had you cornered. *Not that the teachers cared* why *I was late.* I stepped through the front door and scanned for changes. Since it was mid-August, the hall was practically empty, apart from a few scared-looking transfer students. I understood that reaction; Blackbriar was intimidating as hell, and it would probably take them a week to remember where all of their classes were located. Most of the buildings had been named after school benefactors, so that made it even harder to keep it all straight.

Student volunteers sold uniforms in the school store, where you could buy all kinds of branded crap: pens, notebooks, folders, jackets, T-shirts, hats, along with the required school garb. I knew my sizes, so I strode in, mostly wanting to get this over with. I froze for a few seconds when I recognized Cameron Dean, currently facing away from me while he fiddled with the stock. The old, awful humiliation washed over me, until I thought I might be sick.

Choke it down. Otherwise you blow your second chance, along with chunks. Stay calm. This could work to your advantage. If he puts the word out on you, it'll make the first day of school easier.

So I took one breath, two, and thought of Kian. His face sprang to my mind's eye, steadying me. And it wasn't the fact that he was hot that bolstered me; it was that he'd liked me before. *Or so he'd said.*

Cameron had brown hair and sparkling blue eyes, the quintessential all-American guy. He even had a nice smile—with dimples—not that I'd ever seen it before. But the minute I stepped up to the counter, he went into dazzle mode, though he had been dating Brittany King, head queen bee, for almost two years.

"You must be new," he said.

I shook my head, pushing my list of clothing requirements across the counter toward him. It gave me a ridiculous amount of pleasure to say, "Guess again. I didn't come to chat with the help. Could you fill my order, please?"

His smile slipped, as if he couldn't fathom that I hadn't immediately fallen victim to his charm. "I don't actually *work* here. I'm helping the PTA because I'm a nice guy."

"Too good to make an honest living, huh?" My mouth twisted in a scornful smile. "Why am I not surprised?"

"Do you have a problem with me?" he demanded.

Too far, I cautioned myself.

"Only that I still don't have my uniforms." I paused, tilting my head. "Wait, you thought I was serious? Don't you have a sense of humor?"

I had been listening to people say cruel, unforgivable things my whole life, usually to me, and then playing it off like I was the one with the problem. *You gonna cry, Eat-it? Can't take a joke? Why don't you do the world a favor and just kill yourself already?*

And I almost did. Hateful words had a way of worming beneath the skin, until they became the unbearable echo in your head. But I wasn't listening anymore.

"Right," he said, moving to pull my clothes from various piles.

Then Cameron used a calculator to total a bill I could've done in my head. Kind of hard not to mock him, but I managed. I'd blown cold enough for this encounter. Though I'd rather tongue kiss a tailpipe, now I had to convince him I didn't think he was the most disgusting creature ever to crawl out of the primordial ooze.

Maybe I should go out for drama.

I handed him the credit card after he gave the damage. Pausing, he said, "Mildred Kramer? Huh."

"It's my mom's card." Though I was pretty sure that wasn't why he was wearing the I'm-thinking-hard-and-it-hurts look.

"I figured. You don't look like a Mildred."

"She knows I have it, if that's what you're worried about."

Go on and make the connection, genius.

"No, it's not that. We had a girl named Kramer here last year."

"Oh?" Noncommittal reply. "It's a common name."

"I guess. Are you a junior?"

I shook my head. If I wasn't so determined to make him pay, I could almost feel sorry for Cameron, because he didn't have enough cerebral wattage to light up a single Christmas bulb. "Senior this year. I'm surprised you don't remember. You used to pay an awful lot of attention to me."

"Eat-it?" he blurted. "I mean . . . *Edith?*"

"My friends call me Edie," I said breezily.

Not that he would ever number among them.

"Holy shit. What the hell did you *do* this summer?"

I just smiled. "Do you think you could run that card instead of tapping it on the counter? I still need to get school supplies."

Mostly I wanted to get away from him before I started shaking or burst into tears. Remembering what he'd done to me—and how utterly fine with it he seemed—I could hardly breathe for the tightness in my chest. The shame washed high, higher, until it collared my throat, the spiked-leather dog version. Pure inner steel kept me upright and my lips curved into a smile that swore I wasn't on the verge of total collapse.

"Yeah. Sorry." Now he was awkward and fumbling.

Somehow I kept it together until he gave me the ticket to sign. I was an authorized user on my mom's card, so I scrawled on the slip and passed it back. In return he handed me my bag of uniforms. *Still have to figure out how to rock this without looking like I'm trying too hard.*

"See you around," I said.

Smooth strides carried me out of the store and then I practically ran into the restroom, where I leaned my head against the wall, trembling. Slowly the urge to barf passed, but before I straightened up, a girl came in. I recognized her as Jennifer Bishop, a peripheral member of the Teflon crew. She wasn't as popular as Brittany or Allison, but since she was one of them, I couldn't trust her. Jennifer had dark hair and eyes; she looked as if she had Thai heritage, though her last name didn't reflect it.

"Are you all right?" she asked.

"Yeah, I just didn't eat breakfast. I'm a little light-headed." Bending down, I splashed some cold water on my face, then belatedly realized that most girls wouldn't do that because it would destroy their makeup.

Looking in the mirror, I saw that I had, in fact, screwed up my eyeliner. With a faint sigh, I got a paper towel and did what I could to amend the damage. Now I got why girls in the Teflon crew carried around a cosmetics studio. Apparently I still had some things to learn.

"You can use mine if you want." She was touching up her face, but the idea of risking pink eye was enough to make me shake my head.

"Thanks, but I'm headed home now anyway."

"It's Edith, right?"

I was honestly surprised. "Edie. Have we met?"

"No, but I know who you are."

After what Cameron did, that was probably true of everyone at school, to say nothing of the five thousand viewers on YouTube. "What can I say, I'm memorable."

"I hesitate to say this, but . . . you had me worried toward the end of last year. You look amazing now, though. I guess summer break put things in perspective?"

"Yeah." *More than you can ever know.*

"I just want you to know, I had nothing to do with what happened. And I'm really sorry." That was the most I'd ever heard Jennifer say.

"I survived. For what it's worth, I know it wasn't your idea. Talk to you later."

She wore a pained look as I pushed past her, but I wasn't interested in her crisis of conscience. For the sake of my sanity, I needed to get away from Blackbriar and marshal my strength for school next week. Bag in hand, I jogged out of the main building and toward the gate. Guys yelled after me; there were whistles and catcalls, but it didn't make me feel pretty or special. It just made me feel worse, knowing that it didn't matter what kind of person I was, only how I looked.

Eventually, I collected myself enough to head for the T station. In the city, I bought school supplies, and when I got home, my parents were both out. That was par for the course. Since I turned thirteen, I'd spent a fair amount of time alone. I wished my parents had evaluated the social atmosphere at Blackbriar in addition to the academics, but stuff like that didn't occur to them. They saw high school as a hurdle to overcome on the way to an awesome adult life, and I should ignore people who made fun of me. I tried to talk to my mom about it once, and she told me a long story about how things were worse for her growing up and I should be grateful for my advantages. That was the end of me trying to make her understand just how *bad* things had gotten.

Too late now.

Over the next week, I wrote back and forth with Vi, less often to Ryu. I had the impression that he was pretty popular in Japan. It would've made me sad if I thought he was seriously hung up on me, but his quick notes were just about back-to-school stuff. In the mornings, I took to running, mostly because it was exercise I could do with the clothes and shoes I already owned. If my parents thought it was weird that I was up at seven every day and racing through the city

93

streets, neither my mom nor my dad said a word. My new interest in fitness came partly from a desire to keep the body I'd sold my soul for—I hoped not literally—and the rest had to do with burning nervous energy.

The night before school started, I talked to Vi on Skype. "So how's Boston?" she asked, faking a bad townie accent.

"It didn't change since I left it, so that's good. How are things with you and Seth?"

Vi went for fifteen minutes about how awesome he was, and the fact that they were planning to hook up next weekend. I probably shouldn't have asked, if I didn't want the long, detailed answer. Partway through, I tuned out.

When I checked back in, she was saying, "Anyway, his mom says he can't drive to meet me every weekend, and they had a big fight, but eventually they compromised, so we're going every other, and he's paying for part of the car insurance."

"Sounds like a fair deal."

She nodded. "Plus it gives us the chance to make sure we don't fall behind in school. When I'm not seeing him, I'll catch up on projects and extra credit."

Only people from the nerd phylum would say "extra credit" without a sneer or a mocking laugh, but I'd always liked learning what teachers came up with to challenge us. Sometimes it was silly, not hard at all, but it showed you were willing to try. Since I'd had no social life, I was always about a hundred bonus points into A+ territory.

"So," Vi concluded, "I just wanted to tell you to have a great first day."

"You too."

She paused. "Were you listening at all? We don't start until next week."

Oops. It looked like I wasn't a great listener, and I'd missed some stuff that wasn't Seth-relevant, but I'd get better with practice. Except for the SSP, I had more experience hiding from people than talking to them.

"Lucky."

"I'm kind of bored," she confessed.

"Me too."

The waiting was getting to me as well. I kept checking my phone to see if Kian had texted, but nothing so far. It would be a relief to get this mission underway.

Soon after, Vi disconnected and I got ready for bed. One benefit of working out, however, was that I suffered from insomnia less. Despite myriad fears about tomorrow, I fell straight into a dreamless sleep. My alarm blared too early, but I rolled out of bed and went through the regimen I had practiced the week before.

In the end, I decided to go with classic schoolgirl. I wouldn't be wearing thigh-high stockings or tying up my shirt the minute the teachers looked the other way. Instead I wore my uniform nearly as intended: blue knee socks, innocent Mary Janes, two buttons open on the blouse, and skirt rolled up once at the waistband to make it a bit shorter than strictly permissible. I'd seen girls daring much more, however. I did my hair up in a twist, a sexy, tousled one with curls escaping. This look that seemed effortless took me almost half an hour, more with makeup time. But in the end, it was worth it.

At last, I looked like one of the beautiful people, somebody you'd see cruising the halls with the Teflon crew. I had fruit and yogurt for breakfast, brushed my teeth, and waved at my parents, who were barely stirring. They were both kind of night owls, not in the party sense but that they'd stay up late watching documentaries or reading articles in scientific journals while sipping endless cups of hot tea.

"You want oatmeal?" Mom asked.

"No, I'm fine. I ate already. Bye!"

It was time to shift from planning and preparation to payback and penance. By the time I was done at Blackbriar, there would be blood in the water.

THE SHARKS ARE CIRCLING, CIRCLING

W hen I entered DeWitt Hall, where all language arts and literature classes were held, people stared as I walked by. In the old
days, that would've meant the Teflon crew had stuck something on
my back or circulated a new rumor. This time it signified a different
kind of attention, but it was no easier to bear—for different reasons.
Kian probably knew how this felt, and maybe he'd wanted to caution
me about this.

One guy whispered, "Who *is* that?"

"The new and improved Edie Kramer."

"Holy shit."

"I know, right? How do you go from barks like a dog to that in a
summer?"

A girl whose name I didn't know pushed into the conversation
with a scornful "I heard she had plastic surgery. Lipo, nose job, nips,
tucks, lifts, and—"

"You have no idea how much I don't care," the guy said. "Like *you*
were born with that nose, Tara."

I felt his eyes on me as I turned the corner and stepped into my first class. My knees felt shaky, but soon the talk would die down. Then I could make inroads toward my goal. Jennifer Bishop might offer an opening since she'd professed what seemed like genuine regret over what the Teflon crew did to me.

I chose a seat in the middle of the room. The front marked you as a dork and the back said you planned to sleep or text. Since I was trying to reinvent myself, I avoided both classifications. *These people know nothing about you. You're a mystery.* At least, I was hoping there would be a certain mystique surrounding me, and I didn't intend to give anything away. The class filled up and the instructor came in just before the bell. I didn't recognize him, so that meant he was new. I wondered who had retired or taken another job, freeing up this slot.

The girls were suddenly very attentive because this teacher couldn't have been more than twenty-five, and he was hot in a professorial sort of way. By which I meant, he had on a corduroy blazer with suede patches on the sleeves, and he was pulling it off, mostly because he'd paired it with boots, faded jeans, and a striped dress shirt. He had a chiseled jaw, great cheekbones, and black hair that looked like he'd rumpled it in a fit of literary inspiration. I privately suspected it had taken substantial time, plus expensive hair product for him to achieve that level of "I don't care about my hair." All around me, girls gave a soft, collective sigh, and his hazel eyes crinkled in amusement.

He wrote on the chalkboard, "Mr. Love."

And a guy said, "Seriously? That's your actual name?"

"The irony doesn't escape me, and the moniker's offered its share of challenges over the years."

English accent. The female population at Blackbriar had no hope of escaping a giant crush this semester. Coupled with his looks and his slightly bashful air, he was girl Kryptonite. While I registered his definite appeal, he wasn't turning me dreamy-eyed alongside everyone else. That probably meant I was broken.

He drew a line through the name on the board and added, "You can call me Colin. As you might've surmised, I'm from London, and I'm looking forward to sharing my fondness for great literature with you. Now I'd like you to go around the room and state your name, plus one interesting fact about you. We'll start on the right."

I tuned out the introductions, though I did roll my eyes when one girl said her name was Nicole and that she could tie a cherry stem in a knot with her tongue. The guy next to her said, "Call me," but Mr. Love moved the conversation along.

Pretty soon it was my turn. "My name is Edie Kramer, and . . ." *I'm afraid I made a deal with the devil.* "I can recite pi to a hundred places."

"Impressive. And what about you, sir?" I appreciated that he shifted focus to the boy in front of me. Though I would have to get used to it if I truly meant to infiltrate the Teflon crew, I hated being watched.

Eventually I knew all kinds of trivia about the rest of my class and then Colin started the lesson in earnest. He was a good teacher, explaining his expectations up front, how he would evaluate our performance, how much reading and writing we'd be doing, and then his test policies. By far it wasn't the worst first session I'd had.

The rest, until lunch, were a mixed bag. I had a few of the same teachers from last year, but they were all polite enough to pretend I hadn't changed into a new person. By the time break rolled around, my shoulders hurt from the tension. It took all my courage to go into the cafeteria instead of hiding in the bathroom. The place smelled delicious, mostly because we had chefs instead of lunch ladies. There was a wide variety of choices too, but my stomach roiled too much for me to grab anything but salad and yogurt. If I kept up this I'm-freaking-out diet, I'd end up even skinnier, *not* one of my goals.

When I stepped out of the line, I almost bumped into Jennifer. Today, she wore her hair long and straight, glowing with a blue-black sheen. Between that and her flawless skin, she was much prettier than either Brittany or Allison. If popularity was driven by looks alone, Jennifer would rule the school. Since she seemed to have a heart, that would be a good thing.

"I just want to say that I appreciate your apology . . . and I accept. So thanks."

As I moved to step past her, she said, "I don't know if I could be that forgiving."

I'm not. It's a long con.

But I couldn't seem to write off what happened too fast. "Yeah, well. You weren't the one who made all the plans. I mean, you could've stopped it, but I guess . . . it's hard to speak up when all of your friends are involved." That sounded like the right balance of repressed anger and blame.

She nodded. "That doesn't make it okay. I should've gone to the headmaster or a teacher or something. I wish I had."

Me too.

"Well, I'm gonna go. See you."

The words seemed to slip out of her. "If you want, we could eat together."

"Me, with your crowd? I don't think that's such a good idea." Plus, I wasn't sure I could swallow a single bite at the same table with

Cameron Dean. I needed time to get used to the new dynamic and to bolster my resolve.

"It doesn't have to be with them. There are plenty of tables."

"Are you sure they won't see you as selling out to the enemy?" I asked.

She shrugged. "It's the least I can do to make this up to you. They can get by without me. I just . . . I don't want you to eat alone."

I was sure I could join any table at this point and not be run off with torches and pitchforks, but Jennifer seemed to have some guilt to work out. Never let it be said that I refused to let a girl cleanse her conscience. If it made her feel better to see me as a pity project, I could work with that.

"Okay, let's sit by the window." Where everyone could see that Jennifer had taken my side over the Teflon crew.

This should be interesting.

I had only eaten a few bites when a shadow fell across our table. An upward glance identified Allison Vega: brown hair, streaked with copper; bronze skin; green eyes; curvy. Word was, her family had ties to the cartel. That was probably just WASP gossip, though. Rich white people tended to think that there was only one way a Colombian family could make money.

"Are you lost, Jen?" Allison demanded.

She shook her head. "I'm fine, thanks."

The cafeteria denizens were riveted by this discussion, so I went on the offensive. Confrontation didn't come easy to me, but I had been studying their techniques for the last three years. *Call me a method actor.*

"Hey, Allie-cat. You're looking healthy. Did you stop bingeing and purging over the summer?" I said it loud enough that more than a few people overheard it.

"Screw you," she said, smiling.

"It'd be great if you could go. I'm talking to Jen. Thanks." My tone was polite, framed with the saccharine smile that I'd seen Allison and Brittany unleash.

Allison stood for a few seconds, apparently unable to think of a response, then she whirled and went back to the Teflon circle. The people at neighboring tables snickered; they likely enjoyed seeing Allison dispatched with her own weapons. There was *definitely* satisfaction in it.

"Maybe I didn't need to worry about you after all," Jen said. "You've changed."

I smiled faintly. "I'm aware."

After that, my yogurt and salad went down better, since I'd passed the first hurdle. People knew I wasn't the same perpetual victim I'd been last year, and things should get easier from here. I didn't have a clear strategy for infiltration, but making friends with Jen was a good start. From watching other people try and fail, I understood that I couldn't seem to care much about impressing them. They openly mocked those who tried too hard, which was why Davina wasn't a full-fledged member after three years of orbiting their space.

The rest of the day was uneventful. I sat through my classes, listened, and took notes, while gossip washed around me. I could expect more of the same for a day or two, but eventually, they'd get bored with speculating just how much work I had done. I pretended I didn't hear the whispers; it was simple from years of practice, and *now* they were saying nice things.

Assholes.

After school, I sighed at the guy who stopped at my locker and tried to ask me something about Lit class. Since Colin hadn't assigned anything yet, it was a stupid plan for getting to know me better. I stared at him until he stuttered and backed away. For the first time, I glimpsed why Allison and Brittany acted the way they did. I couldn't deny the faint rush of power that sprang from a single glance.

But I don't want to be like them for real.

So I managed a smile. "I have to go. Maybe we'll talk later."

"Sure," he said, seeming relieved.

Then I slipped past him, joining the throng heading for the exit. My backpack was full of textbooks since my dedication to schoolwork hadn't changed. Outside, the weather was sunny, just a hint of clouds, but the humidity made my hair curl. I threaded through the knot of students heading for their cars and passed the gate to where all of the bodyguards and black vehicles were waiting.

Then I drew up short. Kian stood across the street, leaning up against an office building. When he caught sight of me, he straightened, checked the traffic, and jogged across the street. It had only been a couple of weeks, but it felt like forever since I'd seen him. Today, he was dressed in black, but it worked on him and didn't come across as emo.

He wore a faint smile when he reached my side. To my astonishment, he leaned down to brush my lips with his in the kind of casual kiss that boyfriends gave long-term girlfriends. Since that didn't apply to us at all, I froze until I heard some girls behind us talking about how totally hot he was, loud enough that I was supposed to notice.

"What're you doing here?" I whispered.

"I thought it would be nice if I met you on your first day back." The answer radiated goodwill and innocence, but . . . what about the rules that prevented us from socializing? Whatever had happened, his eyes begged me to play along.

"It's an awesome surprise." I stretched up on tiptoes to hug him, murmuring, "What the hell?"

"Later," he breathed into my ear.

Okay, that was supremely distracting. Pressed up against him, it dawned on me that the reason that Colin Love and other crazy-hot guys didn't register on my hormonal radar was because I'd already imprinted on Kian. That could be . . . unfortunate.

"Is this your boyfriend, Edie?" Allison Vega stood behind me, wearing a deceptively friendly smile, but after our exchange at lunch, I knew to expect trouble.

"Yes," Kian said, before I could answer. "I was lucky to meet her this summer."

"Oh?" Allison imbued the single syllable with an insulting amount of skepticism.

He aimed a warm look in my direction. "Normally I wouldn't date a high school girl, but Edie's different."

That's putting it mildly.

"So you're . . . in college?" she guessed.

Kian nodded. "Look, we're in a hurry. But good luck with . . ." He trailed off as his gaze slid over her. ". . . everything."

I stifled a laugh. When he took my hand, I worked not to react, as if we did this every day, when in fact, we'd only done it when he was porting us somewhere. I let him lead me toward the station, but he surprised me by stopping at a red Mustang parked behind all the black town cars and SUVs, a splash of blood against raven wings.

"If I'm going to impress them, I have to go all the way," he said.

He opened the door for me, and I saw Allison and Brittany watching from the gate. The former looked furious and the latter confused. With a mental shrug, I climbed in. He reached across my lap, opened the glove box, and pulled out a small tin. Opening it, he dipped his fingers in the clear gel and smeared it around the frame of his window. Kian tilted his head, indicating I should do mine as well. While I complied, puzzled, he did the front and back windscreens. Then he started the car and smoothly made a U-turn around the cul-de-sac and headed back toward the city.

"We can talk freely now. The effects will last twenty minutes or so."

"What the crap is going on?"

"Circumstances have changed. I've been assigned to you exclusively."

"And you're not supposed to tell me that," I guessed. Which was why we'd soundproofed the car with silicon goo. *God, my life is so weird.* "Let me guess, you're supposed to charm me for some reason."

"I wish you weren't mixed up in this, Edie, but since the alternative is you being dead, I can't wish for that, either."

"Wishes are part of the problem, I'd say. Is this car one of yours?"

He sighed. "Why are you so clever?"

"You went cheap, huh? Sum things up, if time is limited."

"Normally, I manage five cases at once. I grant favors as requested, answer questions when permissible. But my boss called me into his office today. See, he wants your last two burned as fast as possible. He didn't tell me why."

I nodded, listening.

"I was instructed to win your trust, get close to you by any means necessary."

"Which you could be doing right now, by allegedly laying all your cards on the table. Sort of like a double bluff. You tell me enough of the truth to make me think you're on my side while you're manipulating me for your own ends."

"That's possible," he admitted. "Wedderburn suggested I tell you that I'm too into you to stay away, I don't care about the rules anymore."

"I might've bought it," I said quietly.

With effort I hid the wash of humiliation I felt at the prospect of him pretending to find me irresistible. "Explain the soundproofing. Why do they think you've shut them out?"

"To gain your trust," he said quietly. "I pretended to go along with Wedderburn's suggestion about pursuing you. He doesn't know I'm putting all the cards on the table."

"That's why you told Allison you're my boyfriend? In case your boss was listening."

"Partly," he admitted. "But also because I thought it might help you."

"Huh?"

Kian explained, "The guys will think you're a bitch if you turn them all down without giving them a reason. If you have a college boyfriend, it gives you more room to maneuver."

That was certainly true. "What if I wanted to date someone at school?"

"Do you?"

"No. I was just curious what you'd say."

"Am I supposed to be honest?"

"I'd prefer if you were."

"Then . . . I don't *want* you to date anyone else. I hated hearing that you hooked up with Ryu. From your perspective, I haven't known you long enough to feel that way, but—"

"You've been watching me for a while."

His hands tightened on the steering wheel. "I know how that sounds."

"I read a novel where this hit man is supposed to assassinate a woman, but he ends up falling in love with her instead, just from watching her." Maybe that was a stupid thing to say; I wasn't sure how I was supposed to feel.

"I can relate," he muttered. "Anyway, the girls will see you as less of a threat if they're not competing with you for dates."

It was hard for me to imagine that anyone could view me as a potential seductress, but that might be because deep down I was still science-nerd Edie, just wrapped in a prettier package. "Which makes them more likely to accept me. Good thinking. Is this part of making me use my favors faster?"

"Ostensibly it is. The longer it takes to wreak havoc at Blackbriar, the longer it'll be before you start wanting something else."

"Do you have any clue why they want me to waste my last two favors?"

Kian hesitated, risking a glance at me, and whatever he saw seemed to trouble him. "Wedderburn didn't tell me this, but I did some checking on my own. I saw your file."

Ice crept down my spine despite the sunshine. "And what did it say?"

"You have to understand, things at Wedderburn, Mawer & Graf are encoded by department, so I didn't understand everything I saw."

"That's the company you work for? Sounds like a law firm."

"Yeah. And for good reason. They know all about getting away with murder." Kian offered a grim look.

"You're not inspiring confidence right now," I muttered.

He ignored that. "From what I could interpret, whatever you're meant to do, it happens fairly early in your life."

"So they need me to use my favors, so they'll own me *before* I accomplish this mystery goal."

As far as crazy theories went, it made as much sense as anything, but logic hadn't played a big role in my life since I followed Kian off the bridge. Then the faint whisper resonated: *You're dead, you're dreaming, you're delusional.* And I could only work with *this* reality, hard to credit as it might seem.

"Exactly. If they still owe *you* favors when you reach that pivotal moment, they lose the tactical advantage."

"But . . . for your bosses to be sure of all of that, they have to be able to see the future somehow. What're we talking about? Crystal ball? Tarot cards?" If I sounded derisive, it was because this was freaking me out. Too much mysterious conspiracy talk made me feel like screaming, but calm rationality was my chief strength. This didn't seem like an opportune moment to deviate from a functional paradigm.

"They wouldn't invest so much on such uncertain glimpses," he answered.

"So, what, time travel?"

"You accepted translocation, but transtemporal is too far?"

I stared at him. "You're serious."

"My watch doesn't have that function enabled, but those with more seniority have been awarded them. In a promotion or two, I could be working in acquisitions."

"And that means?"

"Jaunting to the future to verify that a projected achievement is every bit as vital as the organization has predicted."

"That sounds pretty cool." The science geek in me was actively enthralled with the prospect of skipping ahead, checking how theory lined up with reality. Once the initial buzz dwindled, a shadowy organization that could pop into the future and evaluate people as if they were stocks whose value might rise or fall according to capricious shifts—I couldn't help but see that as sinister. My enthusiasm dimmed.

Caught up in his explanation, Kian didn't seem to notice. "In fact, there's a department in acquisitions that retrieves tech we use to grant favors like the one you asked for. In the next three hundred years, there will be remarkable innovations in cosmetic procedures—to the point that the average person can give himself a new nose."

"Figures. Did they solve the pollution problem yet?" I shook my head, adding, "Never mind. I'm aware that's a digression."

He flashed me a half smile. "The upside is that I get to spend more time with you. As long as Wedderburn thinks I'm pushing you toward another favor, he won't look too hard at how much we hang out."

"And you can claim you're working on me."

"Exactly."

"What happens if he figures out that you're faking it?"

Kian hesitated. "Don't worry about that."

"Bullshit."

"It won't be good," he said quietly. "But I can handle it."

By this point, the gel on the windowpane was smoking slightly.

I took that to mean that private time was almost finished. "So are you just giving me a ride home?"

"I thought I'd take you to dinner unless you have other plans."

Whoever Wedderburn was, he might be listening in. So I made my response simple. "Can we swing by my apartment first?"

SHADOW DANCE

M y parents weren't back from university yet, so I left Kian waiting in the front room while I scrambled out of my uniform
and into jeans and a T-shirt. I pulled my hair down, conscious that I
was trying to downplay my appearance. I hated the thought that he
might look at me and see his own creation, not *me*. If he was on the
level, he was taking a big risk, pretending to chase me with ulterior
motives, while giving me top-secret info. It chewed at me, not knowing what exactly might happen if they caught him. But he might also
be double-crossing me, doing exactly what I'd suggested in the car.
There was no way for me to be sure.

Still, technically, this was my first date. It was cliché, but I was
excited, even if he might be doing this to please his boss.

I sent a text to my parents, who would probably be astonished
that I had plans involving other human beings, and then went out to
join Kian. "Ready."

"Let's go." He led the way to the car and we drove for a while in
silence.

"You realize the Mustang makes you the total package. Girls will drive me nuts tomorrow asking about you."

"Is that a problem?"

"Only in the sense that I don't know anything."

Kian tilted his head, and it took all my self-control not to brush back the hair that tumbled into his face. "That means I can be anything you want."

"Sounds dangerous. How will I remember what lies I've told?"

"Write it down? Or would you rather know the truth?" He pulled into a small parking lot, nestled behind an Italian restaurant with red-and-white-checkered tablecloths visible through windows draped with twinkle lights. Inside they seemed to be trying to evoke a sense of Tuscany with the textured walls and dark wood. The hostess escorted us to a booth and left us with menus; I couldn't help but notice the way she studied Kian as if he were a chocolate éclair.

I held my answer until the hostess moved out of earshot. "If you're allowed to tell me, I'd like to know the truth."

The appreciative glint in his eyes said he knew I was playing to a potential audience. "You're a special case, Edie. I've been granted clearance to be straight with you."

I grinned. Despite the risks, this was kind of fun, knowing how much subtext simmered between the lines. "Then tell me about the real you."

"I'm twenty," he said quietly. "I was fifteen when I had my . . . moment."

Extremis. When Raoul made him an offer he couldn't refuse. He'd already told me this, but if Wedderburn hadn't been listening in, it was best to pretend that conversation had never happened. Kian couldn't afford for his boss to doubt him. *Or maybe he just wants you to believe he's*

112

loyal to you. But why would he support a girl he just met over the powerful figure who can do unspeakable things to punish him? I had no ready answer.

"Do you want to tell me?" It seemed really intimate, but I still wanted to know.

His voice was soft, barely audible below the music tinkling from the speakers. "It feels like a long time ago. I can talk about it. But let's order first."

I hadn't even opened the menu. "I trust you."

The waitress came over in response to Kian's signal. "We'll start with the bruschetta and then we'll share a Caesar salad and chicken parmigiana. Just bring two plates. We'll divide the food at the table. Thanks."

Once she left, I sat frozen, staring at him. I mean, he'd informed me that he knew everything about me, but it didn't feel real until he ordered all of my favorite things in the same meal. "You weren't kidding about being an Edie expert."

"Work occasionally gives me an edge. You'll be even more wowed when I take you to the Science Museum for a planetarium show."

"Is that in the works?"

His gaze met mine. "It could be. If you want."

"Maybe. So you were about to tell me . . . ?"

His smile faded. "Right. My family had money, up until I was twelve. At that point it came out that my father's empire had been built on a Ponzi scheme."

I dug around my memory, trying to recall where I'd heard the term. Oh yeah, on the news, when the anchorman was talking about fraud and how a fake investment business stayed afloat when the "broker" took money he got later and paid it out to early investors, constantly moving money around. From what I recalled, that could go on for years, but eventually all the stockholders would demand their own payments. I suspected that was when things fell apart for Kian's dad.

"What happened?" I asked.

"Rather than go to jail, he killed himself and left my mother to clean up the mess." He responded in a monotone, like he was talking about something he read, not his own life.

I hesitated, not knowing what to say. "Was it just you and her?"

"No, I had a sister."

"Had?" I asked with growing dread.

Kian closed his eyes briefly and flattened his hand on the table. Impulsively I reached over and covered his fingers with mine, because whatever was coming, it had to be awful. "She came into my dad's study . . . he had the gun—"

"Tell me he didn't kill her."

"Not on purpose."

That painted a picture in my mind. I imagined her rushing over, trying to stop him, them struggling for the weapon. *It goes off, he's shocked and horrified. Then he turns the gun on himself. Bang, bang. Half a family's dead in just a few seconds. Jesus.* I had no idea what to say. *I'm sorry* seemed so inadequate.

He went on, "So then it was just my mom and me, and . . . she leaned, so hard. I wasn't even thirteen. I tried to step up . . . to help. But it wasn't enough and pretty soon, she was hooked on pills. In time my uncle put her in rehab and I went to stay with him and my aunt."

"You said something about his fishing cabin?"

"Yeah. He's hardworking, my uncle. Not like my dad. I tried to restart my life, but it felt like there was nothing but a hole from everything I lost."

"And there was a girl," I guessed.

"Right again. She was the last straw. It took all of my courage to talk to her, and when she said, in front of everyone, that she'd rather die than date me, I kind of . . . lost it. Hitchhiked to my uncle's cabin where nobody would find me. I had already tied the noose when Raoul showed up. Not gonna lie, he freaked me out."

"But he also saved you. So this girl . . . to impress her, you asked to be incredibly hot, you asked for the sports car, what was the last favor?"

His eyes burned with an intensity that stole my breath, locked on mine so I couldn't look away. "Show me how clever you are. Guess."

Before I could, the waitress brought our food and Kian served. After eating only salad and yogurt for lunch, I was starving. I ate a few bites of the chicken while I pondered.

"You wanted her to fall for you, probably so you could shoot her down."

"Spot on. After my last request kicked in, she became completely obsessed with me. Stalked me, in fact. I had to take out a restraining order."

"What happened to her?" I asked.

His expression was flat and dark, completely unreadable. "She killed herself."

A gasp slid out of me, and I nearly dropped my fork. "Jesus, Kian. That's taking payback *way* too far."

He flinched. "I didn't mean for that to happen. I just wanted her to know what it felt like to be rejected. They didn't tell me until later, but in my best timeline, I was supposed to be with her. The opposition interfered, drove her over the edge."

"That's horrible." It dawned on me how dangerous this deal was.

115

So many factors I hadn't calculated before making the agreement. Quietly I stared at the marks on my wrists. *No going back now.*

"I know." He paused, unsure whether he should continue. "When she died, I lost my potential as a catalyst. That's why I work for the company now."

"You say 'work' but that's not the impression I get."

Kian swallowed hard. I guessed I'd trespassed into forbidden territory. His boss likely wouldn't be happy, no matter what he said. So I was surprised when he pulled a pen and notebook out of his pocket, then scribbled an answer. With his watch under the table, he nudged it toward me and ate some chicken parm with his other hand.

Aloud, he said, "It's not so bad."

Yeah, that's the company line. I nibbled at my food while skimming the reality of his response. *My life's not my own.* Indenture *might be the right word, except that means having the chance at freedom someday. I don't. I belong to Wedderburn.* Shock and sorrow cascaded through me. I might've suspected that was the case, but seeing the desolate look in his green eyes as he finished his pasta tightened my chest until I couldn't breathe.

I struggled to keep the conversation going, casting back to a different point. "Wait, what's a catalyst?"

"You're one. It's somebody destined for great things."

"And who gets offered a deal. But . . . *what* opposition?" I seized on that like a lifeline. There were so many mysteries that I couldn't decide what I needed to know most—or what might get him in trouble, if Wedderburn was listening.

A flicker of his eyes told me his boss wouldn't like him focusing on the downside of this arrangement. He was supposed to be wooing me, not scaring me. "It's complicated."

But I couldn't help asking. "What I'm extrapolating is that I could be in danger?"

"That's why I told you not to trust anyone but me. The competition might contact you, just to screw with your head."

Damn. Apparently, when I'd worried that the deal seemed too good to be true, I was on target. Yet if I hadn't, my parents would've claimed my body from the morgue, and I wouldn't even be here. So the complications and risks were better than the alternative.

"Because . . . ?"

"If they shift the equilibrium enough, your fate changes and you cease to be a factor in play. If that happens, you lose value as an asset, and Wedderburn puts you to work."

I thought about that. "So . . . whatever you were supposed to accomplish, it's not happening, because this girl died?"

He nodded.

"And you're trapped because you have no way to repay the favors. That could happen to me, huh?"

"It could," he admitted. "There's no way to be sure what events are pivotal in your personal timeline. You've heard about the butterfly effect?"

"I've read about chaos theory, and I probably qualify as a strange attractor." It was a weak joke at best, but my heart caught at his smile. "I think I see where you're going with this. Basically, there's no way to be sure I'll retain my worth as a catalyst."

"I'm sorry, Edie. I wish I could guarantee your safety." He closed his eyes for a few seconds, as if bracing for intense pain.

I immediately wanted that look off his face. "Hey, it's okay. At least you're honest."

Or is he? There was no way for me to verify any of this . . . unless . . .

"What's your last name?" I hated myself a little for asking.

"Riley. Do you intend to check me out?"

"Do you blame me? Your story might be sympathy bait."

"I don't. Feel free to look it up. You can use my phone if yours doesn't have Internet. The scandal with my dad was pretty well publicized."

Mentally I did the math as I took his cell. If he was twenty, it would've all happened nine years back. So I specified the date in the search bar, along with "Riley Ponzi scheme" and the phone spat back a bunch of links. I picked one at random and read a summary of what he'd just told me.

"Is your mom all right?"

"She's in and out of programs, they never stick. She misses being a socialite but she doesn't have the money to support the lifestyle. So she goes back to using to cope."

"I'm sorry," I said.

"Don't be. Working for Wedderburn, Mawer & Graf has its perks." Judging by the sardonic twist of his mouth, this was more verbal propaganda.

So I played along. "Like what?"

"The house in Colorado. And they don't mind if I take college classes as long as I keep up with my workload."

"Which right now is only me."

I thought about the cabin he'd brought me to, back at the start of the summer. At least they paid well for him to afford a place with a view like that. He was pretty young to own property, and his favors had only included the car, not wealth.

"True. Lucky me." He was smiling, but I wondered how far I could trust him.

Kian might be playing a long game, building rapport for reasons that would become clear only after he sprang the trap. After all, that was what I planned to do with the Teflon crew, so I couldn't believe the warmth I saw reflected in his green eyes. On one hand, he *had* saved my life, but a girl was dead because of him. Though I wanted to, I couldn't trust him.

"Do you talk to your mom much?" I asked.

He shook his head. "I can't be around her when she's using. But I pay for rehab when she chooses to go. Once a year, she has a 'breakthrough,' makes a bunch of promises about how it'll be different, and we start the cycle all over again."

"That sucks." Possibly the least insightful response ever offered.

"Yeah."

"Is it possible for me to tour Wedderburn, Mawer & Graf?" I asked, mostly because I regretted prying, and it was the first topic that sprang to mind.

"Sure. Why?"

"Knowledge is power."

He studied me for a few seconds, then nodded. "I'll talk to my boss and set it up. Just . . . be prepared. If he permits you to access more than the public areas, you'll see some . . . strange things."

"I can hardly wait." The reply was pure bravado. I couldn't let him see how nervous I was, or the fact that I was in way over my head.

After that, we finished our food—it was really good—and he drove me home. I was wary of getting too deep before I had a handle on what I'd learned. Kian tapped his fingers on the steering wheel. The more I learned about him, the more torn I was. Part of me thought that with so much tragedy in his past, he just couldn't be as simple and straightforward as he pretended. It made me feel like he had to be playing me. He cast a few looks in my direction, but I couldn't meet his gaze. Instead I stared out the window at the passing buildings. Once he reached for my hand, but I pulled back and flattened it on my knee. His breath caught, a whisper of sound I barely heard against the rush of the vents.

Smooth, Edie. You hurt his feelings.

By the time he pulled up in front of the brownstone, tension quivered in the air between us. I hardly knew what to say. Finally, I managed, "Thanks for dinner."

"I'll call you." He didn't ask for a kiss or suggest we go out again. In fact, he wasn't even looking at me.

The distance came from me, but crazily, I didn't like it. Sitting here wouldn't solve anything, so I offered a jerky nod and climbed out. It took all of my resolve not to look back, but as I climbed the steps to the entryway, the Mustang roared off. Then I did spin around, watching the red car weave into traffic and turn the corner a block down.

Sorry, Kian.

I plodded upstairs. My dad was home, but my mom wasn't. He still had on his tweed jacket, which made him *look* like a professor, and maybe that was the point. He glanced up from the journal he was reading and asked, "How was your day?"

"Fine. I had an early dinner, so I'm getting started on my homework."

"Good idea."

That concluded the parental talk for the day. He went back to his article as I headed for my room. I did try to focus on the assigned reading, but certain aspects of Kian's story gnawed at me. Guilt plucked at me because I'd definitely cooled off toward the end, communicating my reservations unmistakably. With a muttered curse, I threw down my World History book and opened my laptop. I pulled it across my lap and opened the browser.

First I searched for information about his father, just in case his phone had been tampered with, but I came up with the same results. *Albert J. Riley's house of cards tumbled today. After defrauding hundreds of investors, the self-styled financial genius died at his Pennsylvania home. In a double tragedy . . .* I read on, confirming that Kian had, in fact, lost his sister that day. *Riley is survived by his wife, Vanessa, and his son, Kian.*

But this wasn't enough to put my mind at ease, so I input "local girl suicide" plus the town name and the story came up, short and to the point. *Tanya Jackson of Cross Point, Pennsylvania, took her life today. She had a history of mental instability and she overdosed on her mother's prescription medication. EMTs attempted to revive her, but ultimately failed, and she was pronounced dead on arrival at Cross Point Memorial Hospital.* It seemed . . . bizarre that whatever Kian was meant to achieve, it had been tied inextricably to one teenage girl. What if I screwed up my timeline unintentionally?

You'll end up enslaved to Wedderburn too.

That sent a shiver down my spine. Well, at least now I had proof that Kian hadn't made it all up to engage my sympathies. Reassuring, even as I suspected there was something off about the whole thing. I couldn't dismiss the possibility that he had, in fact, wanted Tanya dead. *Maybe that was his wish, not for her to fall in love with him.* I had no idea if murder could be one of the favors; he'd said it was limited only by imagination and the company didn't seem to value human life very much.

You could ask, a little voice whispered.

Someone at Wedderburn, Mawer & Graf might be willing to talk, though that would reveal that I didn't trust Kian. No way to tell how that would impact the game he was running on his boss about making me fall for him so I'd use my favors faster. *Damn. It's too much to decide tonight.* My life had turned from untenable to unfathomable in the space of a summer, and each step felt like walking across a high wire.

On impulse I searched Wedderburn, Mawer & Graf, just to see what came up. A glossy Web site provided very little information on what the company actually did. The mission statement was about as illuminating as the one in Blackbriar's brochures. *Our responsibility, professionally, is to leverage resources in order to orchestrate diverse opportunities. Our challenge is to proactively maintain information to allow us to innovate cutting-edge mindshare. Our goal is to seamlessly create new technologies to stay relevant in tomorrow's world.* Losing interest in figuring out if WM&G had any products or services, I clicked around the site. In time I found Kian's name on one of the subpages. He was listed as a financial analyst and it gave his e-mail address. I almost added it to my laptop contacts, then I decided we probably shouldn't use company servers.

The executives had pages all to themselves, especially the titular ones. I selected Karl Wedderburn and read his bio. In his picture, he looked like an elderly man with a well-groomed mustache and a thick head of white hair, but there was an unnerving look in his eyes, even in the photo. He looked *older* than the sixty years the picture gave him, and when I narrowed my eyes, it was like the pupils swallowed his irises, leaving only black holes where light should be.

"Creepy," I whispered.

Restraining a shiver, I shut down my laptop entirely. It was possible that Kian's talk about shadowy enemies and trusting no one had worked on me until I was suggestible, but there was just something *not right* about Karl Wedderburn; I could tell that much from that quick glimpse. *And Kian's at his mercy.*

It took some effort, but I finished my homework and went to bed. I was just about to fall asleep when I realized I hadn't thought to check for messages from Ryu or Vi. *Tomorrow,* I promised myself. *First thing.* I couldn't let go of the first two real friends I ever made—and in some ways, my only link to normal life.

• • •

The next day at school, Jen was waiting for me at my locker. "I haven't seen Allison this agitated since her hair got fried with knock-off straightening product."

"Why?" I'd forgotten about firing the first shots at her yesterday. The revenge thing seemed almost petty in comparison to the deep water I was wading elsewhere. It wasn't that I'd forgiven them, more that high school drama didn't weigh heavily against life and death.

"Because you made her look like an idiot at lunch and, apparently, your boyfriend is so hot that she's dying of jealousy."

"I'm not sad about that," I admitted.

She smiled. "I don't blame you. She's my least favorite person in our crowd. Brittany is pretty nice when you get her alone. It's just . . . around other people, she feels like she has something to prove."

"Genius."

"I never said she was bright. In fact, that's part of the problem. Her dad's been telling her 'it's a good thing you're pretty' since she was ten. She thinks her brain is what keeps her skull from echoing. And she kinda . . . hates smart girls as a result."

"Because she thinks she isn't?" I didn't want to learn more about my enemies. If I understood why Brittany acted this way, it would make it harder to bring about her downfall.

"She's not as dumb as her dad makes her feel, but she's not on your level. Now that you're hot too . . ." Jen shrugged. "Anyway, I've been told to ask you to sit with us today at lunch, but I think they're planning something."

"Allison and Brittany?"

She nodded. "I understand if you'd rather not deal with the drama."

"I can handle it." Besides, this was my way in. I felt reasonably sure I could parlay this invite into a permanent place at the table, provided I turned whatever prank they had planned back on them. If they thought I was the same beaten girl they'd abused last year . . . well. I smiled at Jen. "I'm looking forward to it, actually."

Morning classes went quickly, especially since I started with AP Lit. Most of the girls stared at Colin, dreamy-eyed, but I listened to his lecture. He was good, offering insights I hadn't considered on a poem I'd read many times before. The rest of my teachers suffered by comparison. Then it was time for the showdown at lunch.

Jen picked me up and walked with me to the cafeteria. We got food from the line and then went over to the Teflon table. They were such a fixture that they'd claimed it by scrawling on the top with Sharpies, and nobody else ever sat there, even if the whole crew was running late. This time I didn't hesitate when I saw Cameron at the other end. I sat down beside Jen, careful to ignore him, even though my stomach was swirling like a toilet. The nausea came back, reminding me how I'd felt that day, so utterly helpless, and my mouth dry, my throat tasting of vomit.

Drawing from pure determination, I pasted on a smile and said, "Hey, Cam."

Do people call him that? They do now.

"Cameron," he corrected.

I opened my eyes wide as a couple of guys from the lacrosse team approached. "Seriously? You won't let anyone shorten your name?"

"It's because it sounds like 'can,'" Russ Thomas said with a smirk. "As in ass and garbage."

"Maybe you should call him Can. Because he *is* kind of an ass." I paired that with a smile, making eye contact first with Russ and then with his friend Phillip.

A few more people showed up in time to hear Russ say, "I love that. After what you did to my car, bro, I *will* call you Can."

"What did he do?" I asked.

Russ wore a disgusted look. "Barfed all over it. Bitch can't hold his liquor."

"That's . . . surprising." With a twitch of my shoulder, I dismissed Cameron Dean and listened to Russ ramble about the lacrosse team's chances at the championship this year.

I cared minuscule amounts about that, but his attention kept Brittany and Allison from talking to me because every time they tried to start whatever drama they'd planned, he aimed a disgruntled look in their direction and said, "Christ, you can talk to her about how awesome her hair is later."

Which was incredibly offensive, as girls *did* talk about issues more important than hair and makeup, but since it served my purposes, I didn't call him on it. *Not like I'm being myself with these imbeciles anyway.* So if the pretense made me a little sick to my stomach, it was understandable.

As break ended, I said to Russ, "We have the next class together, don't we?"

Sadly he had to think about it. "Yeah, I guess so."

"Want to walk me? I'd like to hear more about lacrosse." I capped my smile, giving just enough warmth to show interest in the sport, not Russ.

Since I have a boyfriend. Who might've killed the last girl who rejected him.

"A budding fan, huh? Absolutely."

Davina watched us go, wearing an expression I couldn't interpret. Once we left the others, I pitched my voice low. "What's the deal with Can?"

He snickered at the nickname. "What do you mean?"

"He seems a little . . . sensitive." I said it like it was a dirty word. To most guys it seemed to be.

"You mean, like he can't take a joke?"

I nodded. "I've seen him dish it out, but . . ."

"Yeah. To tell you the truth, he's kind of a whiny bitch. We roll with him because he's got a sweet house and his parents are never home."

"Interesting." I smiled up at him, making a mental note to repeat that in front of Allison at the first opportunity. I suspected she wouldn't have the judgment to be discreet.

Russ shouldered through the halls, and smaller students got out of the way. I felt like an asshole walking with him. He stopped outside our class and gestured for me to go ahead. It was interesting, like an anthropological experiment, to see that he was capable of using manners with someone he considered worth the trouble.

"You're a nice guy," I lied.

He winked at me. "Don't tell anyone."

"I wouldn't dream of it."

THAT FRYING PAN WAS PRETTY NICE, ACTUALLY . . .

I didn't expect Kian to be waiting for me when I left school and he wasn't. Russ offered me a ride home, but I shook my head. "I don't mind the T. Thanks anyway."

"Where's your boyfriend today?" he asked.

"He has class. See you."

With a wave, I headed for the station, caught the train, and hopped off at Kenmore to grab takeout from India Quality for dinner. The platform was a mess, including the usual spectacle: a couple arguing; a mass of Sox fans jostling while heckling a guy who had on the wrong hat; and a mother scolding her toddler. Through the crowd I glimpsed a tall, gaunt man with pallid, oddly blurred features and thinning hair that clung to his pink scalp in damp stripes. He froze when he spotted me, and at first I thought it must be someone behind me. I half turned, glancing over my shoulder, but there was nobody.

I had to pass him to reach the street, so I fixed my eyes on the ground, shoulders down, out of reflex; that was what I'd always done when someone singled me out for unwanted attention. Somehow, even though I put plenty of space between us, he was right in front of me, blocking my path.

"The dead walk. You're one of them. There's a hole, a hole in the world, and things crawl through. They crawl." His breath was a blast of graveyard rot, his teeth hanging like yellow and black husks beneath dry, chapped lips.

His eyes rolled in his head, going completely white, and he fumbled for my wrist. I jerked back, almost running into a man in a suit coming up behind me.

"What the hell's wrong with you?" the businessman demanded.

I frowned at him and pointed . . . but the spot the creepy dude had occupied was vacant now. Spinning, I searched the whole area and saw no sign of him; his stink lingered, though, proving I wasn't insane.

"Nothing," I said finally.

"Don't forget your meds next time, sweetheart." The asshole brushed by me and I followed, a cold chill creeping down my spine.

It was marginally better in the heat and humidity of a sunny afternoon. *Kian told you not to trust anyone but him. And he said you could be in danger.* Creepy disappearing guy made my flesh crawl. I quickened my step toward the brownstone and tried to pretend my skin wasn't still prickling with the sense that something was very wrong. Sometimes, when I was little, I'd wake up in the middle of the night, sure someone was watching me, but I was never a baby in the sense that I ran to my parents, crying, and begged to sleep in their bed.

No, even at six, I had been methodical, not prone to a wild imagination. I used to swallow the fear that something would grab my ankles just as soon as I put my feet on the floor. The first step was always a bound and then I ran to the light switch to flood the room with brightness, banishing all the shadows. I'd open all my drawers, peer under my bed, check my closet, and silently reassure myself there was nothing to fear. Some nights, I just left the lights on and shut them off before I went to school. But no amount of checking the area today banished this feeling. I saw no one paying me any particular attention; it was all apartment buildings and renovated properties. Not even a single window curtain flickered as I went past. I rubbed my fingertips up my arm, conscious of actual goose bumps.

Yet I knew someone was watching me.

Eager to get home, I mentally apologized to my parents for failing to retrieve dinner and broke into a run. As soon as I stepped in, I felt immediately safer, though I was sure that was psychological. Both my parents were there.

"No takeout?" my dad asked.

"Sorry, I forgot."

With a faint sigh mumble of "teenagers," my dad started cooking. My mom didn't, unless you counted oatmeal. She was pretty ferocious on the subject of gender roles, so she'd bought a bunch of DIY repair books, and she handled all minor maintenance, like broken light sockets or leaky faucets. Since my dad had zero interest in being a handyman, he was happier doing the cooking and cleaning anyway.

"So what're you making??" I asked.

He sounded grumpy. "Stuffed artichokes. How was school?"

"I learned a lot." That was pretty much my pat answer every day.

Unsurprisingly, my mother asked, "Such as?"

I was prepared for the inquisition to take this turn, however, and I summarized what we covered in physics and Japanese. My mother had less interest in World History and AP Lit, though she did lecture me on the importance of writing meaningful papers. "It's good practice for your college applications. How are you coming with those? You need to have your essay shipshape by early October."

"I know. I'll work on it."

"Dinner's in an hour," my dad cut in.

From his conspiratorial nod, he knew he was saving me from my mother's zealous approach to college prep. I acknowledged his intervention with a smile. "Okay. I'll get started on my homework. Call me when it's done."

In my room, I remembered how the creepy guy on the platform had tried to grab my wrist, the one that now bore the infinity mark. I'd kept it hidden from my parents beneath long sleeves, but I needed to invest in some leather wrist cuffs, because eventually Mom and Dad would ask why I never wore T-shirts anymore, even to lounge around the house.

Forcing that worry aside, I powered up my laptop and turned on my phone for the first time all day. There were three texts from Kian and none of them made much sense.

There's something you need to know.

Did he hurt you? I guessed he was referring to the spooky guy in the subway, and I'd give a lot to discover how he knew. I read on.

Whatever you do, don't let him touch you.

Cold crept over me, prickling my skin into goose bumps. More anxious than ever, I texted back, I'm fine. What's going on?

I had messages from Vi and Ryu, but they were reassuringly ordinary, just chatty and full of tidbits about their daily lives. It sucked that I couldn't tell the truth about myself, but how would I begin to explain? I responded to those while waiting for Kian to answer. When he didn't, I tried not to worry. Pretending everything was normal, I opened my lit book and actually jumped when my dad thumped on the door to let me know dinner was ready.

"Coming!"

Thankfully, my mom and dad carried the conversation, discussing some project that needed grant funding. I contributed little, conscious that my phone still hadn't pinged or vibrated. I didn't *want* to worry about Kian, considering how little I trusted him, but he was also my only ally in this mess.

"You look pensive," my dad said.

"Just thinking about college options." Probably I shouldn't have used that excuse, but it was the first thing I thought of after he startled me.

"There are a lot of great possibilities here in Boston," my mom put in. "And you could live at home until you graduate, save up for your own place."

"We can get you free tuition if you go to—"

"I know, Dad. You've made it clear that you'd love for me to go to BU."

"It's an option. Think about it."

I finished my artichoke and escaped before he told me how lucky I was to have such a bright future ahead. That night I finished all of my homework and got ready for bed, but I never heard from Kian. With a faint sigh, I carried my phone to the window and looked out over the dark street. Lights streaked the pavement, leaving patches of darkness that seemed almost sentient. The longer I stared, the more they swelled and seethed with movement until I slammed the curtains shut with trembling hands. Fear had a hold on me when I fell asleep and the next morning, its icy fingers were still wrapped around my throat.

• • •

On the way to the station, I walked into a flutter of pigeons, and it seemed their tiny, beady eyes and flapping wings reflected purposeful intent. I must have looked like a crazy person as I ran from a flock of dirty winged rats, but I didn't stop until I was inside the train car. As it left the station, in the space between one blink and another, I saw the thin man from last night standing on the platform, but when I stared harder, he melted before my eyes, leaving only a dark stain on the cement.

Okay, so I'm going crazy. There are probably pills for it.

At school, I was distracted enough that Colin made me stay after first period. The rest of the girls seemed disappointed that he singled me out instead of them and I imagined they'd daydream in class tomorrow.

I tried not to show my impatience as he asked, "Is something wrong, Edie? I know I've only had you in class for a few days now, but you're usually quite lively and engaged. Today, it was as if you just weren't here."

"I have some things on my mind," I said.

Like where the hell is Kian? And what am I seeing? Not seeing. Whatever.

"Anything you want to talk about?" He fixed a soulful look on me, and I wondered whether he *wanted* girls to fall head over heels for him. Or maybe he just didn't realize how a desperate teenager might read his interest.

"Not really. I have to get to my next class." I hurried off without waiting for him to respond. Maybe I was looking for weirdness, but the new teacher seemed *way* too interested in me after just a few days in class. It was possible he was a run-of-the-mill creeper or that I was reading too much into genuine professorial concern.

"You're so lucky," Nicole said as we left AP Lit. "I'm planning to fail the first exam so he'll tutor me."

"Sounds like an excellent plan," I answered with only a hint of irony.

I tried to pay more attention in the rest of my morning classes, if only to escape scrutiny. Jen was waiting for me at my locker before lunch, so I went with her to the cafeteria, but my plans to cause trouble were on hold in response to more pressing problems: Kian incommunicado, Wedderburn, Mawer & Graf doing God knew what, and mysterious opposition that might try to hurt me to prevent me from doing something years later. If I told anyone, I'd wind up in a mental hospital for sure.

A small voice whispered, *If you don't teach these jackasses a lesson, they'll think they can do whatever they want to people.* Put that way, it seemed more critical to move forward, not because of what they'd done to me, but due to harm they might inflict on someone who wasn't as lucky as I'd been. So when Allison cut in ahead of Jen and me in the line, I took it as a sign. *Gift horse, mouth. I'm on it.*

"Russ said the funniest thing yesterday," I said.

Jen raised a brow at me. "I highly doubt that." Apparently she shared my private estimation of his brainpower.

"He said the only reason you guys hang around with Cam is because he's got a big house and his parents are gone a lot. Is that true?"

The other girl shrugged, her eyes going to Allison, as if to tell me I couldn't trust her. *Well, duh. I'm counting on that.* Regardless of where it came from, this home truth should start a rift between Russ and Cameron. If my observations on social interaction held true, eventually the guys would take sides. And this was only the beginning.

Allison didn't repeat what she'd overheard until just before the warning bell. Wisely, she waited until Russ went to the bathroom and then she leaned over and whispered to Cameron while staring at me. He fixed me with a look that was part confusion, part dread; I met his gaze squarely and smiled. In some deep, dark part of his lizard brain, he recognized me as a threat, but he couldn't reconcile it rationally.

"Talk to you guys later," I said.

After school, as I headed out, I glimpsed Russ and Cam arguing near the guys' bathroom. Russ shoved him, hard, against the lockers, and I smiled. Tomorrow there would be some blowback on me, but not as much as Allison expected. I pressed through the crowd and strode toward the front gate, where I was astonished and relieved to find Kian waiting for me. Pointedly I stopped, checked my phone, then shook it at him; I was tempted to throw it.

He crossed the road toward me. Every time I saw him, it was a shock all over again. On closer inspection, though, he'd definitely looked better. Dark shadows cradled his eyes, and his clothes looked like he might've slept in his car. Before today, I'd never seen him unshaven; scruff prickled along his jaw, giving him a surprisingly rugged look. My fingers itched to touch the copper streaks in his hair, and despite my misgivings about his trustworthiness and his story, I wanted to hug him and then kiss the crap out of him.

"Before you yell at me, exhibit A." His phone was a hunk of melted metal. "I ran into trouble after I texted you."

"I can see that. Why didn't you pop in to see me?" But as soon as the question emerged, I recalled how awkward it had been, the last time I saw him. In his shoes, I probably wouldn't have risked a surprise visit either.

"You said you prefer if I don't do that. I think the word 'creepy' might've been thrown around."

"That was before."

"Before what?"

To my aggravation, I didn't know what to say. Our non-relationship was confusing, especially when he gave me a light kiss for the benefit of anyone who might be watching.

I eventually muttered, "How hard could it be to buy a new phone? Or e-mail me."

"Come on. We won't settle anything standing here and I have things to tell you."

"Me too," I said, thinking of the guy in the subway.

"You go first." He opened my door with careless courtesy and then jogged around to hop in on the driver's side.

I summarized the weird subway encounter and when I finished, Kian wore a ferocious scowl. "So I was right. They've already found you."

"*Who* has?"

"The company is called Dwyer & Fell. They mask another faction in the game, just as Wedderburn, Mawer & Graf does."

"Game?"

"From what I hear, Wedderburn and Dwyer have been competing for centuries."

Pondering the implications, I spoke before I was sure. "But that means—"

"They aren't human." Kian likely saw my uncertainty and filled in the blank.

Understandable. We had too much ground to cover for him to wait for me to make logical deductions when he could supply the answers. But that didn't address the fact that he looked terrible; something bad obviously went down during his long silence.

"So what happened? Are you all right?" I couldn't restrain the expression of concern and he shot me a grateful look.

"A bit singed here and there, no life-threatening injuries. There's no proof Dwyer & Fell are involved, but it's no coincidence that my place burned last night."

Muttering a curse, I shifted in the seat to take a more careful inventory of him. Now that he'd mentioned it, I could see a smear of ash he'd missed on his temple and when I breathed in, I pulled hints of soot and smoke.

"Why are they targeting you?"

"To weaken you," he said quietly. "They're not permitted to go after you directly, but they can attack people close to you. Pawns like me are always the first to go."

"Whereas I'm the queen in play?" I joked, trying to lighten the mood.

I couldn't believe how serious he seemed as he glanced over with grave green eyes. "At the moment, yes."

"I don't understand. WM&G pays you well and trusts you with special assignments. How does that make you a pawn?"

He wore an inscrutable look. "If I'm eliminated, it doesn't hurt Wedderburn. True, the company is out the cost of my favors, but when you consider the scale they operate on—"

"It's a drop in the bucket," I guessed.

"So, to them, my chief value resides in my connection to you.

The game can change at any time, you understand, but right now, *you* have a vital, viable future to protect."

"I'd give a lot to know what future-me achieves and why it's so critical." I sighed. "Seems like it's past time to visit you at work."

"Agreed. That's where we're headed, in fact. Wedderburn asked to meet you."

My heart stuttered in my chest. I'd asked to tour the place, but this was different. His boss *wanted* me there, and it made me nervous. "Any idea why?"

"He has a proposition for you." Though his tone was matter-of-fact, he shook his head ever so slightly.

Right. Whatever Wedderburn wants, I say no. Provided that I believed Kian had my best interests at heart. I wished I could be sure he did. *I can't let myself be taken in by good looks and a pair of sad eyes.* That would make me quite an idiot.

"I hope I can remember what I'm not supposed to know," I muttered.

"Just listen and act appreciative. Wedderburn has a thing for humility. And when he makes his offer, tell him you need time to think about it."

That didn't sound ominous or like bad advice. I might've done the latter without Kian's guidance. I sat quiet for the remainder of the drive, though I stole periodic looks at him, unable to stop reassuring myself that he was really here. Absently I touched the infinity symbol on my wrist. Though it looked like a tattoo, the raised edges felt more like a brand.

"Does it hurt?" he asked.

"No. It just . . ." I couldn't explain it, but it felt as if the thing were *alive* on my wrist and operating independently of me, like it might, someday, force my right hand to do things I didn't want.

More crazy. But if I can't share it with Kian . . .

So I took a deep breath and blurted all of that out. I expected him to stare in shock or even laugh. Instead he swore. "It's happening too fast. They've accelerated the timetable, hoping to push you into burning your favors."

"It's not bothering me enough to make me ask you to take it off my arm." But I stared at the symbol, quietly horrified, like it was an alien using me as its host.

"That's not something I could do anyway. That mark is part of you now."

Before I could ask what he was talking about, he pulled into an underground parking lot. The place was dark and creepy as the car went down, down, down, and it wasn't better when Kian pulled into a spot that had his name painted on the wall. It made me think he was more important than he was telling, and I couldn't escape the possibility that he might've been lying about everything, from his age to his name. While I was sure there *had* been a Kian Riley, it didn't mean he was that person. None of the stories I'd found online had included a picture.

"Try not to be afraid," he whispered as he opened the door for me. "Some of them find it . . . exciting."

ICE, ICE, BABY

Wedderburn, Mawer & Graf had offices downtown, a glittering glass and steel monstrosity some twenty stories tall. The only hint as to who owned the building came in the form of a bronze plaque beside the front door with the names graven in copperplate lettering; the sign looked much older than the skyscraper, burnished with a patina created by time and the elements. Doubtless Kian wondered why I went out front to look around when we'd come up from the garage elevator, but I wanted to get a better sense of where I was.

Call it recon.

The reception area was banal to the point of seeming ironic— with beige upholstered chairs in the waiting area and abstract art in shades of brown. Even the receptionist seemed to have been hired to go along with the room, as she had ash-blond hair and brown eyes, skin that almost matched the walls. And she was wearing, you guessed it, an ensemble in various hues of brown and beige. She followed us with her gaze as we went past her to the elevator, but she didn't speak.

"She's unnerving," I whispered to Kian.

"Iris has that effect on people. She . . . discourages walk-in problems."

"I imagine. It's weird the way she blends in with the décor."

"She'd do that no matter what color scheme they chose." The worst part was, I had no idea if he was kidding, and I didn't want to ask.

The elevator seemed really, really cold, so I exhaled as a test, and my breath showed in a puff of white smoke. "It's warmer outside."

"Technically, we're not in Massachusetts anymore."

While I chewed on that, the car zoomed us to the tenth floor, then the doors dinged and opened. "This is my department."

"Do you have a cubicle with a desk?" I made the joke because I was growing shakier with every step, and I had no idea why. It wasn't just the cold, but something about this building just . . . was *not* right.

From the elevator, I glanced down an interminable white hallway. In fact, the length of that corridor seemed to exceed the diameter of the building, though I wasn't sure how that was possible. Occasionally, I'd dream about an infinite hallway, interspersed with identical doors. Dream dictionaries said halls meant untapped portions of your psyche and closed doors symbolized missed opportunities. In symbolic combination, this place burgeoned with loss and untapped potential. We passed eight doors, all spaced equidistant, and from behind a couple of them, came the sound of muffled screaming.

"You said you were afraid this place would freak me out," I said softly. "Good call."

It felt like we walked for a good five minutes, but when I checked my phone to find out, it had frozen on the time when we entered the building, and no matter what buttons I pushed, it wouldn't respond. I glanced up at Kian and he mouthed, *Later.* Okay, now I was genuinely losing my shit. Only a lifetime of training in the school of If You Cry, We Win kept my poker face intact. I clenched one hand into a fist at my sides, nails biting into my palm.

At last we came to a door at the end of the hallway. When I turned, I could no longer see the elevator from here. This one was distinguishable from the others only in that it had a nameplate on it, K. Wedderburn. I had no idea what madness or horror lay beyond, but Kian entered without knocking. If possible, it was even colder in the office, a big room wrapped with windows on two sides, and those were frosted over so I couldn't see what lay beyond. Some tiny voice inside me whispered that was best.

Wedderburn was even more inhuman than his photo suggested. Oh, he had all the right parts in the correct places, but he radiated a cold that surpassed the chill in the room. His hair was more like hoarfrost and his eyes were pools of black ice. Even his skin looked like it might crack if you touched it. *No wonder they need agents like Kian. They can't travel too easily in the mortal world.* I had no idea why I'd chosen that word, but it fit. This wasn't a human creature, if it ever had been. He was doing something at an odd white metal desk, only it was no compound I'd ever seen before, as it held the opalescent gleam of mother of pearl. While the back framework looked like a computer, Wedderburn had his fingers *in* the screen, stretching and pulling at the surface so that shimmers of what looked like liquid mercury clung his fingertips.

On noticing our arrival, he flicked his hands, so that the computer-thing let him go and he rose with the sound of someone moving over fresh fallen snow. "Ah. Miss Kramer. You are a *fascinating* asset."

"Thank you." I had no idea if that was the right response, but when Wedderburn's cheeks crackled in a smile, I guessed it was.

"I hope Kian has been taking good care of you?"

"He's made it clear that I'm special." Why, I had no idea, and I wasn't sure Kian did, either. WM&G seemed to operate on a need-to-know basis.

There were no furnishings, nothing with which to entertain or make another person comfortable. So I stood in the icy air, wishing I dared reach for Kian's hand. Even though he was supposed to be making me fall madly in love with him, I wasn't sure how far along we were supposed to be, and I didn't want extra attention from Wedderburn. Kian always used a particular tone when he mentioned his boss, and now I understood why. A whimper boiled up in my throat, but I choked it down.

"I see that you're uneasy," Wedderburn said. "I apologize. But certain necessities preclude a more welcoming environment."

If it's warmer, you melt into a puddle of goo? That wouldn't surprise me at all.

"It's all right. I'm more interested in hearing what you have to say than in taking tea."

"Excellent. I appreciate efficiency. Just ask Kian."

Despite myself, I glanced at Kian, who nodded. His expression was as flat as I'd ever seen it. Even his normally expressive eyes gave nothing away. *This is the creature he works for, the one he's trying to save me from.* I wished I could be sure of it, and not fear he was secretly working in tandem to make me do exactly as they wanted.

God, I sound so nuts.

"He said you wanted to meet me," I murmured.

"Indeed. Come around the desk, my girl." The proprietary tone sent a shiver down my spine and I moved quickly to avoid one of his long, spidery fingers lighting on my shoulder.

What had looked slightly like a computer from the other side now looked like nothing I'd ever seen before. It seemed to be part creature, part machine, with a square head, for lack of a better word, and a metallic neck that led down to shoulders and arms that seemed to have been fused with the desk, which might also be alive, as far as I knew. The otherness of it was so appalling I had to look away.

"What is it?" I whispered.

"My interface to the Oracle. Through her, I can sort through various alternate futures, shadow threads, and encourage others."

"Like the Moirae."

"Ah, an educated girl. How charming." But he reacted as if knowledge were a persimmon, unexpectedly tart on his tongue.

"But unlike the Fates, I can only shape or suggest. I cannot cut or create threads."

If you could, you'd have won your game long before now.

He continued, "A shadow on a mortal fate, however, is often enough to blight it. I believe there are those who have been most unjust to you. It seems unfair that you must slog toward vengeance when a mind like yours should be turned to more important endeavors."

"What are you proposing?" I asked.

"Let me take care of it for you."

I thought of the assholes in the Teflon crew and could only imagine what Wedderburn would consider proper retaliation, but I sensed I had to be super careful in how I turned him down. Kian had counseled me to say I needed time to think, but if I didn't nip this in the bud, it would only get tougher to say no later. "While I appreciate the offer, it would rob me of satisfaction not to orchestrate their downfall personally."

Wedderburn sighed. "I was afraid you would say that, but . . . I understand. You will, of course, permit me to be of service in some other fashion. I want to help you reach your true potential, Edie."

With him wearing that insane smile, I feared I might be the next scary dictator in what Kian called my optimum timeline. "Thank you."

"Would you like to see a demonstration?" he asked.

Part of me thought it was a bad idea, but I also couldn't refuse everything. Wedderburn seemed like the easily offended type and I preferred to get out of his office without being flash frozen. So I forced a smile, the same one I gave to the Teflon crew, and said, "That would be amazing."

"Come a little closer."

Kian shifted and pulled in a breath, as if in instinctive protest, but I didn't dare look at him. It required all of my willpower not to shiver uncontrollably and wrap my arms about myself. In addition to the cold, this strange creature also radiated a primordial dread that made my skin creep, trying to crawl all the way off my muscles and bones in horror that no amount of meds or therapy could fix. The whimper in my throat became a silent scream.

"Of course."

Wedderburn turned toward the head-monitor-thing and swiveled it so I could see the liquid mercury stuff. Before he reached inside the frame, it was opaque, but at his touch, it shimmered and turned translucent, so each time he stirred icy fingertips, a new pattern rippled, first a star, then a pentacle, and then it turned into a cephalopod with tentacles lashing in all directions. He speared one with a fingertip and it flowered into a murky image, similar to a convenience store surveillance camera's, only cast in liquid.

Vi.

Like the room around me, my blood iced over. Fear wasn't deep enough for the feeling that swamped me, tighter and knottier than sickness. Outwardly, I kept a cool front, apart from my breathing, but I couldn't do anything about it. My stomach swirled as we spied on her. She was at home, head bent over her schoolbooks. Now and then, she smiled at the candid photo of her and Seth taped to her mirror. *I* took that shot. The scene was ordinary in every possible way, and it was unspeakably wrong for us to be watching her like this.

Beside me, Wedderburn was silent, a faint smile playing at the edge of his lips. "A shadow here . . . or here . . . would change everything," he said conversationally. "Your friend seems to have a bright future."

Seems. That's definitely a threat.

He went on, "It would probably crush her if something happened to her new beau. Ah, first love. I'm not sure she'd recover."

He stirred the surface again, without pulling or changing anything that I could tell, and now we were watching Seth. He didn't have a picture of Vi on his wall, which might disappoint her, but she was the wallpaper background on his laptop. I didn't know if that made it better or worse. Idly Wedderburn flicked the liquid and Seth rubbed his head.

"Very impressive," I managed to say. If I revealed how much I cared, it would go poorly for my friends. I understood that instinctively. The prick of pain on my palms told me I was dangerously close to breaking through the skin with my fingernails. "But surely there are rules about harming mortals who aren't part of the game."

Wedderburn straightened, wearing an inscrutable look. "Are there?"

Oh God. If there weren't . . . if he could kill anyone he wanted, anyone who wasn't a catalyst, then I'd put everyone close to me at risk. *You didn't know. But you can fix this. Somehow.* It was so hard to keep my teeth from chattering, but I couldn't show Wedderburn how rattled I felt. I could easily drop down on the floor and cram my head between my knees while I hyperventilated; only the fact that I needed to help my friends prevented me from melting down completely.

"This has been wonderful," I choked out, "but I have homework. I look forward to our next meeting, sir."

"As do I, Miss Kramer." I noted his reversion to formality, now that the lines had been drawn. I suspected Wedderburn knew that I was not—and never would be—his ally.

Kian didn't speak until we were outside the building. "Are you all right?"

Silently I shook my head and he wrapped me up in his arms. This might be exactly what was supposed to happen, a good cop, bad cop routine, but I leaned on him anyway. I felt like I might never get warm again, even with the late-summer sun shining down on my head. The shivers didn't abate for a few minutes, despite his hands moving up and down my back. People walked around us with nervous looks, as if my distress might be contagious.

"I don't understand. He's supposed to be the *good* guy, on my side?"

"Good and evil doesn't apply here," Kian said softly. "There are only different agendas. I can't say I'm fighting for right, I'm just trying to survive. And I realize hearing that doesn't inspire you to trust me more."

"I doubt you'd tell me that if it wasn't true. Because it *doesn't* cast you in the best light. So at least I know you're being honest."

"Text your parents." He stepped back but left an arm around my shoulder and he guided me to his car.

"And say what?"

"That you'll be back by dinner."

Since I was too freaked to head home anyway, I did as he suggested, then hopped in the car. Kian shut the door behind me and I buckled in. "Where are we going?"

"Someplace we can talk."

• • •

Kian drove out of the city; it was early enough for us not to be caught in rush hour traffic. Half an hour later, we ended up driving along the coast, a swath of land remarkable only for the fact that there was nothing particular here, except the rocky shoreline and the pounding of the sea. Kian pulled off to the side and got out of the Mustang. A path led down from the road.

"What's special about this place?"

"Something in the stone, it's like . . . a blind spot. Neither side can spy on us out here." He tapped his watch with a satisfied look.

"You won't get in trouble?"

He shrugged. "I barely got out of my burning house the other night, and since I'm not a 'fascinating asset,' the company still hasn't done anything about it. I don't much care what they do to me at the moment."

For a few seconds, I wondered if that was just what he thought I wanted to hear. But if this was a blind spot, he had no reason to lie. Maybe this was just his first chance to tell me how trapped and unhappy he was. On the other hand, it might not be a blind spot at all. He could be playing me perfectly—at Wedderburn's instruction. I almost wouldn't blame Kian if that was true; his boss was terrifying.

"You should care," I said quietly. "You're important."

He shot me a warm look, one that quickened my heartbeat a little. But his tone rang with sad finality. "Not to them."

Following his lead, I sat down on the sand, a few feet from the water. The late-afternoon sun warmed my skin, gradually washing away the freezer-death feeling that had sunk into my bones during the interview with Wedderburn.

"So your boss . . . what is he?"

"I'm not sure," Kian answered. "Not human anymore, if he ever was. His name has been on the building for a hundred years, and I've dug up a few pictures of him, looking exactly that way for at least that long."

"Creepy. Does he disappear and then come back younger?"

"No. That's the odd thing. And he never fakes his own death, either."

I'd read books about vampires doing that, then pretending to be his or her own grandchild, but a life eternally encased in ice? That was new.

Kian went on, "But he doesn't go out either. It's all done through intermediaries, and when you have as much money as he does, nobody asks too many questions."

"I imagine bad things happen to those who poke around in his affairs."

"You handled yourself well in there," he said unexpectedly. "Struck the right balance between wariness and respect."

I frowned, trickling a palmful of sand between my fingers. "I don't understand why he offered me payback. Do I hate those assholes? Absolutely. I dream about them finally knowing what it's like, how I felt, but—"

"It was a test," he cut in.

"Of what?"

"Your character. A lazy person accepts all help, even if he doesn't need it. An evil one would've asked Wedderburn to inflict all manner of horrors on his enemies."

"Oh." My breath was shaky when I exhaled. "I can't say I wasn't tempted. A dark part of me would love to see them all broken."

Not just humiliated, but destroyed. That part, I couldn't bring myself to say out loud.

"After what they did, it's understandable. But you'd never actually harm them, no matter what fantasies you play with."

"I wish I didn't have it in me. But I look at Brittany, who held the camera, and I think, *What* would it take to break you? Would I have to mess up her face?" I couldn't believe I was saying that, because it was so ugly, and it made me sick, that I could still be *this* full of hate. I knew for the sake of my own mental health, I had to let it go.

But I couldn't. Not yet. Maybe saying these awful things to Kian would help. He could be my sounding board, and once I vented it all, I could move on.

"Do you want to hurt her?" he asked.

"No. I mean, I don't *think* so. Do I want people to laugh at her? Yeah. I want her to know how it feels. But I'm not thinking about carving her up or anything." I picked up a smooth stone and chucked it toward the ocean. There was no way I could look directly at him and ask this question. "Did you see it? The video they made?"

A pained sound tore from him, and his head dropped into his hands. I could see his fingers tearing at his hair, hard enough that it looked painful. "I was *there*, Edie. My job was to mark your progress, see you skate ever closer to extremis. I could've stopped it. I didn't."

Jesus. I almost threw up. It was bad enough that he *knew*, but this—

"Take me home," I managed to say. "Right now."

"I'm sorry."

"Take. Me. Home."

Then he grabbed my hand and the world speeded up to rushing insanity, and in a single swirl, we were both in my room. That was the last straw; I stumbled to the wastebasket and barfed up my lunch while Kian held my hair. I wanted to hit him—to hate him—but mostly, I was just sick and ashamed that he'd seen. I mean, I'd known he was watching me, but I didn't realize how closely. Afterward I curled up in a ball on the floor, too drained to shove him away when he pulled me close.

"I've seen so much pain in the last three years, logged it, and done nothing to make it better. I'm so sorry, Edie."

"If you don't do your job, what happens?" I asked eventually, head against his chest.

My parents could come in at any time, and I had no explanation ready for who this boy was or why he was holding me on my floor. I didn't care either; the strangeness of the day had sucked it all out of me.

"A human resource that refuses to perform its function is useless." He sounded like he was quoting someone, maybe Wedderburn. "So . . . I'd be terminated."

"As in killed." I had little doubt, but it seemed best to be sure. Considering his obvious guilt over failing to intervene, I didn't imagine he would've chosen inaction, if interference didn't carry an enormous penalty.

"Yeah." He pulled back, as if that wasn't a good enough explanation.

"So essentially, you're apologizing for not *dying* for me. You hadn't even talked to me at that point. No offense, Kian, but I'd rather have you here on my side. As long as we're still breathing, there's hope, right?" Somehow I managed a lopsided smile.

"Oh God, Edie." He brushed his lips across my forehead. We both knew why he wasn't kissing my mouth.

"We'll be okay," I whispered.

How I wished I believed that. It felt like I'd fallen down a well rapidly filling with dark water. As I wrapped my arms around Kian's back, I felt the tremor that ran through him and wondered how long I could hold my breath.

ALL GOOD THINGS

Shadows plagued me, dancing just beyond the range of the street-lights, and since I'd met Wedderburn, I had no idea if they were working for him. And what about the thin man? Did he report to Dwyer & Fell? My head ached.

That night, I pretended everything was fine in front of my parents and then retreated to do homework. In fact, I never went to sleep or turned off my lamp. I was a mess in the morning, bleary-eyed and blessed with bags I could pack my books in. It took longer than usual to make myself presentable, and I had to skip breakfast and run for the train.

So I wasn't prepared when Russ ambushed me at my locker. "What the hell, you told Cam what I said?"

It gave me some satisfaction that they'd nicknamed him Cam, against his will. It said he was no longer calling *all* the shots. My ears rang with an odd tinnitus and I shook my head to clear it, peering up at Russ, whose face didn't seem . . . quite the right shape, suddenly. I stared at him harder and the impression went away. *Just lack of sleep.*

Belatedly, I answered his question. "I didn't. I asked Jen what she thought of Cam, and I think Allison was ahead of us in line, but I would never—"

"Bet it was Allison." His frown cleared. "She's always trying to make Cam like her. She's got this weird rivalry with Brittany. They're supposed to be BFFs, but I get the feeling Allison would giggle if Brit fell down the stairs."

"That's *horrible*." I'd probably laugh too.

"Girls," Russ said, like I wasn't one.

If I cared about him on any level, I'd punch him for being such a dick. Instead I got my books, and for some reason, he walked me to class. It kept everyone else at bay because he had a reputation for being vicious. *He was there when they broke you.* To me it seemed incredible that he could act like it never happened, as if my change in appearance wiped the slate clean.

It didn't. I remember you, Russ.

A girl darted past me with her head down, and at first, I didn't recognize her. She was wearing sweats, her blond hair falling in her face in a messy tangle. Like a snake, Russ lashed out and snagged her arm, whirling her around. He was already laughing.

"Wake up late today, Brit?"

Her head came up on a horrified gasp, and I saw some kind of . . . weeping rash crawling its way across her cheek—virulent red pustules topped with yellow crust—more than just a breakout, a staph infection on crack. Tears glimmered in her blue eyes, so swollen that I guessed she'd been crying for hours. I couldn't bring myself to say a single mean thing, but Russ had that covered.

He recoiled in a move so violent he almost knocked down a passing freshman. "What the hell happened to *your face?*"

"An allergic reaction," she said miserably. "I used a clarifying mask last night, and my skin puffed up a little. By morning . . . it was like this. My mom made me an appointment with my dermatologist for tonight, but she wouldn't let me skip since I have cheerleading practice today."

"Yeah, because everyone wants to see *that*"—Russ gestured at her face and body indicating the big picture—"prancing around. Do us all a favor, get out of sight until your face-sore heals up." He cocked his head. "Huh. In those sweats, you look ass-heavy too. What did you eat this summer, Brit? Your family?"

I should've been elated when tears spilled down her cheeks and she whirled, plunging down the hall in a mad dash to hide in the bathroom. *Now she knows how it feels.* But instead my insides boiled, even though I hadn't done anything to cause this. Shame froze me because I hadn't stopped Russ from saying any of those awful things. I could've spoken up, but I just stood there like a lump.

Incredibly, insanely, he was grinning at me. "Wow, she says meaner shit than that every day, then a little choice truth, and she's a whimpering mess. Weak, huh?"

"I hope the doctor can help her." To my surprise, I wasn't playing a part; I meant it. Looks meant a lot to Brittany, and while I didn't like her, I hated seeing her so shamed. It wasn't nearly as satisfying as I'd expected.

"You're too nice. You should hear what she says behind your back."

That didn't surprise me. Last year, she said it to my face. Frowning, I dodged into my Lit class early, mostly to get away from Russ, who I wanted to kick. A lot.

"You look tired, Edie. Is everything all right?"

I swung around to see Colin propped artfully against his desk. God, everything he did seemed so . . . studied, like he was constantly posing. There were already a few girls sitting dreamily at their desks, and I wished he'd care about their mental and emotional well-being instead. I arranged my stuff, ignoring him until he turned away. It seemed too soon for him to be invested in me as a student, which left a couple of possibilities. He was keeping track of me for Wedderburn . . . or Dwyer & Fell. Though he wasn't as beautiful as Kian, he was attractive enough for me to credit that he'd asked for that face.

You know what they say about those who think random people are involved in a conspiracy and plotting against them. Crazy town.

Putting aside that fear, I focused on my morning classes. Somehow I managed not to fall asleep, though I certainly wasn't performing up to last year's standards. I'd be lucky to pull As if I kept this up. There might even be minuses. My parents would be appalled. Sadly, I wasn't joking.

"Have you seen Brittany today?" Jen asked, catching up halfway to the cafeteria.

"Yeah, before first period. She looks rough."

"I guess she's been hiding in the bathroom most of the day. The headmaster called her mother out of some charity thing to come and get her. Brit was crying her head off when her mom yanked her out of there."

This was exactly what I would've wished on Brittany, a few weeks back. Yet there was no delicious schadenfreude, only a sick sort of regret, tinged in dread. *I just talked about this with Kian. And Wedderburn offered to get revenge for me. What if he won't take no for an answer?*

As we went into the cafeteria, Jen changed the subject, probably seeing that I was uncomfortable. She was trying really hard to make it right, what happened last winter. Unfortunately, there was no way to wipe the slate, and while I appreciated her efforts, I still didn't trust her. Vi was my only real friend, untainted by the shit splattered over the rest of my life. I recalled how easily Wedderburn had drawn her into his web and I shivered; there was no way I'd let anything happen to Vi.

Brittany didn't come to school the rest of the week, but nobody knew why until Friday. At our usual table during lunch, Allison delivered the news in a hushed whisper, as if she didn't intend to repeat it later. Gossip was the water of life to her.

"Her mom told me she's in the hospital," Allison confided.

This news should be coming from Cameron, still her boyfriend so far as I knew. But apparently his interest didn't stretch past a bad skin condition. He wore a bored look, one that rekindled my desire to see him suffer. I wondered if he'd bothered to return Brit's texts or visit her, though I guessed probably not.

"What's the matter with her?" Jen asked.

Russ smirked. "She's got a serious case of butterface. I think it might be terminal."

Allison hit him. "This is serious. She had some kind of skin infection, probably caused by bacteria, but Brit's mom said the doctors aren't sure, because the cultures weren't like anything they'd seen. And now, she has, like . . . *meningitis* or something."

"That's potentially fatal," I said, before I realized how it sounded.

Allison burst into tears and Cameron shot me a daggered look as he wrapped an arm around her shoulders. "Way to go, dumbass."

Her tears dried immediately. From my point of view, she looked a bit *too* pleased to be cuddled up with her best friend's boyfriend, but I shut up. I was still an outsider, even if Russ and Jen liked me. The others talked quietly about putting together a gift basket and sending it to Brit's room, but nobody mentioned checking on her, like, because she had a disease, and hospitals were gross, full of sick people and disgusting germs you could catch. Listening to them, I decided to go see Brittany after school.

I got the information from Jen and took the T to Park Station, then transferred to the Red Line. A few minutes later, I hopped off at Charles/Mass General station and walked the rest of the way, all while wondering what to say when I saw Brittany. Nervous, I stopped by the gift shop and while I was browsing, my phone buzzed with a text.

Where are you? I came to pick you up but you never showed.

Aw. I'd run out much faster than usual, eager to break free of Blackbriar and the stultifying atmosphere. Last year, I'd loved my classes but hated my classmates. This year, it felt as if there was something wrong with the whole campus.

Deciding on a bear in a tiny hat, I paid for the plushie, then replied: I'm visiting someone at the hospital. Didn't know you were coming to get me. Maybe you could work on your communication?

Funny, Kian answered. Unless I say otherwise, assume I'll pick you up, okay?

Just like a real boyfriend, I sent back. That shouldn't make me so happy because he came with a boatload of baggage, but it didn't stop me from smiling as I pressed the elevator button. That silenced him, or maybe it was lack of signal. Remembering the rules from when Great-Aunt Edith died, I shut down my phone and put it away. After stepping off the elevator, I went to the desk. Jen had given me Brit's room number, but I should probably make sure she wasn't asleep or receiving treatment.

"Is it all right if I go see Brittany?" I named the room number, and the nurse nodded.

"I'm glad someone's here. She seems pretty down. It's so tough when they're young."

"Her parents aren't with her?" I'd braced for an awkward moment, where I showed up and they stared at me because I wasn't actually one of Brit's friends.

The woman shook her head. "Her mother filled out the paperwork and took off. I figured she was running home to get some things, but she just . . . never came back."

This was definitely gossip territory, and I wasn't sure if it was against the rules or what. Probably, it was poor judgment, at least, but I encouraged her. "Between you and me, her mom is kind of a bitch."

"I definitely got that vibe." She lowered her voice. "It was like she couldn't even stand to look at her."

"Poor Brit. I'll head in now. Thanks for your time."

The desk nurse was smiling when she went back to her paper-work. I went toward the end of the hall, last room on the left, and opened the door without knocking. My heart thudded like compo-nents hitting the side of a centrifuge. *If Brit was dangerous or contagious, she wouldn't have let you come in. There would be quarantine procedures in place. Right?*

The bed curtain was drawn, even though she had a private room. This was nice, as far as hospitals went. Nervously I set the stuffed bear on her table, next to her pitcher of water. I was tempted to run but I told myself it would be stupid to come all this way and not speak.

"Allison?" she said in a small voice.

Crap. Obviously she expects her best friend.

I swallowed past the lump in my throat. "No, sorry. It's me, Edie."

"What are *you* doing here? If you're here to gloat, go ahead." She waited, as if expecting me to say something horrible. "If you're here to kill me, make it quick."

"No, I . . . I just came by to say get well soon. I brought you a bear."

Her tone when she finally spoke was grudging. "That was nice of you. You can . . . hand it through if you want."

I pushed the stuffed animal through the curtain and caught a glimpse of her ravaged features. What we'd seen a few days ago was *nothing* compared with how she looked now. Part of her nose was just . . . gone, and there were holes in her cheeks. I tried my best not to react but it was tough.

"Anyway, I said what I came to, so—"

"Could you stay for a while? You can watch TV if you want."

Her miserable, lonely tone was too much for me, so I watched an hour of the news while she slept and then I crept out, feeling awful. I couldn't imagine the damage I'd seen healing without extensive plastic surgery for the scarring, and the people in her life were assholes who made *my* parents look warm and emotionally supportive.

It was close to six by the time I let myself into the apartment. My dad had dinner on the table and he looked pissed, though with him it was micro-expressions rather than overt indications. "You're late," he noted. "And you didn't text me."

I wanted to snap at him. "Yeah, I was visiting a classmate at the hospital."

He asked a few questions, likely testing my story, but since it was true, there were no inconsistencies to find. "I wonder where she contracted the infection. Make sure you always wash your hands, Edith."

I sighed. "I do."

My mom came home a few minutes later and took up his attention with more talk about the grant project as we sat down to eat Brussels sprouts and poached halibut. For the first time, I paid attention to the project they were trying to fund. "We've ruled out cosmic strings as possibilities for time travel. The laser research is promising, though."

I froze as my dad nodded. "Let's work on the grant application this weekend."

Any other parents discussing time travel, you'd guess they were crazy or talking about science fiction. When your parents were both physicists, the rules changed. Right now I couldn't imagine working with my mom and dad, but some important achievement lay ahead, not *too* far into my future. Clearing my throat, I moved flaky fish around on my plate.

"You think that's a viable avenue of investigation?" I asked.

Dad smiled at me. "We won't know until we take our research from theoretical to experimental."

"And that requires private sector money." My mom maintained a practical attitude in relation to most things, even when the subject matter sounded pretty incredible.

"Let me know if I can do anything to help." That seemed like the right thing to say, as both my parents lit up like Christmas decorations.

My phone buzzed. Covertly, I checked it under the table. Can you go out Saturday night, 7ish?

Since I had zero plans, it was safe to say I could, as long as my parents agreed. "I was hoping to see a movie tomorrow. Is that okay?"

Both my mom and dad stilled, eyeing me as if I had been kidnapped by aliens and replaced by a socially adequate pod person. "What movie?" my mom asked as my dad wanted to know, "With who?"

"I'm not sure yet," I said. "And his name is Kian. You can meet him when he picks me up."

"It's fine with me," my mom said. "But we'll need to decide on a curfew."

"Is this a date?" My dad was frowning, as if it had only just occurred to him that my altered circumstances presented him with a whole new set of problems.

In all honesty, I had no idea what was going on with Kian and me. But it seemed safest to say, "Yeah."

"If you're finished eating, I'd like to talk to your father. Once we come to a consensus, I'll inform you." It was hard not to laugh at how seriously my mother was taking this, but since that was how she approached everything, it wasn't surprising.

"It's fine, I'm done." Shaking my head, I went to my room and signed on to chat with Vi on Skype.

Her conversation was mostly about school, but just before she signed off, she said something that freaked me out. "Have you ever had a recurring dream, Edie?"

"Not that I can remember."

"That doesn't mean you never have, only that you completed the dream before the REM cycle ended. If you can remember the dream, it means your sleep was interrupted for some reason."

"Oh?"

"Anyway, I was asking because for the last three nights, I've dreamed the same thing." Her expression became sheepish. "There's this ice man watching me but I'm frozen solid and I can't move, not even my eyelids. He creeps closer and closer, like some kind of snow spider, and then when he touches me, I crack into a thousand pieces."

My throat went dry as a bone. "That's—"

"Really weird, I know."

Wedderburn. But I couldn't tell *her* that. Whatever it took, I had to find a way to keep this craziness from bleeding onto Vi. "Can you hang on a sec? I want to look something up."

I kept my cool until I left her field of vision and then the trembling set in. I crouched in my closet. Wrapping my arms around my knees, I dropped my head and let the panic sweep over me. *This is too much. I can't handle it.* My breath came in ragged gasps until I went light-headed, and my heart pounded so hard I was afraid it might actually explode. Gradually I calmed down, knowing I had to get back or Vi might disconnect before we finished talking. But when I went back to my laptop, I was shaky and covered in cold sweat.

"Took you long enough," she said when I sat down at my desk.

I lied through my teeth. "I was digging through a book, but I couldn't find anything. What do you think it means?"

"I'm not sure. I did some checking too, but dream dictionaries are pretty limited. If I had to guess, I'm feeling panicked about choosing a college."

It was as good an explanation as any, especially when the truth wouldn't work. Now I wished I hadn't encouraged her friendship at the SSP, but at the time, I hadn't realized how dangerous a deal I'd made; back then, I didn't understand that players had no qualms about attacking people who knew nothing about it.

"Sounds reasonable."

"You should visit me soon, I miss you. I mean, if you can. If you have time." She seemed uncomfortable, as if it had belatedly occurred to her I might not want to leave my glamorous life in Boston to spend time in Ohio.

"I'd love to," I said.

As soon as it's safe. But I feared that day might be a long time coming.

ANOTHER SATURDAY NIGHT & I SAW A MONSTER

By Saturday at six thirty, I'd completed all of my homework, dutifully proven this to my parents, who seemed to think a daughter who wanted to date might also lie about finishing assignments. And now I was listening to my father give the world's most awkward lecture on how boys were animals and I should not, under any circumstances, trust a person with a penis. I tried to look appropriately impressed by the wisdom he was dropping on me, but it was tough.

"They may act as if they care for you. Respect you, even . . ." My dad trailed off, looking at my mother as if for deliverance.

"Be safe," she said.

"I had the sex class at school." There was possibly nothing worse I could've said.

It wound my father up, so he stammered about love and consideration until my mom finally cut him off in pity. "We trust you," she concluded, though everything my dad had just said offered evidence to the contrary.

"Thanks. I'll be home by midnight."

Half an hour later, Kian knocked. It was probably unwise to consider this a date, despite what I'd told my parents, so I'd dressed in jeans, boots, and a jacket, in case of trouble. With Kian, I didn't spend hours on my hair and makeup. It seemed superfluous since he'd known me before, *and* he'd created this version of me. It wasn't like I could startle him with my beauty.

He was good with my parents, offering a firm handshake to my dad and a smile for my mom. I could tell she was surprised and dazzled—to the point that she almost forgot to ask about his work status and his collegiate enrollment. But he covered smoothly, telling her he worked part-time at a company downtown and he also attended university. The exchange went quicker than I'd have guessed, given it was the first time all around. Soon I dodged out the door with Kian close behind.

"That wasn't so bad," he said as we stepped out of the brownstone.

"You thought my dad would tell you he has a shovel and a handgun?"

"Something like that." He shifted, seeming unaccountably nervous. "I've just . . . I never picked a girl up like that before."

With a face like this, how was that possible? "You don't date?"

Kian sighed. "Work makes it . . . difficult."

"Oh, right. There's no good way to tell your girlfriend that you're up to your neck in a dangerous game. What does the winner get, anyway? Lifetime supply of car wax? Rule the world for all eternity?"

"More of the latter," he said somberly. "But to be honest, I don't think that's *entirely* it."

"Wow, so there's more? High stakes. But how do they know if they win?" I followed him to the car and got in when he opened the door.

"I don't have all the answers, Edie. At this point, you're more important than I am."

"Then I need to find a way to parlay that value into information. Where're we going?"

"There's something you need to see, and this is the best time."

"So this isn't a date." Part of me was glad I'd dressed for trouble, but a tiny corner felt . . . disappointed.

"Did you want it to be?" Kian started the car and drove toward downtown.

I don't know why I said it; possibly my mouth detached from my brain. "Yes."

His hands actually jerked on the wheel, running us toward the curb, and he corrected course quickly, before daring to sneak a look at me. I wondered what he saw in the streaky darkness, illuminated only by passing streetlamps and the occasional flicker of fluorescent light from an open store. For my part, I was watching him in turn, trying to figure out what he'd looked like before. Was he thin or heavy; what flaws had been smoothed away?

"Are you screwing with me?" he asked finally.

"What? No!" I was honestly offended. *God, this is so backward. Isn't he supposed to be able to tell when a girl's into him?* "You remember I asked you to kiss me, right? Maybe it wasn't anything to you, but that was kind of a big deal for me."

After I said it, I wondered what Wedderburn would make of this. Kian was supposed to be making me fall for him, and this was the kind of thing I'd say if his efforts were paying off. So maybe it

166

didn't matter that his boss might be listening to how we really felt. Well, how *I* did, anyway. The constant tension and uncertainty was excruciating.

He didn't say anything straight off but at the first opportunity, he pulled into a convenience store parking lot. After he stopped the car, his knuckles whitened on the steering wheel, but not before I saw that he was shaking. *Okay, what the hell?* Kian didn't look at me, his gaze fixed straight ahead. A liquor store next door had a broken neon sign, so it flashed red across his skin in stutters and skips.

"After my life imploded," he said softly, "I tried not to feel anything because it only seemed to get worse, until . . . well, you know where I hit bottom. And when. Working for Wedderburn is like . . . limbo. I have a life, but it doesn't belong to me. And . . . I don't have a great track record."

First crush equals dead girl, check. That should've given me pause, but I didn't think he had anything to do with that. Maybe there was a hidden monkey's paw after all, or like he'd said, she was a victim of the opposition. Her death got him demoted from catalyst to indentured drone, so it wouldn't make sense for him to get her killed on purpose.

Unless he didn't know his fate was tied to hers until it was too late . . .

"I don't have *any* track record," I answered. "Unless you count that kiss."

He shifted so I couldn't see his eyes. "There was that summer guy, Ryu. Do you still talk to him?"

Are you jealous? But it seemed cruel to ask. "Yeah, now and then."

Should I reassure him? Hard to know when I had no idea what was happening between us or if I should even want the things I did from him.

167

Roughly, he whispered, "Our kiss meant something to me too. But I thought once you knew I could've helped you before you hit extremis, it would change things."

"I'm not pissed, if that's what you mean. I was *shocked*. It's horrible, knowing you saw everything firsthand. But . . . if it doesn't make you think less of me—"

"Why would it? It's all on them, not you." But I could hear the doubt in his voice.

"Then what's wrong?"

"I am afraid." Those three measured words sounded dredged from the bottom of his soul, limned in shadow and salt.

"Of what?"

"Having you. Losing you."

"I don't understand."

I wanted to touch him, and for the first time, I felt bold enough. Reaching over, I brushed the hair out of his face, and he turned instinctively, nestling his cheek into my palm. The heat of his skin felt incredible, as if a small star burned at his heart. I traced downward, conscious that it wasn't his true face I was touching. On the surface, he was heartbreakingly beautiful, but that wasn't the core of him. Instead, he was a bundle of fears and scars, and I was *so afraid* I could love those imperfections.

"It's two sides of the same coin. Right now, there's nothing they can take from me." He lifted his shoulders in a graceful shrug. "Even the cabin was just a place where I lived, so it didn't matter when it burned. WM&G wrote me a check today. I'll buy a condo this time."

This time implied that Dwyer & Fell had gone after him before, probably trying to mess up somebody else's timeline. That raised the question of who, why, and when. Kian had never told me about the other catalysts he worked with, before being assigned solely to me. Maybe one of them got too attached to him, so Dwyer & Fell tried to take Wedderburn's pawn. From that angle, it wasn't hard to understand his reservations.

But I tested my theory to be sure I was right. "If you let yourself care about me, you'll have something to lose."

"It might even be part of Wedderburn's plan. To get me so wrapped up in you that I'll do anything he asks, anything to keep you safe."

Anything was a big, deep hole of a word, an abyss Kian could fall into without ever hitting bottom, and I saw cognition of that in the sorrowful gaze he turned on me. His voice dropped, so low I could barely hear it over the air pushing through the vents. "I'm not far from that point now. God only knows how I'd be if you were mine."

Before I could think better of it, I opened the glove box and pulled out the tin he'd used to seal the car before. I started on my side and he quickly did the same, catching on to my desire for privacy.

I shifted in my seat, bracing for his response. "Maybe we should find out. I don't want to pretend to date you to fool the people at my school. I don't want to fake it for Wedderburn's sake, either." Freezing, I wondered if I was horrible for checking. "Wait, will this count as a favor?"

"Wedderburn might be pissed if he found out I didn't frame it that way, but *he* told me to get close to you. I can finesse this. So come on, Edie, tell me what you want already."

"You. I don't care if it's a bad idea, which . . . it probably is for lots of reasons. Things are already so screwed up and I just want to be happy for a while."

"You think you could be with me?"

"It's always good when we're together. Even when it's scary."

"Oh God. I'll probably regret this, but . . ." He trailed off and cupped his hand around the back of my neck, pulling me toward him in a kiss that put the first one to shame.

He was all tender care mingled with urgent demand. Before I knew it, I was practically in his lap. He ran his hands over my back and shoulders, like he didn't believe he had the right to touch me, but I never felt as if he were admiring his own creation, more like he couldn't get close enough, or couldn't believe I was real.

I knew the feeling.

"You're a coma dream, aren't you?" I whispered, leaning my forehead against his.

"Hope not. This is the happiest I've been in years. But I suppose that's not a strong counter to your claim."

I could've kissed him all night, but he'd picked me up because he had something important to show me. "I hate myself for saying this, but don't we need to be somewhere?"

He wore a smile I could only describe as loopy. "Right."

Kian started the car and merged with the evening traffic. The silence between us was odd, but not awful. He kept glancing over at me and smiling, as if I were a wish he'd made that unexpectedly came true. We were almost there when I realized he was heading for Wedderburn, Mawer & Graf. At this hour on a Saturday, if it was a company like any other, there would be few people in the office building. Somehow I didn't think the devil—or whatever Wedderburn was—kept normal office hours.

"Will this get you in trouble?" The last time we entered the building, he used a code to activate the elevator. With that, plus the tracker in his watch and regular surveillance, I didn't see how he could avoid getting caught.

His smile faded. "I'm not showing you anything against the rules, Edie. This is . . . I've been instructed to offer you this. As a gift."

But he seemed none too sure of my reaction, and I gnawed my lip as he led me through the creepy beige lobby to the elevator bank. Inside, a completely nondescript melody tinkled from poor speakers. Kian pulled out his phone and keyed in a different code by pressing different buttons on the elevator keypad, so many of them that I lost track. Eventually, the doors swished open and we got off. The silence was almost more ominous than the muffled screaming had been. Monochrome seemed to be the unifying theme in WM&G décor; this corridor was gray, unnervingly so, and there was only one door, as far as I could tell. A short corridor led up to it, making me think it must be a huge room, easily the width of the building.

"Before we go in, understand this. The way I changed your appearance wasn't magic, but you shouldn't dismiss the possibility that it exists."

I raised my brows at him. *So many questions, so little time.* I picked one. "But . . . you don't have access?"

"Favors that most catalysts request can generally be fulfilled through future-tech or mundane resources. If they ask for something astronomical, then I get clearance from Wedderburn and he dispenses whatever artifact I need to get the job done."

"What are we talking about here? Holy Grail?"

Kian smiled but he didn't answer. There was an impressive-looking security device attached to the heavy metal door, like the whole setup was worthy of a vault. This time, he didn't touch the pad. A beam jetted out from the doorframe and scanned his face; a holographic image appeared and then it shimmered as his eyes popped open. The floating head rotated as a computerized voice said, "Identity confirmed. Access granted."

The door clanked open.

I wouldn't have been surprised had smoke rolled out of the room, because whatever was inside had to be major. I just couldn't decide if it was kept under lock and key because it was so valuable . . . or so dangerous. Given what I knew of WM&G, it might be both. There seemed to be a shimmer of something . . . as I stepped through; my ears rang with that peculiar tinnitus I'd noticed when Russ's face didn't look like it should. I glanced over my shoulder . . . and the hallway was gone.

"You all right?" Kian asked.

"What was that?" It was an effort to get the words out. "Where are we?"

What I saw didn't bear any resemblance whatsoever to a modern building. The walls were dark stone, worn smooth with endless runnels of water. In fact, the air itself was damp and warm. A fire crackled at the center of the cave. There was no other word that fit. Smoke rose up in a lazy spiral, hinting at the presence of a hidden chimney.

"The better question is when," a drowsy voice answered.

Soon after, a woman drifted into view, clad in a white linen shift. Hair fell in a long black snarl to her knees, yet the sticks and feathers twined in those curls seemed less detritus and more regal adornment. Her skin was pale, marked in intricate whorls that might've been ink or soot. The light was too uncertain for me to tell. One thing I *was* sure of, however; like Wedderburn himself, she had inhuman eyes—no iris, no pupil, just endless gray rings, as if the smoke she breathed had turned into a creature as ephemeral.

Freaking out was beyond me. After a certain point, the shocks left me numb, and right now, an eerie calm had a hold of me. Just as well, panic would leave me unable to think.

"I am the Oracle. Let's see how well you know your history."

This wasn't my specialty, but I had the feeling this was a test. Quickly I sorted through what I knew of ancient mythology. "Ancient Greece. Delphi. Apollo? Not to be confused with the Sibyl or the Pythia."

"Apollo, yes. Some have called him that. Sun god, my ass."

"So I'm right?" I tried a tentative smile, hoping she didn't ask for dates since I had none. On the balance, I'd do better if she asked me to recite the periodic table. That, I could do. There was even a song; I'd performed it for the mandatory junior high jamboree. For some reason, it didn't make me wildly popular.

"Indeed. If you're unfamiliar with the ritual, you present the tribute and then ask me a single question."

Was the Oracle part of the gift Kian wasn't sure I would want? Why? Unless her prophecies drove you crazy or she carried the curse of not being believed—no, *that's Cassandra*. A glance at him told me nothing; he was pulling vials and phylacteries out of his jacket pockets. The Oracle settled on the floor nearby, staring into the smoke; her expression was vacant and rapt at the same time.

"I'll handle the offering," he said softly.

He mixed the liquids and powders into a paste that shimmered with radiance like sunlight shining through harlequin quartz. His hands were graceful as he painted symbols around the fire. I didn't recognize them, but the atmosphere changed. The Oracle straightened, her posture shifting from silent ennui to quivering excitement, and then she crawled around the circle, her tongue snaking out to freakish length. She lapped until all of the runes he'd drawn vanished beneath each slithering, serpentine swipe. Before my eyes, she . . . changed, her skin glowing like mother of pearl, and the smudgy lines drawn on her body sharpened as her lips warmed to a ruby hue. The tangles in her hair became like an intricate tapestry, and what I had taken for twigs and leaves now seemed to be gemstones and gold leaf. The crazy thing was, I wasn't sure when my eyes deceived me— then or now.

"It has been so long." It was both a groan of protest and an exultant cry.

I swallowed hard. Never had I been more conscious of how deep I'd fallen into a situation I didn't understand. So many questions, unsatisfactory answers, and that was when I knew exactly what to ask. If this was a gift, then I'd take full advantage.

"You understand the terms, Oracle. You've feasted. Now answer." Kian stepped back then, leaving the exchange wholly up to me.

The woman-thing turned to me in a sinuous movement. For a few seconds, it was as if she had no spine, as if she were a female torso mounted atop the swaying body of a snake. I blinked through that hallucination, and she had legs again, but the smoke stung my eyes. I was feeling a little light-headed too. Kian set a hand in the small of my back and I exhaled.

Most people would probably ask about their own future, but I needed to know more about the game and its players. Wedderburn wanted me to meet with the Oracle for some reason; therefore, with care, I should be able to turn the situation to my advantage, and nothing was more pertinent than figuring out how to navigate these fiend-infested shadows.

God, I hoped I wasn't blowing my one chance, but this query

seemed like my best bet for an answer of true substance. "Since you're not human, what *is* your nature?"

The Oracle laughed. "Clever, clever girl. So many pilgrims, and year upon year, they ask, *Will I bear a son? Will he be king? Will my true love come?* These are questions written in water, too many futures dancing in the smoke, for I can say yes and yes and yes, then you cross a bridge or do not cross, and the picture changes."

"I'm glad you're pleased."

"Let me tell you the truth, human girl." The Oracle moved around the fire, arms twining over her head, in a complicated yet artful dance. "Before things are tangible, they are ideas. I . . . am an idea someone had, long ago, bound to flesh. Their belief made me real and once real, I had agency."

"I read a theory once—that human belief is a kind of . . . energy, and if that enough people sign on, like with an urban legend, it can actually happen." I didn't say that I had been on a conspiracy site at the time, one with forums for alleged alien abductees, Bigfoot spotters, and other crackpots.

"Humans have long breathed life into nightmares and creatures of legend," the Oracle said. "Some fade. They break apart as a new god rises. Others are eternal and immutable, once unleashed." She bared her teeth in a chilling smile, sharp as shards of bone in a suddenly grotesque face. "How does it feel, knowing that, human girl? That so many of the monsters that stalk your streets are man-made?"

"Good," I bluffed. *Because anything that came from mankind can be undone by us.* At least, I hoped that was true. I had so few certainties left. "Thanks, this was enlightening."

Kian drew me away from the circle in a movement too quick to be coincidental. "We need to go. Now."

"Why?"

He pulled on my hand, yanking me toward the dark mouth of the cave. "Once the question is asked and answered, the terms of the truce are concluded, and the Oracle's free to fight for her freedom. Run, Edie!"

THE ART OF
MAKING ENEMIES

Pillar of salt. That was the only thing I knew about looking back, so I didn't. Something sliced the air behind me, snagging my hair, but Kian pulled me forward. There was a painful tug when the lock ripped free and I dove forward into the darkness. I landed on the floor outside the vault with Kian beside me. He kicked the heavy door shut and then rolled over on his back, breathing hard. Blood trickled from my scalp.

"This might seem like an odd question, but . . . can she *do* anything with my hair?"

"Like what, make a creepy doll?"

"Like . . . sympathetic magic."

"No, voodoo's not among the Oracle's abilities."

That made me feel marginally better as I pushed to my feet. "Why the crap didn't you tell me it would turn into a hunt at the end?"

"I suspected it might freak you out, so you wouldn't be thinking clearly when it came time to ask your question. That was amazing, by the way." He paused, then added, "Don't worry, I would never have let her hurt you."

I accepted that with a nod, but I had so many questions. "Why do some things dissipate and others become permanent?"

He shrugged. "If I had to guess, I'd say it depends on the amount of energy they're fed before the belief fades."

"That makes sense." It bothered me that I had no way to test and verify these hypotheses, and I hated operating under so much uncertainty. But I knew more now than I had before, and I suspected Wedderburn hadn't anticipated that I'd ask the Oracle about the supernatural world. If I had to speculate, I'd bet he suspected I'd want to know about my brilliant, valuable future. Unpredictability was a pitiful advantage, the only one I had.

"Let's get out of here," Kian said.

In the elevator, I asked, "Do you have any idea why the boss man offered me a visit to the Oracle?"

He shook his head. "Wedderburn doesn't explain his motives."

Wedderburn was an inhuman creature, dreamed up long ago, and it might be a waste of my time to try and understand his mind. "I know who he is. At least . . . I'm pretty sure."

"Wait until we're out of here."

I nodded. Kian took my hand as he led me out of the building and I kept quiet until we got in the car. "Safe now?"

"Give me a sec." With my help, he sealed it, using the last of his supply. "Go ahead."

"Father Frost, Ded Moroz, Woden. There's substantial cultural crossover in the stories. And when the beliefs of a large populace overlap, something permanent is created."

I remembered the Oracle's tone when she said, *I had agency.* While humans might've created these things, we no longer controlled their actions. From the look of things, we hadn't for a long time. Set free in our world, they were embroiled in some kind of game, with dire consequences for the mortals who got mixed up in the match.

Like Kian and me.

Wedderburn seemed to view people as chess pieces, which might reflect how the rest of the immortals saw us. I didn't know what else to call them, really. Regardless of definitions, I had to work out the rules of engagement pretty damn quick and identify the key players. Otherwise, creatures like the thin man would catch me off guard. In this scenario, lack of preparation could be dangerous.

It's a good thing I always liked doing my homework.

I thought aloud. "You texted me, warning me about the thin man. Said he had to do with the opposition. Does that mean he works for Dwyer?"

Kian started the car. "He's one of his enforcers, impossible to shake."

"Does Wedderburn have monsters like that working for him too? Why aren't they playing the game on their own terms?"

He nodded as he pulled out of the garage. "For most, it's a question of power and resources. Lesser beings don't have the juice to compete." Before I could ask anything else, he added, "That's all I know. I'm sorry."

"Why isn't the Oracle free to play the game?" I asked, changing tacks.

"She's a forfeit," Kian said. "Caught in amber."

"I don't know what that means."

"Basically, belief in her didn't last long enough to make her permanent. She was real to the ancient Greeks, but to the modern world? Not so much. Wedderburn sent one of his agents back and captured her because she's useful in the game."

"So if she left her cave, she'd . . . dissolve?"

"More or less."

"Then why does she want out so bad?"

"If your choices were oblivion or an infinity alone in prison, which would you pick?"

He made a good point. "Now I kind of feel sorry for her."

"Don't. She would've killed us both, if we hadn't run."

That was probably true of most immortals. I took comfort in his promise to protect me. "What do you call them?"

"Who?"

"Your employers, the two sides in this infernal chess match."

"I haven't had anyone to talk about them with before now."

Taken aback, I fell silent for a moment, trying to imagine that. He had no friends, no close acquaintances, even. "What happened to your liaison? Raoul? Did you get to hang out with him, at least, after your circumstances changed?" I was trying to avoid referring to him as a company drone. More important, I hoped Kian had one person inside WM&G that he could count on.

"Missing," he said tersely, navigating through traffic.

I didn't immediately recognize this part of the city, but I hadn't been paying that much attention as he drove away. "Is that even possible? Don't they monitor all of you?" I pointed at his watch.

"A year ago, he stole an artifact and disappeared." His tone told me how betrayed he felt, like he'd lost his only friend.

From that, I guessed, "Are you discouraged from bonding with other . . . liaisons?"

"They keep us on edge, so we never know who to trust. Early on, you learn that people in the organization may not be who they seem or their allegiances may not be what you thought."

"You've been burned?"

"Just once," he said softly. "I won't make that mistake again."

"Are you sure about me?"

"I know you don't work for Wedderburn."

I smiled. "There's that, at least."

"You're putting things together fast, probably faster than they expect. But catalysts are generally smart as hell or they wouldn't be on track for achieving something important."

Drawing in a sharp breath, I whispered, "You talk like you're not even human."

"I am. The tone is a side effect of learning too much about the game. But I haven't felt like I was for a long time. Even before extremis."

"Help me understand something," I began.

"If I can."

"Why do immortals want power in our world? What's the draw?"

Kian shook his head. "It's bigger than me, Edie. I can't guess what the endgame is, but it's not as simple as *winner gets to destroy the world*. After talking to you, I don't think it's about ruling, either, though that might be part of it."

"Maybe it's entertainment," I speculated.

He shot me a look that said he didn't understand.

"Say you live forever, right? You're real . . . but not truly part of the natural order, forever apart, forever . . . other. You probably feel a certain ambivalence and maybe downright enmity toward your paltry creators. You can do anything, more or less, but over the eons, you get bored. What's the ultimate challenge?"

"Pitting yourself against other immortals and using humans as chess pieces?"

"Maybe the outcome isn't the point. Maybe it's the game. It might seem reasonable by their standards, like we owe them compensation, entertainment at our expense?"

"Sounds reasonable, if by that, you mean completely insane."

I doubted it was so simple, but it was also beyond me not to try and put a puzzle together. "Did they tell you what you would've achieved if Tanya hadn't died and you'd remained on track as a catalyst?"

Kian nodded, taking the ramp onto the freeway. "I went to law school and into politics, became a senator and eventually served on the Supreme Court. Since that's not what I'd choose on my own, I guess she would've nudged me in that direction. I can picture it. She was . . . ambitious."

Before Dwyer & Fell drove her nuts, if that is, in fact, what happened. "It's so weird to hear you talk about a future that will never happen . . . in past tense."

"You get used to it." His smile was fleeting.

It occurred to me that I didn't know much about him, certainly nothing of his lost and quiet dreams. *Time to change that.* "What did you want to do, before?"

He cast me a sidelong glance. "If I tell you, promise not to laugh."

"I won't." The disclaimer made me think it was something juvenile like rock star or astronaut, fantasies that most people had little shot of realizing.

"I wanted to teach college literature and write during the summer."

Hey, a realistic dream. "You can still do that, can't you?"

"I haven't felt like writing for a long time now."

Yeah, I could take a hint from his tone. "So where are we headed?"

"Since the near-death portion of the evening is over, I thought I'd take you out." He risked a quick glance at me. "That's okay, right?"

I realized that he wasn't pretending to be awkward. Though he was a bit older than me, it didn't mean anything in terms of sophistication.

"I'd love that." For tonight, I didn't want to think about the horrors lurking around the next corner. "You said you're taking a few college classes?"

"Yeah." Kian was apparently fine talking about his current course schedule.

"I assume not pre-law."

His smile nearly broke my heart. "Nah, that ship has sailed. I have Death and Immortality; Magic, Science, and Religion; and Symbol, Myth, and Rite."

"I sense a theme."

"It's stupid but I can't help hoping I can learn something that might help."

"Help how?"

"To win my freedom," he said quietly.

Crap, that's right. While I was still a catalyst, Kian had already lost the fight and he would never be free of Wedderburn or his supernatural masters. Little wonder he couldn't bring himself to try for a normal life, especially if the immortals were prone to threatening people's loved ones. If he dated a girl outside the game, fell in love, and got married, he'd live a lie the whole time while worrying that they might be targeted in a power play. *He must feel so alone.* A chill washed over me as I remembered Vi's creepy recurring dreams. At this point, I was one panic attack away from a total breakdown.

And I can't help her from the mental ward.

This might not be date conversation, but I had to find out everything I could for Vi's sake. "Given what you've told me, it seems improbable that there's a single game going on. Dwyer & Fell—"

"It's more like . . . each immortal has a counter. And if you're right about Wedderburn's identity, his opposite would be Apollo, Baldr, Ao, Dažbog . . . There are a lot of different names for the sun god, and most cultures had some equivalent." His sheepish tone told me he'd learned this in the mythology and religion classes he was taking.

"If Wedderburn stole the Oracle from D&F, that makes sense. So there are actually a lot of games going on at once." I wasn't sure how knowing that helped me, but I had to assemble all the pieces until I had the big picture. "So is Dwyer the sun god, or Fell?"

"No idea, but it's as good a guess as any. But I didn't work it out until you figured out who Wedderburn was."

I frowned, thoughtful. "They're *not* gods. That's just how they were created, not their role now." At this point, I was out of inspiration, and none of this helped me protect Vi. "What he showed me in his office . . . he was threatening her. Can he actually—"

"He can."

"So there are no rules regarding mortals who aren't in the game?" Wedderburn had hinted as much, but I'd wanted to believe there must be some safeguards in place. The world was apparently much more brutal and lawless than I'd ever previously imagined.

"Haven't you ever wondered why things seem more screwed up by the week? So much inexplicable violence."

"My parents blame TV and video games." It was a weak joke.

"Mine did too."

"So he could kill her outright. Or he might make a mini-game of it. God, Kian, if he forces Vi to extremis, there will be no deal," I guessed in despair.

"She's a smart girl," he said. "But she's not a catalyst."

It made sense. People with important destinies, who changed the world in some way, couldn't be common. I still had a hard time believing I ranked among that number. My head swam in a bad way, as fear stole over me.

Kian caught my reaction and added, "He won't do it lightly. If he does, he loses leverage with you. Remember, he's a patient creature. Right now he still hopes that you'll burn your favors like I did, and position yourself to be of maximum use to his faction when the time comes."

"That's some comfort." I rubbed my temples, painfully aware of how powerless I was compared to the monsters arrayed against me. "It's selfish, but . . . I just can't handle any more of this tonight. Can we take a break?"

"Sure. What would you like to do?"

"I thought you had a plan when you said you were taking me out."

"There's no planetarium show tonight." He paused, as if unsure whether he should admit this. "I checked."

My heart melted a little. Maybe he was doing exactly as Wedderburn had instructed, making me fall for him, but his awkwardness seemed so genuine. Smooth talk would never work this well with me. I loved feeling like I was the first girl he cared about impressing, so much that he was bad at it. *The first apart from Tanya. Who'd died because of him.* With a frown, I shut that voice up; it would drive me crazy whispering doubts and fears.

"We could see a movie." That was what I'd told my parents. It might not be a bad idea to watch one.

"There's a theater in Cambridge that shows classic films, if you want to check it out."

"That sounds awesome."

That settled, he turned the car toward Harvard Square. It took about fifteen minutes to get there, longer to find parking. The night was clear, though light pollution prevented me from stargazing. All of the weirdness and paranoia seemed so far away as I followed Kian toward the theater. It was a tiny place, compared with the multiplexes, inside what looked like a brown brick house, but the college students wandering around told me we were in the right place. Most of them had backpacks, and there were a lot of bikes chained up outside.

There was no choice as to what to watch; we ended up with tickets for *Enter the Dragon*. I loved old flicks more than modern ones, though I had a soft spot for all sci-fi, especially cult classics like *Highlander* and *Blade Runner*. Kian got in line for popcorn while I realized I had no idea what kind of movies he liked, if he was a reader . . . I knew so little about his personality, other than our shared connection with Wedderburn and the immortal game.

This is so weird. And backward. Life and death aren't usually part of a first date.

"What's your favorite film?" I asked, as he turned to hand me a drink.

"*Casablanca*, followed closely by *Notorious*."

"You're a classic movie nerd." I grinned at him.

"Guilty. I had such a thing for Ingrid Bergman."

Inside, the theater was small and intimate, decidedly old-fashioned. I loved everything about it. During the movie, Kian wiped his hand on his thigh repeatedly until I solved his apparent inner conflict by threading my fingers through his. He pushed out a soft breath and smiled at me, like I'd solved some weighty calculus problem. This quiet moment made him feel *real* in a way that making out couldn't. It was adorable that while he might kiss me in a dark car, he was nervous about how I'd react to a public display of affection, even one so mild.

A hundred and ten minutes later, we filed out of the movie while this ineffable realization sang through my veins: *I just had an actual date with a guy who agreed it was a date.* I could've skipped up the steps into the lobby, no lie; it was childish, I realized, but I didn't care. Silently beaming, I held Kian's hand as he wove through the crowd.

According to my phone, it was nearly half past eleven. That left him enough time to get me home on time, early even. While I would've liked to stay out later, maybe go back to the diner where it all began, I had to keep my parents happy. With so much real danger for them to worry about, though they didn't know they *should* be, I couldn't afford to let them fret over me missing curfew.

"How are things at school?" he asked, as he opened my car door.

His unfailing attention to good manners instituted a whisper of doubt. *You still don't know for sure that he's Kian Riley. He loves old movies. He behaves like a courtly gentleman. Everything about him could be a lie.* Distrust hurt, forcibly piercing my happy glow like spikes of ice. *Maybe . . . he's one of* them.

Still, I tried not to show my sudden apprehension. "It doesn't feel like I expected. I hate being a bitch. And . . . one of the girls is really sick."

"Brittany?"

My blood chilled, frosty fingers tapping at the base of my skull. "How do you know?"

"You mentioned visiting her at the hospital."

Did I? I remembered talking to my dad about it, but I couldn't recall having that conversation with Kian. No, I sent a text, but—*Is he still watching me? Or is the explanation even worse?* This constant suspicion meant that I couldn't even be certain the thoughts belonged to me. What if the opposition was blighting me through some kind of gizmo like the Oracle interface Wedderburn had shown me?

I decided to be honest. "I'm pretty sure I didn't name her when I messaged you."

"It's still my job to look out for you," he said quietly.

"So after I told you I didn't need a ride, you came to the hospital? That's—"

"Creepy, I know." His hands tightened on the steering wheel. "Wedderburn sent me. The watch tracks if I follow orders, remember?"

Given what I knew of his boss, that was probably true. That doesn't mean I like it.

"Then why did you bother asking about school if you're stalking me?"

He swallowed hard, visibly hurt. "Because I wanted to hear your thoughts and feelings, Edie. I can only tell so much from surveillance." His jaw clenched. "You already know I've spent a long damn time watching you. From the outside."

I registered his anger, but I couldn't respond right away. Too many thoughts were whirling in my head, demanding to be heard. Eventually I let the issue drop by saying, "When I went to see Brittany, she looked awful, and none of her family was there. No friends, either." It wasn't full acceptance or forgiveness of him creeping around behind my back, but right then, it was the best I could do.

Kian sounded subdued. "It's one thing when you're alone and you always have been. You get used to it. But to have the awareness dropped on you—your only value is your pretty face, and if you don't have that anymore, what good are you? That's rough."

I recollected telling him how I *felt* about her, dumping it all over him that night on the shore. I'd said, *But I look at Brittany, who held the camera, and I think, What would it take to break you? Would I have to mess up her face?*

Damn. And just look at her now.

That possibility chilled me more than the semi-stalking on boss's orders. I shook my head, shivering a little. There was just no way. *Sometimes bad things happen, nothing to do with you. Allergic reaction, bacterial infection. If karma is real, then Brit's getting what she put into the universe, that's all.*

"Yeah," I agreed. "But honestly, she's not the worst. I still hate Cameron more than anyone, and this week, Russ was an absolute asshole. Like, he has no redeeming features I can see, he's just a waste of oxygen."

I wanted so bad to believe Kian had nothing to do with any of this, and Wedderburn didn't either. *He asked me if I wanted him to take revenge for me. I said no. What more can I do?* My lack of power in this situation could easily drive me crazy. *It's fine, when nothing happens to Russ and Cam, I'll know Kian is innocent.*

"You'll get them all in time."

I shivered. *He didn't mean 'get' how it sounded.*

With suspicion echoing in my head, I was quiet the rest of the way, watching the clock on his dash tick toward midnight. He parked the car at thirteen minutes 'til and then he shifted, facing me. I didn't want to make out when I was so confused; I had the crazy idea that he'd be able to taste the difference. So I leaned over, kissed his cheek and said good night, before he could ask why I was blowing him off, after I'd practically asked him to be my boyfriend earlier.

"I'll see you Monday," I said with false cheer.

After scrambling out of the car, I glanced over my shoulder. I'd been able to refrain when we were running from the Oracle but Kian offered more temptation than I could resist; the streetlamps painted him in gold and shadow, but it did nothing to mask the forlorn cast of his face. He raked a hand through his hair and then started the car. I hurried into the brownstone before he noticed I was watching. It was nuts that I could be so conflicted about him, but the merest hint of pain in his eyes and I wanted to race back and hug him so hard it hurt. The two of us were like magnets with the same charge. No matter how much I wanted to be close to him, circumstances kept shoving us apart.

Not surprisingly, my parents were still awake when I let myself in. My mom glanced up from her notebook, scrawled margin to margin full of complex calculations. "Did you have a good time?"

"Yeah. We went to see *Enter the Dragon* in Harvard Square." I'd found that volunteering information was the best way to forestall more questions.

Dad glanced up. "Oh, that's a good one. Did you know it was chosen as culturally significant and has been preserved in the National Film Registry?"

I grinned, relieved that some things never changed. Trivia was my dad's thing, usually science related—*Did you know, Edith, that there's a wasp that turns cockroaches into zombies and lays eggs in their living bodies?* No, I did not. Upon learning that, I promptly googled the jewel wasp and then spent the night shivering under my covers. Occasionally he popped up with interesting facts in other fields. Entertainment was a new one.

With a grin, I remembered how he used to run D&D campaigns for Mom and me when I was in junior high. Back then, I didn't mind as much that my primary social interaction came from my parents. I was sure it hurt them when I withdrew, but it was hard to hang with them after I started high school and realized that no matter what I did, Mildred and Alan Kramer would be my only option for weekend and evening entertainment.

My mom noticed my expression, and her eyes crinkled into an answering smile. "You seem happier this year. I'm glad."

Considering what I had to contend with, that was messed up in *so* many ways.

BEHOLD A
PALE HORSE

Monday morning, I got up at five thirty and went for a run. The sky was still dark, but I stayed off the side streets; there were other fitness buffs out, and they nodded at me as we passed, though most of them had pedometers and special music players strapped to their arms, along with more expensive shoes and spandex pants. I ran in Converse, sweats, and a hoodie, feet pounding out my confusion and dismay against the sidewalk.

I wanted to trust Kian, but my nature wouldn't let me take him on faith. Maybe I could take a field trip to Cross Point, Pennsylvania, and look for proof. If I saw his "before" picture, I could at least believe he was who he claimed. Sure, he could produce ID, but given the resources at his disposal, that wouldn't prove anything conclusively. But I couldn't keep up the back-and-forth dance, where I drew closer and then I pulled away. It wasn't fair to either of us, and if he was being straight with me, *if*, then he deserved better.

Everyone needs one true thing. I want him to be mine.

As I ran, I heard the scrape of footsteps behind me, not running shoes, more like hobnail boots, heavy and uneven. When I turned, I saw nothing but the smoky shadows cast in the final hour before sunrise, only thin fingers of light clutching at the horizon. The street was empty, but still the footsteps drew closer, and as I spun, I caught the flicker of movement in my peripheral vision. My flight reaction kicked in, so I raced toward the apartment, listening to my heart thump out a warning.

Danger. Danger.

With pure relief, I tore around the corner onto my street and within screaming range of fifty families in the identical brownstones. If something happened, if I called out, someone would hear me. Still, I didn't slow down, sprinting the last fifty feet to my front stoop. I was bathed in cold sweat when I bounded up the steps and into the foyer. The door shut behind me, meager protection from the forces arrayed against me. I skimmed the dark street one last time and just as I was about to write off the incident as my imagination, a stooped figure shuffled into view beneath a streetlight. He *looked* like an elderly man, dressed in garb more suited to the World War I era, right down to the hobnailed boots I'd heard. His mouth was sunken from loss of teeth and he had whiskers growing all over his face, not a beard, more like a human cactus. Over his left shoulder, he carried an empty burlap sack.

He stood across from my house, staring back at me with eyes like drowning, big and wet, and somehow *hungry.* Two children stepped out of the shadows behind him, flanking the old man, close enough to touch, but separate. They too, were dressed in old-fashioned clothing; the boy in knee pants and socks pulled up high, the girl in a pinafore with a dirty ribbon in her hair. And their eyes were black as pitch. The little girl-thing stepped forward.

I whirled to retreat to my apartment and nearly slammed into Mr. Lewis. He peered at me with a somber expression. "Is it you they've come for?"

For a few seconds, I couldn't speak. "Who?"

"The old ones."

"Probably." I couldn't remember ever talking to Mr. Lewis before, but it seemed like he could see the creepy things. I wasn't sure what that said about him. Surreptitiously, I glanced at his wrists, but they were unmarked.

"Do you hear the ringing?"

I gaped at him. The perspicacity of his question shocked all of mine right out of my head. "What, how did you know?"

"Means you've come into close contact with a *powerful* old one. My mum crossed paths with them, told me a story or two before she passed."

Come to think of it, the tinnitus started after I met Wedderburn. Did that mean I had some kind of detection system for immortals now? That might be useful.

Mr. Lewis went on, "Be careful, missy. I'll hang a horseshoe above the front door, but you should say your good-byes. It won't stay them long." With that dire pronouncement, he went into his apartment.

My legs were shaky as I ran up the flight of stairs, partly from the excercise and partly from the weirdness stalking me. Inside the apartment, I took a quick shower and got ready for school. My homework was done, but I had no extra credit so far this year. I imagined my teachers checking my assignments and saying, *It's like I don't even know you anymore.*

At school, people were gleeful, whispering wild rumors about Brittany. "I heard it was mono."

"No way, it's worse. She has VD or something, only she was giving somebody gross a BJ and the infection spread all over her face."

Damn. I tried to ignore them and I avoided the Teflon crew while moving from class to class across campus. It seemed like Mr. "Call me Colin" Love was always watching me, lurking in doorways and corridors with an inscrutable expression, and when I made eye contact, he offered a charming smile.

I'm not buying it. You're one of them. But he hadn't set off my tinnitus. *So maybe I'm just paranoid.*

The one notable thing that happened was I had a meeting with my guidance counselor to talk about college; she also gave me some material about the SAT. At this point, I could register late and take it for the first time in early October. If that didn't go well, there were other test dates spaced throughout the year.

"Thanks," I told her. "We'll talk after I get my scores back."

"You should also consider some extracurricular activities, Edie. Your grades are Ivy League, but the rest of your school life is rather . . ." She trailed off, trying to find a nice way to say I hadn't done anything but skulk and study.

"I'll work on it," I said, though I had no idea how.

In relief I darted out of her office and went to lunch. The others were already at the table, but nobody stopped me when I joined them. Part of me wanted to go sit with some random people and forget about the Teflon crew, but I didn't want Allison to think she'd won. Today, she was practically sitting in Cameron's lap, petting his head to "comfort" him through his sadness about Brittany.

"Did anyone go see her this weekend?" I asked, when the conversation hit a lull.

Silence. Nobody met my eyes and they shook their heads,

mumbling excuses. I ate my lunch and pretended to listen to Russ while the others changed the subject.

The Teflon crew wasn't the same as last year; Brittany in the hospital had created a power vacuum and Allison was scrambling to fill her shoes. With their attention focused inward, they spent less time harassing random outcasts.

"I'm going to see her tonight," I said, just before the bell. "Anyone want to come?"

Another long pause. Then Jen spoke. "I'll go. Is it . . . I mean, how—"

"Bad. But she stays inside her bed curtains most of the time."

"Okay. Should I bring something?"

I thought for a minute. "We can stop and get some magazines on the way up, something with quizzes, celebrity gossip, and bad advice."

Jen gave a relieved smile. "That sounds good. I'm really bad at cheering people up, but I can read."

"Doubtful," Allison sniped.

The other girl leveled a cold look on her. "Who's flunking basic English here?"

"There's only one way to settle this," Russ said. "Vat of pudding, after school."

"I'm out." I pushed to my feet.

"Me too." Jen surprised me by following.

Allison glowered at us while Davina looked intimidated. Last week, Allison and Brittany kept her busy running errands, but with Brittany gone, she was sitting with the Teflon crew, though she didn't seem sure of her place in the social hierarchy. She glanced at Allison, then at the guys, while she chewed her lip.

"Can I go too?" she asked.

"Sure." It wasn't like I owned the hospital or set visiting rules. "Let's meet up at the front doors after school."

"Sounds good," Jen said and Davina nodded.

Allison lifted one shoulder in a bored shrug. "Give Brit my best." Her expression said, *I'll always rule this school, even if you suck up to my former bestie, who used to share the crown with me.*

The day just got weirder from there—with Davina on one side and Jen on the other as I went to class, students scrambled out of our way, like we were new queen bees or something. Davina smirked at me, but it was a conspiratorial look, not a snotty one.

A freshman girl said to her, timidly, "I love your hair."

"Thanks." She tossed the long curls, smiling with genuine pleasure.

Davina had brown skin, pretty features, and great hair. If looks alone were enough to secure entry to the inner circle, she'd have been sworn in years ago. In her shoes, I'd have given up on cheerleading and made friends who weren't such superficial tools. Her motives in courting their approval stumped me.

As I got my books, I fought the urge to bang my head against my locker, but somehow I made it through the day without hitting anyone or getting screamed at by my teachers. When I left Blackbriar, I found Davina and Jen already waiting. I didn't break stride, just beckoned as I went by. Kian would be surprised to find out he'd be driving the three of us to the hospital, but I hoped he'd roll with it.

"You brought presents," Kian said as we walked up.

That was a pretty charming thing to say. Funny, he claimed he had no experience whatsoever, but he could come up with lines like that on the fly? This *is why I don't trust you.* Jen and Davina both beamed, and I stifled a sigh at introducing everyone. Then I smiled at him, trying to decide if he was upset over how things ended on Saturday night. He leaned in and kissed my cheek, which told me the answer was yes.

"I hope you like them," I answered.

"I take it I'm chauffeuring today?"

"If you don't mind. We're visiting Brittany."

"Not a problem." He opened the door and gestured for the other two to get in back.

In the car, I let Davina and Jen carry the conversation, asking Kian questions about his job and what he was studying at the university. *Can't stop gossiping, huh, Allison?* That was the only way they could've known he was in college. He responded politely, with just enough warmth to come across as friendly.

"I'll drop you off out front and then park." He hesitated. "Since I don't know her, it would probably be better for me to wait in the lobby."

Jen nodded. "I guarantee Brit wouldn't thank us for bringing a hot guy to see her when she's . . . not at her best."

"Definitely," Davina agreed.

Wanting to make up for the other night, I leaned over, but Kian gave me his cheek. *Got it. No lip kisses until we talk.* A heavy feeling settled in my stomach as I slid out of the car and pulled the seat forward so the other two could do the same.

"Where did you meet him?" Davina watched him drive off with an expression that suggested Kian was money covered in chocolate.

Grinning, I told the truth. "On a bridge."

Jen sighed and headed for the front doors. "Fine, don't tell us."

This time, I bought magazines in the gift shop instead of a stuffed toy. And like Friday, when I got to Brittany's room, she had no visitors. The shades were drawn along with the bed curtains, and the smell . . . was indescribable. Davina actually took a step back, her nose wrinkling in horror, but Jen clamped a hand on her shoulder and shoved her forward. Her determination to be a good friend boosted her up to a decent human being in my mind.

"Who is it?" Brittany sounded hoarse, as if she had been crying.

"Me, Jen, and Davina. We thought we'd read *Cosmo* and have some girl talk." These were the last words I could've ever imagined saying. Until today, I'd never picked up a single woman's magazine.

"That's nice of you. Is . . . my mom around?"

Damn.

"I didn't see her," Jen said softly.

"You guys don't have to stay," Brittany mumbled, sounding reluctant.

"It's okay," Jen said.

"Let's settle in." Davina was calmer, breathing through her mouth. I could only think, *If it's bad for us, imagine how Brittany feels.*

For an hour or so, we took quizzes like "How to Tell if He's the One" and Jen read aloud an article called "Rocking His World in 5 Easy Steps." It was so bad, it was funny, and to my surprise, I wasn't the only one laughing. Before, I'd always imagined that beautiful girls pored over this stuff seriously, as if it were some kind of bible, but that didn't seem to be the case with these three. Even Brittany was giggling in tiny choking gusts. She might be having trouble breathing, but I was afraid to upset her by peeking around the curtain.

Brittany whispered, "Thanks for coming, you guys. It means a lot to me."

Davina was making a joke when Brittany wheezed and then there was a wet sound, a splatter, and I leapt to my feet. No time to think about whether she'd want me to—I yanked open the curtain and even in the gloom, I saw so much blood, blood everywhere, staining her gown, her sheets, pouring from her mouth in a river of red. Jen came to my shoulder and screamed while Davina fumbled for the call button.

I wheeled and ran to the door, banged it open and yelled, "Nurse! Doctor! Somebody, we need help in here. Oh my God, hurry!"

The machines attached to Brittany were going crazy, and pretty soon, there was a team with a crash cart shoving us out the door. Jen was shaking and Davina was so pale she looked green under the fluorescents. My skin felt like it was too small; I couldn't sit still, so I paced while they worked.

Eventually, a nurse shooed us down to a waiting area. "You can't loiter here, you'll bother the other patients."

"I had no idea she was so sick," Davina kept saying.

Jen was silent, a look of horror locked in her eyes. What was left of Brittany's face . . . dear God. I'd seen pictures on the Internet that horrible, but . . . *no more, I can't.* With shaking fingers, I texted Kian some directions, along with, Come up. Please. I need you.

Five minutes later, he found me. He dropped into the chair next to me and wrapped his arm about my shoulders in a move so natural, *I* could believe we'd dated all summer. I could get lost in his lies every bit as easily as in his eyes. And that scared the shit out of me.

"What happened?"

"Brit's really bad. She started hemorrhaging right in front of us," Jen answered.

Without thinking, I reached for Jen. She held on like she was full of helium and in danger of floating away into an empty sky. On her other side, Davina looked like she needed comfort too, so Jen put her hand out. We sat like that, not talking, just holding hands, while hospital staff came and went. Nobody would tell us *anything*.

Around half past five, Mrs. King stumbled into the lounge. Her eyes were nearly swollen shut, and I could tell she hadn't been sleeping. I had seen her from a distance at school functions, but the coiffed society matron bore little resemblance to the distraught, disheveled mess who collapsed in the chair next to Davina. Mrs. King scrubbed trembling fingers through her tangled hair and repressed a sob.

"I went home to shower," she whispered. "And to try calling her dad again. He's in Singapore this week."

Davina reached out and took the older woman's hand, looking like she had no idea what to say. None of us did. Finally Kian murmured, "Are they treating her?"

Mrs. King nodded. "They wouldn't let me stay. The nurse called and I got back as fast as I could. It was rush hour."

She started crying then and Davina patted her on the back. The only sound in the waiting area came from Mrs. King's soft, choking sobs and my own breathing. *Kian didn't do this. He'd have to be an utter monster to sit here with Brittany's mom if he had anything to do with her condition.* Still, a knot formed in my stomach until I wanted to scream.

Belatedly, I texted my parents. It was a school night, yeah, but if they thought schoolwork was more important than somebody's life, then their priorities were seriously screwed up. At six thirty, I went down to get coffee and sandwiches, mostly because it was something to do. Passing out food and drinks and pretending to eat carried us past seven. I wasn't sure when she started, but Mrs. King prayed, though I wouldn't have taken her for a religious woman. Prior encounters had made me think she was cold and controlling, but maybe she was one of those mothers who pushed because their standards were set high, not from lack of love.

Around eight, I was sitting on the floor, propped up against Kian's knees, when the doctor—at least I *think* he was a doctor—came into the lounge, along with the nurse who had gossiped with me the first time I visited. They both wore such grave expressions that I was worried. Tension tightened my shoulders until my skin felt wrapped in razor wire.

Then the doctor said, "Mrs. King, let's talk privately."

Jen squeezed my hand hard as Brittany's mom left. She followed the trio with her gaze, then took a deep, shivery breath. "What should we do?"

I had no idea.

Davina said, "Let's wait until she comes back. Maybe Brittany's stable now or they need her to sign a form for more tests or something."

Twenty minutes later, Mrs. King stepped into the waiting room, looking absolutely ravaged. "Thank you three so much for coming and for . . . being with Brit. If you hadn't been here . . ." Her voice broke, so she tried again. "It's . . . over. You can go home now."

"She's . . . gone?" Jen choked out.

Before Mrs. King could respond, the hospital staff pulled her away again. Numb, I eased to my feet. Kian herded us to the car and offered to drive the other two girls home, even though they lived in different parts of the city. It was late enough that traffic wasn't horrendous. I got out when we dropped Jen off and hugged her. She held on for a long time. When we got to Davina's house, I did the same. Her mom was standing in the doorway in a golden wash of light, and Davina ran to her outstretched arms like I could never do. My mom wouldn't think to open them.

"Is this because of me?" I asked as he put the car in drive.

Kian should've answered right away with a firm denial. He didn't. "I don't know."

"Did I *do* this somehow?" A shriek bubbled in the back of my throat as I saw that crimson splatter over and over, out from the raw hole that was Brit's mouth, cheeks eaten away, so much pain, so much. Her eyes were wild with it and swimming in fear.

"Of course not. You'd never hurt anyone, Edie."

You wanted them all to suffer, a little voice whispered in my ear. *So it begins.*

Whipping my head around wildly, I caught a glimpse of red eyes in the side mirror. On a smothered cry, I checked the backseat but there was nobody. *Just a reflection of some taillights. Monsters don't live in reflections.*

Or maybe they do.

It was too much. I fought the tears for a full minute according to the clock on the dash, but in the end, I lost. Kian eyed me but he didn't pull over until we got close to the brownstone. Then he parked up the street from my apartment and reached for me.

"I don't know what the hell's going on, but I'll look into it. I'll keep you safe."

His hands roved my back, gentle and soothing, and I cried for the life Brittany had lost, the one he'd signed away, and the future that might not even be mine anymore. My eyes felt sore and swollen when I finally calmed down. I couldn't remember losing it like that in front of *anyone*, ever, and that made it impossible to look at him.

"This sucks," I muttered.

"Remember what I said? I meant it. I'll never let you down when you need me."

"Why? I was kind of an asshole to you the other night."

"We'll talk about that later. Right now, I'm walking you upstairs. Under the circumstances, I'm sure I can convince your parents to let me stay a while."

"But it's a school night."

"Trust me," he said.

If only I could.

I should've told him that night about the bag man and the spooky children. But I didn't; I forgot about them in the deluge of other problems.

That was a mistake.

A GRIEF LIKE FEAR

Tuesday, word had already spread. The minute I stepped into school, other students surrounded me, some of them sporting black armbands. Farther down the hall, Davina and Jen were mobbed. Jen looked horrified while Davina couldn't seem to decide if the attention was good or bad. An onslaught of questions bombarded me.

"I heard you were there when she died."

"Was there a lot of blood?"

"Someone told me Brit was possessed or something, and—"

"What is *wrong* with you?" I demanded.

Before I could bitch at the vultures, an announcement came over the PA system. "Morning classes will be canceled. Instead there will be an assembly in the auditorium and then grief counselors will be available to those who need them. If you were close to Brittany King and need a mental health day, you will be free to contact your parents."

At lunch I sat by myself for the first time this year; the rest of the Teflon crew had gone home. At least, I thought that was the case, until Cameron plopped down across from me. His tray had beef and noodles on it but he showed no sign that he meant to eat anything; instead he dropped his head in his hands. He looked like shit. The circles beneath his eyes were so dark, it looked like he'd been punched in both eyes, and there were scrapes and bruises on his knuckles. I didn't ask if he'd been fighting or hitting inanimate objects. For all his assholery the week before, it was clear he was taking Brittany's death hard.

I raised a brow. "What're you still doing here?"

When he raised his head to meet my gaze, his eyes were red and bloodshot. "My parents are in Europe. There's nobody to sign me out."

"Ah." I couldn't bring myself to be more sympathetic, so I picked at my lunch. When I'd pictured Cameron getting what he deserved, I never imagined anything like this.

"They're gone, like, *all* the time. The housekeeper works five days, but I'm pretty much on my own, nights and weekends."

I didn't want to talk to him when he was acting like a decent person. Before, he was just a one-note jerkwad who seemed to get off on making my life a living hell.

"At least you have a lot of freedom." That was a stupid thing to say.

"And I spent most of that time over at Brit's. She has an actual family, you know? Her mom is kind of crazy and her dad's a dick, but they'll miss her. It should've been me."

For a few seconds, I stared, unable to believe such a thing had come out of Cameron's mouth. "Don't say that."

"I thought she'd get better, so I didn't go see her. She died thinking I didn't care." He bit out a curse.

"You loved her?" Kind of astonishing, I'd suspected those two were together because they were both hot and nobody else at Black-briar met their exacting standards.

"Yeah," he said in a dull voice.

Against my better judgment, I spoke some consoling words and counted the minutes until the bell rang. I wasn't subtle when I hurried away from Cameron, but for the first time, it wasn't because his presence made me sick with shame. Pity swelled inside me instead but I didn't think he'd want it.

In my afternoon classes, the teachers crafted impromptu lessons about death and loss; the lectures were more like group therapy. And in my last class, an actual grief specialist came in, introducing himself as Greg Jessup. He had apparently been making the rounds. The counselor had us move our desks into a circle, and he asked us lots of questions about our feelings. At first, people were reluctant to speak, and then it got deep. Since there were so few of us still in school, I guessed it made it easier to be brave.

"It makes you think," a guy named Stuart said. "I mean, I wasn't friends with Brittany or anything, but it's sad. She was so young."

Another dude nodded. "Yeah, man. It could happen to anyone."

Could it?

My heart pounded nearly up into my throat while fear and horror battled inside me. As if he could sense it, Greg turned toward me. "Do you want to share with the group?"

"Not right now, thanks."

Like everyone else, I admitted to being sad, but I didn't say how scared I was or how much nascent guilt was churning in my gut. That period seemed endless. Consequently, I was glad as hell to get out of Blackbriar at quarter to three. The few students left trickled out of the front gate, and I was among the stragglers. Kian had been amazing the night before, though things were a mess between us. I felt bad about letting him stick around while I cried on his shoulder as my parents hovered, made tea, and said ridiculous things that were supposed to cheer me up.

I was used to looking for him as I came out of school, and it was an incredible relief to find him waiting. His reaction when he spotted me was a beautiful combination of pleasure and yearning, quickly dimmed to a more neutral expression, as if he didn't want me to know how happy he was. Yet he still crossed to me and enfolded me in his arms, not a perfunctory hug but a real one, and I held on tight, heedless of people trickling by.

"Bad day?"

"You could say that." And it was about to get worse.

I can't do this to him anymore. In my head, there was a messy jumble of wariness, longing, and suspicion. It wasn't fair to Kian and I couldn't handle additional weight on my conscience. Already, my body felt like it was made of glass; the next blow would break me.

In a rush, I blurted my doubts in a single breath. There was no way I could meet his eyes after that. I expected him to stiffen up and shove me away, but he waited until I finished. Then he lifted my chin gently.

"I get it," he said. "You have no way to be sure of me."

"Of whether you're really Kian Riley, one of Wedderburn's monsters in disguise, or if you're really loyal—"

He kissed me, quick as a blink. *To Wedderburn.* Too late, I understood why he couldn't let me say that out loud.

"Does that answer your question?"

I pretended his kiss had assuaged most of my doubts, beaming up at him.

He went on, "If you want to meet my aunt and uncle, we can do that this weekend. They still live in Pennsylvania, near Scranton. It'd be a long day trip, but doable. And I do have some things that will prove I'm Kian Riley, if that will help."

"Like what?" Maybe this couldn't assure me that he wasn't manipulating me for his boss, but it would help to know he wasn't some immortal creature in handsome human skin.

Definitely a step in the right direction.

"Old yearbooks, for one."

"They survived the fire at your place?"

"I have a bunch of stuff from my old life in storage. I'm not sure if you noticed, but the cabin wasn't very—"

"Lived in?"

"Exactly." He continued, "I can't prove everything to your satisfaction. Some things you have to take on faith. But . . . *be* with me, Edie, or cut me loose. I can't take not knowing how you'll treat me from day to day, especially when I'm so far out on the ledge."

"That's fair," I said softly. "Then can we swing by your storage unit? You know everything about me and I only get glimpses of the real you."

"We'll go now, if you have time."

"Thanks."

I stretched up on my tiptoes and he met me halfway, kissing me with a heat and tenderness that stole my breath along with another chunk of my heart. Maybe it didn't matter how smart I tried to be, how cautious; in the end, I couldn't resist him. I wanted so bad for Kian to be the real deal; I didn't know if it was the fact that he'd saved my life or changed it, and then there was that kiss . . . *I'm afraid I'm falling in love with you.* Though I didn't say it aloud, something must've shown in my face because his gaze softened and he smoothed a hand through my hair.

Nothing but shivers.

"Come on, it looks like rain."

He drove to a storage place on Massachusetts Avenue, built of pale corrugated metal and accented in red. His stuff was upstairs in a long corridor outfitted with identical units. Kian unlocked one halfway down the hall and raised the blue door. Though it was small, no more than five by five, it was only half full. A sure stride carried him toward a box set apart from the others and he sat down, cross-legged, and opened it up.

Unaccountably nervous, I sat down beside him. "What's this?"

"My school stuff." He pulled out four yearbooks first and then a sheaf of certificates, a couple of small, dented trophies.

I picked one up and read ACADEMIC BOWL CHAMPION. The other was for BEST ACTOR. "Interesting. I didn't know you were into drama." It was troubling to learn that he'd won an award in an area that proved he had the skills to play me. *Stop that. You're here to find reasons to trust him, not doubt more.*

Kian touched the gold statuette, wearing a melancholy expression. "It wasn't my first choice, but I needed to pad my college application; I can't sing, and I hate team sports. At the time, I didn't realize how little control over my future I had left. Wedderburn waited until I graduated to spring the news."

I imagined Kian applying to college, not realizing he'd lost his status as a catalyst and how he must've felt when he found out. "Is that standard?"

He nodded. "They have no use for underage agents; too many questions from mortal authorities and irate families."

"That makes sense." *So I won't know if I go off track and fail my purpose until I graduate.* "And from their perspective, a year or so doesn't seem like long to wait."

"Pretty much."

Putting aside the trophies, I examined the dates on all the year-books and picked up the earliest one. "Freshman year?"

He winced slightly and put his hand on the cover. "Edie—"

"I don't care, okay? I want to see who you were."

With a sigh, he pulled back and let me open the book. I flipped through the ninth graders, poring over awkward faces dotted with zits, braces still on, glasses not yet exchanged for contacts. Now and then I spotted the future beautiful people, not because they were already perfect, but they had fewer physical faults to overcome. It made my life easier that the class pictures were alphabetized, so I flipped to the Rs.

There you are.

The other Kian wasn't heavy, as I half expected. Instead, he was thin to the point of gauntness with thick Coke-bottle lenses and ter-rible skin. The buzz cut didn't help; neither did the weirdly patterned button-up shirt with the over-large collar. Looking at this picture, I'd never guess he came from money. He was dressed like he'd bought his clothing at a thrift store. But what really got to me was the dead, hopeless expression in his eyes.

I am alone, that look said. *And it will never get better.*

A year after this picture was taken, he tried to kill himself.

He shifted, staring up at the ceiling. "It's bad, I know."

"You're still you," I said. "And . . . I'd have dated you when you looked like that. If you'd asked me."

A shiver went through him, relief or pleasure, or I didn't know

211

what. He put an arm around me and leaned his head against mine. "I would have, if I'd had the nerve. Remember at the diner? Before I optimized you, I said you have pretty eyes and a nice smile. But more important, you're smart and brave and—God, stop me, before I say something ridiculous."

I laughed softly. He was a person to me now, one with a sad past and a dark history, but he was real. He wasn't a monster; he couldn't be. Not with such awkward, painful signatures in his yearbook that said he had been almost as friendless as me. Most of them read, "To a smart guy" or even more damning, "Have a great summer." I also noticed he had more comments from teachers than people his own age.

Another thing we have in common.

"You went for the ideal version of yourself, huh?"

He nodded. "It was Raoul's suggestion . . . and why I offered it to you."

"I'm glad."

Nestled against his side, I worked through the rest of his box, unearthing certificates for academics and a bad poetry journal. That, Kian yanked away from me with red tinting his cheeks. He wore a hunted look.

"Please don't open that."

"You write poetry?"

"Nothing worth keeping. And not for a long time."

"Read me something," I demanded.

I'd never been close enough to anyone to feel comfortable being so bossy. With Kian, it seemed . . . safe. He paged through the notebook and mumbled, "I dream of sunlit streams / And moonless tides. / Of infinity / Among dark rocks. / I dream of quiet souls / And divinity / That breaks like a wave / Over me. / And instead of drowning, / You pull me in; / I swim."

I was good at identifying themes and explaining them to teachers, but I had never listened to a poem and *felt* anything before. That didn't mean Kian's work had literary merit, and . . . maybe it was because I knew what his life was like when he wrote it, but I understood the words from the inside out.

"You were so sad," I said softly. "Wondering if there's a god, looking for someone to stop you."

He drew in a sharp breath. "You see too much."

"I want to see everything."

This is happening. This is real.

I came up on my knees and hugged him; sometimes it felt like we were two halves of the same soul, and that was so stupid it made me feel like I lost IQ points just for thinking it. His arms tightened around me and he buried his face in my hair. For a few seconds, I imagined what this would've been like with him thin and me fat, if it would've felt better, worse, or just . . . different. Sometimes I felt like an impostor in my own body.

"When Wedderburn told me to get close to you, I was, like, *shit*. Because anything *he* wants isn't good for the people involved."

"There has to be a way that this doesn't end badly," I said. "We'll find it. You said I have to be with you or cut you loose. I'm ready, I'm not scared anymore."

He exhaled against my hair. "I'm glad. Because it kills me when you look at me like I'm one of the monsters."

His hands trembled on my back and he tucked his face against my neck. His breath was hot and damp, misting on my skin. Any other moment, that would've been exciting, but he was shaking, his breath coming in quiet gasps. I touched his hair, alarmed.

"Kian?"

"I'm so sorry. You have *no* idea how awful I feel. I close my eyes and I see what they did to you, and I should've stopped it. That moment haunts me. I wish I'd kicked Cameron's ass. I don't even care that it means I'd be gone, as long as you'd be all right. But—"

"If they hadn't forced me to extremis then, they'd have done something worse, and you'd have died for nothing. Bottom line, I burn my favors, like Wedderburn wants, because my liaison doesn't care. I end up dancing like a puppet on his string. You're the reason I'm even remotely in the game. So stop torturing yourself."

"I don't think I can. That's all I want, you know. For you to be okay." His voice was low and hoarse, ragged as if he'd spent a whole night screaming. The intensity he radiated was thrilling but also scary.

"You have to care about other things. Yourself, your life, your freedom."

"Sure, Edie." He said it too readily; I didn't believe him.

For long moments, I just held him, hoping I could hug the hurt out. Comforting him made me feel stronger, though, like I could let go of my shame and pain to make Kian feel better. Eventually I sat back enough to kiss him. His lips tasted faintly of salt.

"That's enough personal history for the day. Want to take me home?" Belatedly I realized how that sounded, and heat washed over my cheeks.

Oh God, why?

"More than you know."

"That was quite a line," I managed to say.

His green eyes settled on my face, shining with such fervor that I might've burned from it. "It's only a line if I don't mean it."

I had no answer for that. Silently, my cheeks still on fire, I helped him restore order to the storage unit and we went down to the car. "Why wasn't all your stuff at the house?"

"Partly because I wanted a new start and Raoul warned me not to keep precious things too close." That sounded ominous.

"Because you could be targeted by Dwyer & Fell?" I remembered him saying they'd gone after him before, and they just burned his house down. Damage like that could destroy all happy mementos of his former life.

"Yep."

"Great, now I have something else to worry about. I don't know if our insurance will cover ulcers at seventeen."

He smiled, as I'd intended him to. The car started with a purr and he pulled smoothly into traffic. On the ride home, Kian told me a little more about his aunt and uncle, concluding, "I'll call them and see if we can come for lunch on Sunday."

"Lunch?"

"Dinner would get you home too late. It's almost five hours, depending on traffic."

"No, it's okay. I mean, unless you just want me to meet them. It's a long way to drive to reassure me . . . and I already believe in you."

His throat worked visibly. "It's been a long time since anyone said that to me."

"I'll say it again if you want, slower this time." I tried on a flirty smile, and to my relief, I didn't feel like an idiot.

He grinned at me, thanking me with his eyes for not making a thing about the fact that he wore his heart close to the skin. "Let's not pack too much excitement into a single day."

My mom and dad were waiting when I got home. They were weird and solicitous, as if Brittany and I had been friends for years. My dad made my favorite soup—homemade chicken noodle—and my mom produced a carton of ice cream. Tonight, however, I limited myself to a single scoop instead of filling a huge bowl. Both my parents were weedy academics, not prone to overindulgence in anything, except esoteric ideas. As we ate, I brought up my college application, and as expected, that occupied them until I could escape.

"Thanks for dinner. It was really good."

They exchanged one of their looks, then my mother spoke. "Will you be all right tonight? I've been asked to do a guest lecture, and there's a cocktail party afterward—"

"I'm fine," I assured them. "I'll do my homework and maybe Skype with Vi."

"Who's that again?" My dad was frowning.

"I met her at the SSP. She lives in Ohio."

"Oh, right." His brow cleared. Any kid who could get into the science program was apparently good enough for me to chat with online.

"If you're sure," my mom said, pushing away from the table.

After that, she got ready in a hurry while my dad and I washed the dishes. Twenty minutes later, she came out in her standard black dress, having dotted her cheeks with blush and put on red lipstick that didn't suit her. Last year, I wouldn't have known that.

"Have fun." I shut the door behind them and turned the deadbolt.

Though I'd been alone countless times before, this felt different, somehow. Strange noises rumbled in the apartment, nothing I could identify, and I couldn't settle on my assignments. I roamed from room to room, checking in closets and looking under the beds. Soon I'd be rummaging through cupboards and making myself a tinfoil hat. Brittany's specter haunted me, whispering accusations that sent shivers down my spine.

"It's your imagination," I said out loud.

My voice was supposed to reassure me, but the strange tinnitus was back, ringing so loud that I thought it was the phone for a few seconds. Then I realized it was, but it sounded like it was inside my skull. I ran to answer it, and when I picked up, there was only a single high-pitched note. I slammed the phone down and unplugged it.

Then it rang again.

Fear pounded a tattoo in my ears as something heavy hit the front door, hard enough to shake it on the hinges. My thoughts went frantic and disjointed. *Shelter. No windows. Cell phone. Call for help.* I sprinted down the hall to the bathroom, slammed the door behind me, then I leaned against it with all my weight, listening to the pounding. My hands trembled as I dialed the 9, then the 1. As if whatever it was sensed trouble, the noise stopped.

I listened for a full minute. Nothing. Silence.

Exhaling, I turned, started at a glimpse of myself in the mirror, then smiled in relief. My reflection did not smile back.

THE EYE OF A
LITTLE GOD

can't get help from *911* for this.

Cold suffused the room in a silent swirl, until my breath wafted like fog between me and not-me. Every instinct said I was in mortal danger, but I was afraid something worse lurked outside. Just because the thing had stopped banging, it didn't mean it wasn't there.

I backed up a few steps, until I stood near the door, but my mirror image never moved. "What do you want?" I asked.

"Your life." The voice was warped and strange, a drowning mouth full of water.

I didn't know if she meant she wanted me dead or to swap places, trapping me on the other side. No matter how you viewed it, I lost. As I tried to control my heartbeat, she lifted slender fingers to trace a pattern on the wrong side of the glass, and the surface rippled, stirred, as if she might conceivably crawl through. That was enough for me. I banged open the bathroom door, slammed it shut behind me, and bolted.

Wait, what's the smart move? Danger outside. Danger inside. Can't call 911.

If the thing could break the door, wouldn't it have already done that? My life depended on working out the answers, and nothing had prepared me to solve this particular equation. While they couldn't kill me, they *could* hurt me, or drive me to do something stupid in sheer terror. I took one breath, another, forcing myself to be logical when impulse suggested I should run and scream.

There are rules in play. What are they?

That was part of the problem. I didn't know the regulations, how to avoid breaking them, or how to report a violation. But then, I wasn't really a player, more of a pawn. In chess, the pieces couldn't wave from the board and bitch over how they were handled. Actually, that analogy gave me some insight as to my position.

I'm not even a person. I'm a . . . what did Wedderburn call me? An asset.

Okay, so . . . what do I know? Thinking it through kept me from panicking. In a lot of lore, monsters had to be invited or permitted to cross your threshold. Therefore, reason dictated that I was safer at home than I would be running around after dark. Plus, there were human maniacs to contend with as well.

Briefly, I considered calling Kian; he'd stay with me until my parents got home. In the end, I decided not to. I preferred not to get dependent on him. My chest ached as I went to my room. As I settled down, I listened for any sign that the creature outside the apartment had come back, but everything sounded still and quiet. There were no noises from the bathroom either. If the mirror-girl had been able to get out, she'd be here by now.

Yet I wasn't fully at ease; my nerves jangled like an alarm clock. Before starting on my homework, I googled mirror ghosts and then covered the one in my room with a sheet, just in case they *were* portals. I read something about witches trapping spirits in mirrors and how ghosts needed a connection with someone living to pass through. *So she can get out only if I'm too scared to run? Good to know.* Apparently in Serbia, Croatia, and sometimes Bulgaria, they buried the dead with a looking glass, so their spirits couldn't roam around and haunt the living. I didn't like the ramifications of what could happen, though, if some maniacal grave robber dug up corpses all over Eastern Europe and smashed those mirrors.

Don't you have enough to worry about already?

The apartment was quiet now. Apparently staying calm and toughing it out had been the right choice. In junior high, I used to play a lot of video games and sometimes there were puzzles, where one wrong step meant insta-death. That was how I felt right then. It took all my concentration to work through my assignments, solve equations, and answer questions, when school seemed like the least of my worries.

It was almost nine by the time I finished, and as I was about to close my laptop, I was surprised to get an IM from Ryu. A quick what-time-is-it-in-Japan search told me he was probably in school, maybe messing around during IT. It was hard to send Skype messages in other classes since teachers usually made students shut off their phones. I answered right away, as we hadn't talked live since I got back, and his e-mails were sporadic.

Me: hey, what's up?
Ryu: nothing, just have a free period and I'm in the computer lab
Me: cool, how are you?
Ryu: not bad, school is tough this year

My fingertips hovered over the keyboard. So many things I could say, but eventually, I replied with, *on my end too, and not just academics. A girl from school died yesterday. I was visiting her at the hospital when it happened.*

Ryu: damn. Are you okay?
Me: it was pretty rough, but I'm hanging in

I could tell from the pause that he didn't know what to say. We weren't as close as Vi and I had become over five weeks of rooming together. So I changed the subject.

Me: was wondering if you could help me out
Ryu: not sure what I can do from here, but absolutely
Me: I have a friend with a tattoo and she won't tell me what it means. It looks kinda like a Japanese kanji, though
Ryu: send pic if you have one

I took a snap of my wrist with my phone, then e-mailed it to him.

Ryu: that's weird
Me: what is?
Ryu: it looks like a kanji but it isn't. I've never seen this symbol before
Me: huh. Well, thanks anyway
Ryu: if you want, I can do some checking, see if anyone has seen that
Me: it's not that big a deal

I regretted that impulse; this might be dangerous. Given how Wedderburn was threatening Vi, I should've known better. I cursed silently and blamed the scary version of me in the mirror. *The fight-or-flight hormones numbed my brain, I guess.* To cover my worry, I asked Ryu if there were any likely girls this year, and that kept him pinging me for a good ten minutes; as it happened, the answer was yes. I hoped he hooked up with someone cool. I was glad we'd shifted smoothly from summer fling to Internet bros. We chatted a bit more before his free period ended, and I got ready for bed.

My parents came home an hour later; I heard them unlock the door, along with the low murmur of their voices as they tried not to wake me. The normalcy of it all seemed suddenly precious, compared to the rest of my life. They had no idea there were monsters in mirrors or thin men who smelled like graves. More to the point, they had no clue I might be responsible for a girl's death. Tears burned like acid in my throat.

My folks believed in cause and effect, rational science, and they would be horrified if they discovered how chaotic creation was and how much damage mankind had done. Then again, my mother was a cynic, so maybe she wouldn't be surprised. For a few seconds, I stared at the ceiling, wishing I could tell them, show the marks, and share the whole story. But the line had been drawn between them and me; I could never again stand beside the blissfully ignorant. My eyes were open, and I couldn't unsee the shadows on the wall.

In the morning, I skipped my run, remembering the hobnail boots. *I'll go after school.* At Blackbriar, more people had on the mourning armbands and someone had posted pictures of Brittany all over her locker, sort of like a shrine. Cameron wasn't around; neither was

Allison, but Jen and Davina both waved at me. As I got my books, the headmaster made an announcement about the funeral, including time and place for services, and then he segued into the usual crap about fund-raisers and respect for school policy, which seemed irreverent. *Yeah, yeah, dead girl, but what about the chocolate sale?*

"Have you seen Russ?" Davina fell into step with me on my way to class.

"Not for a while."

"People are pretty upset," Jen said.

I nodded, trying to figure out why these two were hanging around with me. Granted, Allison and Brittany hadn't offered many spots in the Teflon crew to the competition, so the guys outnumbered the girls. So maybe it was that they didn't have anyone else?

"I still am," Davina whispered. "God, it was just so . . ."

Awkwardly I patted her on the arm. In another minute, I'd be saying "there, there" and offering her a hot beverage. God, I sucked at social interaction with everyone but Kian. Sometimes it felt like he and I were two of the same species, stranded among aliens.

Jen said, "I'm glad she wasn't alone, though. I think . . . it was kind of nice, wasn't it? Right up until the end."

"Would it be weird if we hung out?" Davina asked. "The three of us. I don't want that to be the last thing we do together. That probably sounds strange and superstitious."

Jen looked as if she was relieved Davina had suggested it. "If you want, you guys can come over on Friday."

Is she seriously inviting me to a sleepover? Brittany dies, and . . . But honestly, I had no idea how to parse this, no frame of reference for how freaked I should be. Greg the Grief Counselor said I shouldn't be ashamed of my feelings, whatever they were. Mostly, I was sad and confused, interspersed with fear and guilt. It had to be a coincidence, bad luck, karma.

"I don't have any plans," I said aloud.

"Tell me what kind of movies you like to watch and I'll take a look on Netflix." Jen seemed a little more cheerful, smiling at Davina and me.

"Romantic comedies," she said, just as I answered, "Science fiction, any kind."

"Even bad ones, like *Sharknado*?"

I grinned. "I'd watch it again."

"Then I'll find a good rom-com and a bad sci-fi. Sound fun? We can drink to Brit and talk about stuff."

"Awesome," Davina said. "Kind of like a wake."

Jen nodded. "I guess."

"I don't know how many stories I can contribute," I warned them.

Most of my experiences with her weren't positive. I wasn't happy something so horrible had happened to her, just the opposite, but I had no funny, adorable anecdotes waiting in the hopper, either.

I shifted uncomfortably while Davina studied me. "Doesn't matter. You were there, so you need to come. Catharsis."

"Okay. You talked me into it."

"You can ride home with me. So tell your super-hot boyfriend he doesn't need to pick you up." Jen was smiling, though, and not using the bitchy tone Allison would've imparted to the comment.

"I will. Catch you guys at lunch."

We split then and I went to first period, where Mr. Love was smoldering at the girls who had doubtless turned up half an hour early in hopes of getting time alone with him. The problem was, like, seven of them had the same idea today. *That guy's a lawsuit waiting to happen.* Yet I couldn't say he was looking at them inappropriately, just radiating a Lord Byron poetic intensity and talking with just the right hint of pretension.

"You look fetching today, Edie."

"Do I?" I glanced down at myself, seeing the same uniform and the same hairstyle I'd been wearing since the start of school.

"I hate that girl," Nicole whispered, she of tongue and cherry-stem introduction fame.

Maybe I should've let it go . . . but no. I didn't turn over a new leaf and infiltrate the Teflon crew just to let *other* people roll over me. So I dropped my backpack on my desk and strolled over to her desk.

"Why?" I asked politely.

"Excuse me?" Her eyes went wide, as she glanced at friends on either side of her.

"You just said you hate me. I'm asking why. Or am I supposed to pretend I didn't hear you?"

Before she could answer, the cause of our problems intervened. "Girls, it's almost time for class to begin. Find your seats, please."

Yet as I sat down and got out my notebook, I noticed a pleased gleam in Mr. Love's eyes. With proper encouragement, his female students would fight over him in earnest. When I went to snap at Nicole, I didn't even *care* about his tousled hair or stupid smile. God help those who did.

His lecture was interesting, per usual, and we discussed the imagery in a poem. I'd always found "La Belle Dame Sans Merci" to be overrated and somewhat misogynistic. The knightly ass had no more style than to hump a woman in a hedge, and then wondered why she left him? Fairy bullshit allegory aside, his behavior answered the question.

Afterward, I waited until the rest of the class had gone. Pausing at his desk, I stared hard at Mr. Love, who stirred beneath my scrutiny. "Is something wrong?"

The tinnitus kicked in, and it only happened when I got close to something inhuman, monstrous, or immortal. I slammed a palm on his desk and muttered, "I know what you are."

Well, not exactly. Not yet. But his presence meant trouble and Very Bad Things.

"I beg your pardon?" He wore innocence like a white mantle, dusted in gold.

No matter. That was all I said; it was enough. Gauntlet thrown, I hurried to my next class, hoping I hadn't just made a *huge* mistake.

●　●　●

On Thursday, I went to Brittany's funeral. Pretty much the whole school did, and they gave us a half day, I suspected because the Kings had donated a lot of money to Blackbriar over the years. It was a closed-casket service with pictures of her on top of the coffin. Brittany's younger sister sang and Allison tried to deliver the eulogy, but she broke down halfway through her speech. Cameron sat with Brittany's parents up front, and he looked worse than he had the other day, like he wasn't sleeping at all.

After the services, I paid my respects to the family and Mrs. King hugged me. "Thank you for coming."

"I'm sorry for your loss." That felt like the wrong response, but I didn't know what else to say. I stood for thirty seconds, letting her hug me and then I stepped back. No matter what Kian said, I still felt guilty. My head felt like scrambled eggs, and I was full of crazy theories, like what if I asked for the power to make the Teflon crew pay, and then my third wish was for a memory wipe of that request, so I didn't have to live with the guilt. Surreptitiously, I checked my wrist. *Only one hash mark atop the infinity symbol.*

I didn't sleep much that night.

Friday, I went to school late, so I could skip first period. I didn't feel like dealing with Mr. Love's scrutiny. Since I'd dropped that warning, he had been different, watchful and cold. The other girls hadn't noticed, but they were purblind where he was concerned, seeing only the carefully disheveled hair and keen insights into poems we'd read before.

Apart from pictures of Brittany hanging near the main office, things got back to normal. Classes resumed their usual curriculum and the teachers were determinedly cheerful. At lunch, the cafeteria was back to full capacity, though people were quieter than usual, less yelling, less wandering between tables. Most of the Teflon crew was back. After hesitating for a few seconds, I took my lunch to the table, thinking, *I should try to make some real friends.*

As I sat down, I noticed Russ was still absent. Davina, especially, seemed worried about him. "Has anyone heard from him?" she asked.

I was still feeling horrible about Brittany. Plus, he wasn't on my list of people worth giving a crap about, but I only shook my head. Surprisingly, the rest of the crew didn't know anything, either. Davina turned to Cam. "I thought you guys were supposed to be tight."

"Excuse me for having other things on my mind. My girlfriend just *died.*"

She looked like he'd slapped her. "I'm just . . . worried. It's not like him to—"

"You're so funny," Allison cut in. "I bet you think you're actually dating. On the DL, right? So you don't have to 'deal with drama' from everyone else?"

Davina sucked in a shaky breath. "You don't know anything about it."

"I know *everything*. You're not his girlfriend, you're his bike, available anytime he feels like a ride." Allison glanced around and seemed to take offense at our expressions. "What? It's not a secret. Russ is always adopting strays and letting them think they have a shot at being one of us."

"*Bitch*." Shoving back from the table, Davina grabbed her tray and looked for somewhere else to sit.

Without making a conscious decision, I stood up. "There are some chairs over there. This table reeks."

I didn't realize we had started a mass exodus until Jen joined us; I glanced over and saw the guys looking at Allison as if she were the shit on their shoes. And then Cam said clearly, "Jesus Christ. I have *no* idea why Brit was friends with you."

Then they left the table that they'd staked out freshman year to sit with the three of us, leaving Allison alone. Her cheeks were hot with rage or shame, her eyes dark as thunderclouds. She lowered her head and went back to her lunch, but the other students were smirking at her. Her behavior was odd, like she felt she had to be extra mean to make up for Brittany's loss.

"That was too far," Cam said, and the other guys nodded.

Like you'd know. But obviously he had a different rulebook for girls like Brittany. She deserved better than I had. I stared hard at him, remembering.

To her credit, Davina didn't say anything about Allison; she was focused on Russ. "I've texted twelve times and he hasn't answered. Is he replying to anyone else?"

Cam checked his phone. "Nope. And I'm sorry for what I said before."

God, I hated seeing him act . . . human, apologizing to people. In my mind, he was a horned, cloven-hoofed monster with no redeeming qualities. One by one, the rest of the table scrolled through texts and then shook their heads.

"I'll call Russ's house. I'm sure his mom can tell me what's going on." Cam waited while it rang, then said, "Mrs. Thomas? This is Cameron Dean." A pause. "Yes, it's awful." Another pause. "Thanks, I hope so too. I was wondering if Russ is sick. I can bring his—what?" He stopped talking, eyes widening. "No, I haven't seen him in days. And he wasn't at Brit's funeral, either. No, I'm sorry. Yes, that's fine. I'm *sorry.*"

Shaken, he dropped his cell on the table as a bad feeling swelled in my stomach. "What's wrong?" I asked.

Cam answered, "Russ told his mom he was staying with me for a few days . . . because of Brit. So I didn't have to be alone. His parents thought he was at my place this whole time."

"Oh my God." Jen's face paled. "Shit. So he's . . . *missing?*"

Hearing it put into words, Davina burst into tears.

THE SLEEP OF
REASON

That afternoon, I went home with Jen and Davina. Jen's mother was a beautiful Thai woman who spoke perfect English. She looked as if she might've been a former model or actress, which explained Jen's good looks. Ms. Bishop was also polite and charming, delighted to meet Jen's new friends. Or so she said; I was inclined to believe her. She drove us to a restored three-story Victorian out near Beacon Hill. That alone told me the family had money, but the inside was breathtaking, tastefully decorated in an East-West-fusion style that was calming and warm.

"I'm sure the three of you don't need me to hover," she said, hanging up her jacket in the hall closet. "So Jen can show you to her room, but let me or the housekeeper know if you need anything."

So it's that kind of house.

"Come on." Jen went through to the hall, the walls a pale cream that contrasted beautifully with the dark wood of the staircase.

I'd always liked our apartment; it had character, but I had the feeling I was about to feel inadequate. We went up two flights to the top of the house, where Jen had the whole floor. Walls had been torn down to create an enormous suite with oval windows all around. The ceiling slanted on three sides, and she had a full-size bed with a couple of futons placed on the other side of a rice paper and bamboo screen to create a small TV room. She also had a mini-fridge and an electric kettle. Add in the big en suite bathroom, and I saw no reason why she'd ever need to leave.

Apparently Davina shared my minor awe. "You could live up here."

"I do, pretty much."

"Your mother seems cool, though." I understood why some teenagers wanted privacy from their parents, but Ms. Bishop didn't strike me as a helicopter mom.

"She's fine. But my parents have a lot of parties. My dad is an entertainment lawyer and it's 'part of his job to schmooze.'" Jen sounded like she was quoting him. "So I'm glad I have my own floor, otherwise they'd drive me nuts with the constant noise."

"Any celebrities?" Davina wanted to know.

"Depends on what you mean by that. D-list, sometimes, people who were in soap operas ten years ago and are trying to get endorsement deals in Japan or Thailand."

"Not too exciting," I said.

Jen grinned. "Trust me, I'd be downstairs if any real stars were in my living room."

"So what're we watching tonight?" Davina asked.

"I found an Anna Faris movie for the rom-com and a terrible SF about a time-traveling T. rex for the sci-fi portion of the evening."

Davina cocked her head, seeming thoughtful. "The one where she's freaking out over how many guys she's slept with?"

"Yep."

I had no idea about romantic comedies, unless they had been made before 1960, but I couldn't stop grinning at Jen's SF choice. There was no way I could've done better myself. "Sounds perfect."

"First, maybe we should talk about what happened with Brit." Davina perched on the edge of the blue futon. "I'm still kind of freaked out."

"It's hard not to be," Jen admitted.

"I've been having dreams." Davina stared at the floor. "I haven't told my mom or she'd have me in counseling so fast it'd make my head spin."

Jen smirked. "I thought everyone at Blackbriar had a therapist and a personal trainer."

It was meant as a joke, but I felt pretty sure Davina and I were in a different tax bracket. She mumbled, "I'm on scholarship."

"Wow, really?" I was impressed.

Davina nodded. "I have been since the beginning. I'm pretty sure that's what Allison has against me. Her parents are nouveau riche, so she's kind of sensitive about it, like being polite will infect her with poverty."

"Did you seriously just say 'nouveau riche'?" Jen asked.

"You know it's true. People who just got their money always act the worst about it. They want so bad to be accepted by the blue bloods, to hang out with the right crowd—"

"Allison is kind of bitchy to everyone, though." These were all nuances completely undetectable to an outsider, namely me.

Jen said, "She got boobs early and everyone except Brit froze her out. So now she shoots first. Constantly. She's always at DEFCON three, looking for a fight."

"So a preemptive strike, so to speak." I'd never thought about it before; the Teflon crew seemed to have actual reasons for their behavior. Honestly, that never occurred to me. I'd figured they didn't need any motivation to be mean—that like summer and winter, they acted as nature dictated.

"Basically. Allison used to be best friends with Nicole Johnson, but then she developed and guys started paying attention to her. It pissed Nic off, and they stopped hanging out a few years back."

"Allison is a bitchzilla these days, no lie, but it sucks that Nicole ditched her over something that wasn't her fault. It's not like we can control when we get boobs." Davina glanced down at her own chest. "Or if, in my case."

"Whatever," Jen said. "I bet your mom is never on your case about gaining two pounds. Whereas if I even look at carbs, I get a lecture."

Wow, and I thought my parents were a pain in the ass. At least my mom never bitched at me about getting fat.

"What's that look about?" Davina asked.

I didn't want to tell the truth. "My parents teach physics at BU, so—"

"That explains a lot," Jen said.

I guessed she meant that it accounted for my complete lack of physical awareness last year. And she would be right. Most girls had a mom who talked to them about hair and makeup at some point, if only in passing. Mine was completely devoid of typical feminine interests; it balanced since she was a brilliant scientist on the verge of an earth-shaking breakthrough. People always thought their discoveries or inventions would change the world. I had a suspicion my mother was on track to do it.

"Yeah, well. Better late than never, right?"

Jen seemed to read my discomfort with the topic. She glanced over at Davina.

"You guys want a drink?"

"Some water would be great," the other girl answered.

"Still, sparkling, or mineral?" She apparently had all three in her mini-fridge. Talk about hospitality.

"Sparkling," Davina decided aloud.

"Same," I said.

Jen got out three bottles of sparkling water, then she turned on the TV, but none of us were in the mood to watch; it was more background noise than anything. I might be wrong but I didn't think Jen had ever hung out with Davina like this before either. We were united in that we'd seen something horrible together, and while it didn't precisely make us friends, it did offer a bonding moment that nobody else shared. I might not know these girls very well, but they understood what those moments had felt like.

"So . . . ," Davina said. "Brit . . ."

Dropping her gaze, Jen drew her knees up to her chest and wrapped her arms around them. "I can't get her face out of my head. When I try to get to sleep, I see it over and over."

"For me, it's the blood," Davina whispered.

There were so many things I couldn't share, not the least of which was my suspicions that it hadn't been a natural death. "It happened so fast. One week, she has a terrible rash and then . . ."

"That's terrifying too," Davina said. "I'm kind of scared to try any new brands of makeup now."

"Her parents are suing the cosmetic company," Jen put in.

Yeah, that'll help. I clenched a fist, trying not to reveal the chaos in my head. Guilt warred with sadness while regret danced around in circles. *But you don't know for sure it was your fault. Or Kian's. But if it was Wedderburn . . . God, it's all so tangled.*

"Maybe we should just . . . not think about it for a while," I suggested for my own sanity. "If that's possible. It might help if we had a better memory together to replace it with." God, I hoped that didn't sound as dumb as I suspected. It reeked of Hallmark greeting cards and I expected them both to throw something at me.

Instead both girls were nodding. "That makes sense," Jen said.

Davina got out a magazine and we paged through it, looking at clothes and deciding what items were fug and which were overpriced. That carried us for an hour, and by that point, I felt pretty comfortable. The housekeeper came upstairs then with a tray of finger foods: white cheese, various cut fruits, carrots, celery, and jicama, along with some cold cuts and whole wheat crackers.

"Dear God." Jen sighed. "Any other girl has a sleepover and she gets to have chips and cookies and popcorn. Not me. Sorry about this, guys."

"I don't mind. It looks good, actually." I wasn't just being nice. It was much fancier than anything I got at home, especially arrayed on the teak serving tray.

Davina grinned. "I love the radish roses."

"Nobody likes radish roses," Jen said. "Radishes are disgusting."

"I didn't say they were delicious. But they *are* adorable."

We ate, and I listened while they talked about people from school. Apparently Nicole Johnson tried to make a move on Mr. Love, and got shot down. *That won't end well,* I thought.

"Are you serious?" Davina asked. "I mean, he's fine and all, but he's at least twenty-five. Something is seriously wrong with him, if he wants to date a high school girl."

I offered, "Date might be the wrong word."

"You mean like a professional cherry-popper? We had one in my old school, kept a score card and everything. Asshole." Davina made a face.

Around six, Jen put in the romantic comedy, which was much funnier and more entertaining than I expected. Note to self: Don't judge modern movies prematurely. As the movie ended, my phone buzzed with a text.

"Is that your man?" Davina asked.

I checked. "Yep."

"Oooh, what'd he say? Is he sexting you?" At home, Jen was much more chill than she seemed at school. She unwound enough to try to steal my phone.

I held it away from her and read out loud, "'Is it too needy to check in and see how you're doing? If so, this is a mis-text. If not . . .'"

"Funny and hot," Davina said.

I smiled as I typed back, It's not. And I'm good. Thanks.

He replied immediately. See you tomorrow night?

Yeah. What time?

Pick you up at seven.

When I put away my phone, both of them were smirking at me.

"What?" I demanded.

"You should see your face." But Davina's expression softened like she thought whatever she'd seen me reveal about Kian was a good thing.

"We are *not* talking about her man all night," Jen cut in.

And I was grateful. "Cool. Let's watch the time-traveling T. rex instead."

That was bad SF at its best. I laughed until my stomach hurt, and so did the other two. I shouldn't have been startled to find that they weren't so different from me, but I'd started thinking of the people at school as a separate species, so it was tough to shift my thinking. Halfway through the movie, Jen broke out her secret stash and added vodka to our OJ.

Things got blurry after that. They told stories about Brittany, and I cried along with Davina and Jen; I regretted so much that I never got to know the girl who would strip down to her undies and steal a rose on a dare or drive twenty miles to buy a case of beer because she'd promised to make Davina's first party the best one ever. Jen told me how when Cameron was sick—and there was nobody at his house—Brit went over and made chicken soup and then cleaned up the vomit when he couldn't keep it down. How could such a nice girl do what she did to me?

And how could I do that to her? *If* I did.

People can be monsters too.

It was half past midnight when Davina drunkenly suggested we try the Bloody Mary mirror thing. For a few seconds, I froze, and the giddiness dissipated almost instantly. Jen was already heading for the bathroom with some candles.

"I don't think that's a good idea," I said.

In my head, I heard Kian say, *Sometimes you call things. And then they don't leave.* I remembered the girl in *my* bathroom mirror, and I wondered how to stop this. Circumstances might've thrown me together with Jen and Davina, but I liked them. As of yet, I didn't trust them as I did Vi, but it would come, in time, if they didn't turn on me or stab me in the back.

Provided they don't die horribly.

Jen stopped in the doorway. "Why not? It's kind of a sleepover tradition, along with light as a feather, stiff as a board, right, D?"

The other girl nodded. "Are you scared or something?"

"Obviously." It seemed better to tell the truth. And if they'd seen a quarter of what *I* had, if they knew what I knew, they'd be petrified too.

"It's just an urban legend." Jen tried to reassure me.

Davina wrapped an arm around my shoulders and dragged me to the bathroom. "Don't worry, I'll protect you."

Before I could say another word, she snapped off the lights and Jen lit the candles. The tiny flames cast spooky, flickering shadows on the dark tile walls. In normal circumstances, Jen's bathroom seemed modern and elegant, done in black and white with red accents, but right then, the room looked like something out of an asylum with three faces seeming disembodied in the mirror. Jen lifted her candle, so that the scent of cinnamon wafted up; she leaned forward until her nose nearly touched the glass. I recoiled, but Davina was behind me. She put her hands on my shoulders, like that would settle me down.

"Bloody Mary," Jen chanted, and Davina chimed in.

I didn't say a word; I couldn't. Fear crept up my spine on caterpillar feet as the other two whispered. They were smiling until the glass darkened. Our images distorted, warped sideways, and then it was like the creature in the mirror wiped us out of existence. She was a wraith of a thing in a ragged white nightdress, her face all bones and eye sockets, with a mop of tangled dark stringing down her cheeks like damp seaweed. The dead girl on the other side pressed her fingertips to the glass in front of the candle, and the flame winked out. When she smiled, it was like staring into an open grave. Jen shrieked and stumbled, dropping the other candle; it rolled across the floor and went out, bathing the room in shadows.

"Shit." Davina scrambled for the door, unsteady on her feet.

I shoved Jen after her, then I grabbed a towel from the rack behind me. Quickly, I covered the mirror and turned on the overhead light. It took all my courage to stand my ground, but I counted to ten and waited, listening. The silence was broken only by the gasps and whimpers coming from Jen's bedroom. My hands shook as I reached up to pull the towel down; my muscles locked in anticipation of the need to fight or flee, but when I looked in the mirror, it was clear. I leaned forward, touched the surface, and nothing happened.

"What's with you two?" I asked, going back to the bedroom.

Jen eyed me like I was crazy. "Didn't you see . . . ?"

"What?"

"The thing . . . and the candle." Davina paced, breathing too fast, and if she kept it up, she'd hyperventilate.

"See, that's what happens when you suck down that much vodka and then play with matches." I couldn't afford to have them ask too many questions, so I grabbed Jen's arm and tugged her back into the bathroom, now illuminated by plenty of overhead light. "See? Nothing."

"You really didn't see anything?" she asked.

"Just some shadows." Hopefully, this lie wouldn't drive her into counseling.

"Huh."

Davina came up behind us, tipping her head in puzzlement. "So . . . it was like a shared hallucination?"

"What else could it have been?" Innocent expression, as I tried to slow my heartbeat and stop shaking. I had no idea what might've

239

happened if I had been wrong about covering the mirror; my best guess was that it interrupted the connection to the other side.

But if the nightmare has a link to Jen's mirror now . . . damn.

"I don't know." Jen looked at Davina, who shrugged.

We talked a little more after that, but the others were subdued, and we stayed together to brush our teeth. Later, Jen gave us some bedding, so Davina and I could make up the futons. I settled down, but as I lay there, I was afraid to shut my eyes. The ragged edge of disaster loomed closer and closer, as if my life was constructed on a fault line, and there were aftershocks constantly shifting me toward the precipice. Jen's steady breathing filled the room pretty fast, but a glance at Davina told me she was wide awake, and she didn't look like she'd be sleeping anytime soon.

"Edie?"

"What?"

"You were lying, I know you were. I'm not asking why, but you did something in there. And you *expected* something to happen."

I didn't deny it. Instead I whispered, "Remember me saying it was a bad idea?"

"Yeah. So you've had weird stuff go down before."

"I'm really tired." I dodged the question. "If you don't mind?"

"No, it's fine. But . . . thanks." That was the last word she said before she turned over and snuggled in.

It took much longer for me to relax. Around 2:00 a.m., I rolled off the futon and went to the window. Darkness wreathed the streets, so there was only the streetlamp casting a golden circle on the pavement. I was increasingly apprehensive about reflections, so I wasn't thinking at all about the old man with the bag. And then he was there, outside on the sidewalk, gazing up at me. The two creepy children stood on either side, their eyes cast upward, all black and unblinking. Their silent attention seemed ominous, as if they were marking the house somehow. A shiver of dread went through me when I realized the boy's shirt and the girl's pinafore were stained with blood.

Silently, I shook my head. Whatever they wanted, I had to keep them from getting it. I blinked, once, twice, hoping they were the hallucination I'd claimed when Davina and Jen summoned Bloody Mary. In that split second when my lashes swept down and up again, the little girl-thing scratched against the windowpane, standing on nothing at all.

She spoke in the tinkling voice of an old doll, one with a cracked porcelain face and dead, unblinking eyes. "Let me in. This won't take long."

YOUR FRIENDSHIP
IS KILLING ME

The glass between us frosted, such a thin barrier of protection, but when I mouthed the word *no*, she disappeared. Davina stirred on her futon and I ran back to mine, half afraid of what else might creep out of the dark and of the monsters my unconscious mind might create. *You need other people to believe for your nightmares to be made real.* But that didn't comfort me much.

I didn't sleep. Each tick of the clock, I wanted to call Kian. I didn't. *Be brave. Be strong. They need your permission to come in. Right?*

If they didn't, then life would get ugly, fast.

Early the next morning, Jen's mom fed us a healthy breakfast of egg whites, fruit, and yogurt, and then I got the hell out before they noticed how haggard I looked. Davina's mom was picking her up later, so I hugged Jen and then Davina, thanked everyone, and ran for it. But I stopped on the sidewalk beneath the streetlight, staring at the dark imprint of man-size footprints that seemed to be *burned* into the cement. Of the two children who accompanied the bag man, there was no sign. But I read dire portents in the shape of his shoes:

This is mine now and I will return.

Nausea born of foreboding rose to the back of my throat, but I choked it down and started walking. Soon I broke into an uncontrollable run, wishing I could scream as well, but people were already staring since I had on jeans, not sweats or spandex, and I was carrying a backpack. All told, I hoped they'd conclude I was late, not crazy, but truthfully, if I had on a hoodie, they'd probably suspect me of antisocial crimes.

My body was covered in cold sweat by the time I got on the T; luckily, there was a guy singing to his shoe, so that took precedence in the weirdness hierarchy. I got off at the usual stop and went home. My parents had papers spread *all* over the table, yellow legal sheets covered in complicated equations, along with rough sketches of how something or other could actually be built.

"Did you get your funding?" I asked.

"Don't know yet. It'll be a while," my dad answered.

"Was it fun at Julie's?" Mom wanted to know.

"Jen. And it was different. We watched movies, ate healthy food." *And called up something monstrous in the mirror. You know. The usual.* Since my mom lacked all appreciation of whimsy, I didn't joke about it. She'd take me seriously and assume I was experimenting with psychedelics, and then I'd get a lecture about the importance of sticking with natural recreational drugs.

Dad protested, "*My* food is healthy."

"But you never make me radish roses."

"Oh, fancy. I don't do fancy." He seemed appeased.

After a little more conversation, I escaped on the homework excuse. Nobody but my parents would believe I planned to study at 10:00 a.m. on a Saturday, which was why it was kind of nice having professors in the house. They saw nothing weird about it.

After retreating to my room, I researched the bag man. In Latin American countries, he was known as "the old man with the sack" and he abducted children. Sometimes he ate them and left only the bones. Other times, he cut off their heads and stuck them in the bag, savoring the brains and making grotesque bowls out of their little skulls.

"Jesus," I whispered.

And he's stalking you. What the hell.

To take my mind off it and to make the lie a little bit true, I did my Intro to Japanese worksheet. That turned out to be a gateway assignment, as nerd habits died hard, and I couldn't stop until I worked my way through the list. Schoolwork might be the only thing keeping me sane at this point since I could block off the threatening terror and confusion and sheer helplessness I felt with regard to the rest of my life. I had just finished up my last project when Vi popped up on Skype.

I answered the video call request with a smile that faded when I saw her expression. She looked like sickness, death, or sorrow, maybe some horrendous combination of the three. "What's wrong?"

"Edie, is this . . . you?"

"I don't—"

"This link, just a sec, I have it on my tablet." She put it in front of her laptop and touched the play icon on the screen.

The moment it loaded and I saw the first few seconds, I knew. The grungy room, normally used to store chairs and things for PTA meetings and parent days, was empty, as everything had been moved to the cafeteria, extra chairs for the winter festival. Each year, there was a theme with booths and decorations, and it was kind of like an open house. This was the first time I'd seen the video, though I knew it had been uploaded.

Title: *Dog girl in training*
Description: *This girl is a dog. And she knows it. Watch her act like one. It's hilarious! Pls like and subscribe, more awesome vids to come.*

I couldn't speak to answer her as memories scoured me raw. It took two of them to get the job done. While Brittany distracted me by being nice, friendly even—she *apologized* for all the harassment before—Cameron had spiked my water, just some roofies, no big deal. I drank it just before last period. When I stumbled out of class, they were all waiting. Sick and dizzy, I knew, I *knew* I had to get away but I didn't have the strength or coordination.

So they took me.

To the bare room with the dingy floor and gray cement block walls in the basement. They could've done *anything* to me down there. Cameron put a black spiked dog collar on me and had me crawl around on the floor. He led me by the leash and said, "Bark for me, there's a good girl. Bark, Eat-it. Bark."

It was all there, on shaky camera phone. Me, on all fours, me barking, me leashed, collared, and crying, begging for them to let me go. I heard the echoed laughter all over again through my laptop. A hard shudder rocked through me when Cam dropped the dish of dog food in front of me. The fat version of me was weeping, red-faced, snotty

245

tears, as I lowered my chin to the brown goo and lapped it up. The laughter got louder and louder.

Vi stopped the video. "Edie?"

"Yeah," I said quietly. "That's me."

With some logical corner of my mind, I was calculating. It was more than six months from the time this video was posted until the time I met Vi. A hard-core diet could, theoretically, produce results similar to what Kian had with his future-tech shaping gloves. Given how upset I was, it seemed unlikely that Vi would question my makeover.

"Such assholes. And what the hell, why would anyone send me this?"

I sucked in a breath, fighting for composure. Tears stood in my eyes, but I didn't let them fall. Shame was a hot coal trying to burn its way out of my chest. Every day at school since the last before winter break, I went to class and people followed me, barking. They put dog biscuits on my desk. Someone tied a leash to my locker. Every. Single. Day.

I had told the school counselor how I felt . . . not that I was suicidal, but that things were just getting to be too much, and she said something like, "Some people just have trouble socially, Edith. Maybe if you . . ." Then she listed all the ways I could stop being the dog girl: if I worked out or bought makeup or went to a salon. I took her words to mean the problems were my fault, and that was what broke me.

As to why anyone would e-mail that to Vi, I had some ideas. "To remind me who I was. And to let you know too. It'd be awful if you didn't realize you were hanging around with the Beantown dog girl." Somehow I didn't burst into tears, though the humiliation hadn't lessened; there was still a raw stripe inside me. From what Kian told me, this was in character for Dwyer & Fell, an underhanded tactic to destroy my current contentment and drive me away from my optimum timeline. I remembered him saying, *The opposition interfered, drove her over the edge.* Dwyer & Fell might think if they drove a wedge between me and Vi, it would weaken my support network. Kian had also said, *If they shift the equilibrium enough, your fate changes and you cease to be a factor in play.* So any way they could make my life worse, they were likely to give it a try.

Though I tried to fight the wave of memory, I remembered what Cameron had said, as he dumped me behind the school. I had fallen hard, scraping my palms and knees. He stood over me, looking like this was the most fun he'd ever had. More tears trickled down my cheeks.

"Come on, Eat-it. It's just a joke. Not like we raped you." He'd strolled away as I barfed up a can of dog food.

"Wow," Vi breathed. "I'm glad I don't go to private school."

Surprised, I choked out a shaky laugh. "I'm sorry you—"

"Hey, no. They can eat shit and die."

I almost agreed with her, but then I remembered Brittany's face. No matter how I felt about her, I hadn't wanted her *dead.* So I smiled at Vi when she changed the subject and told me about something she was working on, a robotics project. I had less interest in that, but she carried the conversation long enough for me to pull myself together.

"Thanks," I said finally.

"That's what friends are for. And if you want me to come kick some tail, I will totally put together a posse."

"What's your gang called, Vi-Z?"

She snorted. "I thought I'd offer. Anyway, I'm deleting this crap.

Let us never speak of this again." By her tone, I could tell she was quoting something, but I wasn't sure what.

"Talk to you later, Vi."

"Don't let the Neanderthals get you down."

"They don't, anymore." In fact, there was one less in the world.

I closed my laptop and took a shower, but I couldn't lose the uneasy feeling that something could be lurking outside the curtain, staring at me from the other side of the mirror. So no more long, luxuriant scrubs—this time, it was fast and unsatisfying, much as my dad had described virginal sex during his super awkward talk the other night.

Afterward, I got ready for my date, which involved a clean pair of jeans and a shirt Kian had never seen. I didn't have a ton of clothes, and shopping wasn't high on my to-do list, considering the stuff going on. Not sure what it said about me that I wasn't rocking and weeping. But before I left, my computer beeped again with another call from Vi.

That's weird.

But I answered, figuring she forgot to tell me something important. "Long time, no talk."

"I just want you to know, I'm not crazy. Whatever they say later." That was such a weird greeting that I put down my hairbrush.

"What the hell. Vi?"

"I told you about those dreams, right? Well, it's happening when I'm awake now too. I see everything encased in ice. Just now, I went to ask my mom something and she was all blue, enveloped in ice, and I couldn't wake her up. And then, like, she wasn't, it was all in my head or something, but—"

Wedderburn. That word blazed in my brain, more dreadful than any curse.

"It's fine, you're just stressed. Calm down, okay?"

"I can't! I'm losing my shit and I'm only seventeen. Instead of college, I have a bright future ahead of me coloring with crayons and writing things on the wall of my cell. The weird thing is, I never even *liked* snow that much, but now I see it everywhere I turn. The other night, my dad was sprinkling salt and I kind of fell into watching it, so it was like I was lost in a blizzard and I didn't answer my brother for, like, five minutes. My parents blame Seth."

I have to fix this.

Aloud, I said, "Drink less caffeine. Have an herbal tea at night before bed and meditate or something."

"I don't think waking dreams are normal." She sounded so sad and scared, and considering how amazing she had been a few hours before about the damned dog video, I wanted so bad to help her.

This can't turn out like Brittany. I felt like a plague carrier, spreading darkness and death in all directions. Whether that was true, I didn't know, but a scream prickled in my throat. I swallowed it like a cactus and imagined I tasted blood.

"Psht. Who wants to be normal?"

That made her smile. "Fine. I'll try your new age-y crap before I dump this on my mom. God knows she has enough to worry about with Kenny starting junior high." She went on to tell me about her brother's host of mental problems, most of which required medication.

"Better?" I asked.

"Yeah. Thanks."

"That's what friends are for." I repeated her words from earlier, trying to sound calm and reassuring.

She paused for a few seconds, and I wished I could reach through my laptop to hug her. "My friends here aren't the same. You know?"

"Sure." Because I knew it would make her laugh, I said, "You're my sister from another mister."

"Totally. I'll keep you posted on whether the tea and serenity stuff makes a dent in my crazy."

"Later."

This time, when I closed my computer, I tapped out a text to Kian. Come early, it's urgent. Favor related.

Five minutes after I sent that, he ported into my room. "Edie, don't rush this. You can have five years, free and clear. Take them."

"I can't. Wedderburn is terrorizing Vi. Isn't that . . . cheating or something?"

"Not by their standards."

"You didn't tell me they could do this when I first signed up for the deal."

He lowered his eyes, cheeks washed with red. "You didn't ask." Then his voice went low. "I'm sorry. I wanted to warn you. I did. That's the second thing I feel guilty about in relation to you."

I almost asked what the first one was, and then I remembered that he felt horrible about not *dying* for me. *Crazy, beautiful boy.* Though I'd tried to absolve him, clearly Kian agreed with Voltaire: "Every man is guilty of all the good he did not do." *Even if it meant paying the ultimate price.*

He went on, "But I . . . also wanted to save your life."

"It doesn't matter. At this point, I'm ready to use my second favor."

"Edie—"

"Will you grant it or do I need to go over your head?" I was dead serious.

"I'm listening," he said, resigned.

"First I need to ask a clarifying question."

"Go for it."

"Can I include multiple people in a request? Like, if I want to protect all of my loved ones from the game?"

Kian shook his head. "By immortal standards, that would require a favor for each of them. You could pick two people, at most, and that would burn your last two."

"Dammit." But Wedderburn had given no sign that Ryu or my parents had registered with him, so maybe I shouldn't borrow trouble. "Fine. Then this is what I want: He needs to keep Vi out of this. She gets to have her happy life without being bothered. I don't want the fact that we're friends to screw her up. Can you do it?"

"This is exactly what he wants," Kian warned.

"I still have one favor. He hasn't railroaded me all the way yet, so that gives me a little leverage."

"Your mind's made up then." He looked as if I'd confessed to having brain cancer when he tapped his watch, one of the myriad buttons whose function I didn't know, and Wedderburn's face appeared above it in 3-D holo.

"Yes?"

Kian repeated my request, though more elegantly. For the first time, I could imagine him on the path to law school and eventually the Supreme Court. It was sort of odd, since he wasn't actually that person, but there were echoes. People were mirrors turned inward to infinity, where all choices and roads not taken led to an endless shifting of self.

When Wedderburn smiled, I wished I could reach through the ether and throttle him. "This is easily done. A commendable gesture on your part, Miss Kramer. Your friend's future is safe, assured by your altruism, and *you* are one step nearer to your destiny."

"Bullshit," I said.

I hissed as my wrist burned. Another line, this one crossed the infinity symbol in the middle, where the two halves met. Two out of three favors burned. Fear bubbled inside me at shifting that much closer to Wedderburn's clutches, but I didn't regret protecting Vi. It chafed that I'd played into the icy devil's hands, but what else could I have done?

"Think what you like." Wedderburn's tone radiated pure satisfaction. "It has been a pleasure, as always."

When the holo vanished, Kian's shoulders slumped. "I wish you hadn't done that."

"He was making Vi crazy. How long before he got bored with the cat-and-mouse thing and did something worse to her?" No way to prove it, but I suspected Wedderburn didn't listen when I told him not to intervene with the Teflon crew. If so, Brittany's death was on me. *But it could also be D&F, trying to drive me nuts with guilt.* My head throbbed.

"I don't know," he said quietly. "Their sense of time doesn't align with ours, usually. They're capricious, but . . ."

"What?"

"They have long attention spans. I've known creatures to stalk one person for years, just appearing and watching, appearing and watching, feasting on their fear."

"Until that person winds up eating pudding from a cup for every meal and living in a room with upholstered walls? Because nobody will believe them."

Kian stepped closer, and I went into his arms.

"It makes me want to interview a bunch of people in mental hospitals and find out what they know."

He grinned. "I guarantee that's not the future Wedderburn's pushing you toward."

"That's hardly a deterrent. He says I'm on track, but who the hell knows? According to you, I won't find out until I graduate."

"Worst matriculation present ever."

"It's hot when you use ten-dollar words." I smiled up at him, ready for a kiss, until I heard one of my parents coming down the hall.

"Edie? Who are you talking to?" my dad asked.

"I'm on Skype," I called, while motioning for Kian to disappear.

"Ah. Say hi to Vi for me."

With a regretful look, Kian ported, leaving me to wait for him to pick me up the old-fashioned way. When he arrived via the front door, he was a little late. Both my parents inspected him for the second time, and my mom grilled him about his science background. I suspected she might show him the door if he showed too many liberal arts tendencies. Most likely, his poetry journal would get him evicted.

"Ready?" Kian asked, after fifteen minutes of convo with my parents, which was like eight dog years.

"Yeah, I'll see you guys later." With a wave, I followed him out and down the stairs, where we found Mr. Lewis staring at a giant nail protruding over the front door.

"Something wrong?" I asked.

"Yeah. Some no-good bastard stole my horseshoe."

At first, I had no idea what he was talking about and then I realized he'd mentioned hanging one up for protection. "That's a problem."

The old man leveled a grim look on me. "More for you than me, girlie."

"Why's that?" I asked, while Kian glanced between us in dawning startlement.

"Because now they can come in."

FINDING THE LOST

"Could you text Kian and ask him not to pick you up today?" From Davina, that was a surprising question, but she had been a little different today, possibly as a result of our whispered conversation at the weekend sleepover, after Jen fell asleep. She'd followed me to the bathroom after lunch and was pretending to put on lip gloss while I washed my hands.

"Why?" Maybe it qualified as cynical, but I wasn't agreeing to anything without asking. My life was currently in too much of a mess for me to take on more complications blindly. Brittany's death danced in the corners of my mind while monsters lurked in the shadows, waiting to catch me unaware. Lately my head was a scary place to live.

"I need to look for Russ, and I was hoping you'd go with me. I can borrow my mom's car, but I don't want to leave the city alone."

"How far is it?" There was a limit to what I could get away with on a school night.

"About an hour and a half."

"I can text my dad and tell him I'm studying at the library with you if you're willing to corroborate."

Last year I'd have bet my vintage TARDIS that any member of the Teflon crew, even a perpetual floater, didn't know what that meant. Davina nodded. "Absolutely. And it'd be awesome if you were willing to tell my mom the same thing."

"Not a problem." That settled, I tapped out a quick message to Kian saying I didn't need a ride after all, but he didn't reply.

Apparently he has a life.

"Thanks for doing this." She paused, lowered her voice to add, "The others don't get it, but Russ actually cares about me."

I hadn't seen any evidence of it, but she seemed secure in that conclusion. "I'm sure he's a nicer guy than he lets on."

"Exactly. When we're alone, he's really sweet. Did you know he plays piano?"

"Absolutely not."

"He'd kill me if he knew I told you. Don't let on, okay?"

"I won't." Unlike Allison, I didn't want to cause trouble for Davina.

"Thanks. I'll see you after school?"

I nodded and she hurried out of the bathroom, much more cheerful. Pausing at my locker, I sent my dad a message. Working on a project with Davina at the library. Home later than usual.

How late?

Not sure. I'll have dinner out.

Remember, I know what time the library closes.

My dad was sharp. While I'd never given him any reason to distrust me, he remained cognizant that I might suddenly start lying at any time, an anomaly he would doubtless blame on hormones and their

256

response to people with penises. Since Russ presumably had one, my father wasn't entirely wrong, just not right in the way he'd imagine.

Afternoon classes passed slowly; I turned in assignments and took notes, though not my usual meticulous ones. Davina was waiting when the last bell rang. She jittered with energy as she walked to my locker, surprising me with her nonstop narrative. Before, I always got the impression she was shy, but that might've resulted from being shut down by Brittany and Allison. Possibly she felt like we'd bonded, after the hospital and then the sleepover weirdness.

"I don't know if you heard," she said, as we headed for the front gate, "but Allison is holding tryouts to fill Brit's spot on the squad."

"You're the alternate. Aren't you supposed to move up automatically?"

Her chin firmed as if she was clenching her teeth. "That was how they conned me into being mascot for the last three years."

"That's bullshit. How is she getting away with it?"

"The short version? Her dad has more money than mine. So when she comes to Coach Tina with how she's *so* concerned about the performance of the squad in competition, too many fliers, not enough foundation, blah blah, and an open audition is best—that her dad will be very happy to buy new uniforms, even a new bus, if necessary—as long as Allie gets the support she needs."

"Wow." I had no idea what to say. "You need to perform so well that you land a spot anyway, then a freshman can be mascot this year."

"That'd be nice. But the teachers who pick the squad always seem to choose me as alternate." Her smile was ironic. "I wonder why. Maybe if my family bought textbooks or new computers or donated a pool, I'd miraculously make the squad."

I smirked. "On your own merits."

"Naturally. It'd be three years of hard work and relentless practice that finally shattered that glass ceiling."

Deciding I liked Davina, I made up a new school slogan on the spot. "Blackbriar, just enough diversity to prevent litigation."

She laughed and grabbed my arm, dragging me toward the T. At school, I'd never had friends, of either gender, who hauled me around like that. My throat tightened a little.

Davina got us to her house fast, where she wheedled and begged her mom for the car. In the end, it took some creative lying about the many heavy books our project required, and she agreed to get some groceries before her mother handed over the keys. This was a big, old car with a powerful motor that roared like an aging lion when she started it.

I buckled in, hoping she was a good driver.

Davina seemed to know what she was doing, heading out of the city on the interstate before the worst of the commuter traffic locked the city down. I didn't say much because on some levels, this seemed crazy. Russ had obviously disappeared for a reason; I mean, if he had been kidnapped, he wouldn't have lied to his parents about being at Cameron's house. The farther we got from the city, the more nervous I became. There was no guarantee that Davina wasn't working with Wedderburn or Dwyer & Fell. Either way, it could be bad for me.

"Where are we going?" I asked, mostly to see if she'd tell me.

"His dad owns a house in New Hampshire. Sometimes Russ took me out there."

That didn't sound like the behavior of a guy who cared about a girl, more like how he'd act if he was hiding her. I didn't say that; Davina was barely keeping her concern in check as it was, and she was driving. I didn't have a license.

"Nice?" I imagined a lake mansion, six bedrooms, as many baths, and a boat house.

"It's remote," she said thoughtfully. "Peaceful, though. Smaller than you'd expect."

"Maybe it was leftover from before they had money."

Though I was kidding, she said, "Probably."

Conversation died in her preoccupation, and I lacked the focus to press on. The more distance we put between Boston and me, the less the infinity mark on my arm liked it. All around the symbol, the skin felt hot and inflamed, like the brand was reminding me I had obligations. *I know, one more favor.* Odd, because when I went away for the SSP, it didn't bother me at all. That was before Wedderburn decreed that I needed to burn through my requests, though. As time wore on, I actually had to lace my hands together to keep from wrenching the wheel and turning the car back toward the city.

We passed the state line without any problems, though I noticed Davina worrying her lower lip. The roads got smaller and rougher until we turned onto what I guessed was a long, private drive. Trees framed the rocky path in an archway of foliage, mostly green, tinged here and there with gold. If Davina didn't seem sure of the route, I'd assume we were hopelessly lost as she turned the car deeper and deeper into the woods. By this time, the sky was darkening to purple, clouds dotting the horizon like bruises.

Just when I was about to question her sense of direction, the rutted track opened to permit a glimpse of an A-frame house nestled amid the trees. Beyond I caught the glint of water. It was a quiet, picturesque place, but my arm felt like I had been stung by a hundred bees, and when I lifted it to the dying light, my skin around the mark was red as blood. Hastily, I jerked my school blazer down as Davina parked.

Right next to Russ's silver BMW.

As I climbed out of her mom's beater, she grabbed my left hand and held on until it hurt. "Do you think he's here with someone?"

Shit. Do I think he'd skip school to cheat on you? Absolutely. Do I want to say that out loud? Nope.

"I have no idea" seemed like the kindest response.

Our footsteps crunched over the weeds and gravel choking the driveway, then we hit the wooden steps to the front deck. Inside, the house was dark, and I couldn't see much despite the immense windows. Apart from the wood frame on the sides, the front and back seemed to be glass. Davina rummaged for the key in a potted plant and let herself in. Eyes wide, she beckoned me to follow.

The smell hit me at once. She stopped in her tracks, and as one, we tipped our heads back. Russ wasn't cheating on her. Nor was he breathing. He spun in a slow circle from a noose, hanging from the rafters above. Horror flooded over me like a wave of dark water.

That's how Kian tried to die. It can't be a coincidence.

Davina opened her mouth to scream and I dragged her outside; she hunched over and I suspected she would barf, but instead she grabbed her knees and drew in a few shaky breaths. I put my hand on her back, too shocked to know what I should be feeling. A few seconds later, it occurred to me we had to call 911 and I said so. She didn't argue with me, though it would mean our parents finding out we'd lied about the library.

"You do it," she said in a thin voice.

"Okay. Go sit in the car. I think we should stay out of the house."

The 911 operator asked me a number of questions, and I had to ask Davina for the address. At last the dispatcher said she was sending a policeman to our location and we should get in our vehicle and wait. I did that gladly since I had no intention of sitting in the house.

"My grandmother said these things come in threes," Davina whispered.

"What do you mean?" I asked.

"That once the bad spirits woke up and the dying started, it didn't stop until they took three souls."

"I hope not." Over the last few months, I'd learned not to dismiss such things. Hell, if enough people believed it, the worst would come true.

"I think I'm cursed." Davina hesitated, eyed me with a sharp look. "Or maybe *you* are. I never had shit like this until I started hanging around with you."

That's my worst fear.

Aloud, I said, "You think I gave Brit a flesh-eating virus and hung Russ?"

At that she burst into tears and I spent the next ten minutes hugging her. We were in her mom's car, crying together, when the state police showed up. There were two of them, looking bored and clearly expecting a high school prank. Old and young, tall and short—it was like whoever paired them up thought opposites made the best partners. The small, portly one stepped forward.

"The young man's inside?" A nice way of putting it.

I nodded. "We unlocked the door but we didn't touch anything."

"Let us check things out and then we'll be right with you."

Off they went, but it didn't take long before they were outside, and the younger one made a call on the radio. *Not a trick, officer. This is the real deal, unfortunately.* That started half an hour's worth of questions

261

and then other people arrived, including the county coroner. By that point, Davina and I were on our phones, explaining things to our folks.

To say my dad was displeased? Understatement. "You used to be such a smart girl. What in the world has gotten into you? You *lied* to me and left the state. What if this boy had been dangerous? You two might've found him lying in wait with a gun. If your friend suspected he might be there, why didn't she tell his parents or the headmaster?"

Because she loves him, I thought. *And she didn't want him to get in trouble if he was just skipping a week of school. She was hoping she could save him.*

It took another hour before they let us go, and by that time, a cavalcade of luxury vehicles had started to arrive, Russ's family, most likely. From Davina's panicked expression, I could tell she wanted to be gone before she had to face his parents. The state police dismissed us soon after. She got us out of there and back onto the main road, knuckles tightened on the steering wheel.

"I know nobody believes it, but he was different with me. We'd sit out on the deck behind the house and talk."

"Sounds like you were close," I said.

"Not at first. In the beginning, he was using me for sex. I *knew* that. But I just liked him so much . . . I thought if we spent time to-gether, he might feel the same way."

"Did he?" Even if her side of the story was only one she was tell-ing herself, it might help if I listened.

"Yeah. Back in June, we'd come out here, have our fun, and he couldn't wait to bail. But by the end of August? He wanted to stay for hours. We talked and he'd hold me. Sometimes, this summer, we came out here and didn't hook up at all."

"Sounds like he cared about you, Davina."

"Not enough to tell me what was wrong. I didn't even notice he was sad."

"It's not your fault."

But I had something else on my mind. Come to think of it, when Russ paid attention to me, I never noticed that he had any particular interest in more than a captive audience for his lacrosse lectures. It definitely wasn't like he was hitting on me.

"Actually, when I hung out with Russ, he *did* act like he was taken." She flashed me a sad smile. "Yeah."

Strange driving down this dark highway, thinking about the Russ I never knew, who played the piano and spent long hours on the lakeshore, cuddled up with Davina. Now I never would meet him, which was too damned bad. An ache rose in my chest, pinioned by dual weights of fear and dread. *What if this is my fault?* I couldn't escape that specter, no matter which way I turned. *You wanted revenge. Wedderburn offered. You declined. But what if he doesn't take no for an answer?* I'd thought it before, but with two casualties in this secret war, the connection grew harder to ignore.

I'm the common denominator.

I refused to believe it was Kian. Then I remembered saying *Russ is such a total waste of oxygen.* To the boyfriend who wore death and despair like a pair of black wings, shadows that prowled in his wake. *You promised to trust him.* But it seemed illogical to ignore the evidence; he and I were the only ones who knew what I said about Russ. *Spies, someone listening in? But he said that gel guaranteed privacy.* I pondered for a few seconds. *Then he must've been wrong. Kian wouldn't kill Russ just because he pissed me off. If my hatred was lethal, Cameron Dean would've been the first body on the ground.* Still, it was hard not to wonder if Kian was lying . . . about so many things.

Putting those thoughts aside, I asked, "How much trouble will you be in?"

She shrugged. "When I tell my mom he was my boyfriend, she'll intervene with my dad. They'll scream at me, hug me, ground me, send me to counseling. Then she'll spend a week cooking my favorite foods and trying to keep me out of bed."

"Will it work?"

"Probably not."

"You're holding together pretty well right now."

My arm felt better at least, now that we were headed in the right direction.

"Getting us back to Boston is my job. After that, I can fall apart."

"I wish I could drive, but—"

"It's okay. This was my idea."

"Still, I'm sorry."

There was nothing more to say, so Davina drove in pained silence. Every now and then, her breath hitched, but her eyes were dry as she took us from New Hampshire to Massachusetts and back into the city. She dropped me off first and I hugged her, not knowing what to say. It was almost like we were sisters in sorrow by this point, but it wouldn't surprise me if she switched schools and chose never to see me again.

"Thanks for coming with me."

"I wish it hadn't ended like this."

She ignored that. "I'll see you next week."

Taking that as my cue, I hopped out of the car, in no hurry to climb the stairs to our apartment. If my dad's response was anything to judge by, parental doomsday awaited.

It was the first time in my life I could remember getting in trouble. *First Brittany, now Russ. How do I stop it? Oh God, how do I live with it?* A whimper slid out of me as I went up the stairs. After I let myself in, I found both my parents waiting on the lumpy sofa.

"Edith," my mother said.

Then something happened that I could never have expected. I would've been less shocked by another ice age. Both my mom and dad got off the couch and hugged me.

A DEMON,
DREAMING

True to her word, Davina didn't show up at school the rest of the week. The following Monday, Blackbriar issued an official statement that another student, Russell Thomas, had died, but they didn't release any additional information or disclose that it had been suicide. I didn't tell and I doubted Davina did either, but the rumor mill got word anyway. The most popular version was that Brittany had been cheating on Cameron with Russ, and when she died, he killed himself in grief.

If Cameron looked bad before, he was a wreck this morning. It looked like he had slept in his uniform and he'd given up eating and bathing. I noticed people circling around him in the hall, as if his funk might be contagious. *This is exactly what you asked for,* that tiny, insidious voice whispered. I squeezed my eyes shut and rested my head against the cool metal of my locker. My stomach hurt while my pulse pounded out a damning rhythm.

Guilty. Guilty.

The telltale heart refrain stretched my nerves to the breaking point. As the day wore on, the shadow over the school darkened. Mr. Love seemed inappropriately cheerful, whistling in the hallways and beaming broad smiles as if he could lift people's spirits just by existing. He paused as he spotted me and watched me walk away, the smile fading to a whitened compression of lips. There was something horrible in his eyes, none of the studied and careful concern, more of a dreadful anticipation, like when a storm chaser straps into his van, knowing destruction is imminent.

Or you might be imagining things.

As promised, Nicole Johnson had failed a couple of quizzes, so she was always in his classroom: reading, studying enrichment materials, or doing extra credit. There was nothing overtly wrong with it since he left the door open and she sat at her desk, but Nicole didn't look right anymore. Her face was pale, eyes blank and circled with rings. It bothered me most that she'd stopped tending her once-shining blond hair, so now it hung in lank strings and she no longer wore her uniform with sexy flair. *That's just not like her.* But if I tried to warn anyone, they'd think she was just depressed and nursing a hopeless crush.

"Talk about giving up." Allison spoke at my shoulder, studying Nicole with disdain. "It's pathetic and embarrassing to watch."

"What is?"

"Nic pining over Colin, like she has a shot."

Like you do with Cameron? With effort I choked the bitchy reply because lately it seemed that every horrible thing I whispered came true in some form. I didn't want to believe the horror was inside the house, so to speak, but if *I* was the source of the darkness at Blackbriar, then I had to keep my mouth shut.

"She looks sick," I said.

"No shit." With a curl of her perfectly lipsticked mouth, Allison brushed past me and headed to her next class.

But I didn't mean it as she thought, not that Nicole was disgusting. On closer inspection, she seemed pale and weak, physically ill. *Like something's sucking the life out of her.* I was willing to bet Colin Love was the leech draining her dry.

During lunch, I went to the library instead of the cafeteria. Unable to believe I was about to do this, I sighed and typed two words into the search bar: psychic vampires. Each time someone went by I covered my screen, guilty as a sophomore trying to disable the browser locks to look at porn. But I read all kinds of crazy stuff about creatures who fed on energy, not blood, and didn't have the weaknesses associated with the traditional kind. *They seem completely human, but tragedy, discord, and despair follows in their wake. You will know these demons because they are not born of woman and have no navel.*

"That's the dumbest thing I've ever heard." I tapped my fingers on the cubbyhole that held the computer I was using.

"What is?" Jen asked.

I jerked, surprised to find her at my shoulder and already reading the screen. *Shit.* My mind went blank, and I waited for her to head off to tell everyone how crazy I was.

"You write fic too?"

I didn't answer, and her tentative smile widened into a grin. "Come on, it can't be worse—or weirder—than mine. I have like a hundred and eighty thousand words devoted to Draco."

"Wow." The light came on. Obviously I knew about fanfic, and I read it for my favorite pairings, but I'd never written any. "Uhm. Actually this is research."

"For a story?"

Relief spilled through me, softening my locked shoulders. "You got me. I've never done any creative writing and I thought it might help to do some reading first."

"It's best to jump in," Jen advised, perching on the chair next to me. "If you think about it too much, you'll get nervous. Just make everything up and check your facts later."

"Okay."

I wasn't sure if that was good writing advice, but she seemed really excited, so I put the computer to sleep and followed her out of the library. Break was almost over anyway, and she had a lot to say about my alleged project.

"From what you were looking at, I'm guessing it's paranormal. I can't remember if I've ever read about psychic vampires, but bloodsuckers were really popular for a while. Do your mind-leeches sparkle?"

I thought of Colin Love and his air of predatory malice. "Nope."

"That's probably best if this isn't fanfic."

"No, it's original." *And completely problematic. I can't take much more.* If the opposition was behind this, then they were winning. Honestly, for me, that would be the best possible outcome, because it meant Kian hadn't betrayed me, and I'd brought the darkness through the deal, not careless, malicious words. It would be easier to bear if that were so. *If bad things were happening because of Wedderburn, because I wished them true . . .*

I shook my head and gave Jen my full attention.

"If you want me to look at it once you finish, I'll be happy to. I'm in an online group, but it'd be cool to have a local crit partner too. We can trade feedback."

"If I ever do. Right now it feels like there's no solution to my problem." That wasn't what I meant to say; it just came out.

"Oh, are you stuck on the plotting?"

"Definitely."

"Then tell me your scenario and I'll see if I can figure it out. I'm really good at this. There's a professional writer in my group, and I help her sometimes."

"It's kind of complicated."

"Then we can Skype about it tonight."

Remembering Vi . . . and Ryu, I wasn't so sure it was a good idea to confide in Jen, even on a theoretical level.

"Maybe. Hey, there's Davina. I haven't seen her since—"

"Yeah." Her face lost the animation my supposed story had generated. "We should hang out with her."

I nodded and headed toward the other girl. Though she had always been thin, there was a new air of fragility about her, as if one more blow could break her. *The Teflon crew are dropping fast.* The impulse came on too strong to resist; right there in the hall, I hugged Davina and she gave as good as she got.

"Thanks. I didn't see you at lunch."

"Yeah, sorry. I didn't know you were coming back today."

"I didn't want to, but my mom said a week was as long as she was giving me for a boyfriend I never introduced to her."

That's on Russ.

"I doubt my mom would give me a day, even if she did meet him," Jen said.

"I need to talk to you two." I'd never skipped, but we could hide on campus. The grounds were spacious enough that if you didn't pass the gate, it was impossible to find you before class ended.

"I don't want to be here anyway," Davina muttered.

Jen didn't answer, but she must've been curious because she

270

followed me out. There was a steady stream of students walking between buildings, but I didn't turn toward the Stinkatorium or the science complex. Instead I found us a quiet corner, nestled in the trees, out of sight from the main building. The groundskeeper was working on the other side of the property today, so we had some time. In the distance, I heard the final bell ring.

"So what's up?" Jen asked.

I took a deep breath. Now I'd find out if they were really my friends. If not, my insanity would hit the fan and splatter all over school by the end of the day. The prospect didn't even bother me, as things had gotten so screwed up that the idea of people saying mean things seemed like the *least* horrible consequence.

"I don't think it's a coincidence, what happened to Russ and Brittany." With judicious editing, I managed to tell the story without making it sound ridiculous. I concluded, "If you notice, it all started after that new teacher arrived."

"You think Mr. Love is doing terrible things to students?" Davina sounded skeptical.

"I don't have any proof," I said. "But I'm concerned about you two. I mean, if I'm right and he's taking revenge for someone else, then something bad could happen to you and Davina. In all honesty, Allison and Cam should be worried as well."

But I don't like them well enough to warn them.

"Should we talk to them?" Jen asked.

I nodded. "I doubt they'd listen to me, but I hope they'll take you or Davina seriously."

"We'll try," Davina promised.

I had no idea if the Lit teacher had anything to do with this, but I couldn't dump a supernatural conspiracy on them, especially with me

271

at the center. If I mentioned sides and game pieces, immortal monsters, diabolical corporations, and faceless evil, they'd just point and laugh before leaving. Davina and Jen traded a look while I dug at my cuticles, aware how sketchy this sounded. But their prior response seemed encouraging.

"There *is* something going on," Jen said softly.

Davina was nodding. "The school feels different this year."

So I wasn't the only one who'd noticed. "I was so sure you'd both tell me I've been reading too much horror."

"Then there was the thing you claimed you didn't see at my house," Jen went on. "By the way, you're full of shit."

"I'm sorry. I didn't know what else to say."

Jen peeled a strip of bark from a nearby tree. "I can't believe I'm even asking this, but . . . do you think Mr. Love is a brain limpet?"

I could almost resent how well their minds worked, considering how naturally pretty they were too. "Yeah. It sounds crazy, I know."

Davina shook her head. "Nothing has been right since school started. Russ changed as soon as we hit Blackbriar."

"All I know is, I don't want anything happening to the two of you," I said. "If there's any way you can get out of Boston—"

"I'll see what I can do." Davina didn't look hopeful, though. Given her scholarship, her parents would probably feel as if leaving would be the same as throwing away her future.

Jen said, "I might be able to convince my parents to let me visit my grandmother in Thailand, especially if I claim I had a dream about her. My mom's a hardass but she's really into signs and omens."

"If you can't get away, just . . . be careful, okay?"

"Definitely. I'll keep an eye on Mr. Love too." Stepping out from the trees, Davina shaded her eyes with one hand. "It looks like we've got company."

I saw him too. The groundskeeper turned us over to the teacher in charge of miscreants, who then escorted us to see the headmaster. I couldn't muster up a smidge of regret for missing class, however, as this had been a matter of life and death. We all listened to the lecture, but he went easy on us because it was a first offense, and he allowed that we were probably upset.

"Very," Davina said with tearful eyes, and she wasn't faking.

He dismissed us in time for last period, along with an admonishment not to let it happen again. I worried through my last class and practically sprinted to my locker to get my stuff. It felt like ages since Kian had picked me up after school last week, but there had been no date this weekend since I was grounded. The joint hug from my parents had been startling; my punishment was not. For good measure, they'd confiscated my computer and my phone, so I hadn't heard from him either.

Today, Kian was waiting as close to the gate as he could without being on school property. Two strides carried him to my side and he pulled me into his arms. Burying my face in his chest, I breathed him in, lemons and spice from his soap. He kissed the top of my head and then we moved toward his car.

"Missed you," he said.

"I'm still on restriction for another week," I said.

His gaze ran over me like it had been much longer than a weekend. "I can take you straight home . . . or I can show you my new place."

Temptation sashayed toward me and flashed a come-hither look. It was so easy to give in, such a relief from the relentless awfulness of my life otherwise. "I can realistically claim about an hour before my parents guess we took a detour. Will it take long?"

"Not if I leave the car here. We can swing by the condo and then I'll take you home via Express Way." The faint smile curving his mouth told me he was proud of that pun. Better yet, anyone who overheard us wouldn't think it was a weird thing to say.

Luckily, showing me his new apartment fell under the heading of company business. I imagined Wedderburn rasping a cold chuckle as Kian charmed me according to instructions. *But that's exactly what's happening.* God, I hated myself for each little pinprick of doubt. Kian had taken so many risks for me over the past weeks and had never shown a hint that he was on anyone's side but mine. I pushed all of the bad feelings out on a long breath.

"Let's go."

For the sake of appearances, he moved the car away from the school and parked on a residential street a few blocks away. Then he took my hand and pressed a button on his watch. We ported immediately, the world zooming out of focus in a stutter-skip that always unbalanced me. I stumbled a few steps, my head spinning as I took in pale walls and hardwood floors. A glance out the window told me I wasn't far from Fenway.

"You got a place in my neighborhood?"

"I want to be nearby." The ache in his voice made me want to kiss him.

Kian walked me through; it was a two bedroom with a galley kitchen—nothing remarkable, but less isolated than the cabin. The furniture looked as if he'd bought someone's rental property, including all contents. I supposed that made sense. But the result was another impersonal place, nothing unique to Kian.

"It needs some color. And some clutter. You need to set out your trophies and hang up your certificates. Put your books on the shelves. Dump your poetry journal on the end table. Start *writing* again. In other words, stop hiding who you are in a storage unit."

He went to the window and leaned his head against the glass. I could taste the sadness in him, heavy and rolling like the sea. "If I do, then the next time something awful happens, I lose everything. I'm not as strong as you seem to think."

Neither of us is unbreakable. We shattered, but we put the pieces back together, and I love the way your fractures shine. I came up behind him and put my palm between his shoulder blades. A quiver ran through him at my touch; sometimes I felt as if he were a piano tuned to my hands.

"I don't think you're a superhero or anything. But . . . sometimes you have to draw the line and fight for your ground. *Fight*, Kian. Take something for your own."

He whirled then, lightning in his eyes. *"You're* the only ground I won't yield, Edie. Everything else is dust, and each time I walk away from you, I'm afraid it's the last. You don't know the deals I've made, the—" Swallowing hard, he clenched a fist. "Never mind. I shouldn't have said that."

"I think you'd better tell me exactly what you mean."

He stepped into my space and tangled his hands in my hair, tipping my face up. I should've insisted on an answer, but when he looked at me like *that* it was impossible for me to think. *"You're* mine. How's that?"

"It's good," I whispered.

"I'll fight for you. I'll draw all the lines around you. I've"—he brushed his lips teasingly, delicately, across mine—"never felt this way before."

When I went up on tiptoe to kiss him back, kiss him more, he spun me and pressed me against the window. I twined my arms around his neck and held on; the longing was honey sweet and ferocious like a storm. He tasted me and I ran my hands over his shoulders and down his back, digging in with my fingers, because this feeling just couldn't be real. Kian made a soft sound against my mouth, a growl or a whimper, and I shivered against him.

"I should take you home," he whispered. "Or I won't at all. I want you to stay."

"I can't. Not yet."

"I know. Your life is complicated enough."

Shaky nod, as I reached for him. He claimed my hand and whooshed us to the alley we'd used to depart for the SSP. "I'll never get used to that."

"And I'll never get enough of you." Kian devoured another kiss and another, until my knees went weak. Until meeting him, I hadn't known longing for another person could come as a physical ache.

"Wow." I swallowed hard and then hurried away before I begged him to take me back to his apartment.

It was crazy that I had to weigh everything now in terms of cause and effect. A night with Kian would be amazing, but I had enough stress in my life. When we slept together, I wanted the timing to be right. After waiting this long, sex shouldn't be one of my regrets.

NORMAL IS
ANOTHER COUNTRY

Blackbriar might be under a cloud, but for the rest of my imprisonment, it didn't storm. The silence made me uneasy, however, and things were lonely at school, as Davina and Jen were MIA. I hoped that meant they'd persuaded their parents to send them elsewhere, at least for a while. I checked my messages, but there was nothing in my in-box.

Vi was still around, at least. Tuesday night, we talked on Skype. "How are the dreams?" I asked.

"After I sent off my college applications, they totally stopped. Must've been stress."

I suspected it had more to do with burning my second favor, but relief cascaded through me so hard, I got a headrush. "I need to send my stuff in, deadlines are approaching."

"I figured you'd be done already."

"No, I'm still putting the package together. I can't get my essay right." Truth was, I hadn't even tried to write one.

"Don't let it paralyze you. Just pick a theme and run with it."

"Thanks. I'll see if I can get everything out next week."

We chatted a little longer, then I disconnected to get ready for bed. When I went to the bathroom, I left my bedroom door cracked, but when I came back, it was closed. My heart skittered in my chest like it was full of mice. For a few seconds, I stood in the hall, staring.

"Something wrong?"

I spun to find my mother standing behind me. "No, I was just thinking."

"About how ill-considered your behavior has been lately, I hope."

"Obviously."

Normally she wasn't good at picking up sarcasm, but both brows went up. "Edith, you haven't been yourself this fall. Do you want to talk to a specialist?"

I had no idea what she meant by that. "A psychologist or a brain doctor?"

"Whichever you think would be most helpful."

The secrets I had locked in my head would only land me in the psych ward, if the shrink pried them out of me, and an MRI couldn't solve these problems. So I shook my head. "Sorry, Mom. I think the college admission process is getting to me."

Any mention of university usually diverted Mom into a lecture, but she didn't take the bait this time. "Do you have a minute to talk?" She sounded oddly tentative.

"Sure." Bemused, I followed her into the living room. Before sitting down, she made us both a cup of tea.

"I feel like I don't know what to do with you anymore."

"That's an ominous beginning. I've been more trouble than usual lately, but—"

"I don't mean we're on the verge of shipping you off to boarding

278

school." She fiddled with the fringe on the afghan dangling from the back of the couch. "It's hard for me to say this, but I perceive I haven't been what you need, emotionally, as a mother."

Oh Jesus. A year ago, I would've loved to have this conversation with her. Now it was too late, though not for the reasons she feared. I fidgeted, picking up a pillow and clutching it to my chest, as if stuffing and fabric was a shield for awkwardness.

"You're fine," I mumbled.

"That's nice of you, but it's not true. I thought if we sent you to a good school and let you form your own emotional attachments while giving you space that would be enough. I can see now that it wasn't."

Part of me wanted to ask where this epiphany was before I ended up on the bridge, but I swallowed it along with a sudden ache in my throat. "I'm not sure where you're going with this."

Her face fell, but she soldiered gamely on. "I want us to have a better relationship, a closer one. We have science in common, at least. I don't know much about your new interests, but I could stand to be more physically fit. Maybe we could work out together? There's a nice facility at the university . . ." She bit her lip, sad and hopeful at the same time.

Nice olive branch, Mom. I could either accept it or set it on fire. Since I hadn't run in the morning since the creepiness started, I nodded. "We could go a couple of times in the afternoon and then maybe on Saturdays?"

"I'd like that. And . . . I wouldn't hate it if you have time to teach me some things about doing my face. For parties?"

No more fugly red lipstick, Mom.

"That would be fun." Not a word I typically used to describe anything related to my mother. "You're an autumn, you know."

Her unshaped brows shot up. "I'm a what now?"

"One step at a time."

She wore a tentative smile, and I studied her. Her hair was a frazzled russet, badly in need of a good cut and some deep conditioning. For as long as I could remember, she had worn it in a messy knot. She was round, but not seriously overweight; she had the body of someone who didn't move around a lot, understandable given how much of her time she spent writing on whiteboards and poring over legal pads.

"Would it be all right if I hugged you?"

For some reason, that choked me up. Tears rose to my eyes as I set aside the throw pillow. "You don't have to ask. You can, anytime you want."

I wish you did it more.

She smelled like lilac talcum powder when she reached over and squeezed me around the shoulders. "Your father and I love you very much. And we're so proud of you, Edith."

Exhaling in a shaky rush, I put my head on her shoulder. Her lumpy cardigan scratched my cheek, but it was a good five minutes before I moved. "Let's hit the gym Thursday afternoon, okay?"

Mom actually looked misty when she nodded. "I'll meet you there. We can swing by and grab takeout for dinner afterward, give your dad a break from cooking."

If I was teaching her about hair and makeup, then I should ask to trade. "Maybe, if you have time, you could show me something about electrical sockets? And plumbing?"

"I'd be glad to. A woman should never—"

"Depend on a man if she's capable of learning how to do something herself."

She looked so surprised when I finished her sentence, then she burst out laughing. "It's good to know I haven't been shouting my wisdom down a well all these years."

"Nope. Night, Mom."

Wednesday was a good day, maybe because I was happy, and I just . . . didn't think about the problems squatting on the horizon. Even pawns on a chessboard needed a day off now and then. I pretended I had Pandora's box inside and shoved all the horrible feelings into it. On Thursday morning, Davina came back to school, and it astonished me how relieved I was. I wove through the crowd toward her.

"You back?"

Glumly she nodded. "I talked my mom into letting me see a therapist, but the traitorous bastard said the best thing for me was to get back on the horse that threw me."

"Huh?"

"Coming back to school will prevent me from forming some kind of aversive phobia." She yanked down a pink sign-up sheet with more than a hint of violence. "Oh, look. Allison's gone wheels-up with her *coup d'état* and tryouts are tomorrow afternoon. I haven't practiced at *all*, so I'll be lucky to be mascot, after three years of taking their shit. God, sometimes I hate them *so* much."

"Why didn't you just make new friends?" I asked.

"Russ," she said miserably. "God, I'd liked him since I was a freshman and he barely knew I was alive."

"You don't have to go out for the squad. Let Allison have it."

She shook her head, wearing a ferocious frown. "Screw that. If I don't make it, then it's like I wasted *all* of that time and she wins."

"What can I do to help?"

"Try out with me."

I cackled, until I realized she was serious. "Why, to make you look better by comparison when I fall on my butt?"

"Partly," she admitted. "But also for moral support. *Please*, Edie."

"What the hell." I liked Davina, apparently well enough to make an ass of myself in solidarity. "How long does it last? I need to tell Kian I'll be late tomorrow."

"Depends on when they call you to perform, but allow an hour."

"Awesome."

"You need an original cheer and then you'll also be scored on how fast you learn the routine, along with the rest of your group. I don't suppose you can do a backflip?"

"I can *walk* backward. Sort of."

Davina smiled and slung an arm around my shoulders. "I would *not* be okay if you weren't around this year. I'm glad we're friends."

She had no idea how much those four words meant to me . . . or how scared I was that something evil might be listening. I was like some kind of disaster demon, one touch, and the contagion spread, inky tendrils of malevolence creeping toward those I cared about. Still, I didn't shift away because Davina needed the contact as much as I did; it took all of her bravado to pretend the stories about Russ weren't breaking her heart, mostly because none of them included a whisper of what they'd been to each other for one sweet, short summer.

"My mom and I are hitting the gym this afternoon," I said. "Maybe you could come along and afterward, you and I can work on something for the tryout?"

"Let me ask," she said. "I'll get back to you at lunch."

Company at the table was thin: just Cameron, Davina, Allison, and me. Russ's lacrosse pals sat elsewhere, as if they sensed the dark cloud hovering over the Teflon crew. Since Russ had bound them together, they'd separated into sub-cliques. Everyone was quiet, and after eating, I left, disturbed by the wreck Cameron had become. I understood his grief; in a short time he'd lost both his girlfriend and the person he'd thought was his best friend. A pang went through me at how I'd used Allison to deliver Russ's barb about why they hung around with Cam.

"I'm with you," Davina said, catching up as I hurried toward my locker. "I'm thinking we find a new table. I don't even like anyone who's left. Well, besides you."

"Yeah. Sometimes you have to know when to let things go."

If only I'd learned that lesson sooner. But the promise of revenge got me through the weeks after the bridge and by the time school started again, I had some distance. If I hadn't cared about getting even, I might not have taken the deal. *Is your life worth so many others?* It was too heavy a question to carry, so I set it aside and crammed it inside the metaphysical crate in my head.

"My mom said we can hang out, by the way. But she wants yours to call her, just to confirm we'll have parental supervision."

"That's what happens when you lie and go to New Hampshire instead of the library," I said, imitating my dad.

"I'm well aware, trust me."

Before I went to class, I texted Kian that I didn't need a ride. I felt bad making him chauffeur me around when I had plans with other people, so I told him I'd be with Davina and my mom at the gym. He replied, I wouldn't mind giving you and Davina a ride but it's fine. I'll move my stuff out of storage today instead.

That made me smile as I replied, Does that mean you'll read me another poem?

Maybe.

When I put my phone away, Davina was smirking at me. "Girl, you so can't get enough of what he got."

"You learn that grammar at Blackbriar?"

"Obviously."

I smiled at her. "See you after school."

We met up at the gate; Davina arrived first and we took the T to my place. She soaked everything in with an interested look. "I can tell your parents are teachers."

The jumble of science journals and notepads no longer registered on me, but to someone else, it probably looked messy. "Professors, actually. Physics." I'd mentioned it before, but maybe it didn't sink in.

"Damn. No wonder nobody can touch you in that class."

Since I'd invited her at the last minute, she needed workout gear. My T-shirt and yoga pants were a little big on her, but since the point was to sweat, it didn't matter. It was odd having her in my room—two worlds colliding—but she didn't say anything about all my scientist posters or my piles of books. Relieved, I texted my mom: I'm on my way with Davina. Be there soon.

Okay. I'll head over.

Introductions were awkward since my mom *knew* I went AWOL with Davina, but she fixed it with, "You must think I'm a bad influence, but I want you to know I'll never ask Edie to do anything like that again. I hope you'll give me another chance."

Mom smiled. "Everyone makes mistakes, Davina, and yours was understandable. I'm glad to meet you."

"Do you mind calling my mother to reassure her I'm with you?" She dialed and offered her cell with a sheepish look.

"Not a problem." Mom waited for the call to connect, then said, "Hello, this is Mildred Kramer, Edie's mom. I'm verifying that the girls are here. We're working out this afternoon." A pause. "Absolutely."

Davina took the phone back. "I should be home by seven, latest. See you then."

Faculty got a discount at the fitness and rec center, so my parents kept our membership active, though only my dad used it regularly. He said doing mindless reps helped him think through thorny problems. We bypassed the classes and went directly to the equipment, where we spent forty-five minutes sweating. Afterward, I felt good, loose and limber.

"Still up for choreographing a routine?" Davina asked.

"Absolutely." That might be an overstatement, but I *had* promised.

After her shower, my mom watched us with an expression of bemusement. "Are you two in a talent competition?"

I laughed. "In my case, more like un-talent."

"You're not . . . horrible," she said, probably trying to be supportive. "You just need practice. Davina has obviously put more time into . . . whatever you're doing."

"It's for cheer tryouts," Davina answered.

My mom froze, as if I had confessed to a secret meth addiction. "Is this true, Edith?"

"I'm not really trying to make the squad. I'm just going to support Davina."

"Ah." Apparently she could get behind feminine camaraderie. Mom sat down on a mat nearby and half watched us practice for another hour while tapping on her tablet.

By the end of that time, *I* was no better, but Davina seemed to have her routine down. We didn't have any clothes to change into anyway, so I said, "We can go now if you want. Thai takeout for dinner?"

Mom nodded. "Pad thai sounds good."

"I wish I could stay, but my folks are expecting me." Shrugging, Davina made a what-can-you-do face.

Outside, I gave her a hug. "See you at school."

"Do you want us to walk you to the station?" Mom asked.

Davina grinned. "I've been on the T by myself before, but thanks anyway."

Since it was getting dark, my mom insisted. Davina seemed torn between appreciation and annoyance. At the subway steps, she merged into the throng of college students with a cheery wave. I talked my mom into a haircut on the way home and then I dragged her into a store that sold mineral makeup. I knew she wouldn't stick to a complicated beauty regimen, but dusts and powders wouldn't take long. All told, by the time we picked up the Thai food, it was pretty late, close to eight before we got home. It was also the most fun I could remember having with my mom in years.

"We have to do that again soon," she said. "Saturday afternoon?"

"Definitely. I'll show you how to use the stuff we bought, if you want."

She hugged me again, this time without asking. "You probably think I'm odd for not knowing any of this, but . . . I remember once, when I was eleven, my mother got me *only* beauty products for Christmas. She got me a curling iron, hair spray, fancy brushes, hot rollers, eye shadow. When I opened all my packages, I pretended to be thankful, then I went to my room and cried. I thought she was saying that I wasn't good enough or pretty enough—that it wasn't enough for me to be smart."

Wow. I never knew that. "So you turned your back on all girlie stuff. I get it."

"But . . . it's fun with you."

"I don't let it rule my life or anything, but I like feeling pretty."

"So do I," Mom admitted quietly. "But I never thought I was, so no point in trying."

"You should never give up," I said, conscious of the irony of me saying that. But I had come to believe it.

"So when you came home this summer, I was taken aback. It felt like you were trying to tell me something. Then I realized I was transferring old hurts. If I'd known you were interested in a makeover, maybe we could've worked on it together. I just never wanted to make you feel like my mom did me. I always wanted you to feel that however you are, it's okay with me."

"Thanks, Mom." I was almost crying, unable to see for the stinging in my eyes.

In that moment, I desperately wanted to tell her everything. Fear for her safety kept me silent, along with remorse over what I might've done. She seemed to think so highly of me; I couldn't stand to tarnish that image. To give me time to recover, she patted my head and went to talk to my dad. I went to my room for five minutes to settle down.

Dinner was lively; I actually paid attention when they were talking about the new project and to my surprise, I had ideas to contribute. My mom made notes while my dad treated me like I was a genius. *I could get used to this.* If working with my parents led to my optimum future, at the moment, I didn't feel like fighting.

Now and then, the Pandora's box in my head slammed from side to side, thoughts of Brittany and Russ trying to escape. I didn't let them. There was no other way I could cope. *I have to push forward. If I quit, they win.* Stubbornness kept me in school, still turning in work.

Friday, cheerleading tryouts went every bit as bad for me as I'd anticipated. I didn't screw up my personal routine, but I had zero aptitude for learning choreography. Though I didn't fall down, that was about all that could be said for my performance. Davina, on the other, was like a rocket, bright, on point, and utterly graceful. If the teachers who picked the squad didn't put her on the A-list, then I could only assume they had already accepted bribes from parents who wanted a cheerleader in the family.

"You feel good about your chances?" I asked her afterward.

"You know . . . I do. Thank you." She hugged me.

That made the ordeal worth it.

Saturday morning, I had the SAT. Fortunately, I was no longer grounded and I didn't have to explain that the test I claimed to have aced last spring, I never took. I felt like I did well, but I wouldn't find out for a while. Then I met my mom for lunch near the university, and after our food settled, we went to the fitness center, nothing extraordinary, but these were things I'd rarely done with my mother.

This is normal. Feels like another country.

But . . . I could get used to living here.

THE DARK SIDE
DOES NOT HAVE
COOKIES

A week later, Davina and I stood in front of the list Miss Tina, the cheerleading coach, had just posted. Girls clustered around, making it impossible to see, so I pushed my way to the front as the crowd thinned. Occasionally excited squees popped up, but most of the hopefuls trudged off with their dreams crushed.

I ran my fingertip down the page. "There you are on the varsity list."

"No way." She bounced forward and then danced in a circle when she confirmed.

Unsurprisingly, I didn't even make alternate, but since that wasn't the point, I didn't care. "Happy?"

"Yeah! Surprised, though. I honestly thought this crap was fixed."

Maybe some slots, but Blackbriar cared about trophies, which meant they needed some athletic girls on the squad. Otherwise, they'd be screwed later in the year. She got out her phone, already dialing to tell her mom. This was the happiest she'd been since Russ died.

I'd expected Kian to make up for lost time, but he was busy with classes—or so he claimed. Instead of spending time together, I got texts and Snapchats, like we were in a long-distance relationship.

That week I also got an e-mail from Jen.

Hope you're happy. I'm in THAILAND. With my grandmother.
My mom told her about what happened to Brittany and now
I spend my mornings lighting candles in shrines and temples.
I'm finishing the semester online, but Blackbriar is holding my
spot. I'll be back after winter break.

We miss you, I sent back. And I'm sorry if this was all in my head. If
so, I'll get help.

Her answer came the next day. I don't think it was.

That was all she said, but it reassured me that she didn't hate me for sending her into exile. Mr. Love still watched me and Nicole looked more and more like a ghost, but the rest of Blackbriar got back to normal. Every night, Davina had cheerleading practice and, like Kian, I joined drama, not because I wanted to act, but it might help with college applications. I also spent more time with my parents between working out with Mom and talking about the laser array they were working on. Their theories on time travel and alternate realities were kind of fascinating, especially when paired with actual hypotheses.

With his increased workload and me in extracurriculars, I saw Kian even less; he picked me up twice a week, Mondays and Fridays. Sometimes we went out on weekends, but he seemed . . . different. Since he'd showed me his apartment, there was a new distance between us. Though he'd told me he was unpacking his boxes, he hadn't invited me over again to see how it turned out.

The resulting quiet felt more like the calm before the storm than a permanent peace. While I planned for college, studied, and spent time with my mom, I feared the silence would be shattered by a scream—or a disaster of such epic proportions that the enemy needed time to put all the pieces in play. Kian's remoteness only reinforced that impression. He denied anything had changed and he said the right words, but sometimes I caught him looking at me with an ocean of grief shining from his eyes. His words came back to me in quiet moments:

I am afraid.

Of what?

Having you. Losing you.

But I couldn't let sorrow or worry keep me from living. Otherwise all of this had been for nothing. So, even knowing things weren't . . . right, I had to persevere. I'd never give up again.

• • •

A week after I took the SAT, I confronted him about it. "Kian, what's going on?"

"Nothing, why?"

"You're different."

He just smiled and kissed me.

No matter what I said, he refused to open up. So I resigned myself to letting him tell me what was wrong in his own time. The distance hurt, even as it reassured me that I could trust him: I suspected he was shielding me from something bad . . . and I let him.

I wish I hadn't.

It took about three weeks for my SAT results to arrive, and I grabbed the envelope from the mailbox before my parents saw it.

Hiding in my room, I opened it alone, relieved to find my scores were high enough to get me into my school of choice, provided the rest of my application package lined up. I spent the next week scribbling my essay and then I sent the packets, grateful I could do most of it online. I used my mom's Visa to pay the application fees, and then it was oddly anticlimactic. Replies should start in January; I finally felt like maybe I had made up for lying to my parents for all those months.

Apart from the tension between Kian and me, things were looking up. I still felt terrible about what happened to Brittany and Russ, but the tinnitus I had noticed around him made me question whether it was my fault. And if his death wasn't related to me, maybe her illness wasn't either. *I want so much for that to be true.* Some days, I could almost convince myself that was the case, and it let me carry on. But wishful thinking didn't explain Mr. Love at all, so I couldn't entirely accept the coincidence theory. Deep down, I was waiting for the third calamity, like Davina's grandma predicted.

The day before Halloween, I noticed that the bizarre events had slowed way down. They didn't stop entirely, or I would've caught on faster; sometimes I glimpsed the thin man on the subway platform, but he didn't approach me. Belatedly, Kian's words echoed in my head: *You don't know the deals I've made*—to keep me safe or to stop the attacks? I was afraid to ask if he'd contacted somebody at Dwyer & Fell. God only knew what Wedderburn would do if he suspected Kian was a traitor. But maybe I had already gone off course, so the opposition had no reason to stalk me anymore. If so, I wouldn't find out until graduation when Wedderburn informed me that I'd become a waste of time, and I could earn my keep by offering deals to people in extremis.

Sadly, that might be the best-case scenario.

With that possibility whirling in my head, I was glad when Davina distracted me by bounding up to my locker wearing a smile. I still caught a melancholy look now and then, but since the rumors were now centered on Nicole Johnson instead of Russ and Brittany, it was easier for her to pretend not to be heartbroken. I thought it best to go along.

"What's up?" I asked.

"Party at Cameron's tomorrow. His parents are never around, but this has their stamp of approval, so it's high-end, big-budget scary. I wasn't even sure he'd do it this year."

"No invites, not even online or whatever?" Since I had attended zero parties in my life, I was well aware that I might sound stupid.

Davina shook her head. "Pretty much everyone knows about it. If you know how to get to the house, you don't get kicked out on Halloween."

"Costumes?"

"Definitely. You'll go, right?"

"Why not?" I could work out with my mom on Saturday afternoon, talk physics with my dad . . . and miss date night with Kian.

I don't even know if he'll mind. My heart ached.

"Sweet. My mom can drive us, if you want. I guarantee she won't let me have the car, and she'll want to make sure I'm going where I claim I am."

"The party won't be loud enough to make her change her mind?"

"Not if we get there early enough. I'll pick you up at half past six."

"Sounds good."

After school, Kian picked me up at the normal time, but he was even more preoccupied than usual. I seized on that as an excuse not to say anything until he parked outside my apartment. I'd never broken a date with him before, so I had no idea how it would go. If he acted like he didn't care, that'd be worse than hurting him. *Well, for me.*

"We still on for tomorrow night?" he asked.

At this point, we were regulars at the classic movie place in Harvard Square. A pang went through me as I shook my head. "Actually I'm going to a party with Davina."

Maybe I should invite him? We did have plans first.

Before I spoke, he smiled. "I have a term paper due anyway."

"For what class?"

"Magic, Science, and Religion." The easy answer made me think that he was lying, but it wasn't like I could demand proof. "Don't worry about it. We can go out next weekend."

"As long as you don't mind," I said.

"It's fine," he answered, smiling. "I want you to have friends. To have a life."

That sounded so much like, *Good luck with everything, Edie.* It felt like he was opening his hands, letting go of me. But I'd know if we were breaking up. Wouldn't I? Somehow I smiled and nodded, kissed him and climbed out of the car. My chest was tight, but I had no explanation for it.

Upstairs, my dad was working in the living room. He mumbled something as I went by, but he was deep in concentration and just lifted a hand that said, *I'm aware that you live here.* In my room, I tried not to think about Kian; instead I poked through my stuff, trying to decide what would work as a quick DIY costume. Briefly, I considered Ophelia, but that was too macabre, even for me, since I'd have been a dead girl floating in the river for real, if not for Kian. Plus, I didn't have any white flowing gowns.

"Dad!" I yelled.

"Hm?"

"Can I borrow one of your old lab coats?"

"Anything you find in my closet, you can have, if you don't bother me for an hour." Dad sounded vaguely impatient.

He and Mom had agreed they needed to be home more, or I might repeat my trip to New Hampshire. I didn't mind the attention, but it made my dad cranky, especially when it was his turn to play warden. However, since I'd been letting myself in for five years, it made for a nice change to have someone in the house when I got home from school.

"Anything, huh?"

From various boxes, I dug out a white lab coat, left from my dad's grad student days. He worked out when he remembered but even so, he wasn't nearly as thin as he had been then; my mom called it science-geek svelte. That went into my pile of costume components, along with protective goggles and a plaid bow tie. I had some black pants and if I added those to this stuff, plus my school shirt, I could mess up my hair and go as a mad scientist. It wasn't sexy or even cute, but it suited my personality more than devil's horns and a red leotard. All things considered, that also seemed a little on the nose.

Three hours later, a Skype request popped up from Ryu. I checked the time—early in Japan, so it was probably before school on his end. I accepted, smiling when he appeared on my laptop. His room was messy in the background, but his expression demanded my attention; he looked serious, nervous, even.

"What's wrong?"

"Tell your friend to be careful. She's mixed up in some scary shit."

"Huh?" *Oh, right.* I told him the picture I sent was a friend's tattoo.

Worry surged through me, mingling with anger that I had been rattled enough by the mirror girl to ask him about the mark.

Fortunately, he took that as a request for clarification. "It took me this long, but I was curious, so I didn't stop digging."

"Dammit, Ryu. I told you not to bother." *Now you might be on their radar if you weren't already.*

He made a rude gesture at his screen. "You're welcome. Anyway, do you want to hear what I found or not?"

"I guess."

"Good. I don't have much time before I have to catch my train. It's not a kanji per se, but a gang symbol, and it seems to be favored by men with ties to the Yakuza."

That tracked with what I knew about the immortals and their game. They chose individuals with great destinies, and from what I understood of the strategies, the Yakuza often made connections with powerful people in order to smooth the path for their operations. But I couldn't tell Ryu that. Best to pretend I didn't know anything about it.

"Wow, really? I wonder if she knew that when she picked it out?"

"Probably not. These things end up listed wrong, so some hipster wants the Chinese symbol for peace, and he gets the one for soup. Then Chinese people laugh at him."

Despite growing unease, I snickered. "That would be my luck."

"If you decide to get some ink, do your own research."

"I'll bear that in mind."

"One last thing," he said, as I reached to click off the call.

"What's that?"

"The mark has a fairly sinister meaning. The guy I talked to down in the market said it literally reads as 'Property of the Game,' and if I ever meet anyone who's marked with it, I should run like hell. Edie, is your friend in trouble?"

I closed my eyes briefly. "Maybe."

"Well, try not to get pulled into her drama." A woman called to him, likely his mom, and he yelled a reply. Then he leaned forward. "Talk to you later."

My screen went blank.

I stared at my left wrist, assessing the statement of ownership. Kian had warned me the marks couldn't be removed, and the infinity symbol hurt when I left Boston with Davina. Therefore, whatever I was supposed to do, it happened here. *So if I try to move—or go to school elsewhere, will it burn that bad, trying to keep me on track?* Obviously that must be a built-in guidance system, courtesy of Wedderburn.

With a muttered curse, I took a shower as if I could wash away my problems. That night, I chatted with Vi, and then I slept in on Saturday, nearly until noon. My mom woke me up to head to the gym. It was cool seeing how people reacted to her new look. Mom was rocking an asymmetrical bob and she'd started using both bronzer and lipstick in the mornings. A couple of professors totally checked her out as we rolled into the fitness center.

"Mr. Goatee has a thing for you," I said.

"Edith." She spoke in a chiding tone, but a smirk curved her mouth as she glanced over at the balding, forty-ish guy working on the elliptical across the way.

"Hey, I didn't say *you* were interested in him."

"These past weeks have been really fun," she said.

"Agreed. I'm glad you took the first step." There had been a lot more hugs in the past three weeks than in my whole life combined; I was looking forward to a bunch more.

"Me too."

After we sweated and showered, we took the T east. Fifteen minutes of walking and we splurged on lobster rolls and clam chowder, well worth the trip to James Hook & Co. The trailer made the setup look sketchy, but it was a pretty day, sunny enough to make it hard for me to believe some of the shit that had happened recently. Outdoor tables turned the meal into a bistro experience, and it was awesome watching people go by, even if the ambiance was a little . . . industrial. The Old Northern Avenue Bridge reinforced that impression.

Mom raised her drink. "It feels like we should celebrate. To new beginnings."

I smiled and tapped my soda can against hers, then dug into the delicious food. Halfway through my roll, I decided it was well worth fifteen bucks or whatever she paid. We took a walk before heading home in time for me to get ready for the party. Since my costume was simple, that was easy.

When I came into the living room, my dad made me pose for a picture. Both he and my mom laughed at my take on the mad scientist since my hair was more punk rock than eccentric genius. Still, it was better than showing up in my uniform and saying I was a schoolgirl. Davina arrived five minutes late and her mom came up with her, which delayed our departure another ten minutes.

"I'm Mrs. Knightly." She shook hands with my parents. She was a pretty African-American woman in her forties, well-dressed in a suit that said she hadn't changed out of work clothes yet.

They made small talk for a few minutes, and finally Davina lost her patience, dragging her mother toward the door. Mrs. Knightly lectured us on the way to Cameron's house about the importance of making good choices.

"I won't pretend I don't know there's going to be alcohol there, just don't come out so drunk that you puke in my car. Also? Don't leave your friend's place, and don't drink anything you didn't pour yourself."

"Got it," Davina said.

The drive took forty-five minutes, and the sky darkened as we crossed the city. Now and then, I caught sight of kids with their parents going door to door. This one night of the year, adults got away with marching around in vampire regalia. *They're probably on their way to costume parties too.* Bizarre, this was the one night of the year when the monsters could mix freely with humans and not draw a second look. Inexplicably, I shivered.

In the posh suburbs, Mrs. Knightly parked in front of a house fronted by a stone wall and a looming gate. "What time is curfew?" She sounded like this was a trick question.

"Midnight," Davina replied.

Her tone softened. "You two try to have fun, okay? I know it's been a tough year, but you have to put it behind you."

Easier said than done.

For Davina's sake, I'd try not to spoil the night. She was dressed as a leprechaun in a short green skirt, ankle boots, black tights, leotard, glittery makeup, and a tiny green bowler. Before I could say she looked good, she dragged me out of the car with a promise to be waiting here at precisely twelve.

The drive was asphalt, leading up to a classic new-money house, all modern convenience and no elegance, less charm. "Wow. That's . . . big."

"Right? I think I hear music. Come on." Davina led me around back, where there were lights strung up. The patio doors stood open and the interior flashed with black lights, casting weird, zombie-ish shadows over all the faces. Right now, the crowd was light, but we'd arrived early on purpose.

"Where's the booze?" she asked a random guy in a hockey mask.

The mass murderer pointed at a tin tub full of some murky mixture that looked too much like real blood for my comfort. "Seriously?"

He shrugged. "It's vodka and Kool-Aid, relax."

There was no way I was drinking that, but I took a cup so Davina wouldn't think I was a pain in the ass with a mental age of forty. "Is that a DJ over there?"

"Yep. No expense spared. Later, monsters will jump out at us and everyone runs around screaming. The party doesn't end until somebody calls the cops."

"But is there cake?" I was trying to be funny with the whole cake-is-a-lie meme.

"That's only propaganda. The dark side does *not* have cookies. Come on, let's rock."

FOR EVERY ACTION,
THERE IS A PUNCH
IN THE FACE

The Halloween bash got wild pretty fast. Nobody seemed impressed by my mad scientist gear, but plenty of guys tried to hook up with Davina. She blew them off to stick with me, which I appreciated since I didn't really know anyone else. By ten, people were hammered, taking off their clothes, making out with questionable partners and barfing in the bushes, usually not all at the same time. Awkward was my middle name as I skulked around the fringes; I had rarely felt more out of place.

I'd thought she was kidding, but a mob in monster masks poured out of the house at eleven. Drunk girls screamed and ran, turning the backyard into pure chaos. Between the shouting and music, I couldn't think. Davina was dancing on the patio, so I waved to her and gestured that I was going to the bathroom, but from what I'd seen, it was worse indoors. Every available surface was covered in people grinding. Given the other costumes, I could live without seeing more side boob tonight.

Should've gone out with Kian.

The thought didn't cheer me up as I rounded the corner of the house, looking for half an hour of solitude before I dragged Davina out front to wait for her mom. I found a gazebo nestled at the back of the property, where it was dark and quiet. The monsters playing tag on the lawn hadn't discovered it yet. With a sigh, I sat down on a padded chair before I realized I wasn't alone.

"Not enjoying the festivities?" From the smell, Cameron had been drinking long before his guests arrived.

"It's not really my thing."

"Mine either. Not anymore." With the careful movements of the totally shitfaced, he set his plastic cup on the floor. "Want to go for a walk?"

With you? Hardly trembled on the tip of my tongue, but his face was so ravaged, I couldn't kick him when he was already on the ground. "You obviously want to be alone, so let me find somewhere else to hide."

But he wasn't listening to me. "I don't understand how everything went to hell so fast. Last year I had everything. Last year—"

"You hurt me because you could."

He recoiled like I had punched him in the face. Part of me considered it; no matter how much I wanted to move on, I *couldn't* forgive him. Cameron stumbled to his feet, and I jumped up, putting some distance between us. On seeing my reaction, he stopped short, his hands up in some clumsy gesture I couldn't interpret. Out here, the shadows were too deep for me to read his expression.

"Edie—"

When the howl rang out, at first I thought it was more special effects for the party, but Cam looked blank, and two red eyes opened

302

in the darkness behind him. I raised a shaking hand to warn him, and he stumbled. A growl rumbled from the shadows.

"Wild dog?"

"I don't know," I whispered.

"If you run, I'll distract it." He turned slowly.

"That's a terrible plan. You can't even walk straight."

But it happened too fast for me to make it more than two steps. Smoke dogs swirled around Cam's ankles, real and not-real, hounds born of night with fangs like obsidian and eyes likes windows into hell. With each snap of their teeth, he faded a little more, not blood but shadow, until he was only an outline with a hand thrown out toward me.

"I'm sorry," the wind whispered. And then it fell silent too.

A single black dog stepped out of the smoke; this one had full shape and definition, probably gained from the life it stole from Cameron. It studied me with ember eyes, sniffed once, and then trotted away. Teeth chattering, I ran forward, patting the chair where Cam had been sitting, the floor where he'd set his drink, but . . . he was just . . . gone. My teeth chattered as I whirled and fled, back toward shrieking monsters and giggling girls.

What the hell just happened? Who can I tell? There was no body, no blood. Halfway there, I had to sit down with my head between my knees. That was where Davina found me, half an hour later. Probably thinking I was drunk, she hauled me to my feet, but when she didn't smell booze, she tapped my forehead.

"You high?"

"No. I'm freaking out."

"I can see that. Let's get you home, little hermit crab."

Maybe I should've corrected her and explained that it wasn't the

303

party that turned me into a trembling puddle of goo, but I couldn't find the words. So I sat in the back of her mom's car and shook, right up until they dropped me off. My thoughts ran in an endless, panicked, disjointed loop. *Cameron is gone. Cameron is never coming back.* And I was the only one who could give his parents peace of mind, but they wouldn't *believe* me.

I saw it, and I wouldn't either.

I mumbled my way through the parental inquiry, but my dad seemed reassured that I was sober and still wearing a bow tie. Hat tip for his savvy; it was hard to imagine hooking up without taking it off. Five minutes later, I escaped to my room while this fact battered against my brain: *You had just thought that you couldn't forgive him . . . when the hellhounds appeared. You're doing this. Somehow.*

Because I didn't know what else to do, I typed "hellhound" and then "black dog" into the search bar; it told me a bunch of legends and lore, including the fact that these dogs were nearly always a portent of death. Since it *killed* Cameron, that seemed logical. But I never heard any of that before just now, so why would my angry thoughts summon them? Pacing, I raked my hands through my hair. *Now that's the real mad scientist do.*

I need to do *something. This can't continue.*

Briefly, I considered the solution I'd chosen before, but I couldn't even complete the thought. *I want to live. Maybe it's wrong, but I just can't. Not now.* A true heroine wouldn't hesitate to give her life for someone else, but I wasn't painted with that stripe. Just as I'd come to that place out of weakness, now that my life was good, I couldn't throw it away, even to save people.

My knees gave out after a while, and I huddled in front of my bed. Around one, I came up with the half-baked idea of going to see

Kian since he was only a few blocks away, but reason poked me. Not only would that be stupid and dangerous, I could tell him what happened without leaving the apartment.

So I got my phone and typed, *You there?*

Yep. How was the party?

Can you come over? By the time I locked the door, he was in my room. "That's handy." Odd. My voice didn't sound shaky at all.

"You don't ask me over for ninja visits unless something's wrong." He replaced the distance with concern. Five seconds later, I was in his arms. While I recounted Cameron's last moments, he stroked my back. I finished by asking, "What did I *see?* Is he dead?"

He hesitated. "I've never witnessed anything like that. But if the dogs took him, I suspect the answer is yes."

"What am I supposed to do with that?" I demanded. "What about his parents?"

"I have no idea. I wish I did."

A whimper escaped me. "It's . . . I think *I'm* doing this." Before he could interrupt with hollow reassurances, I repeated what I had been thinking the instant before Cameron disappeared—how I couldn't forgive him. Then it was like my dark reflections translated to instant judgment. "Now tell me that's a coincidence."

"It seems unlikely."

"I can't deal," I whispered. "I'm *so scared* right now."

Kian murmured something into my hair and tugged me toward the bed. I knew better than to imagine he'd picked this as the perfect time to make his move, so I followed, and he cuddled me against his chest. No telling how long it would take for the party to wind down and for anyone to realize Cameron had vanished. But unlike Russ, there was no body for anyone to find.

If anyone looks.

"I'd do anything to get you out of all this," he said softly.

"That's what I'm afraid of." I was just upset enough to tackle the way he had been acting. Again. "What're you hiding from me?"

"How long have you known?" At least he didn't try to deny it.

I thought back. "Since just after we went to your new place."

"I need to give back that trophy for best actor." He attempted a smile, but too much pain dragged down the corners of his mouth, resulting in more of a grimace.

"Please don't do anything stupid."

"Good advice, if it wasn't already too late."

"Kian, *tell* me."

"I made a deal for your protection," he blurted.

A spate of words I didn't even realize I knew—in all-new combinations—tumbled out. "With who?"

"He's not in the game, but he has leverage. He's not interested in competing with other immortals. His interests are more . . . varied." That wasn't an answer, and he knew it.

Maybe *who* wasn't the right question. "Exactly what did you use for collateral?"

In the old stories, humans made all kinds of dire bargains with elder beings. Swaps included the soul, a first-born child, all the love in your heart, or a particular memory. The taut silence ended when I smacked him. Inexplicably, he smiled.

"It's not a big deal, Edie. I was already serving a life sentence. So it doesn't matter."

"It does to me." I fixed him with a look that promised I wouldn't budge until he confessed, but Kian shook his head.

"Knowing certain things would make your life worse. This is one of them."

"Before, you said 'I want you to have a life.' And you looked *so* sad. Is it because you signed away what little freedom you had left? For me?"

"Stop talking," he said firmly.

I wasn't in the mood, at first, when he started kissing me, but Kian's mouth changed that. Even though his physical closeness felt good, it didn't change my sadness. When Kian left an hour later, my sorrow still went bone deep, because our kisses tasted of loss and endings. The Pandora's box in my head exploded, peppering me with emotional shrapnel: Brittany, Russ, now Cameron. The guilt spread through my system like a poison, and I couldn't even rely on Kian to be straight with me. Our relationship could survive all kinds of stress, but *not* his silence or his secrets, and I didn't want to watch us die like I had Cameron. That night, I cried until my head ached.

Things didn't look better in the morning, possibly because my eyes were almost swollen shut. An hour of cold compresses reduced the damage enough for me to leave my room. Sunday my parents slept in; I couldn't talk to them and a day in isolation wouldn't help, so I shoved some things in a backpack and headed out. One of my favorite places in the city was the Victory Garden on Boylston. During the day, it was a great place to walk when you had nowhere else to be and, more important, it was free. During the worst time of my life, I'd spent hours hiding there and pretending I had a social life. Today, the character of each plot didn't charm or relax me. I wandered aimlessly, shoulders bowed beneath the awareness that Cameron was gone, and it was *my* fault.

I wish I knew what I accomplish that's so important. The immortals were batshit crazy if they thought I could see things like this and then stay on course toward a shining future. *Of course, maybe that's the point. You don't know who killed Cam. If Dwyer is watching you, he might've decided that guilt would drive you nuts.* If that were true, maybe I didn't manifest the death dog after all. It wouldn't save Cameron, but then I wouldn't have to live with knowing I was a heinous person. But I'd ping-ponged over who to blame before.

Despite the brisk breeze and the sunlight, I spun in place, suddenly wary. The people wandering the garden this late in the year were mostly old. A few gardeners had planted pumpkins and had Halloween displays not yet taken down. Bales of hay and gourds, mostly, though there were ghosts made of white sheets and fat-bellied witches from plastic trash bags. I didn't see anyone who rang my alarm bells.

Until something rasped, "Hello, pretty-girl skin."

The thin man had spoken to me once before and I would never forget that sound, or the waft of the grave that poured from his mouth. I whirled, making sure he was out of reach. *Kian said not to let him touch you.* But he wasn't close enough. Yet. People passed all around us, probably guessing I was admiring the autumnal colors in the chrysanthemums before me.

"What do you want?" I growled the words, low, hoping nobody would notice the crazy girl talking to the flowers.

"I bring a message from my master."

"And who's that?"

"The Lightbringer, of course."

A scared click of my brain, and I suspected he meant Dwyer, who Kian had guessed must've been known as the sun god. "Make it fast."

Pure bravado, because what would I do if he attacked? Before,

308

when I tried to escape, he appeared in front of me in the blink of an eye. My heart pounded out a terrified rhythm. *If I can't run, maybe I can fight.* Too bad I had no idea how.

"He is waiting. Waiting for you to breathe your last," he rasped. "Your death is already written. But you cheated, pretty-girl skin. Now you're a hole in the world, and you let other people fall in your stead. How long before you become one of us?"

With awful, empty eyes, he reached for me. This time, I understood the futility of running, so I did the only thing I could. I touched him first.

Madness. He doesn't take your life. He steals your mind instead.

My brain spilled over with cascading flashes of pain and violence, red splatter, black dog, crawling maggots, a bird eating a fish head. The images twisted and bled, burrowed deep until I couldn't think, and still it wasn't finished. Despair, decay, dread poured into me, endless rivers of poison, until my vision grayed, replaced by shadows, echoes of footsteps running away, away. I tried to call out, but a bony fist about my throat choked my voice.

For a few seconds, I saw how this ended—me gibbering in a padded room while nurses shot me full of tranquilizers, and then I glimpsed the other end of the tunnel, where this vacant thing hunched, avid for my pain. Channeling everything toward me left a vacuum on the other side. *Simple physics.* Trembling, I fought the only way I could— with my own dreams and memories, hopes and longings. I shoved back hard, until slivers of me plinked into the empty well. *Spelling bee, DNA model, trip to the Grand Canyon, first kiss, A+ in calculus*—I swam against the toxic stream, carrying my life, my identity with me.

You didn't touch me, I told him silently. *I touched you. That makes you mine.*

When I couldn't bear more without screaming myself hoarse, the thin man vanished. My eyes snapped open; I was on the ground, surrounded by worried onlookers. A middle-aged woman I had noticed tending a garden nearby crouched beside me.

"Are you diabetic? Epileptic? Do you have medicine?" She spoke slowly, like I might not be able to understand her.

I shook my head, coming up onto my knees. "I'm all right, right and tight."

Dizzy, I scrambled to my feet and rushed away, staggering with each step. I heard an older man say, "Probably a tweaker. Cops don't patrol this place like they should. You know I've found needles down by the water?"

Sadly, being mistaken for a junkie was better than them thinking I was nuts. Near the exit, my legs went watery. I grabbed on to the fence and forced myself to stay awake through sheer force of will. With agonizing languor, the tendrils receded; my brain felt as if it had pinpricks all over it. But it was mine, wholly mine, and if I'd had the strength, I would've shouted in triumph.

Like a drunkard, I stumbled home, and it took me the better part of an hour, though I wasn't far in terms of physical distance, but I kept having to rest before my legs gave out: curbs, benches, other people's front steps. I didn't realize I was sitting near Kian's building until he strode down the street toward me. Rarely did I get the chance to observe him when he didn't know I was looking; in this unguarded moment, his mouth was compressed into a grim, pale line, and his green eyes held the weight of a promise he refused to share. Women checked him out as he went by, but he never turned. Not once.

In fact, not expecting me, he hurried past and then whipped

around, like he might've imagined me. I managed a weak smile. "Hey, way."

"Are you waiting for me?" he asked, butterfly-tentative.

"Nope."

"Then what are you doing?"

"Sitting." I sounded giddy, goofy, even, I couldn't stop giggling. "Hitting."

"Edie?" He crossed to me in a few steps, leaned in with a look of dismay gradually dawning. "Jesus Christ. I smell him on you."

"True blue. I've been dancing with the devil in the pale moonlight, didn't go down without a fight."

His voice trembled. "Did it touch you?"

"Don't fear the worst, I got him first. I can't fight monsters with guns or knives, but it seems I can with my mind." With trembling hands, I made dual finger-guns and fired. "I fought the law and *I* won. See, this is *my* wheelhouse, son."

Why the hell am I rhyming all the things? That's probably not a good sign.

"You can't survive touching the thin man." Kian seemed frozen with horror. "At least, not with your mind intact."

I smiled up at him, though my face felt stiff and strange. After a few seconds, I shook off the Cockney rhyming daze, keeping my reply simple as weary pride bloomed.

"But I *did*."

THE PAWN IN PLAY

t was nearly a week before my brain recovered fully from my encounter with the thin man. In the meantime, I flunked my first test ever. Ironically, it was in Intro to Japanese. Ryu laughed when I told him, while Vi was quietly concerned. I pretended to be nonchalant while panicking in secret. The truth was, I'd tried studying, but my mind was like a saturated sponge, incapable of absorbing any new information.

Slowly, however, the side effects wore off and my head returned to normal. Rather than have my parents find out, I begged my teacher to let me take a makeup test or do extra credit. She wasn't on board with grading extra projects, but given the problems at Blackbriar recently, she cut me some slack because she'd seen me with Brittany and Russ. Now with Jen gone and Cameron MIA, she saw the writing on the wall. The second time I took the exam, I got a B. Not my usual A+, but I kept that score. Under the circumstances, I had to perform some triage, cut myself some slack for not pulling A+ s when my life was imploding.

When word circulated that Cameron had taken off, I wanted to tell someone what I knew, but I had no idea what to say. The truth would get me locked up, and admitting I was with him when it happened might turn me into a murder suspect, though they couldn't convict me without a body. The dog-girl video gave me clear motive, and gossip could be vicious. So I choked down my desire to confess and kept quiet.

Two weeks into November, things went from bad to worse at school. It started in first period; Nicole was sitting at her desk as usual. No matter how early I arrived, she was *always* there, and I was starting to wonder if she slept in Mr. Love's room. He was talking to a couple of other students, but I sensed that he was aware of her . . . and darkly amused. Allison strolled in—why, I had no idea since she didn't even have Lit—and propped a hip against his desk. In comparison, she was a tropical flower whereas Nicole had become a sepia photo.

Allison said something to Mr. Love, pitched too low for the rest of us to catch, but he laughed quietly. Nic's head came up, and her eyes narrowed. She stormed from her desk to his, scowling at Allison, who threw her a mocking look. Then, deliberately, Allison touched Mr. Love on the arm to catch his attention.

Nicole snapped. With a snarl, she whipped a switchblade out of her pocket and slashed. Allison skittered back but not in time; red bloomed through the sleeve of her blazer. Another girl screamed while someone else ran for the headmaster. Allison wrapped a hand around the wound and I shrugged off my jacket, offering it to her as Mr. Love grabbed Nicole's arms. *Too slow, asshole. You wanted this.*

Nic screamed the minute he touched her, the raw, wordless cry of an animal in pain. At first she struggled and fought like a crazy thing, but by the time the headmaster arrived, she was sobbing with snot streaming down her chin. In the chaos of so many people talking at once, trying to explain what happened, I escorted Allison to the nurse. But we were only halfway there when she unwrapped my blazer from her wounded arm and gave it back.

"Are you sure that's a good idea?"

"I'm fine," she said. "Just a scratch."

The blood that gushed from that slice said otherwise. "I'm pretty sure you need to go to the hospital for some stitches."

Her green eyes held a mocking light. "Do I?"

Then she showed me the blood-smeared skin. Sure, it was stained red, but there was *no wound*. "That's impossible."

"Not so much. *They seem completely human, but tragedy, discord, and despair follow in their wake. You will know these demons because they are not born of woman and have no navel.*" With a faintly feline smile, she tugged up her school shirt to show me smooth skin.

Jen saw you looking up psychic vampires. And it was Jen who brought you into the group. Is she . . . did she . . . ? I had no proof that she was actually in Thailand, and I hated the fear and doubt that swamped me.

"It's tough not knowing who your true friends are," Allison said sweetly.

"*You?* I was so sure it was him," I blurted.

Her lazy smile didn't shift. "He's a monster, but not one of ours."

I glanced at her wrists, but they were unmarked.

"What faction are you?" I demanded.

She smirked. "Don't you get it? Every game needs spectators."

"But . . . my ears don't ring around you." To my surprise, she didn't seem confused.

"Some of us are . . . natural to the world, not dreamed up by humans. And we don't set off alarm bells in those predisposed to sensitivity."

"Ah." That made sense. "But . . . Russ, before he died—"

"Humans who are feeding a nightmare become attuned to the predator."

"I'm not sure what that means."

She rolled her eyes. "You know how a chameleon changes colors?"

"Yeah."

"It's like that, only in a parasitic exchange the human gives off a . . . false positive. To someone like you."

Allison fixed her blouse and sauntered toward the main office. "I'm done tutoring you now. Thanks for the help." Such pleasure in the last two words.

How does—whatever she is—reproduce? No belly button. Quickly I ran through what I knew, biologically speaking. *Parthenogenesis, asexual, gemmules, sporulation*—that one gave me a shivery twinge—*budding, regeneration. Dammit. It's not like I can figure this out now.* I had so many questions, though she'd answered a few.

Obviously I had miscalculated, so I raced back to Lit class, where things had calmed down a little, but no learning took place that morning. Since one student had attacked another, the police questioned everyone and they took a dim view of why there were no security screenings like in public schools; they didn't seem persuaded that affluent students were less prone to hurting each other, given today's events. The headmaster wore a hunted look as he foresaw his prestigious school reputation swirling down the drain. In the end, he dismissed us early, probably so he could consult his attorneys, find out about liability, and decide the best spin on this mess when he talked to the board.

Instead of rushing out along with everyone else, I headed for Lit. Part of me suspected the instigator would've already run off, but I found him packing his briefcase like nothing had happened. When he saw me in the doorway, he smiled.

"What can I do for you, Edie?"

"I may not be able to prove you did this, but there will be questions. They'll dig into your relationship with Nicole and see how much time she spent with you."

He didn't profess innocence or confusion, as I half expected, but when he spoke, he lost the British accent. Instead, he sounded guttural, like an enormous thing, speaking from man-skin. "Darling girl, you claim to know what I am, but you have *no* idea. Run along now, before I teach you."

I made the thin man back off. It'll take more than you to frighten me. That was bravado, but it kept my feet planted.

"I don't think so. You're done here. If you come back tomorrow, I'll find a way to make you pay." That was a bluff; since I had no idea what the hell he was, I didn't know how to punish him.

He rushed me. It never occurred to me to fear a physical attack, but he swung at my head and in reflex, I threw up my left arm to block. Red light sparked from the kanji brand on my wrist, flinging him halfway across the room. Mr. Love landed hard and whacked his head against the desk. In a normal human, that might've been enough to kill him, but he staggered to his feet, cracked his neck in a grotesque fashion, popping the broken column back into place and rolling his shoulders. But he didn't come at me again.

Instead he studied me with an expression of growing delight. "Ah. So *you're* what drew me here, little queen."

"I have no idea what you're talking about."

"Don't feign ignorance, it doesn't suit you." His gaze lingered on my mark, the one that meant Property of the Game. "Do you suspect what lies ahead? I wonder."

"Are you part of the opposition?"

He laughed, a rumbling sound like thunder. "Not all of us choose to play. Some of us prefer to watch . . . and make wagers. I think I'll bet on how long you'll live."

"Are you related to Allison somehow?"

He shook his head. "But you know that already. Testing me?"

"What *are* you?"

"Your kind dreamed of me, so I came. I'll let you work it out." He strolled past, whistling, so cheerful I resisted the urge to throw something at his back. At the doorway he paused to add, "When I don't return, don't imagine it has anything to do with you. Instead, rest assured that I got what I came for."

Since I'd be crazy to take him at his word, I followed Mr. Love out of the building. The halls were deserted, just the click of our shoes. He looked so normal in his overcoat, briefcase in one hand; I might never believe what my eyes told me again. The immortal—whatever he was—headed for the front gate without looking back. His shoes tapped briskly against the walkway and I rushed after him.

Overhead, the sky was gray with threatening rain. Fat droplets spattered my face, and though I looked away only for a second, when I checked the front gate again, he was gone. There was only a huge black bird wheeling lazily above the trees. With bright, beady eyes, it dove toward me, claws outstretched, and I swung at it with my bag. Its raucous cry sounded almost like laughter.

"Well, that was donked up," Davina called, running up to me. "Was that crow rabid? I swear, this school gets weirder by the day, and my mom will have a shit fit when she finds out about Nicole. I'll be lucky if she doesn't homeschool me."

"Maybe that would be safer."

"Can't argue." She proffered a red umbrella.

As I stepped under the brim with her, the clouds opened up, spattering my bare legs and soaking my shoes and socks. That fast, it was pouring rain with the wind carrying it along in slanted sheets.

Davina shivered. "Man, I hate November. You want to come over for a while? We can study together."

"If my mom says it's okay." It was hard to stay close enough to her not to get drenched while making the call, but I managed, and by the time we got to the station, I had permission to hang out until five.

On the train, she didn't say much, but that was a defense mechanism, best not to attract attention. You never knew when pervs would take accidental eye contact as encouragement—and since we were both young and pretty, the danger was twofold.

Afterward, as we walked to her building, the rain slowed enough for it not to be miserable. Davina led the way and unlocked her front door; nobody was home, which explained why she'd wanted me to come. After the crap at school, I wasn't on board with cozying up to my own thoughts, either.

She dumped her backpack by the door, and headed for the kitchen. "I can make tea or hot chocolate, the powder packet kind."

"I'm sensing you want a warm beverage."

"Hot chocolate," she decided.

The kettle took five minutes to whistle, then we mixed the instant chocolate and added marshmallows. Davina's place was warm and inviting, full of crafty things like handmade pillows and throws. It was obvious that she didn't come from money, but I felt more at home here than in Jen's ultramodern mansion. Once we finished our drinks, she beckoned me to her bedroom and shut the door behind us.

"I might be a little slow, but I'm pretty sure I've put the pieces together."

"We're not studying?" Whatever she thought she knew, it wouldn't be good.

"You were in full meltdown when we left Cameron's party. Then, a few days later, we find out that nobody's seen him since that night. What did you see, Edie?"

"You wouldn't believe me if I told you."

"Try me."

Call me paranoid, but not until I checked something. "Let me see your belly button."

Davina raised a brow, but she pushed up her shirt to reveal an innie. "Is this like reading tea leaves or something?"

I released a nervous chuckle. *What the hell.* So I filled her in, explaing how Nicole attacked Allison, the cut sealed over, and she had no navel—then Mr. Love went nuts on me. I pretended to have no idea how these events were related. For her safety, I left out everything related to the game; I was afraid too much information might make her a target, and I only had one favor left. There was no way I could protect everyone as I had Vi, much to my dismay.

"This shit is full-on crazy," she said finally. "You mentioned you thought Mr. Love was shady, but this—"

"I *know.*"

"Don't take this the wrong way, but can I see *your* belly button?"

I giggled as I showed it to her, and the situation didn't seem as

319

grim if we could laugh. Though I couldn't give her the big picture, the conversation cheered me up. We didn't come up with any solutions, but I felt less alone. At quarter past four I got up to leave.

"You know I've got your back at school, right?"

"Yeah. Thanks."

"See you tomorrow, unless the place burns down. Which wouldn't surprise me."

I hurried down the sidewalk, trying to get to the station before the rain started up again. If anything, it was darker than it had been, a worse storm was on the horizon. There was scant foot traffic in Davina's neighborhood on the six-block walk to the T station. A few birds nestled on ledges of buildings; even more perched on the wires and they stared as I quickened my pace. Maybe I was imagining it, but they turned their heads almost all the way around, just watching.

I ran the rest of the way.

On the train, it was better, until I noticed the shadows following the car, tendrils of darkness slinking along the block walls. Each time we left a station, they swelled and drew closer, only to be driven back by the bright crackle of fluorescent lighting at the next stop. I hopped off a little sooner than I should have. Rain or no, I'd walk home from here.

The lull in the weather held just long enough for me to get to my street, then the sky dumped buckets on me, not just stinging rain but hail too. Ice pelted me, raising red welts on my skin, and I was panting when I got to the front stoop. Shoving through to the foyer, I almost ran into Mr. Lewis, who was inexplicably carrying a hammer. He said something about a horseshoe and wind chimes.

"What?"

"I can't find one," he told me. "An old one is best, one that's grown rusty and strong over the years. I put up wind chimes, but the building manager made me take them down."

"Wind chimes?"

"To keep the old ones out," he reminded me impatiently.

"Why can *you* see them?" Nobody else could who wasn't part of the game.

"Those who are close to death can see beyond the mortal caul." That didn't help a whole lot, and I guessed he read that in my expression. So he clarified, "Stage-four lung cancer. I don't have long."

"I'm sorry."

He shrugged, as if that were the least of his problems. "I've got a mezuzah here. Don't know if it'll do the job. The rabbi at the synagogue might've been humoring me."

"Thank you for trying to keep us safe."

The old man smiled at me. "What else do I have to do?"

As I headed upstairs, he hung the scroll case, muttering about the need for precision. My mom was home since it was her turn to stand guard over me. I got in just before five, proving I could be trusted. She smiled at me, setting down her pencil. From what I could tell, she was truly trying to build a better relationship with me, and I loved her for the effort.

"How was school?"

If I don't tell her, she'll find out from Blackbriar. So I said, "Scary," and then told her how an obsessed student assaulted another girl over a cute teacher. Her eyes widened and she pulled off her glasses, absently polishing them on her sweater as she listened. I concluded, "So that's why there's blood on my jacket. It's not mine."

"How horrible! This term has just been . . . *tragic*. What's changed, I wonder?" From her expression, she was half a step from launching an experiment with control groups to determine why Blackbriar was no longer the safe haven she paid for.

"I wish I knew." That wasn't entirely a lie.

"Are you all right? Do you need to talk to someone?" How ironic she kept asking me that *this* year.

"I'm okay," I said.

Then I fled to my room, supposedly to work on assignments. She must've filled my dad in because he was especially solicitous when I came out for dinner. They were both trying *so hard* to be more emotionally available; it didn't come easy since their natural state was to be completely absorbed in whatever research had captured their attention, and I basked in the surety that they did love me, even if they sometimes sucked at showing it.

As soon as I thought that, my wrist blazed. *So it's better if I think my parents don't care?* Why that would influence my future, I had *no* idea. As always, I had on a hoodie in the house. Since my parents preferred to keep the heating bill low, they didn't question it. Summer might offer problems in that regard.

Later, I didn't feel like talking to Vi, so I e-mailed her instead of signing on for our usual chat. I went to bed early, disturbed by the heat in my right arm. The feeling was similar to when Davina and I went to New Hampshire. Eventually, I fell into a fitful sleep, plagued by nightmares of the thin man.

I woke with a start, but I wasn't in my bed. Instead, I stood in the kitchen, a knife in my right hand. A thin trickle of blood spilled from my abdomen, a clean slice through my pajama top. With a stifled cry, I dropped the blade in the sink, ran water over it, and then bolted, aware I needed help, but there was no one to save me. If I called Kian, he'd try to bargain for my safety, and I couldn't bear for him to sacrifice anything else for my sake.

I am alone.

In the bathroom, I raised my shirt to inspect the slice. *Not deep. Shallow, like I'm a cutter.* The implication scared me more than the actual wound. *It's a warning. They* can *get to you.* It took all my composure to tend the wound and tape some gauze over it. Remembering the girl in the mirror, I didn't linger there for fear of what I'd see. Retreating to my bedroom didn't make me feel safer—only trapped, with nowhere to run.

Teeth chattering, I turned up the heat, which steamed up the room. Trickles of moisture ran down the foggy panes like tears, and then one by one, handprints appeared on my windows, like something lurked beyond my sight, waiting to get in. I imagined it watching me as I slept. A whimper escaped me as I crept closer, expecting to see the little girl-thing, but there was only mist. I touched the cool glass and discovered what I feared most to be true.

The palm prints were on the outside.

ANTICIPATION
OF EVIL

The next day, state employees descended on Blackbriar and inter-
viewed a bunch of us, but in the end, they concluded Nicole was
unstable, and it wasn't the school's fault. Allison wore a bandage for a
few days, and only I knew that she didn't need one. Three days after
the incident, the headmaster announced that Mr. Love had resigned
his position, though not due to wrongdoing. We were encouraged to
send farewell cards, which would be forwarded to him.

A retired teacher took his place and she paid more attention to
the ball of yarn in her tote bag than she did us. That was fine with
me; I could use another free period. Administration promised there
would be a permanent replacement when winter break ended. I hoped
he or she was human; that seemed like a reasonable expectation in an
educator.

By the time Thanksgiving rolled around, I was ready for a four-
day weekend. Kian picked me up; I waved at Davina as I got into the
car. It occurred to me that I'd gotten my revenge—the Teflon crew
was wrecked. As it turned out, Allison literally wasn't human, and the

rest were dead or missing. The weight of it hit me all over again. *Be careful what you wish for. It might come true.* And I hated that I could forget my culpability, even for a moment.

"You look upset," Kian said, starting the car. He listened to what I had to say, then he shook his head. "Don't blame yourself. Nothing you did caused this."

"Is that better? If I had died—"

"Don't say that. Don't you dare."

"What?"

"Talk like you're nothing. For me, the world would be unbearable without you."

His certainty smoothed over the guilt like a balm.

"That's how I feel about you," I said softly.

And that made his secrets more painful, since he seemed so distant, committed to protecting me rather than being *with* me.

A smile curved his mouth that I'd best describe as blissful. "As long as you do, I can stand anything."

"You shouldn't have to."

He ignored that, weaving through traffic toward our neighborhood. Since he lived in the area too, I felt less guilty about using him for transportation. I mean, it wasn't like he had business near Blackbriar, but I enjoyed the way other girls looked when they saw him waiting. Sometimes I feared he was an illusion or a hallucination from which I must inevitably awake. Of course, if that meant all of the horrible things, all the demons and monsters were bad dreams too? Maybe I could live with losing Kian.

Maybe.

My heart hurt just thinking about it. As if he sensed it, he reached over and covered my hand with his. On impulse, I raised his palm and kissed it. His fingers closed convulsively, and he cut me a sharp look.

"While I'm driving? Really?" God, that look curled my toes.

"Sorry. I'll be good." I cast around for a topic that wouldn't distract him. "What's your favorite color?"

"That was random. Why do you want to know?"

"Just tell me."

"Blue."

That answer made me smile. "Mine too."

When he parked outside our brownstone, he leaned over for a kiss that broke all records for hotness and threatened to set my uniform on fire. *Maybe he's part djinn*, I thought dizzily, as he tunneled his hands into my hair. He tasted sweet and fresh, everything I wanted wrapped up in one person, and I could've crawled on top of him then and there. *Bad hormones, bad.* Intellectually I understood that our pheromones were shaking hands and that our chemical compositions must be compatible—and that was all. On a pure girl level, I just *wanted* him. So I told my brain to shut up and we kissed for ten minutes, until he was breathing hard, and I was trembling.

"Can I come up?"

The question elated me. Maybe there was still hope for us, together.

"My mom's probably home," I warned.

Rueful smile. "That's fine. Just . . . give me a minute."

Oh. Wow. It was impossible for me to restrain a smirk. "No problem."

Five minutes later, we got out of the car and headed into the foyer. Right away, I noticed the mezuzah was gone. Like before, only the nail remained. A shiver went through me as I trotted up the stairs, Kian close behind me. He set a hand on the small of my back while I dug for my keys, but—

The door stood open, half an inch.

My blood chilled.

"Let me go in first." Kian tried to push past me but I shook my head.

"We'll go in together or not at all. Maybe she just got home."

"My mom used to leave the door ajar if she was carrying groceries." By his tone he knew that was unlikely.

Yet I couldn't help but cling to hope. Silently I counted to three before nudging the door wide. The way the apartment was laid out, I had a clear view through the living room to the kitchen, where I saw my mother's feet, motionless on the tile floor. Kian tried to hold me back, but I yanked free and ran to her, my breath a tight and silent shriek in my chest. Recycled fabric bags were spilled all around her, broken eggs and bottles of juice mingling with the blood—*oh my God, so much blood*—I crumpled. Kian caught me. When he carried me out of the apartment, I didn't fight. Inside my skull, the screams echoed in endless loop.

He took her. The bag man came. He took her head.

I was only half aware of Kian banging on Mr. Lewis's door and asking him to call 911. The old man complied at once, and Kian carried me out of the building, cradling me on his lap on the front steps. He rocked me, and I held on, but I couldn't cry. Everything was tight and dry; my mind simmered with the madness of it. *The bag man will have your brains for his soup, your skull for his bowl, and he'll drink you dry.* Mr. Lewis brought a blanket out for me, and Kian wrapped me in it. The fleece did nothing to banish the cold.

I didn't respond. I couldn't. Across the street, I saw the old man with the bag, and it bulged with a new and hideous weight. Beside him stood the two black-eyed children. The girl-thing's pinafore was smeared with blood. I fought free and jumped up, racing toward them. They vanished before my eyes as the screech of car brakes yanked my attention to the street. Kian hauled me back to the stoop, shaking, while the driver shouted out his window at me.

"That was . . ." Kian tightened his arms on me.

I wasn't listening. "Kian . . . did you see them?"

He glanced around my shoulder. "Who?"

"Never mind." My head was a mess; I couldn't think.

"What's your dad's number, Edie?"

I shrugged, dazed and shivering.

Kian was gentle in plucking the backpack from my shoulder. Silently, he rummaged in the front zip pocket until he found my phone. A few clicks, and he was talking to my dad. His voice was a low rumble but I couldn't make out the words. *Buzz, buzz, buzz, go away. I don't believe this is real. I won't. This isn't my life.*

"I'm ready to give you up." There was some sadness in the admission, but if keeping Kian meant living this, then the nightmare had to end. "The dream is over now. I need to wake up."

No more coma dream. Back to reality. Back to being an ugly girl with no friends, no boyfriend. But I'll still have my mom.

"God, Edie," he whispered.

I'm sorry, the wind whispered. I felt a sad, familiar presence all around me, raising the hair on my arms. Through dry eyes, I stared hard at the street I had lived on all my life. "Cameron?"

But there was only a stained newspaper tumbling down the sidewalk. And Kian was still here, holding me, with a face like an angel and a dark shadow in his eyes. In the distance, sirens screamed toward us.

When I said I wanted this to stop, I anticipated sitting up in a hospital bed, IV in my arm, both of my parents at my bedside. *You tried to kill yourself. You failed. You're in a coma. Wake up, now. Wake up.*

"She's in shock," Mr. Lewis said.

"Could you make her some hot tea? Plenty of sugar."

"Of course." The old man moved off.

A few minutes later, or maybe hours, Kian put a warm mug in my hand. I drank the tea because it was there. I couldn't wake up; there was no exit from this that didn't end in policemen putting tape on my front door. Two officers showed up and then an ambulance, but it was oh-my-God too late. They carted away her body, covered in a sheet.

"We have to ask you some questions," the older cop said gently.

I stared up at him. There was no tinnitus. Allison hadn't registered on my faulty ears, either. The irrational desire possessed me to demand to inspect all of their belly buttons. *Another death, and I can't tell the truth. Or maybe I can. Maybe it doesn't matter anymore.* I opened my mouth, but Kian squeezed my hand. He warned me with his eyes not to open that can of crazy and upend it all over the nice humans. I understood now why he said it like that; it was what you called people who walked around with blinders on. I might've started life that way, but I didn't feel part of the collective anymore.

He took her head. Why can't I cry?

"Okay," I said finally.

"Her dad should be here soon," Kian put in. "Maybe you should wait for him."

"Is she a minor?"

329

He nodded. "Eighteen in February."

"Then let's secure the scene and wait for the detectives to arrive." The younger one followed his partner upstairs, leaving us on the front step.

Ten minutes later, my dad dashed toward us, his chest heaving. I'd never seen his face that shade before. He hunched over for a few seconds, hands on knees, before he could get the breath to ask, "Edith?"

It was all the questions wrapped into one. Kian loosened his arms, but I didn't get off his lap. My mom was the one who asked if she could hug me, and I couldn't get the words out at first. My dad's hair was a mess and his glasses were fogged up. He took them off so he could see us better.

"Mom's dead," I said. Two words, heavy as osmium.

"Oh God, honey." From his expression, I could tell he didn't know what to say, what to ask, and my words were balled into a Gordian tangle.

"Are you Alan Kramer?" A man in a wrinkled suit stood outside the brownstone, wearing a grave but purposeful look.

"Yes."

"Please come with us. We have some questions for your daughter."

In the end, they asked Kian and me several times exactly what we saw. We recounted the story separately and together. No, we didn't see anyone fleeing the scene. Yes, we both had class before coming home. Kian picked me up at Blackbriar; we came straight home. I resisted the temptation to give the detectives a description of the bag man. It was late by the time we finished, and our apartment was a crime scene.

"We'll . . . get a hotel room," Dad said. "We can stop at a pharmacy and buy some essentials, like pajamas and toothbrush—"

Kian cut in, "You're welcome to stay at my place. I'll sleep on the couch."

He seemed older than twenty at the moment, but age was more than chronology. I didn't have the strength to doubt him, so I clutched him close instead. I turned to my dad. "If you don't mind, I'd rather do that."

"Okay." It was so strange for him to acquiesce that readily, like my mother had been the reason for the steel in his spine.

Kian drove us to his apartment from the precinct and parked a few blocks down. On the way, I stopped at a corner drugstore. They had toiletries and I found T-shirts and novelty shorts to sleep in. Silently, I dropped the few items into my dad's basket and he paid. Nobody felt like eating, and just as well, because Kian had cup noodles and a box of tea. He made each of us a mug, and my dad seemed every bit as shell-shocked as I felt.

He didn't lecture us about staying up too late or give me a speech about how Kian wasn't to be trusted. Instead, he kissed my cheek and went to the guest bedroom and shut the door with a quiet, final click. Bereft, I sank down on the sofa.

"This isn't a dream," I said to Kian.

Sadly he shook his head.

The dam burst. Tears streamed down my cheeks as the ache for my mom blossomed in my chest. I remembered our lunch. Lobster rolls. *It feels like we should celebrate. To new beginnings.* Now, like the Teflon crew, she was gone, but—

I never wished for this. I never did. Never.

Mom, no.

I protected Vi instead of my mother; that was my choice. But all this time, I thought the man with the sack and the awful children were hunting *me*. If I'd known, I would've used my favor to make sure she was safe. *I'm so sorry, Mom.* I imagined them knocking on our door, after Mr. Lewis's protective measures failed, hiding their nightmare skins under an illusion of normalcy. *Mom would've invited them in.* But if I'd warned her, she wouldn't have believed me.

She never wore makeup because she didn't feel pretty. So why try? If I hadn't gotten to know her better, I never would've learned that about her . . . or the curling iron story about my grandmother. My mom always had ink stains on her sweaters. She . . .

. . . died in a pool of blood. Did she suffer? Or was it quick?

She never taught me about electrical wiring. I never showed her how to do her face with the autumn mineral makeup we bought together. *I can't, I can't, I can't—* Kian wrapped his arms around me, but he didn't try to staunch my sobs. He stroked my back, my hair, and let me weep until I couldn't breathe.

"They'll never know. The case will go cold, someone will file it."

"You said . . ." His voice caught. "That you were ready to give me up. If there was anything I could do, if I *could*, I'd trade places with her for you."

Hard shudders racked me from head to toe. "Idiot. No swaps, no deals. I want both of you. I don't want this, Kian. I can't have *this*. I just want it to be over. I don't want to play this game anymore."

"It can't be undone," he said, as if I didn't *know* that. But maybe in our world, there were certain mutable realities, and death was more of a swinging door. "Sometimes people use favors to bring loved ones back, but . . . they're never right. I'm so sorry."

Oh.

"Is there any way to make him pay?" The words came before I could stop them, before my brain could remind me that it was my quest for revenge that had carried me here.

"Who?"

"The old man with the sack." I realized then, I'd never *told* him. He knew about the thin man, but this monster, I had kept all for my own.

It might not do any good, but I told him everything then. *Too late, too late.* My muscles locked, as I waited for him to yell at me and tell me this was my fault. But his face paled instead. He covered my hand with his, eyes grave.

"If Dwyer sent him, there was *nothing* you could do. Telling me wouldn't have changed anything. It kills me to admit it, but I bartered away my last coin keeping you safe." He didn't mean currency, of course, but the last thing any immortal would want, whatever that was. "I wish I could've protected your mother too, but it doesn't work that way."

One person, one favor, I know. Hope you didn't sell your soul for me. That would mean he couldn't escape his masters, even in death. *I don't want to be the rocks in your pockets, dragging you under. Oh, Kian, don't let me drown you.*

I might. And you'd let me.

"Don't look like that," he begged.

"Will you read me something?" Glancing around his apartment, I saw he *had* taken my advice. Everything he had left from his old life, he'd arranged—books on the shelves, journal nearby with a quality pen, and his two small trophies sat above the TV. Despite the heart breaking over and over inside me, it was almost enough to dry my tears.

Almost.

"Like what?"

"Another poem. Something beautiful."

"I have one I wrote for a competition. It's less . . . emotional, more about pretty imagery and theme. Maybe that one?"

"If you wrote it, I want it." Breathing was onerous with lead on my chest. I ached as if I had fought an avalanche and lost. Somewhere, the old man with the sack had my mother's head, and the wind spoke with Cameron's voice.

This is madness. No. This is Boston.

Hysteria tapped against the glass wall I'd built around this fragile calm. I didn't let it in. Kian grabbed his notebook and then settled down with me tucked against his side. With a crisp snap, he opened to a page already marked. "My mother loved this one."

"I'm sure I will too."

"It's called 'Firebird.'"

"Stop stalling and read." I put my head on his shoulder.

He huffed out a breath. His shifting told me he was nervous. For some reason, his jitters calmed mine. It grew easier to breathe. I closed my eyes, letting his voice wash over me.

"Pointed beauty, sienna, umber, the sky in autumn rage;
Slim maids weep their hued tears,
a touch of lace, bright mantle of their undress.
Crisp, air a-bite with apples, rich with winter.
Mother's lament for fled daughter, angry arms,
accusing heaven's twilight; wispy kiss, mourning mist beneath our boots.
And how should I, walking this old earth, think to tread those paths?
Human, humbled by these elders turning down thin hands,

We stand and breathe, remembering that bird, fluttering
with color in these dark boughs, remembering
Its conviction of passage—it must fly or die."

"Beautiful. I love it. It's about the foliage turning in the fall," I said. "And how much you wanted to be free."

He nodded, closing the book. "Now, I know it's an illusion. Nobody ever truly is. There are prices to be paid, obligations to meet."

I met his gaze, sure of only one thing. "That's not true. When the time comes, we have to be like that bird. Fly or die, Kian. Promise me."

He kissed me instead of answering, but if I had to drag him over the cliff with me, so be it. *Whatever it takes, we'll fly.*

WHAT IS GONE
BECOMES REALITY

There was no holiday those four days.

My dad dealt with the practicalities, and Kian *tried* to do Thanksgiving with lunchmeat turkey slices and instant potatoes, bought at a convenience store. Along with canned peas and white bread with butter, it was pretty much the saddest feast anyone ever tried to eat. I didn't cry until he busted out the weirdest dessert ever—some kind of cookie layered with pudding. Then I hid in the guest room until I calmed down because it should've been my dad doing the cooking while my mom and I set the table.

Kian tapped lightly. "I'm sorry. I tried."

"It's not the food. You weren't planning to have guests for Thanksgiving." Or ever, from the look of his cupboards.

"I usually go to my aunt and uncle's house."

"Are they worried about you?"

"I told them I'd be with my girlfriend. I think my aunt was . . . relieved."

I frowned, wiping at a trickle of tears. "Why?"

"I'm a reminder of the old scandal. She never liked my dad and she hated having me in the house. For my uncle's sake, she pretended I was welcome, but . . ." He shrugged. "She wasn't sorry when I graduated and moved to Boston."

"Why did you?"

"Wedderburn called me here," he said simply.

I tried to imagine getting my diploma and then learning the deal I'd made was now worthless, and that the bright future they'd hinted at was no longer viable, therefore I could expect to spend the next sixty years in servitude. It was like being a spy, only without the satisfaction of knowing you were risking your life for the greater good. This was blind obedience with no hope of escape or understanding.

"How was that?" I asked.

"By that point, I didn't care. My senior year when Tanya died, I went numb. And I stayed that way until the first time I saw you."

I ducked my head. "If you say stuff like that, I will shatter into a million pieces and you'll have to sweep me up."

He sank down on the bed beside me, but I was conscious of my dad in the other bedroom. If he came in, I didn't want him to think . . . anything. So I stood up.

"Living room?"

"That's fine. I can put on a DVD."

"Do you have *Casablanca*? That way, if I cry, I can blame the movie."

"Not a problem."

We settled in to watch and partway through, my dad joined us. I could tell he had been weeping too, but nobody acknowledged it.

The weekend went slowly. I missed some school days for my mom's funeral. The whole university showed up, which was nice for my dad, less so for me because of all the hugs I got from strangers.

My eyes were dry that day; I had wept myself out at Kian's place. I bought a new black dress and I hated it, but I wore it with black tights because *everything* was black. Except the sun. It had the nerve to shine, after days of rain, and I hated it too.

Davina and her mother came to the service; I was grateful, but it also reminded me that she still had a mom. The knife dug in and twisted, around and around, until it was an effort to hold my smile in place. I imagined it had been carved into my face, blood trickling from my mouth, and my cheeks ached. I hugged another stranger.

Kian held my hand through the prayers, songs, and speeches. I clenched hard when the minister started talking about the afterlife. We had never been a religious family, and my mom would laugh over his talk of being called home. I tuned everything out, until Kian tugged on my arm, telling me it was time to stand up and say good-bye. For obvious reasons, it was closed casket, pictures arrayed on top.

Like Brittany.

My dad grabbed my other hand, and they flanked me as we approached the coffin. It was high quality; my dad picked it out. I flattened my hand on top of the box that held what was left of my mother. Beside me, my dad did the same and Kian stepped back, letting us grieve. Then we took our places by the door, so the pall-bearers could do their work.

Kian drove us to the cemetery. God knows what my dad and I would've done without him. Taking a taxi seemed disrespectful; so did public transportation. An hour later, there were more words, more prayers, and a handful of dirt raining down. *She's really gone.* Someone put a flower in my hand and I pitched it into the grave. I stumbled on the green carpet, meant to look like grass so the gaping hole didn't hit so hard.

People said, "It was a lovely service," as they filed past.

I nodded but I didn't *see* them. They all wore the bag man's face. Dad and I stayed until everyone had gone. Mom's headstone was in place, but nothing was carved on it. That seemed so very wrong.

"We should go," Dad said finally. "We can come back after the engraving's done. Leave some flowers for her."

"She hated cut flowers," I muttered.

It was true. I remembered her saying it was cruel to snip and put them in vases, laying waste to their beauty. *Better to let them bloom and die, as they're supposed to.* Did that mean my mom believed in fate? I wished I had told her about the bargain, about my place in the time-line, but I had been ashamed of my weakness, boiling with guilt. Now it was too late. Repeatedly, I reminded myself that she was a scientist, and if I'd spilled everything, she wouldn't have been on guard; she would've put me in a mental ward, so I'd be locked up and she'd still be gone.

"What verse did you choose?" Kian asked.

My dad turned to him, probably grateful for the distraction, as we walked toward the car. "'Our death is not an end if we can live on in our children.'"

My throat closed. I recognized the quote at once; I had been reading about Einstein obsessively since I was a little girl. The tears spilled over as Kian wrapped an arm around my shoulders. I squeezed my eyes shut until the urge to sob passed.

"That's perfect," I whispered. "She would l-love that."

Dad couldn't smile. He tried. The glint of his own tears shone through the lenses of his glasses. He took them off, polished them on the sleeve of his coat. "I don't know what we'll do without her. Every-thing . . . will break down."

"Then we'll fix it. I'll learn."

But she won't teach me. All the moments we might've had together, they're gone now.

"There's a cleaning crew coming to . . . sort things out." *To scrub up her blood.* Dad went on, "The police have released the apartment, but we can't live there. I asked around, and we—*I*—have a colleague at the university who knows someone willing to sublet to us, half a mile from the old place. I know it's not ideal, but—"

"No, that's fine. Do we need to pack?"

"Mr. Lewis volunteered to help us. If Kian doesn't mind, we can swing by for the boxes and . . ." Trailing off, it was clear he had no idea what to call the move. It wasn't something either of us wanted.

"Get settled?" Kian offered.

I could've kissed him. "Do you mind?"

"Of course not. And I can get takeout if you're hungry."

Dad shook his head, but even though I didn't *want* to eat, we both needed to. So I said, "That would be good."

Nothing is. The sun shone on until sunset, swirls of purple on the skyline dotted with city lights. As I climbed out of the backseat in front of the brownstone, the wind whispered, *I'm so sorry.* Cameron's voice, at my shoulder, made me whirl around, but I didn't see him. There was only Mr. Lewis waiting on the stoop. My dad took Kian while I opened the trunk. We packed it with our clothes but not Mom's, my dad's research and various books that Mr. Lewis thought I might want. The rest would keep.

"What's the address?" Kian asked.

In a husky voice, Dad told him and we pulled away from the curb, leaving my old life behind. The new building was red brick, sharp and featureless, with uniform lines and no window boxes full of autumn flowers. Though I wasn't sure, I thought it might be December now. During the days prior to my mom's funeral, I lost track of how often I ate and slept, though mostly the latter.

This unit was on the first floor toward the back. We had a nice fenced patio and two bedrooms, decorated in classic rental unit. So much beige and brown. The pictures on the walls looked like abstract poop. Kian helped us unload the car, then he dodged out to grab some food and brought back stir-fry noodles. Like the other two, I ate in silence. There were no words for any of this.

"I have some work to do," my dad said eventually. "Feel free to stay as long as you like." The last, to Kian.

I guessed he trusted him now. So did I. At any point, he could've bailed on us, left me to deal with the fallout on my own. Coping would've been much harder without him to smooth the rough spots, do what I couldn't. If not for him, my dad might've starved.

"All right. Thank you, sir."

Dad shook his head. "Thank *you*."

Then he went to the smaller of the two bedrooms and closed the door with a click. At first, I didn't understand why I was getting the master suite until I realized it had a huge bed. *He doesn't want to sleep alone in* that. I wished I had the kind of relationship with my father where I could run to him and hug him so hard it hurt his ribs and my arms, but we were stiff with each other, like strangers.

Kian and I watched a documentary about bees on cable, but around nine, he pushed to his feet. "I don't want to go, but I feel like I should."

"It's okay. I'll be fine." That was a colossal lie, but I had to stand on my own two feet. I'd leaned on him enough over the past couple of weeks.

"Are you going to school tomorrow?"

"Yeah. I don't want to spend the day here alone. If I know my dad, he'll retreat to the lab, so he can focus on work."

"Maybe that's not a bad thing."

It can be if you neglect all other aspects of your life. Worried my dad might overhear, as the walls weren't exactly thick, I didn't say so aloud. Instead I walked Kian to the door and stretched up to kiss him. My heart wasn't in it, but he didn't seem to take it personally. He brushed his lips over my forehead in response.

"If you need anything, text me. I'll be here in two seconds. And I do mean *anything*, Edie." His tone was so serious, so earnest, that I actually smiled.

My face didn't crack. My heart did a little, and sweetness spilled out. I no longer had any hope of resisting or protecting myself from future harm. He was the only star in my firmament, shining in darkest night, so I could always find the path.

"I'll bear that in mind. Thank you."

Once he left, the new apartment seemed very quiet. I wasn't used to the noises in this place, the humming fridge or the creak of the neighbors walking around upstairs. After turning the dead-bolt and latching the chain, I retreated to the bedroom, the type where grown-ups argued, fought, and complained bitterly over the ashes of their failed ambitions. I'd never slept in a queen bed for more than a few nights when we traveled.

"So all this is mine now, huh?"

And here you are, talking to yourself.

I hadn't talked to Vi since it happened, and her e-mails were now verging on panic. Though this was the last thing I wanted to do, I pinged her on Skype. She answered on the second beep, disheveled, frowning in worry. "You okay?"

"No," I said.

In the baldest words possible, I told her. *Now it's real. I have to live with it.*

"Oh God, Edie, I'm so sorry. Let me talk to my parents. I bet they'd let me come to Boston for the weekend. I don't know what I can do, but I really want to be with you."

Tears spilled out. I had no control, only a broken overflow valve. I was so tempted to say yes, but seeing her would hurt more. Vi could be here, safe, and my mother wasn't. I could've used a favor to save her, but I didn't know I *needed* to. Not fully understanding how far the players would take the game—that was my mistake, and I had to live with it.

Taking a deep breath, I shook my head. "Not right now. Things are really unsettled."

"Are you sure?"

"Yeah. I don't think my dad could handle visitors."

"Oh, right. I should've thought of that."

"I have to go."

"Okay. Call me if you need anything."

"Thanks. I will."

It was early, but I went to bed after talking to Vi. The new apartment permitted me to sleep without dreaming, and in the morning, guilt stormed my battlements. I failed the saving throw and cried in the shower, trying to be quiet so my dad wouldn't hear. After pulling myself together somewhat, I put on my uniform and found him already in the kitchen. No oatmeal this morning—we might never eat it again, because it was my mom's favorite breakfast food: steel cut, hearty, topped with brown sugar, crushed walnuts, butter, and raisins. He served me a fried egg sandwich instead, and I ate it, mostly because he must've run out to get a few groceries from the corner store before I even woke up.

"Thanks," I said.

"Have a good day at school."

We both knew that was unlikely, but if I didn't play along with his determined pretense, then we both might start crying and go back to bed. While it sounded appealing, as a long-term coping strategy it had little to recommend it. I trudged out the front door and down the station, ten minutes farther than before. The numbness was wearing off, so my mother's loss throbbed like a rotten tooth.

Teachers treated me with kid gloves at school. So did the student body. Apart from Davina, it was like I had a circle of sadness warding everyone off. We sat by ourselves at lunch, and she tried really hard to cheer me up. I smiled at the right moments, but I suspected she knew it didn't help. I appreciated the attempt, but also when she stopped. Her own loss might be less recent, but Russ lingered in her eyes, a haunting of what might've been.

"Want to get drunk?" she asked, as we left school that afternoon.

"I don't think it would help. We'll catch up this weekend, okay? Thanks for coming to the service, by the way. It meant a lot to have you there."

"You'd do the same for me." She went toward the T while I looked for Kian.

Oddly, I didn't find him. I waited for five minutes, then I got a text. *I'm so sorry. I can't make it today. I have something to do.*

The message raised all my hackles. He was so protective, I couldn't imagine anything short of life or death diverting him. It had to be Wedderburn . . . or the mysterious other *he*, with whom Kian had made a deal for my sake. In that moment, I made a snap decision, and I took the train downtown instead of going straight home. On the way, I sent word to my dad, so he wouldn't worry.

I'm with Kian. Will be home for dinner.

Mom's death had driven his concerns about whether I could be trusted back underground. Or shit, maybe if he didn't believe me, he felt like he had nothing left. Whatever the reason, he answered, *I'm bringing home Japanese. You like yakimeshi, right?* I smiled as I sent back, *Yep.*

• • •

I hurried through the front doors of Wedderburn, Mawer & Graf, where I found Iris in the lobby, working the reception desk. Today, everything was red and black instead of bisque. And as Kian had predicted, her look had shifted to match. Crimson hair cascaded past her shoulders, and her eyes gleamed like onyx. I didn't think I was imagining the predatory light that shone in them.

"Do you have an appointment?"

"I do *not*. Ask if Mr. Wedderburn has time to talk to me anyway." The honorific burned my tongue, as I'd much rather call him that asshole or that bastard.

"Have a seat while I check."

She radiated disapproval and kept me waiting for almost half an hour. At last she said, "You're a lucky girl. He'll see you now."

"Imagine my delight."

I had never gone upstairs on my own, and I didn't have an employee badge or security clearance, so she tapped on her keyboard, then gave me a slip of paper. "Don't lose this." Her tone implied I was an imbecile, likely to do precisely that.

Ignoring her, I hurried to the elevator before I lost my nerve.

Remembering how Kian did it before, I entered the code and pressed my desired floor. The elevator accepted the security check and away I went. The motion pushed my stomach up into my throat, so I was queasy and cold when I stepped onto Wedderburn's floor. I thought I'd find Kian in his office, but when I entered, there was only the cold man himself, lying in wait.

In a motion that crackled like icicles spearing into the snow, he came around his desk to greet me. He seemed . . . jolly, and that was one of the worst things I'd ever seen. "Before you begin your business, Edie, let me convey my condolences for your loss."

That was an unexpected blow. On some level, I grasped that he was keeping tabs on me, monitoring his investment. But I hated knowing he had seen me break down so completely. The tears I shed for my mother belonged to me and me alone. I squared my shoulders, refusing to let him get to me.

"Do you know who did it?" That wasn't why I had come, actually, but with the question posed, I waited to see how he would answer.

"It's tragic, but sometimes terrible things happen. 'To what serves mortal beauty?'" He lifted a shoulder in an eerie, crackling shrug. "From a poem, I think, about how man must fade. Sad for you, no doubt, but sometimes it's simply . . . fate."

"You're saying it was just her time?" My tone sizzled with skepticism. If I hadn't known about the old man with the bag and his awful children, I might've taken the words at face value.

"I may be terribly old," Wedderburn said in an ominous tone. "But I don't claim to know all things. For instance . . . where is your beloved this afternoon?"

DAMNED IF YOU DO

Kian burst through the door with a panicked look, as if Wedderburn might be doing something unspeakable to me. "I'm here," he said, breathless.

I turned, aware we were on shaky ground. Without being sure where he'd been, I couldn't even lie to cover for him. And Wedderburn knew it. Still, I put my hand out and Kian took it. His fingers were cold beyond bearing, and they trembled in my grasp.

"Sorry to trouble you. Are you done, Edie?" His urgent tug on my hand said I was.

In coming to headquarters, I'd intended to ask about Kian, but now that he was here, it was impossible. So I nodded. "Thanks for your kind words about my mother."

As Wedderburn nodded in dismissal, Kian dragged me out of the office and toward the elevator. He was on the verge of a full collapse, something I'd never seen before, and I didn't resist when he zoomed me past Iris and out to the car. He wasn't parked in the underground garage; we speed-walked several blocks and he wouldn't answer any question I asked until we were inside the Mustang.

"Seal it up," I ordered.

Fortunately he did, or we would've had our first real fight. I made a mental note to ask where he'd gotten a new tin of the stuff, but there were more important issues to discuss. He was shivering so hard that I wasn't sure he should drive, but when I said so, Kian shook his head. "H-have to get you away from there. Give me five minutes."

My trepidation increased with his silence, but eventually, he pulled over and rested his head on the steering wheel. Confused and feeling helpless, I rubbed his back. He was the stubbornest person I'd ever met, and the only solution was to wait him out. A few minutes later, he straightened and reached inside his jacket and silently passed me a packet of papers.

"What's this?"

"It's faster if you just read it."

"Okay. But afterward, you have some serious explaining to do."

"I will, I promise."

These pages had the look of official documents, stamped and coded in a system I didn't recognize. The words themselves were clear; this was a *contract*, ordering the death of one Mildred Kramer, signed by K. Wedderburn and witnessed by S. Mawer. I read it over three times, but it didn't make any sense.

"Why?"

Kian handed me another file, marked Acquisitions. I understood now why he had been so eager to get out of the building. When he said he had something to do, he was *spying* for me. My stomach churned with sick dread as I skimmed this dossier. A lot of it was hard to interpret, having to do with eddies and currents, but this phrase seemed unmistakable.

In Edith Kramer's optimum timeline, her mother dies. She works alongside her father to complete the project. All research shows that the outcome hinges on that pivotal event.

"It's time travel," I said, suddenly sure. "That was the project my mom and dad were working on when she—" I couldn't finish the sentence.

But Kian was nodding. "I think you're right."

"But . . . that doesn't even make sense. They're using technology my dad and I develop *right now*. How can they use something I haven't invented yet?"

"Wedderburn made a deal with an immortal who has temporal powers. From what I hear, it was expensive, so he wanted his own method of mucking about in the time stream."

"So he went forward, stole our tech, and brought it back for his own use in the game."

"Pretty much. And now he has to make sure you stay on the right path, or this whole version of the universe will be wiped out."

"Jesus. No pressure." Now I was shaking too.

"It's not like the world would *end*, Edie. Not for everyone else. Things would just . . . shift, like two steps to the right or something."

"After all the mystery, it's a relief to know what's waiting for me. But . . . to make sure he wins and I remain a viable piece in play, Wedderburn had my mother *killed*." I curled one hand into a fist. "And then he said he was sorry."

He looked as if he wanted to reach for me, but he feared how I would react. "I had no idea, I swear."

"I know. You're a pawn, like me."

At that, he shook his head. "Not even that. Not anymore."

"What do you mean?"

"The other night, you said you couldn't take this. I know how much you want out. You remember how I said Raoul stole an artifact and disappeared?"

"Yeah."

Calmer, Kian put the car into gear. "I lied to you, Edie."

"About what?" I couldn't look at him, tracing the edge of the dash. Maybe I'd rather not know; I couldn't lose my one true thing, not now.

"When I said I was taking those classes in hopes of figuring out how to win my freedom? That's bullshit. I've only ever been looking for a way out . . . for you."

"I don't like where this is going."

"So in my Religion and Magic class, the professor mentioned a protective icon. Most of the class sleeps through his digressions, but I took notes. And then I searched the database at WM&G."

"You found something?"

Kian nodded. "I tried to get it for you. It would've let you follow in Raoul's footsteps, but . . . I failed. The security was too tight, so I grabbed those files instead. When Wedderburn finds out—"

"He'll know you're not loyal. Jesus, what have you *done*?" I got mad because I didn't know what other emotion could serve, certainly not the tsunami of fear sweeping over me.

"It won't be until tomorrow, I think, when he gets the reports. It would've been worth it if I had succeeded. I'm sorry."

I took a second look at the file, but there was nothing about what had happened to the Teflon crew. Apparently, Wedderburn took me at my word when I declined. Maybe Kian was right when he guessed that Dwyer was trying to drive me crazy by hurting the people around me. There was nothing to confirm or deny the speculation, however, in these files.

"Then . . . we have one night left together. Just one."

"You've given me so much more than I ever expected," he said softly.

There had to be some way out of this maze, but my brain wasn't firing on all cylinders. I fell silent, the closer we got to my place. *How am I supposed to go upstairs, eat Japanese with my dad, and act like nothing's wrong?* I wanted to cry, break things, and scream until I had no voice left.

"There's no point in hiding things from me anymore," I mumbled. "So what did you promise in return for my safety? And who's the third player?"

He smiled then. "You're so persistent. I love that about you. Try not to feel sad about the situation with Wedderburn." Such a stupid word for his imminent death, *situation.* "I didn't have that long anyway."

"Kian! For the last time, *what* did you promise? And to who?"

"My life," he said simply. "When I made the compact with the Harbinger, he gave me until my twenty-first birthday. Six months with you, so worth it to be happy that long, knowing you'd be all right after I was gone."

"Since you said that with a straight face, the world's lucky you're never serving on the Supreme Court because you're definitely the stupidest person on the planet. How does this work? If Wedderburn executes you, won't it cause problems with this Harbinger?"

The idiot actually grinned. "God, I hope so."

"This isn't funny! I *won't* be okay if something happens to you. Don't you get that?" The weight of the look he aimed at me said *when* not *if*, but I couldn't face it. "I won't give up. I promised myself I never would again. There has to be something I can do."

"Even if you could protect me from Wedderburn, my time will be up in six months."

"If you don't shut up, I will seriously punch you. Let me think."

But no answers came to me. Kian had dug a grave and in the morning, Wedderburn would shove him into it. When he stopped outside my apartment, it was almost six, and I was barely choking back tears. I didn't want to get out of the car, but I couldn't make my dad worry, either. *You're all he has left.*

"Here's the plan," I said. "I'll have dinner with him, then go to my room like I usually do. I'll text you."

"You can call, if you want. I think we've reached that point in our relationship."

"Stop it." I hated that he could smile, but he seemed pleased with the fact that he'd drawn all the lines around me, just like he'd promised. *And he's fighting for you with his life.*

Kian, no.

"Sorry I interrupted. You'll text me . . . ?"

"And you'll pop in to get me. I want to spend the night at your place, but I don't want to freak my dad out. You can bring me back in the morning."

If he thought I was going to school, however, he was nuts. I'd stay only long enough to make sure my dad left for work. Whatever happened with Wedderburn, I'd go with Kian, and we would face it together. Surely I could fix this, somehow.

352

"If I was a better person, I'd say no. But I don't want to spend my last night alone."

This time I leaned over to kiss him, silencing the words that tunneled into my heart until I couldn't feel anything but pain. *This isn't happening. This is not real.* But like with my mother's death, I didn't wake. I got out of the car and went into our apartment, where I ate yakimeshi and pretended I wasn't dying inside.

Dad talked about his work, and each unconscious pause told me he was waiting for my mother to chime in, responding to his theories. I did my best to fill her shoes, but I wasn't sure I succeeded. It seemed improbable that I could ever invent anything that resulted in time travel. Around nine, my dad went to his room and shut the door. That was my cue to do the same.

In the master suite, I locked up and called Kian. "Come get me."

He did.

Bittersweet memories assailed me, the first time he traveled with me like this. Tonight we could go anywhere and who would punish us? "Is there anything you want to see? Anywhere you want to go? There's nothing preventing us now."

To my surprise, he shook his head. "I only want to be with you. I'd run if I thought it would do any good, but they can track me through the watch. The thing only comes off if I die or Wedderburn removes it."

"We could stop your heart." I was only half kidding.

Weirdly, he appeared to consider it before shaking his head. "If you failed to bring me back, it'd eat you up. You can't be the one who kills me, Edie."

"I know," I whispered. "But I can't give up, either."

"You're unbelievably, fantastically determined to save me. Come here." Lacing our fingers together, he led me to his bedroom.

The bed was neatly made with a navy-and-white-striped comforter, pillows propped up against the simple headboard. I didn't hesitate when Kian drew me down with him. With every part of me, I wanted to be close, closer still. But he didn't kiss me, as if he feared I'd misinterpret his intentions.

"Is this where you tell me it's your last wish not to die a virgin?" Worst joke ever, but otherwise, I'd spend the next eight hours crying.

I can't do that to him. I'll use that time to think and to soak him in.

"What makes you think I would?"

"Ouch. I thought you said you don't date."

His lips quirked. "You think people have to date to hook up? That's so cute."

"Maybe you're not the droid I'm looking for."

He kissed the top of my head. "I wish I could say I never have, but—"

"No, it's okay."

"You can ask."

"Do I want to know?"

"You're the only one who can determine that."

"Then I guess . . . yes. Tell me. Not how many, when or where."

He settled me against his chest and turned on the TV, more for background noise. I liked his bedroom better than mine. "I got lost in the attention. Before, I was so nervous, and after, it was so easy. The first time I had sex, I'd only known the girl for, like, four hours."

"And I bet it was magical," I said drily.

"She was drunk and I was in a hurry. If she remembered more about it, I doubt she'd come back for seconds."

"No offense, but that's pretty gross."

"I know. That's why I didn't do it again."

"Is that why you haven't pressed?" Kian had given me signs that he wanted me, and that it wasn't easy to stop at times.

"No. I figured you'd tell me when the time was right. Before I made the deal to protect you, I had all the time in the world."

I considered asking about the Harbinger, but did it really matter? One emergency at a time, and Wedderburn constituted the pressing problem. After I got him out of this mess, then we'd deal with the next crisis. Kian might've already accepted that he was terminal, but I'd do *anything* to save him. Too many people had already died because of me.

Part of me wanted to sleep with him, but with so much darkness looming and my mother's death close at hand, I'd never recover if *this* was my first time. So I didn't offer. Sex should be about love or pleasure, not sadness. Unless you listened to my dad, in which case, it should only be undertaken to save the world from a meteor. Or something.

I started, "I can't—"

"I wouldn't, even if you said yes."

"Can we make out?"

"I'm willing to go that far." His smile reached his eyes for the first time in months. This was the reason behind his emotional distance; now that I knew how far he'd gone for me, Kian could be himself again.

Kian slid onto his side and I faced him. This was different from kisses in a parked car or furtive moments on the sofa. He cupped my face in his hand as my lashes drifted down. Shards of glass slid in and out of my heart as I realized he'd given me my first kiss, and I might be giving him his last. His mouth brushed mine, once, twice. I laced my hands in his hair. He kissed me deep and deeper still, a lush sweetness blooming between us, more than chemicals, more than chemistry.

He ran his hands down my back, tugging me closer. His muscles felt lean and strong beneath my hands. Sex was a bad idea, but if he kept touching me, I'd soon be willing to make him my favorite mistake. As if he had the same thought, he buried his face in the curve between my neck and shoulder, breath coming in hot puffs.

"Hurts," he managed. "How much I want you."

"I know." I had the same ache, growing stronger with each brush of his mouth.

With shaking hands, he held me to him. I wrapped my legs around his, only half knowing what I was doing. "Stop. Edie, stop."

But neither of us did. It felt too good.

"Okay. Okay." Kian muttered the words, trying to calm down, but I didn't let go.

"This. Not sex, this." And I moved, showing him what I wanted, what I could accept.

Our clothes were still on, and I couldn't breathe for wanting him. He groaned as he rolled on top of me, giving in. It might not be enough for him, but for me—yes. Definitely. I shifted and rocked, until I shivered uncontrollably, unable to believe it could be this wonderful with all of my clothes on. His mouth was on mine, and he arched on top of me, breathing me in. One push, another, quick and convulsive.

"Jesus." He scattered kisses all over my face.

"This is my promise to you. When I'm eighteen? We'll revisit this subject." *Not* sleeping with him was my way of keeping hope alive and proof that I didn't accept his fate.

We held each other until it became necessary to clean up. For me that wasn't a problem, but he showered and changed. His expression when he came out of the bathroom was priceless. Love flooded through me, though science might argue this was only a result of the endorphins.

Gravitation is not responsible for people falling in love. Another Einstein saying, one of my favorites—and until this moment, I had no idea what it meant.

"You look pleased with yourself," he mumbled.

"There are a ton of reasons why I shouldn't be . . . but at the moment, they all seem really far away."

"I know what you mean." He padded to bed, barefoot, and snuggled me against his chest, my favorite place in the world.

As I listened to his heartbeat, a possible solution knocked at the edges of my brain, but I was exhausted. Epiphany danced around the perimeter of my mind, refusing to coalesce. Kian ran his fingers through my hair, a sweet cycle that sent shivers through me. I kissed his shoulder; he made a delicious noise.

"Was that too much?" I asked.

"I wouldn't have tried to get you to do that . . . but it was perfect. Are *you* okay?"

"No virginal remorse on my end. Hey . . ."

"Hm?"

"Since we watched *Casablanca* the other night, can we watch *Notorious* now? You said it's your other favorite."

Obviously pleased that I'd remembered, Kian got up to put in the DVD. "This is your chance, ask for anything. It's impossible for me to say no to you right now."

Don't die. Don't leave me.

But those were cruel favors to ask, not within his ability to grant. And those were the terms, right? *What we ask will always be within your power to fulfill.* The revelation brightened, like a new lightbulb, and then it fizzled and winked out. *Dammit. You're supposed to be smart. Figure out how to help him. He's in this mess because he cares so much about protecting you.* And I couldn't even get mad at him over it.

"Just the movie."

"You probably think I'm weird for liking the oldies, huh?"

"No. But I'm curious what got you started on them."

"Our housekeeper," he answered, surprising me. "On Saturday nights, she always watched the late show, and I was a lonely kid. At first, it was mostly the thrill of staying up past my bedtime, but I came to love the classics as much as she did."

"Do you still talk to her?"

He shook his head, and without him saying so, I realized that she was gone. Not like his mother, in and out of rehab. But *gone*. Like my mom. Rather than say something stupid, awkward, or insensitive, I scooted over, so he could sit next to me. The mattress dipped.

Kian put an arm around me, clicking play on the remote. Ingrid Bergman came to glorious life while Cary Grant was smooth, inscrutable, and charming. They both had undeniable glamour, maybe because I didn't know about their cheating habits or their secret addictions. Beside me, Kian was smiling, lost in the movie, but every now and then, he kissed my temple, reminding me that we were together.

You are my one true thing, I thought. *Always.* In time, I might love someone else, if the worst came to pass. But he would never be Kian, and I hoarded these moments like a dragon on a pile of shimmering gold. We watched his favorite film until my eyelids grew heavy, and I drifted before I learned whether Devlin loved Alicia.

In my heart, I knew he did, even if he never said the words.

A SACRIFICE
TO LOVE

woke alone.

Immediately I knew that was wrong, and dread cramped my stomach. I rolled out of Kian's bed and ran to the living room. Foreboding turned to sickness, and I trembled as I padded toward the note taped to the door. Perspectives in the room seemed off, so that the paper got larger and larger, until it loomed bigger than the door, as if it was so heavy that it should pull the door inward into a hole that would swallow them both. Blinking my eyes repeatedly made Kian's neat handwriting resolve from teary swirls into comprehensible language. I hated this note, even before I read it. But I had to know what it said and what he thought constituted an adequate good-bye.

Edie,
I wasn't truly alive until I met you. It's funny
how spring always follows winter, even when

you've given up all hope of ever seeing the sun again. But it rises. "Why does the sun come up, or are the stars just pinholes in the curtain of night?"

At that line, a quote from *Highlander*, I choked back a sob and it was as if he knew I would react that way as I read on.

Don't cry for me, but I do hope you'll remember that we were good together and you were always beautiful in my eyes. From the start, you mattered, even when I was trying to play by their rules. So do me one final favor, if I have the right to ask anything—live for me. Your future is wide open and without me, you'll achieve remarkable things. I won't see your potential ruined and you enslaved to Wedderburn. I'd rather die.

There's one more thing I kept from you, a file I didn't show you last night. In no future, if you're with me, do you complete your mother's work. I'm the sacrifice that must be made. And I'm willing.

You will succeed. You'll repay the favors. Then your life will be your own. And that's all I care about now. My time is done, one way or another, so let me choose how I go. I have always, always wanted to be your hero.

Kian

My heart cracked wide, threatening to spill a river of tears. *In every way that matters, you're already my knight in a shiny red car. How can you not know that?*

"No," I said aloud. "Damn you, *no*, bastard-asshole martyr, I don't accept this."

Fury lent me strength; I raced into the bedroom and grabbed my purse. My cell phone tumbled out of the front pocket. As I bent to pick it up, it rang. I recognized Vi's number, and I knew she must be worried. It had been a couple of days since we'd talked.

Already moving toward the front door, I answered it. "What's up?"

"Are you all right?"

"What, is your spider sense tingling?" Classic question parry since I didn't want to worry her. She knew little about my actual life, but it warmed me that she cared. My red winter coat was hanging in the closet in the foyer; I shrugged into it and exited Kian's building.

"I don't know, I'm just . . . concerned about you." She sounded puzzled, like she couldn't explain it. "You were really quiet last time we talked. With your mom and everything . . . maybe you should spend the holidays with me?"

People should trust their instincts more. You're right to have a weird feeling, Vi.

"I can't leave my dad."

"Bring him. I already talked to my parents. He can sleep in the den and you can have the trundle bed in my room. It'll be good. Come on."

"Maybe."

I couldn't tell her the truth as I ran toward what might be my doom. Early Saturday morning, I didn't have to fight commuters, just a few runners, mothers out with children, and people gearing up for

Christmas shopping. Dodging around the other pedestrians, I raced toward the station.

"Thanks. I . . . just want you to know that your friendship means a lot to me." That was the kind of thing you said as part of a farewell like the one Kian wrote to me.

"You're starting to freak me out. You sound all grave and . . . final."

"I don't mean to. Look, Vi, I can't talk now. I have to be somewhere and I'm about to dodge into the subway."

"Okay. Call me later?"

"Sure." *If I'm alive.*

At least Vi would miss me if this rescue mission went wrong. Davina probably would too. And my dad, God, I couldn't even think about my dad. With shaking hands, I texted him. It was barely dawn, so he likely wasn't up yet, but he should find my bullshit about going for an early run reassuring.

I don't want to leave him alone. I'm supposed to help him. Optimum future, my ass.

Finally, I tapped out a message to Davina, nothing dramatic. Just, *thanks for being my friend.* Which might scare her, but . . . I knew the risks of confronting Wedderburn and interrupting the grand gesture Kian had planned. I hoped I got there fast enough to do . . . something. What, I had no idea; I hadn't planned that far ahead. My head throbbed with tension and trepidation. Too much shock and grief apparently impaired cognitive function, because I did *not* feel at the top of my game.

The ride downtown seemed interminable and the tunnels were full of living shadows that slithered after the racing car. Long dark fingers crawled toward me, but I stared up at the lights overhead, letting them shine into my eyes until I saw spots. *I won't let the darkness in. I won't. I'm not crazy.* I didn't realize I was mumbling this aloud until the old guy nearby moved away by several seats, but I was beyond caring what anyone thought.

The thin man watched me race off the car, across the platform, and toward the stairs, but he made no move to stop me. Only the smell of corruption lingered in my nostrils as I blew past. It was too early on a Saturday for businessmen to be out, but there were service workers in uniforms and homeless people layered against the cold. A few of them raised their heads when I raced by, staring at a spot just over my shoulder, until I wanted to scream.

No breath for it. Keep moving.

Iris was at the desk in the lobby, red as blood, terrifying as always. "How good to see you again, Miss Kramer. Do you have an appointment?"

"Wedderburn will want to see me," I said, hoping it was true.

She didn't take my word for it, of course; she rang upstairs to check. In some ways, it was reassuring that even supernatural creatures clung to protocol and procedure.

I'm not too late. I'm not.

To my astonishment, Wedderburn must've asked her to put him on speaker. His voice snapped from the intercom. "Yes, send her up. There's something I want her to see."

If it's Kian's body . . . the careless cruelty of it would unmake me. But then, that was Wedderburn's specialty. *Ice doesn't care who it harms.* My knees quivered and I locked them, holding on to the reception desk for support.

Kian, you ass, I don't need a hero. I just want you.

Wearing a deep frown, Iris scrawled a code. Like before, she warned, "This will get you to the proper floor and nowhere else. It will only work once."

The elevator was spooky in silence, no tinny music today, but it moved so fast I heard the rushing air beneath it, as if I had been sucked up into a monstrous maw. I half expected teeth to crunch down and smash me like a bug in a can. At last, the car stopped and I got out. Wedderburn strode down the hall toward me, unusual. I had never seen him out of his office. When I realized Kian wasn't with him, I choked down a tide of angry questions.

"How delightful of you to come," he said. "I was starting to worry that you'd overslept and we'd have to start without you."

Without another word, he led me back to his office and threw open the door. I braced for the sight of Kian in a pool of blood; my brain was ready for it, Dr. Oppenheimer whispering in my ear, *The optimist thinks this is the best of all possible worlds. The pessimist fears it is true.* But it *was* the best of all possible worlds. Kian whirled, alive, breathing— breathing and glaring—but *alive*. His jaw tightened, and his eyes went livid with a ferocious blend of fear and anger.

Wedderburn shut the door behind him with a restrained snick. Displeasure radiated from him like frost snapping from winter-withered leaves. He paced, so that his movements reminded me of the back-and-forth sweep of a blade across a weighted trap. Sooner or later, the axe would fall.

"You're here to bear witness to his judgment?" he asked. "Brave of you."

"Not exactly," I started to say, but Wedderburn wasn't listening.

"There is no doubt. Kian Riley serves you now, not me. And a tool that cannot be trusted to its purpose is irrevocably broken and must be discarded."

Shit. I knew exactly what that meant.

I said desperately, "He doesn't serve me. He *cares* about me. Surely you can understand the difference."

"I gave him an order . . . and he did not follow it. Instead, he told you the whole of my plan and tried to help you escape, using *my* resources. I have the report here." With icy irritation, he tapped the page on his desk. "That is . . . disloyalty. I saved his life, you know."

Kian didn't say a single word in his own defense. By the set of his shoulders, he was ready to accept the consequences. Though I didn't blame him for it, he carried the weight of what the Teflon crew had done to me, the last day before winter break, and he regretted not giving his life for me then. I could hardly breathe for the pain tightening my chest. I had lost too much already.

Wedderburn turned to his desk and pushed a button. A tone sounded, then an inhuman voice said, "What do you require?"

"Send in the clown."

At first, I thought it was a hideous, macabre joke, another of Wedderburn's evil games, until the door banged open and a clown stood in the doorway. I narrowed my eyes on the smudged, faded "makeup," then realized the cracked and flaking skin was imprinted with a huge red mouth with a white oval around it. The thing's nose was bulbous and tinted red, and it had frizzy orange hair sticking out in all directions. Baggy clothes and giant shoes added to the disturbing picture, but that wasn't even the worst part. In his hand, he carried a black case, and at Wedderburn's nod, he opened it, revealing a shining variety of knives in all shapes and sizes: curved, straight, serrated blades, some more like scalpels, others for skinning or boning.

"Which one?" When the clown-thing spoke, it revealed sharp yellow teeth and a long pink tongue that snaked out to wet its mouth as it glanced between Kian and me.

Wedderburn inclined his head with an icy crackle. Kian held his silence, imperturbable in the face of death. In fact, a faint smile curved his mouth, as if he were glad to do this for me. Only this wouldn't solve anything, and I wanted him with me, not as a martyr whose picture I could clutch and weep over.

"Wait," I blurted.

"You have no cards to play," Wedderburn said.

Inspiration struck; epiphany finally clarified into certainty. "That's not true."

Kian's eyes widened and he shook his head, frantic. He tried to intercept me, but the clown wouldn't let him.

You know me so well. But you're not stopping me.

"I'm ready to ask for my final favor. Since Kian isn't allowed to fulfill it, as you've disavowed him, then that falls to you, right?"

Wedderburn fixed on me an enigmatic look, steepling his fingers. "Correct."

I hesitated, thinking about my dad and Davina, who might need protection down the line. But those were maybes. This was Kian's definite death, here and now. I *could not* watch him die when I had the power to save him.

For someone like me, there could be only one choice.

"Edie, don't. Let me go. It's better this way. If you're with me, you'll never achieve what you're meant to, and you'll end up indentured. I told you in the note—"

"Then I want Kian set free, now and forever, *truly* free, untouchable by any immortal in the game. No tricks, no shadows on his timeline. *Free.*"

As I spoke, Wedderburn nodded, and a final line appeared at the bottom of my infinity symbol. Just like the first two, it burned as if someone held a soldering iron to my skin. I hissed as the sting faded. *Asked and answered, now Kian and I have matching ink.* Curling my left hand into a fist, I reached for Kian with my right. He looked as if I'd died for *him,* and I just didn't know it. Yet he stepped to my side and laced his fingers through mine.

"Your services won't be required," I told the clown-thing.

"Today," it corrected. "Ultimately, my services are *always* in demand."

"You may go." Wedderburn didn't watch as his executioner strolled out. Instead, he was focused on me. Incredibly, he was smiling. "You've just won me a great deal of money, Miss Kramer, along with a fair amount of prestige."

I froze. "What are you talking about?"

"From start to finish, you've behaved exactly as I predicted you would. A handsome boy, a forbidden romance . . . well. This outcome was inevitable. For a clever girl, you've been a bit of a disappointment in some respects. In others? You performed beautifully."

"Because you wanted me to burn my favors. And I have." Realization swept over me, along with a steaming hot burst of chagrin, but I couldn't let Kian die.

"That's been my goal from the start. If you think I care how you used them, then you don't understand my strategy at all. Now, darling girl, you are precisely where I want you."

He turned to Kian. "This doesn't solve your problem with the Harbinger, though, does it? Since he's not part of the game. But . . . that's not my concern. I'll have your watch back now, if you please."

The cold one touched a metal wand to the wristband and the thing fell off like a dead insect. I shivered. "The two of you may go."

"Wait," Kian protested.

Wedderburn leveled an awful smile on him. "Enjoy your freedom. I'll ensure the others know you're no longer in play and may not be used for ancillary maneuvers, either. Go. Be human." He packed a world of scorn in the last word.

I tugged on Kian's hand. "Let's get out of here."

This might not be a victory, only a reprieve, but I practically ran out of the office and I didn't stop shaking until we reached the lobby. Iris came around the desk to block our path; she wasn't smiling. The receptionist held out a hand expectantly.

"I've been informed that your employment has been terminated, Mr. Riley. I need your passcard back. Your security codes and clearances will be revoked immediately. I have also been instructed to inform you that if you appear on this property without a written invitation from any of the partners, I'm to have you arrested."

"I understand," Kian said, digging into his wallet and turning in his badge.

He seemed dazed as we stepped out into the wan winter light. People hurried about, their business-coat collars pulled up and scarves wrapped about the lower halves of their faces. I had never noticed how much the same everyone looked in their black coats, like a flock of ravens fluttering in the same direction. Some of them tapped at their phones as they moved and the motion put me even more in mind of pecking birds.

I pulled him toward the T station since he didn't mention his car being parked anywhere nearby. If I guessed right, he hadn't brought it, not expecting to need a ride home. "Let's go to your place."

That roused him and he fixed furious green eyes on me. "What the hell did you do?"

"The best I could. There was no other way to save you."

"Now you're at Wedderburn's mercy. Trust me, that's *not* where you want to be. Edie, you could end up—"

"Indentured. I know. But maybe I won't. I refuse to believe who I date has that big an impact on my future. Anyway, I don't care. The most important thing is that they can't hurt or control you anymore."

"That's completely beside the point."

"Not to me."

"Damn you," he whispered.

Then, with the people swirling past us, he drew me into his arms and rubbed his cheek against the top of my head. "Don't you get how this works? I was supposed to save you."

"Says who? The favors were mine to use on whatever I want most. And, Kian . . . I need you with me."

"Just when I think I can't love you more—"

"You . . . love me?"

"God, yes. I'm in so deep . . . and now, you have no use for me. You're still in the game, what do you need with an awkward, human boyfriend?"

"I'm human too," I reminded him. "And . . . I'd do anything for you. I just did, in fact. In case you haven't figured it out . . . I love you too."

"But I'm a liability, Edie. The ones in the game can't touch me, but immortals are devious. They could contract with noncombatants like the Harbinger, and now that they know I'm your Achilles' heel—"

"So I'll buckle on some ass-kicking boots—"

Kian cupped the nape of my neck and leaned in. His lips brushed mine, once, twice, then he nuzzled a path over my jaw to my ear. Rush of warm breath, and he kissed the side of my throat. Not what I expected, better, because it was tender as a rosebud yet not too much for the people surging around us. Gazing up at him, I swallowed hard.

"Wow."

"You said something about my place?"

"Yeah."

He slid his hands down my arms and turned our wrists to look at the matched set of marks. "I don't know what's coming, but I'll be there with you."

"That's all I could ask."

"You're a miracle," he said softly.

"Einstein said something like there are two ways to live: as if nothing is a miracle or as if *everything* is. And the fact that I'm alive? *That's* the miracle. If I've helped you at all, it's only because you saved me first."

Kian cradled my face in his hands. "Whenever I'm ready to give up, there you are, hauling me to my feet." I opened my mouth but he said it for me. "I know. We'll be okay. As long as we're still breathing, there's hope."

I didn't kid myself it was over. Dwyer & Fell would challenge my place in the timeline—try to derail me while Wedderburn plotted, schemed, and protected his queen. At the end of next semester, I could end up indentured . . . or worse. The thin man was still out there, along with the old man with the sack, the black-eyed children, the clown executioner, and doubtless other monsters that I hadn't encountered yet. Like Kian, I'd burned all my favors too fast and it might come back to haunt me.

At the moment, I didn't care. I smiled as another Einstein saying sprang to mind—my new credo. *You have to learn the rules of the game. And then you have to play better than anyone else.*

So I will.

As I followed Kian toward the station, snow sprinkled down, a dusting of white courtesy of Wedderburn, letting me know I wasn't beyond his touch. Kian's hand was warm wrapped around mine, his wrist naked without the watch that had been his master. A chill wind skated over me; I turned, staring up at the glass-and-steel monstrosity where the bitter-cold god hid from the modern world, like so many other ancient, terrible things.

And I whispered, "Game on."

AUTHOR'S NOTE

I've always been fascinated with anthropological phenomenon, how certain divine archetypes permeate civilizations in wildly diverse geographic regions. Humans have been inventing similar stories to explain the natural world for eons. Urban legends intrigue me in the same way—tales repeated mouth to ear, winging through phones and forums, until people are convinced that a young couple has really been murdered in the woods by a man with a hook for a hand and that you can, in fact, summon things in a darkened mirror. Fear is a visceral emotion, impossible to banish from modern life. At the heart of us, we are still primitive creatures warding off evil with flaming brands.

Which brought me to this idea: Imagine a world where, if enough people believe in them, the nightmares come true. The delicious awfulness of it worked on me until I had to combine all of these factors and write it as *Mortal Danger*. I had a blast researching various mythologies and creating new characters based on old legends, like Wedderburn. I'm sure you're all wondering about the Harbinger, who you'll learn more about in the sequel. I also trolled the Internet, mining for gold, and that's where I found Slenderman. The thin man is *my* version, given life by everyone who read stories and repeated them as if they were real. I found *so* many creepy things that they wouldn't all fit in one book, so there are many shocks and gasps yet to come. The Immortal Game is messy and convoluted, full of monsters and magic, science and sacrifice. I hope you enjoy it as much as I do, though the stakes are terrifyingly high and *no one* is safe.

In some ways, this is a deeply personal book. Confession: I have walked in Edie's shoes as a weird and awkward outcast myself. I too, have stood on that emotional ledge and wondered if anyone would care if I checked out. Many of her thoughts were mine first, and despair should never be taken lightly. Please understand that suicide is not an ending to pain, it only creates more. If you're feeling this way, please seek help. If there's nobody in your life to talk to, there *are* people who will listen: suicidepreventionlifeline.org. I muddled through alone, but it's not the best option, and I want better for all of you. Dear readers, whatever you're going through, it's not your fault, and time can mend it, if you fight on. The sadness passes, even when you think there's no hope. But you have to be fierce; don't let anyone take away your inner light. You are important. You matter. And if you quit before you've begun, the world will be lesser for it. I'm glad I didn't let the bullies win. I'm glad I'm still here, writing stories for all of you. Thank you for reading them.

ACKNOWLEDGMENTS

Thanks to Laura Bradford, who lets me lead with my heart. I can be impulsive, but she never tries to turn me away from whatever direction I'm running in. That's why we work so well together, because I need that freedom, or else I lose the joy.

Next, I must express my utmost appreciation for my amazing editor, Liz Szabla, for not asking me to pull my punches. Sometimes my books hurt, but they're *supposed* to. She's also great at making sure the complicated worlds in my head translate clearly for readers on the page. I love everyone at Feiwel and Friends; the whole team does an amazing job from cover art to interior design, marketing, sales, and event planning. Jon, Jean, Rich, Elizabeth, Anna, Molly, Mary, Courtney, Allison, Kathryn, Ksenia, Ashley, Dave, Nicole . . . there are more incredible people pushing me toward greater success and I'd like to hug each and every one of them. Your work makes mine possible, so thank you so much.

Kudos to my lovely copyeditor, Anne Heausler, and my proofreader, Fedora Chen. Because of their talents, my books are beautifully polished, a feat I could never achieve on my own. Thank you both!

Now I roll out the star-studded list of those who helped with

Mortal Danger, encouraged me, or answered questions: Rachel Caine, Lish McBride, Donna J. Herren, Leigh Bardugo, Bree Bridges, Yasmine Galenorn, Marie Rutkoski, Lauren Dane, Robin LaFevers, Megan Hart, and Vivian Arend. There're also the two invaluable writer loops that keep me sane, and I can't forget Karen Alderman and Majda Čolak, my two beta readers. Thanks to the talented Cara McKenna for her early read of *Mortal Danger*; she was my local Boston expert. Any mistakes or liberties are my own. You've all contributed to my success, and I adore you for it.

My husband and children—they listen to me rant, then offer hugs, hot tea, and solutions to plot problems. I couldn't do this without them. Hear that, beloved family? You're the best.

Readers, it's just you and me now. I think of you savoring my stories and kick my feet in glee. This is everything I've ever wanted, and each time you put your faith in me by opening one of my books, you're making my dreams come true. And with all my heart, I thank you.